THE ISLAND ESCAPE

Kerry Fisher lives in Surrey with her two children, a very tolerant husband and a naughty black dog. *The Island Escape* is her second novel. She'd love to hear your views, so please visit her website at http://www.kerryfisherauthor.com, follow her on Twitter @KerryFSwayne, or join her on Facebook at https://www.facebook.com/kerryfisherauthor.

D0332897

Kerry Fisher

The Island Escape

AVON

AVON

A division of HarperCollins*Publishers*
1 London Bridge Street
London, SE1 9GF

www.harpercollins.co.uk

A Paperback Original 2015

1

First published in Great Britain by
HarperCollins*Publishers* 2015

Copyright © Kerry Fisher 2015

Kerry Fisher asserts the moral right to
be identified as the author of this work

A catalogue record for this book is
available from the British Library

ISBN-13: 978-0-00-757025-6

Set in Sabon LT Std by Palimpsest Book Production Limited,
Falkirk, Stirlingshire

Printed and bound in Great Britain by
Clays Ltd, St Ives plc

MIX
Paper from
responsible sources
FSC™   **FSC C007454**
www.fsc.org

Find out more about HarperCollins and the environment at
www.harpercollins.co.uk/green

Acknowledgements

I've had so much support since my first novel, *The School Gate Survival Guide*, was published last year, that it's difficult to know where to start this time in expressing my gratitude. I've had such a lot of encouragement from readers, so I'd like to say a huge thank you to everyone who's tracked me down on Facebook/Twitter or left a review on Amazon to let me know they've enjoyed my novel – it really does brighten my day. I also want to give a big shout-out to the book bloggers – they work so hard to promote authors and I stand in awe of how many books they manage to read and review.

Setting the first few scenes in a police station has made me ridiculously grateful that I didn't have a whole crime novel to check for accuracy. I've had some very generous help from Tracey Blair, Mandy Bewicke, Gary McDade and Alan Tebboth. They saved me from lots of police procedure errors – any remaining ones are entirely down to my taking fictional liberties.

I'm incredibly lucky to know lots of lovely authors who've helped me along the way, though special mention has to go to my writing buddy, Jenny Ashcroft. Without her, it would all be much harder. A big thumbs-up to Harriet Benge, who also gave me very useful feedback early on.

I have to give a big cheer to my children for keeping the 'Yeah, yeah, we know you're working but can you take me into town/Is there any bread/Can I use your computer?' requests to a minimum, especially in the intensive editing phase, and to my husband, Steve, for just being a good man who wants me to enjoy what I do.

I couldn't possibly overlook my agent, Clare Wallace, at Darley Anderson, who looks after me so brilliantly. It's a bit embarrassing that I'm much older than her but only half as wise. Finally, it's been a privilege working with the Avon team, especially my editor, Helen Huthwaite, who helped me sculpt *The Island Escape* into a book I could be proud of. Or – just in case my dad is reading – a book of which I could be proud.

For Steve, Cameron, Michaela and Poppy

Roberta

I was wearing the wrong bra for sitting in a police cell.

It was sod's law that I'd chosen today to try out my early Christmas present from Scott. But I hadn't dressed thinking the police would confiscate my blouse as 'evidence'. I'd dressed thinking that sexy underwear might put my husband into a more festive frame of mind.

When we arrived at the police station, the officer who'd arrested me, PC Julie Pikestaff, led me into the custody suite. I was more used to suites containing champagne and roses.

PC Pikestaff quickly explained why I'd been brought in to the custody officer behind the counter, sighing as though if it weren't for me, she'd be stretched out on a sun lounger in St Lucia. 'She'll have to take her shirt off. We need to bag it up.'

The custody officer ferreted around under the desk and handed Pikestaff a white boiler suit, saying, 'She can put this on once you've booked her in. Take her cuffs off.'

The creak in my shoulder blades as I brought my arms in front of me reminded me that I needed to go back to Pilates. The stunned disbelief that had enveloped me on the journey to the police station was starting to evaporate. That boiler suit epitomised how low I'd sunk.

I tried to find the voice I used at parents' evenings when teachers were evading my questions, but I could only manage a croak of despair.

'I'm sorry,' I said. 'I can't wear that.'

People like me only came to police stations to report stolen iPads or missing Siamese cats. I was already trying to salvage any scrap of pride I had left. Rustling around in that wretched space suit might finish me off completely.

Pikestaff waved dismissively. 'Look, it's just something to cover you up while your blouse is examined for forensics. No big deal.'

Before she could say anything else, two policemen burst through the door, struggling to restrain a couple of girls in their mid-twenties. One had dyed black hair, thigh-length boots and the tiniest red miniskirt. The other was in a neon-pink body stocking. The Lycra had given up trying to contain her rolls of fat, her boobs spilling out like boxing gloves. The girls snarled and flailed as much as their handcuffs would allow, straining to get at each other in a torrent of abuse.

I glanced at Pikestaff. She looked bored rather than shocked. Another run-of-the-mill Thursday night.

Except for me.

These two women made Scott's outbursts look like tea and scones with my mother's patchwork club. The woman in Lycra spat at the policeman, saliva splattering onto his jacket. The other one was trying to stab anyone she could reach with her stiletto boots. No wonder Pikestaff was unperturbed that a middle-aged woman like me was having a wardrobe crisis.

She shuffled me over to the end of the counter, while I tried not to gawp round at the rumpus behind us. I prayed she'd keep that pair of devil women well away from me.

With my Home Counties accent and aversion to miniskirts, the only common denominator uniting us was an unfortunate choice of meeting venue. The F-word didn't trip off my tongue either, though Scott was no stranger to it.

When it was aimed at me, I felt the word land.

Pikestaff set out a sheet in front of her. I stood next to her, feeling as though I should make conversation, but what could I say? 'Do you get many middle-aged, middle-class women in here?' 'Is it always this chaotic on a Thursday night?'

I couldn't hold back my tears any longer. I took a tissue from the box on the counter, a nasty cheap affair that disintegrated, leaving me picking bits of paper off my face.

Pikestaff ignored my pathetic little sobs and started running through my details. She scribbled away, stabbing an impatient full stop onto the paper after every answer as though there was a particularly salacious murder to solve just as soon as she could wash her hands of me. 'Age?' Thirty-nine. 'Colour of eyes?' Brown. 'Distinguishing features?' None. 'Empty your pockets, please. Then I'll just need to search you.'

I looked at her to see if she was joking. There didn't seem to be anything funny about her. No wedding ring. I wondered if she had children. It was hard to imagine her soothing anyone to sleep. The disappointing contents of my pockets amounted to a Kleenex. She patted me down. Did she really think I had a knife tucked in my trousers? She rattled a plastic bag open. 'I need your belt and jewellery.'

I dropped in my belt and bangle. I hesitated over my necklace. My Australian opals. Scott had brought them for me all the way from his native Sydney, his first trip home after Alicia was born, thirteen years ago. I wrapped the necklace in a tissue and placed it in the corner.

I threw in the big diamond solitaire Scott had produced with a flourish on our fifth anniversary. 'Show that to your father,' he'd said. 'Told you we'd survive without his handouts.'

Every time I looked at it, it reminded me of my father's disapproval.

Pikestaff was still making notes. Judging by the concentration on her face, no 't' would escape uncrossed.

I slipped off my wedding band. The skin underneath was indented. Pale and shiny after fourteen years in the dark.

'You're allowed to keep your wedding ring,' she said, barely looking up.

I held it for a moment, absorbing its mixture of memories, then slowly slid it back onto my finger.

I handed her the bag and she scrawled away, listing the contents. She thrust the paper towards me. 'Sign here, please.' My hand was shaking so much I could barely form the letters of my name.

'You have the right to a solicitor. Would you like me to arrange one, or do you know someone?'

'Solicitor? No. Thank you.' I'd never even had a parking ticket before. Surely this wasn't going to escalate into a proper full-blown police investigation? I was convinced that, sooner or later, one of Pikestaff's minions would scuttle up and tell me I was free to go.

Pikestaff frowned as though I didn't have a clue. 'Do you want to tell someone you're here? You're allowed a phone call.'

Fright was taking the place of rebellion, but I declined. Scott knew I was here. That should be enough.

Surely that should be enough.

With a final flick of her papers, she picked up the boiler suit and said, 'Right. Let's take you down to a cell to get changed.'

My own incredulity, plus the shocking racket from the two women who were still taking it in turns to bellow obscenities, clouded my ability to think. Were they actually going to lock me up and make me strip?

4

'Couldn't I keep my blouse? Can't I just sit in here until all this gets sorted out? I promise I won't go anywhere.'

I think I was expecting her to make an exception because I wasn't slurring my words, didn't have any tattoos, and had had a shower in the last twenty-four hours.

She shook her head and opened a heavy grey door. 'Your shirt's considered evidence because it's got blood on the cuff. There's no point in arguing, we have to remove it. By force if necessary.'

I did that eyes-wide-open thing, trying to get my tears under control, but they were splashing down my cheeks then soaking into my blouse as I trailed along after her, just another Surrey miscreant to be dealt with before tea break.

Every cell door had a pair of shoes outside it. All too soon, it was my turn to feel the cold concrete beneath my feet. My patent boots looked out of place amongst the trainers and stilettos. Pikestaff stood back to let me enter, then followed me in. Pikestaff pushed her straggly blonde hair off her face. 'Your shirt.'

I gave in. My pride was already at an all-time low. I wasn't about to embark on an unseemly tussle with a policewoman, so I stripped off my blouse and thrust it at her without meeting her eye.

She put the boiler suit down on the mattress. 'Are you sure you don't want to wear this?'

'Quite sure, thank you.' I squared my shoulders, trying to ignore the fact that I was standing in front of someone I didn't know in a bra with more lace than substance. Judging by the disdain on her face, Pikestaff was more of a walking boots and headscarf sort of woman.

'Suit yourself.'

The silent stand-off fanned a tiny spark of rebellion inside me. She had no idea about my life, none at all. Let her pass judgment about what sort of woman I was. Let the whole world.

Something shifted slightly in her face. I recognised the signs of a last-ditch effort. 'Come on. Put it on. You don't want to end up being interviewed in your bra. There's CCTV everywhere.'

I tried to imagine walking through the police station with a mere whisper of black lace to protect my modesty. I pictured a crowd of officers pointing at the CCTV monitor and making jokes. To my frustration, my nerve buckled. I shook out the silly boiler suit and stepped into it. As I zipped up the front, resignation overwhelmed me. I didn't look at Pikestaff in case I found smug satisfaction on her face.

As she left, the door reverberated shut like a scene from a budget police drama. I tried to distract myself by thinking about people facing a lifetime in jail for their beliefs and what it would be like to wake up in a tiny cell every day for years. Instead I became obsessed with whether I could get out of here before I needed to use the vile metal loo in the corner. I racked my brains to remember when I'd last had a drink. A glass of wine before dinner, about eight-thirty. That was three hours ago. I prayed I'd be able to hold on all night.

I perched on the mattress, trying not to touch it with my bare hands. I wondered if Alicia was asleep. I hated the thought of her going to school in the morning all strung-out and exhausted. The memory of her bewildered face as the police marched me away, that teenage bravado long gone, threatened my fragile composure. I hoped she'd heard me shout, 'Don't worry, darling, it's just a bit of a misunderstanding,' over my shoulder as I ducked into the squad car. I hoped – probably in vain – that Scott had been more interested in comforting her than making sure she understood that 'I'd driven him to it'.

He couldn't really have intended for me to be sitting here in this airless pit, though. Every time someone opened the door outside in the corridor, the smell of stale urine wafted around. I saw the occasional shadow move past the opaque window to the outside, convincing myself every time that it must be Scott coming to save me. A man was singing 'Why are we waiting?' in the cell opposite. Whoever was next to me was trying to batter the door down. I kept jumping at every crash.

After what seemed like an eternity, a fetid gust signalled the arrival of someone. The metal shutter was pulled back. Then a dark-haired policeman I hadn't seen before came in, carrying a paper cup. Another person to feel humiliated in front of. Sitting there in a garb more suitable for carrying out a crime scene investigation made normal interaction impossible. I didn't even dress up for fancy dress parties. The hairs on my arms lifted with static as I crossed them over my chest.

'Are you OK?' His voice was gentle. None of Pikestaff's hostility.

I shrugged, then nodded.

'Here.' He handed me the tea. 'Can I give you a word of advice? Don't turn down the duty solicitor.'

'Why? I shouldn't even be here.'

'I'd have one, just in case. It can be a bit weird on your own the first time. It is your first time, isn't it?'

'Yes.' I wanted to add, *Of course*.

'Get someone to help you who knows the ropes. I shouldn't tell you this, but they've taken a statement from your husband.' He bit his lip and glanced at the door. 'He's going to press charges.'

I gasped. I didn't think anything Scott did could shock me any more. I was wrong. Just a day ago I'd thought we were in a calm period. We'd discussed Scott's next trip to Australia to check up on one of his building ventures, had a curry and watched the news. Then we'd gone upstairs and had sex, good sex.

And now he wanted to take me to court.

My God. I was actually going to *need* a solicitor. Lord. That meant rights and tapes and statements. I started shaking. Up until then, I hadn't really believed Scott would go through with this charade. I wanted to throw myself around the policeman's legs and beg him to get me out of here. I dug deep. And strangely enough, thought of my father and his favourite mantra. 'You can get anywhere with a bit of back-bone, Roberta, it's what defines the Deauville family.' I don't think my father ever expected me to grow a backbone to use against *him*, but I was grateful for it now.

I swallowed and concentrated on breathing. 'Could you organise a solicitor for me, please?' My voice wobbled. 'And I think I'd better phone someone.'

He nodded. 'I'll let them know at the desk.' He put his hand on my shoulder. 'Stop shaking. You'll be OK. Who do you want to phone?'

I dithered. Who would have the *Get out of jail free* card? Scott? Beg him to come down and tell them it was all a stupid joke? That obviously wasn't part of his plan. My mother? No, she could transform serving up a Sunday roast into a national emergency – 'Oh my God, I've forgotten the horseradish. Just a minute, get started, it will all go cold, nothing worse than cold food, come on, get eating.' Me, my bra and the police cell would probably put her on Prozac for good. My father? I wasn't sure whether he'd rush to my rescue or say, 'Serve you right'.

The policeman looked down at me, waiting for an answer. I trusted him. Even his name – Joe Miller, according to his name badge – was solid. GI Joe. He looked like the sort of chap who knew how to fix a dripping tap, who could change a tyre without swearing, who could accept there might be an opinion in the world that was different from his.

'I'd like to call my best friend, Octavia Shelton.'

He ushered me out of the cell to a side room and I told him the number to dial. I knew she'd be in bed. I imagined her spooned up to Jonathan, all fleecy nightshirt and woolly socks. I was always teasing her about her utilitarian choice of bedwear. Scott would never have put up with it. She seemed to take forever to answer. GI Joe announced himself as calling from Surrey police, quickly saying there was nothing to worry about – though that, of course, depended on your perspective. He handed the phone to me.

Relief coursed through me. Octavia would get it sorted. She always did.

Octavia

I hated the bloody phone ringing in the middle of the night. Good news could always wait until morning. My first thought was Mum. I'd never liked her living alone in that big house after Dad died. I was awake on the first ring; it just took me a little longer to find the flaming handset under yesterday's jeans.

I was still trying to get my head around the Surrey police announcement when Roberta came on the line. She sounded strained, as though she was being forced to speak in front of a hostile audience. As soon as she said, 'Arrested', she started blubbing and couldn't get proper sentences out. I got 'Scott' and 'solicitor' and something about bringing a T-shirt. I ended up speaking slowly into the receiver, not sure whether she could even hear me.

I told her I'd be there as soon as I could, already grabbing a jumper from the end of the bed. Then the police officer came back on the phone. When I asked if I'd be able to see her, he told me that 'detainees weren't permitted visitors while in custody'. That did freak the shit out of me. Even though he said he didn't know how long it would take for Roberta to be 'processed', I decided to go down anyway.

I pulled at Jonathan's wrist, trying to read his watch in the dark. Nearly one o'clock. He shrugged in his sleep. I shook him. Then again, much harder. The whole family could be hacked to death with a machete and Jonathan would just tug the duvet a little higher. In desperation, I held his nose. I thought he might suffocate before he opened his eyes. Panic that Roberta might be in real trouble made me pinch hard.

When he did finally gasp into life, he squinted around as though he'd never woken up in our bedroom before. If the house had been on fire, I would have saved the three children, dog, hamster and been back for the giant African land snails before Jonathan had worked out where he was.

'Roberta's been arrested. I'm going to the police station,' I said, while he was still peering round, mole-like. It really hacked me off that my husband could breathe life into any ailing computer but had the slowest thought processes on the planet when it came to getting to grips with the bare bones of a midnight phone call.

'Arrested? Wha-? What's happened?' He started getting out of bed, almost knocking over his water glass. 'Is she hurt?'

I shook my head. 'I don't think so.'

'How long are you going to be?'

'I don't know, she couldn't really speak. Not sure what's happened, something to do with Scott.'

'God, bloody Roberta. She can never have a drama at a civilised hour, can she?'

'She can't help it. Let's hope she hasn't murdered Scott,' I said, tying my hair back with one of Polly's school hairbands.

'Can't see that the world would be a worse place if she had done away with that arrogant git.'

'Don't say that. Anyway, go back to sleep.' I wasn't up for a rant about how Scott thought he was the dog's bollocks with his great big banger of a house, even if it was the truth.

He snuggled down again but stuck out his hand to squeeze mine. I held it for a second. He was warm, as always. I flicked away the grain of resentment at having to turn out on a freezing December night to hoover up the shards of someone else's life. Just for once I would have liked Jonathan to come and help me de-ice the car, make sure the stupid Volvo started. I snatched up my handbag and hoped Roberta hadn't done something very silly.

Though God knows, Scott deserved it.

Roberta

By the time I knew I was going to be released, I'd been swabbed, fingerprinted and photographed like a common criminal. I'd explained everything to a solicitor, then again to yet another policewoman who kept telling me that she knew how difficult this was for me.

Actually, she didn't have the faintest clue. Everything about Scott had been complicated: meeting in Italy when he was on a gap year and I was an art student, the ensuing courtship that survived to- and fro-ing from Australia to England, our differences in culture, manners and upbringing.

Not to mention everyone else's opinions on the subject.

I'd tried to be that obedient girl, destined for a future with a City boy. But I was no match for Scott's persistence. He'd torn through my staid world, bringing spontaneity and irreverence. Springing out on me in the university library, straight off the plane from Australia. Spraying 'I love you' in shaving foam on the Mini my dad bought me for my twenty-first. Asking me to marry him in Sydney's Waverley Cemetery, overlooking the sea.

This softly-spoken DC Smithfield probably thought I was a spoilt housewife, clinging on to a wealthy husband so I could shop for shoes every day. I didn't have the energy to explain that we'd toiled away together, building up Scott's property business, renovation by renovation.

By the time I signed the caution, accepting my guilt, I was punch-drunk, too exhausted to care about anything as long as I could lie down soon on a bed that wasn't in a cell.

DC Smithfield told me that they'd have to finish processing me outside the custody suite because they were dealing with some 'violent detainees' in there. I wasn't about to start splitting hairs over my preferred exit location. She led me into the normal part of the police station, where I'd once come to report the lawnmower being stolen from our shed.

And to my delight, Octavia was sitting there. My whole soul lifted as though I'd been staggering along with a box of encyclopaedias and had just found a table to rest it on.

She rushed over. 'What the hell's going on? Are you okay?'

I threw my arms round her, breathing in a trace of White Musk, the perfume oil she'd been wearing since we were about thirteen. I'd be able to pick her out blindfolded. Octavia was quick to prise me off her. She preferred the Swiss Army knife approach to drama.

She stepped back to look at me, taking in the boiler suit. 'Jesus. Didn't know you'd be dressed as Frosty the Snowman. Did you get the T-shirt I brought in?'

I shook my head. The detective constable looked apologetic. 'I'll check what happened there. Anyway, you can get changed back into your own clothes now.'

'Have they finished with you already?' Octavia asked. 'I thought I might be here all night.'

'They did me first while they were waiting for the others to sober up.'

DC Smithfield gestured for me to wait while she found the paperwork.

I sat with Octavia, relief flooding through me. She leant into my ear and whispered, 'Tell me you didn't kill him.'

I glanced towards the desk and kept my voice low. 'God, no, nothing like that. It's all resolved now. I just need to collect my belongings. Things got slightly out of hand. It was six of one and half a dozen of the other.'

'So what did happen?' Octavia said.

'Same old, same old.' A sudden weariness engulfed me. I was tired of talking about what had happened, of thinking about it.

Octavia was shaking her head. 'Hardly same old. You've never been arrested before.'

'Same old, but one step further. Scott was furious because I'd let Alicia wear an off-the-shoulder T-shirt to go to the cinema. It wasn't a sexy thing, just an ordinary T-shirt. He thought it was too tarty.'

'So?'

My stomach clenched as I remembered Scott shouting in my face, his Sydneysider accent becoming more pronounced.

'The Australian side of the business isn't going well and he's been a fight waiting to happen recently. I carried on cooking dinner, refusing to get dragged in. He wouldn't let it drop, kept on and on, right at me, how I'm so self-obsessed I can't see that my daughter is turning into a little floozy, and I'll be lucky if he doesn't disappear back to Australia with her, the usual stuff. I tried to push him away but he was standing there, holding me back with one arm and laughing.' I paused to stop the sob leaking out into my voice. 'Then he said it was probably a good job that we hadn't had any more kids as I was such a hopeless mother and I just lost control.'

A look of disgust flashed over Octavia's face. 'Vicious bastard.' She squeezed my hand. She was one of the few people who understood how much my two miscarriages still hurt, over a decade later.

15

'I picked up the frying pan and cracked it into the side of his head. The edge caught his forehead and it poured with blood. You know me, I was lucky not to faint. I shouldn't have done it. Though if I'd known he was going to send me here, I'd have cracked it a bit harder.'

Octavia flickered out a smile at that. 'Whoo-bloody-hoo. Poor little Scott got a bit of a bang on the head, bless his little cottons. Presumably he didn't bleed to death and stain the limestone?' As the words left Octavia's mouth, I saw her lips twitch. I started to giggle too, a spirally sort of laughter that made a good alternative to crying.

Octavia grew serious again. 'So how did you end up here?'

'He phoned the police. Said I'd assaulted him. So Watermill Drive had the glorious spectacle of blue lights flashing outside our house and me being escorted away in handcuffs. No doubt the Surrey grapevine is quivering as we speak.'

'He called the cops on you? Did they not look at the fact that he's about fifteen stone with arms like hams and you are, what? About eight stone? Bloody hell. I suppose they don't count all the times he's locked you out or sworn in your face? Talk about a piss-up in a brewery. No such thing as common sense in British policing, then.'

Octavia's shoulders went back. For one horrible moment, I thought she was going to march off and start grabbing a few ties over the reception desk. I was poised, ready to grip her arm. Luckily, they were busy dealing with a drunk who was complaining that his bike had been stolen and collapsing into hysterics every time he tried to spell his name.

I attempted to answer her. 'Scott's behaviour has never been serious enough to report. And I shouldn't have hit him.'

'He bloody deserved it. Anyway, it doesn't take a brain box to work out that he could probably stand up for himself. What was it? A scratch? I've got a plaster in my bag. Perhaps I'll pop over there and put some ice on his little head while

I'm at it. Maybe he'll piss off back to Sydney and do us all a favour.'

'Don't. His mother arrives tomorrow for Christmas.' I looked at the floor.

Octavia stared. 'Tomorrow? Make her stay in a hotel. You can't go home as if nothing has happened after this.'

'I have to. It's Christmas and I am not ruining it for Alicia. When it's over, I'll work out what I'm going to do. If anything.'

Octavia was shaking her head. 'You can't stay with him now. You just can't.' It was astonishing how much disapproval I'd managed to engender in my life.

I shrugged. 'It's not as though I've got a proper criminal record. It's just a caution.'

'A caution? What for?'

'Actual bodily harm.'

'Actual bodily harm? For a scratch and a bit of a bruise? That's bloody ridiculous. What an arsehole.'

'I shouldn't have allowed him to antagonise me. I'm sure he didn't mean what he said about the babies. You know how devastated he was at the time. And a caution doesn't mean anything unless I want to work in a school. Which obviously I don't.' I tried to smile. I loved my own daughter but had nothing like Octavia's natural affinity with kids.

'Could you have refused to accept the caution?'

'Yes, but if he didn't drop the charge, then it would have gone to court.'

'Scott wouldn't have done that, surely? Maybe he liked the idea of you sweating in a cell for a bit. He should have married some brainless drip, who never stands up to him. What would all his beefy business mates say if they found out his missus had clouted him one with a frying pan? He'd be a laughing stock.'

Octavia knew that Scott had a quick temper but I'd been economical with how often and how ferociously we'd argued. She simply wouldn't get it. She'd always seen marriage as a pie chart of household chores, parenting and work, with the tiniest sliver of romance and passion. The rollercoaster ride of love and anguish that I'd experienced with Scott was alien to her, though we'd never plumbed these depths before.

Octavia had her hands on her hips, waiting for me to explain.

'Scott made a statement. He said he would definitely press charges, so the solicitor advised me to admit "the offence", as he called it, and agree to the caution. I just wanted to get out of here.'

Shock washed across Octavia's face. She spoke in a low voice. 'Robbie. Where is all of this going to end? Are you going to stay with him until he's sucked every last bit of joy out of your life? Perhaps next time he'll get you sent to prison. You can't go on like this.'

'I know that.'

Octavia was expecting me to be like her. Make a decision, there and then, pack suitcases and be gone. I owed it to Alicia to get through Christmas, at least one more time. It was a massive leap from accepting that I couldn't live like this to separating from Scott permanently. If he went back to Australia, I'd probably never see him again. My growing-up history, the bedrock of my adult life, would be wiped out at a stroke.

There would be plenty of people celebrating that.

'Do your mum and dad know you're here?' Octavia asked.

'No. I decided I didn't need to burden them with this latest escapade. I think I've probably heard enough "*Oh darling!*" to last a lifetime.'

'You wouldn't consider going to stay with them for a few days?' Octavia asked.

'Definitely not.' There wouldn't be enough room in Surrey to accommodate such a vast quantity of 'I told you so's.

'Come and stay at mine, then. Bring Alicia. I'll put Immi in with Polly. You can have her room,' Octavia said.

'I won't, but thank you. Alicia's been looking forward to spending Christmas with her grandmother for months and I'm not going to disappoint her. Scott probably didn't mean to push it this far. It's a cultural thing. You know how he feels about people respecting him. I suppose smacking him over the head with a frying pan wasn't quite the adulation he thought he deserved. I imagine he'll be grovelling apologies when I get home.'

Octavia rolled her eyes. 'Respect. He doesn't know the meaning of the word. Whatever he says now doesn't take away from the fact that he's downright bloody cruel. Are you really going to go home and act like nothing's happened? *Cup of tea, darling? Polish your shoes?*' She was throwing her hands up in frustration. '*Blow job?*'

Black. Or white. That was Octavia. I usually envied her decisiveness. And I loved her for her loyalty. But right now, I wasn't in the mood for a lecture on the absurdity of my life. I could see her point. I didn't know how I was going to go home and put my Happy Christmas face on.

But going home I was.

Octavia

I sat on the bench watching Roberta sign for her stuff. I was reeling from the idea that my friend, my funny, gorgeous friend, now had a police record. I had no doubt that a week from now she'd be blaming herself and make out that Scott landing her in the clink was no big deal, simply the inevitable downside of a passionate relationship. God knows why a woman like her put up with a man like him. This was the girl who got a new boater and lacrosse stick every year while us scholarship girls were fannying about in grey gym kit and blazers several sizes too big. The girl who carried off her posh name with such ease, whereas I still cursed my working-class parents for landing me with the cumbersome 'Octavia' in the hope that I'd be 'someone', someone who'd require a name that stood out. Roberta was the girl who never had to sit out at school dances, who should have glided into the perfect life, bubble-wrapped from care, struggle and worry. But she could never pick the easy option.

I watched her talking to DC Smithfield and another policeman. The faint sense of guilt I always felt surfaced again. At heart Roberta was a goody-goody, all dainty teacups, poncey art exhibitions and god-awful obscure authors. But she'd been desperate to be my friend at school, joining me on my shoplifting jaunts, though never stealing herself, hanging out with me while I smoked my dad's fags at the park, helping me pierce my ears with a needle we'd sterilised in some hot Ribena. The fact that my dragon tattoo was on my arse rather than my shoulder was down to Roberta taking charge in the tattoo parlour.

If she hadn't met me, she'd probably think that taking back her library books late was a walk on the wild side. I'd introduced her to the joys of rebellion and that had led her straight into the arms of Scott, the biggest rebellion of all. I wondered, not for the first time, if I could have done more to stop her marrying him. On the few occasions I'd broached the subject, she'd made it quite clear that if we were to stay friends it was a case of 'Love me, love my feckless, repugnant choice of husband'.

I looked at my watch. Nearly three o'clock. I was going to be knackered for open day at work the next morning. I needed to be firing on all cylinders to convince sceptical parents that my outdoor nursery with its dens and mud kitchens would inspire their toddlers far more than plastic saucepans and dolls' prams. Bed would be good right now. The dark-haired police officer was emptying a plastic bag and passing things to Roberta. I strained my ears to hear what he was saying and managed to catch, 'Is there somewhere you can stay for the time being until you get things sorted out?'

I wondered if he'd be so bothered about a chubby, brown-haired woman with the beginnings of a double chin and no ankles – just feet stuck onto legs.

Roberta flicked her long black hair over her shoulder. The gesture was familiar. I knew she'd be dropping her head and raising her eyes, those dark brown eyes that whistled men to her. She had no idea how attractive she was. Yet another thing Scott had squashed out of her.

'I'll be fine, don't worry. My friend is going to take me home,' Roberta said.

He handed Roberta a leaflet. 'Don't forget about the domestic abuse helpline. You don't have to put up with it, but we can't help you unless you report it.'

The words 'domestic abuse' shocked me. We'd both dismissed Scott's outbursts as him 'having a short fuse'. Roberta's catchphrase was, 'You know what he's like.' But the policeman was right.

I walked up to the desk and tried again. 'Please come back with me. You can text Alicia from mine.'

'No, it's OK. I'd better get home and check on her.'

I glanced at the police officer. I wanted him to forbid her to go back. For him to have the argument with her so that I didn't have to. His eyes flicked to Roberta, then to me, in a way that was more than just a casual taking-in of scenery. The pressure had somehow switched to me to prove I could make Roberta see sense. I couldn't bring myself to disappoint the Plod. 'Robbie, Alicia will be asleep by now. You can talk to Scott in the morning when everyone's calm.'

I glanced over at Plod. He was nodding. I looked at him expectantly. It was on the tip of my tongue to say, 'Come on, mate, you get your shoulder behind the elephant and give it a shove uphill. I've been pushing for over a decade now, so a bit of a hand any time soon would be a right old bonus.'

Roberta had that set face on. She managed to look tear-stained, fragile and defiant. I was quite sure that I would have looked like a lump of defeated corned beef had the tables been reversed.

Plod finally waded in with a feeble, 'It's sometimes better to let the dust settle, Mrs Green. Why don't you go with your friend?'

Roberta smiled warmly and thanked him, without actually

answering. DC Smithfield led her into a side room to get changed, carrying her boots for her. Everyone wanted to look after Roberta.

Except the bloke she married.

Roberta

Usually Octavia kept a very tight silence when I tried to explain away Scott's bad behaviour. Now, as she drove me home, she'd abandoned all pretence, adopting my mother's helpful stance of 'But what about . . .?' as though that particular set of soul-sapping doubts would never have occurred to me.

I turned away from Octavia and watched the trees flash past in the dark. I knew he could be a bastard. I didn't need telling.

'You can still change your mind and come to mine,' Octavia said, without taking her eyes off the road. The immense effort she was making not to overrule me engulfed us, killing all conversation.

Octavia was so generous but I knew what Jonathan would be like. He'd pretend to be happy about me staying, then walk into the kitchen with a little too much purpose, radiating huffiness like a cat ejected from the warm spot in front of the fire. He'd snatch up my coffee cup before I'd finished and pass me my handbag every time I put it down somewhere. In this fragile frame of mind, I knew I'd also struggle with the chaos of Octavia's household in the morning. The children would be wandering about spilling Coco Pops everywhere, while Jonathan followed them around with a dustpan and brush. I never understood how Octavia could stand the children screaming with laughter, Charlie on his drum kit, often with Stan, their huge Alsatian, barking away, far too big for their little house. And that was without the TV on in the sitting room and kitchen.

I'd trained myself to find one child noisy enough.

No, I didn't want to go to Octavia's. I wanted to disappear up to the second floor of my own home and lock myself in the guest suite. Every bit of me yearned to snuggle under a clean duvet, pull down the blackout blinds and blank everyone else out.

Octavia rolled to a halt under the big chestnut tree outside our house. 'Shall I come in with you?'

'No. You've done enough, thank you. I'm not going to talk to Scott now, even if he's still awake. Don't wait. You're going to be worn out at nursery – go and get a few hours' sleep.' I gave her a big hug. Everyone needed someone they could call in the middle of the night.

I pointed the fob at the electric gates, got out of the car and walked up the lonely drive of my life, the cold slicing into my lungs. My key wouldn't turn in the front door. I stood fiddling with it for a moment, but I knew. Of course, I knew. Scott had dropped the latch.

Bastard.

Octavia's car still hadn't moved. Her concern was beginning to smother me. I wanted her to go so I could sift through the debris of my life in peace, even if it meant sleeping in the summerhouse.

I flicked the fob at the garage door and it rolled back. I waved at Octavia, forcing a smile, making shooing motions with my hand. This time I heard the creak of her ancient suspension as the car lumbered into reverse.

I picked my way past the gas barbecue and huge gazebo Scott used for summer parties, in his guise as the neighbourhood Lord of the Manor. The door into the utility room was unlocked. Not a total bastard, then. I put my boots in their little space on the shelf and tiptoed upstairs. The house was still. I prayed that Scott was asleep. The morning would be soon enough for that confrontation. Our door was shut, thank God. I looked in on Alicia, bunched up into a tight ball. I smoothed her hair, tucked the duvet round her and hurried to the top floor.

I could smell the stale air of the police station on my skin. The en suite shower was singing its siren call to me but I didn't want to wake Scott. Before I did battle with him, I needed some sleep. I stripped off my clothes, then hesitated. I put my underwear back on. Some discussions couldn't happen naked. I climbed under the duvet, my shoulders and neck releasing tension into the fat, downy pillows. Contrary to my expectations, sleep sucked me down into immediate oblivion.

And Scott catapulted me out of it.

He strolled into the room, clean-shaven, favourite blue shirt, handsome. A more sophisticated version of the spirited surfer boy who'd enchanted me in Venice nearly nineteen years ago. Far too flaming refreshed for someone who should have been lying awake, guilt-ridden and repentant.

'Hi. What time did you get back?' He sounded as though I'd been up to London for cocktails with the girls. He put a cup of tea on the nightstand. I was failing to match the affable man in front of me with the vindictiveness of the previous evening.

My head felt as though someone had filled it with stones. My eyes were dry and gritty. It was years since I'd gone to bed without cleansing and moisturising. I was blinking as though I'd been living underground, my mind slowly ordering the events of the previous day.

'I don't know what time. About three-thirty, maybe, no thanks to you.' I was scrabbling for accusations and anger. I had expected to fly at him, grab him by the perfectly ironed collar of his shirt and shake an explanation out of him. Instead, I was like the split beanbag in Alicia's den, a million little polystyrene balls littering the floor, leaving an empty casing in a heap. I waited for him to piece together some fragments of the puzzle that had transported me to that pit of a police station.

Instead Scott drew the curtains a fraction, running his finger along the sill. 'I've never understood why this room suffers so much with condensation.'

I hadn't either, but unlike Scott, that conundrum was number four thousand and twenty-nine on my list of immediate worries. Silence sat in the room. I just wanted him out of there, so I could have a shower and pull myself together. 'You're up and about early.'

Scott rarely scheduled any meetings before ten-thirty. 'Mum's landing at 11.30. You never know what the traffic's going to be like round Heathrow.'

I started. Adele! I had to get up, get going. The cleaner had changed her bed, but I needed to sort out some toiletries, towels, pop out for some flowers. I wanted to check that Alicia was OK before Adele swept in, taking over with her incessant chatter.

Scott standing there so nonchalant filled me with fury, giving life to my limbs. I felt as though I might leap out of bed and start snatching pictures off the wall to crash over his head. My throat had tightened so much, I wasn't sure I could force enough air through it to produce speech.

'Just so you know, I'm staying for Christmas. For Alicia's

sake. Over the next few days, I am going to forget what you did to me and do my best to carry on as normal. But when your mum has left, we need to have a serious talk.' My jaw was so tense, I could feel my wisdom teeth grinding together.

I expected him to bristle and start off down the 'Don't threaten me' route. He shrugged a brief acknowledgement. I waited for an apology or an excuse. Something that indicated that he understood I wouldn't just brush this under the carpet along with all the other hurts that had gnawed away at the great monolith of love we'd started out with. This time he'd pushed me too far. Instead he said, 'After you left yesterday, I took that quiche you were making out of the oven and put it in the fridge. Wrapped it in silver foil. Hope that was OK.'

Quiche. My God. I'd been in a cell half the night and we were talking about quiche. We'd be auditioning for *One Flew Over the Cuckoo's Nest* next. It was like being trapped in a reality show where the participants were selected on their ability to behave like lunatics. I could easily have obliged, launching myself at him, pummelling his chest and clawing his face with sheer frustration that all the love that we'd treasured, fought for and defended, lay shattered around us, with barely enough strength to plead for one last chance.

Scott walked towards the bed as though he was going to kiss me goodbye.

Before I could react, he stopped a couple of feet away and waved. 'I'll be off then. See you later.'

Either he'd read my face or he saw that there was something of the great unwashed about me. Scott was a man who liked his women fragrant, plucked and waxed. I didn't know whether I could go back to being that person now. I tried to imagine going downstairs, packing my stuff and walking out of the door.

The problem was I couldn't conjure up any images in the black beyond.

Octavia

There weren't many days when I regretted setting up my holistic nursery but today, two days before Christmas, was one of them. My eco-ethos meant I couldn't fob off the kids with sticking a bit of glitter on a few polystyrene stars. Instead, we'd done a full-scale expedition down to the woods to gather 'material' for decorations. This had led to a couple of four-year-olds getting covered in dog poo, a little girl collecting rabbit droppings to use as food for Rudolph and another boy sitting in a puddle pretending he was a duck. The morning had ended up being less about decorations and more about turd control.

By the time I'd picked the girls up from my mother's and popped into the supermarket on the way home, I was officially knackered. My heart lifted as I squeezed the car in next to Jonathan's Rover. His company had obviously found a little Christmas cheer and let them go early. He could help me lug in the shopping. I'd fought my way round Tesco trying not to barge into people who'd left it until the twenty-third of December to decide they needed a Christmas pud. I'd got all the basics in place but I liked my vegetables fresh. Immi and Polly had bickered from start to finish: the illogical mind of an eight-year-old pitched against the pedantic tendencies of the ten-year-old. They were still having a ding-dong over who was having the chocolate Santa on the Christmas tree. With the last pinch of patience I could muster, I told them to ring the doorbell to ask Daddy to come and help. Charlie eventually came to answer, bringing with him the distinct smell of an unshowered teenager who's been glued to a screen all day.

'Where's Dad?'

'He's in bed.'

'Is he ill?'

'I don't think so, just said he was really tired and needed a lie-down.'

I'd give him a lie-down. As usual, Jonathan would rock up to Christmas without writing a single Christmas card or chasing the end of the Sellotape, let alone coming into contact with a supermarket trolley or a vegetable peeler. He'd then dice with death on Christmas Eve by saying, 'Did we send a card to the boss and his wife?'

I slammed the boot shut, shoved a couple of carrier bags at Charlie and stomped up the stairs. I burst into our bedroom to find Jonathan in his Y-fronts, face down on the bed, shoulders rising and falling with the rhythm of deep sleep. I shook him.

'Jonathan. Jonathan. Do you think you could give me a hand to bring the shopping in?'

He gurgled and snuffled his way back into consciousness.

'What are you doing in bed? I need help with the bags. Now would be good.'

Jonathan rolled over and groaned. 'Can you get Charlie to do it?'

'I can, but given that you've got the afternoon off, perhaps you might like to move your lard and lend a hand rather than tipping up on Christmas Day wondering how the fairies did such a marvellous job. I've had a gutful of the girls going at each other, so feel free to chip in.'

He pulled himself into a sitting position and ran his hands over his face. 'I haven't got the afternoon off.'

'What's the matter with you then? Are you ill?'

'No.' He hugged his knees into his chest. 'I've been made redundant.'

All my aggression seeped away. Guilt rushed into the space left behind. I hadn't seen that coming. I didn't know what to say. I sat down on the bed and reached for his hand. 'Bloody hell. When did they spring that one on you?'

'As soon as we got in this morning. Called in five of us, one after the other.' Jonathan's voice was flat, monotone. His face was pale and blotchy. I hoped he hadn't been crying. One of the things I loved most about Jonathan was that he was solid. Resilient. Which was just as well because my wifely qualities were a bit sparse in the knee-patting category.

'Why you? They were telling you how crucial you were to their management strategy in your last review.'

'Cost-cutting. We need to be able to compete with the Asian market and there are plenty of bright young things coming in from university who can do what I do, maybe not better, but certainly cheaper. Seems that experience in computing isn't as important as I thought. So "Cheers, mate, thanks for all your hard work, of course there'll be a period of 'consultation' but don't forget your jacket on the way out."'

'Wankers. They've always been out with the old and in with the new. Think of all those bloody Bank Holidays you've worked because there was no one else they could trust to keep the systems running.' I could understand how people stormed back into their former workplaces and smashed everything up. I needed to step away from the mallet myself.

I snuggled up to him. 'Poor you.' I couldn't imagine Jonathan without a job. That's what he did. Got up and went to work every day. He took a boffin-like pleasure in being 'in computers', a geeky delight in the 'sounds very clever' comments from people who didn't want him to elaborate further in case they had no idea what he was on about. Shock was giving way to practicalities. How would I cope with him in the house every day while I rushed three children out to school and went to work myself?

The volcano effect was my forte – the most pressing thing came to the priority surface. Jonathan, on the other hand, spent any time when he wasn't being a workaholic tutting over milk cartons opened in non-date order, spoons in the fork section of the cutlery drawer and tea towels gaily discarded on the back of chairs. Disorder caused him pain, whereas the kids and I didn't even notice.

When I'd unexpectedly found myself with the proverbial bun in the oven, aged twenty-two, I'd been grateful for Jonathan's practical approach to life. Over the years, though, the über-organisation Jonathan required became a barrier to having fun. God forbid a trace of paint, glitter or glue should sully our kitchen table after a craft session with the kids. His latest obsession – putting the honey on a little square of kitchen roll in case it left a sticky ring on the shelf – made me want to drizzle it around the skirting boards and stick Stan's dog hairs in it. The idea of Jonathan lying in wait when I trollied in after work, leaving a trail of shoes, coats and bags, didn't spell harmony for us.

It seemed the wrong time to mention the little matter of money, but I'd never been good at picking my moment. We couldn't survive on my wage as a nursery manager.

'Did they give any indication of your package?'

'Statutory pay.' He looked down at his hands.

I didn't want to turn the knife by asking for an exact figure – though my mind was working out a savings versus mortgage payment ratio – but anything statutory didn't sound good. It was too late to do any Christmas cost-cutting. I was regretting the XBox splurge, cross with myself for letting Charlie suck me in with his 'everyone's got one'.

I found a smile. 'Never mind, love. On the upside, you won't be called in on New Year's Day and you can have a proper holiday, a real rest. There'll be something out there for you, something better. In the meantime, it'll be great to have you at home.'

I turned to hug him. 'Sorry,' he whispered.

I kissed the top of his head and went downstairs to heave in the shopping.

And yes, I had sent a bloody Christmas card to the boss and his wife.

Roberta

'Happy Christmas, beautiful. Thought we'd get the day off to a good start.'

Seasonal goodwill to irrational men and jailbait wives was shining all around, from Scott's perspective at least. I was still sleeping in the guest suite. When Adele had arrived in her usual whirlwind of news from Down Under a couple of days before, Scott and I had embraced an entente cordiale worthy of the Middle East, all 'Coffee, darling? Sauv Blanc or Chablis? Soup or salad?' As soon as Adele and Alicia were in bed, I'd retreat up to the second floor, with barely a hiss goodnight.

Now here he was, holding out a glass of pink champagne, like every other Christmas.

I took it, resting the delicate stem on my stomach, trapped between so much and so little to say. Scott took a large swig from his glass, then sat on the edge of the bed.

I knew that look.

He pulled back the edge of the duvet, looking playful and cheeky, the same sun-kissed maverick I'd met in Italy where I'd been studying art history a lifetime ago. He was nothing like the boys I'd known before who twiddled away at me as though they were trying to tune into Capital Radio, downing pints and not thinking beyond their summer bar jobs. I'd spent three days resisting having sex with him before he headed off on his bus tour, promising to write. Octavia – as usual – had teased me something rotten. 'Australian sex-god meets Britain's answer to Mother Teresa. You won't hear from him again.' She was wrong. At twenty-two, Scott knew what he wanted from the world – money, property, status – and me.

'You've got a gorgeous body,' he said, leaning over to kiss my neck. I turned my head away.

'Come on. We always have sex on Christmas Day.'

'This isn't like any other Christmas Day though, is it?' I said.

'It could be.'

'How can it be? Really, Scott, how can it? Do you understand this goes beyond one of our normal rows? That you have actually overstepped a line?' I slammed my glass down on the nightstand.

'You know I didn't mean it. I got carried away in the heat of the moment. I'd had such a tough day. The bank pulling the plug on that property up in Queensland, that venture capital guy messing me around. I took it out on the wrong person. I'm really sorry. I shouldn't have said what I said.' He paused. 'It still does me in, too, you know. I would have loved those babies.'

There was no mistaking the tight knot of rage in my stomach, even though I wanted to believe that he was sorry. God, I was desperate to accept he was so sorry that he was coming apart at the seams, trembling in his shoes about whether I would forgive him this time. However furious I'd become in the past, I'd never truly considered leaving him.

But then he'd never taunted me about my babies before.

A door banged downstairs. Alicia would be getting ready for our present-opening ritual. I shrugged, unable to voice any thoughts that wouldn't inflame me further. Christmas morning wasn't the right morning to embark on a big discussion because I had no idea where it might end. Octavia had been right all those years ago: Scott was too unpredictable, though that was rich coming from her.

It was one of the things I'd loved about him.

I sipped my champagne, feeling the bubbles spread their soothing tendrils through me.

Scott was the picture of contrite. He smoothed a strand of hair behind my ear. I shook him off. 'Come on, doll. I made a big mistake. What can I do to make it up to you?'

I drew my knees up to my chest. I could still feel the stickiness and grime of that police cell no matter how many times I showered. 'Nothing.'

'It's Christmas. Let's enjoy ourselves. For Alicia's sake.'

I wavered, unsure whether Scott was just trying to weasel his way out of trouble or was genuinely regretful. I did want Alicia to have a lovely day.

In case lovely days were suddenly in short supply.

Maybe, over time, I could forgive him.

He swung round to face me, his index finger under the silk shoulder strap of my nightie.

But definitely not yet.

'No. Just no. Get off.'

He stood up, backing away, hands raised in surrender. 'OK, OK. No need to turn nasty.'

Pot. Kettle.

I got out of bed. 'Come on, we need to get downstairs. Alicia still gets excited about presents.'

Scott drained his glass, shaking his head as though I was completely irrational. He paused at the door. 'I hope you're not going to spoil today by sulking.'

I waited until he'd disappeared downstairs to hurl a pillow at the wall.

I heard Alicia shouting down the landing. 'Mum? Mum? When are we doing presents?'

I called down to her. 'I'm up here. Shower's not working properly in our bedroom. Be down in a mo. Can you see if Granny Adele wants a cup of coffee?'

As soon as I arrived in the kitchen, Adele was right there, getting in the way of the fridge, standing in front of every cupboard I wanted to open, like a dog I'd forgotten to feed.

'Where's Scotty?' she said. 'He used to love Christmas, first one up. When my Jack was alive, we'd all get up at six to make the most of the day. I used to buy kilos of potatoes, parboil them, fluff them up in the colander. And Jack, he was in charge of the turkey. We used to get it from Mr Saunders. His is the house on the corner of our road, you know, the one with the blue gates and the boat-shaped bird table on the front lawn . . .'

Endless detail rained down in the strong Scottish accent Adele had retained despite emigrating to Australia in her late teens, fifty years earlier. I put the coffee machine in motion and nipped into the loo to text Octavia. She'd sounded wrung-out when she'd filled me in on Jonathan's redundancy the day before. With three kids who all came with a bewildering array of after-school activities, I knew they struggled to keep their heads above water even when Jonathan was earning. I wondered how I could persuade Octavia to let me lend her some money.

Happy Xmas – hope you are OK. All bearably festive here. Kilted kangaroo bouncing about but calm everywhere else. Going out for lunch shortly. When can you escape for a walk?

We'd always gone out for a walk on our own on Christmas Day. As teenagers, we'd examined each other's new eye shadows and compared appalling knitwear. In our twenties, I'd tried to play down Scott's extravagant presents. Even when we were broke, he'd still decorated the tree with little love messages, souvenirs from places we'd been, postcards of paintings I loved. Once Charlie was born just after Octavia's twenty-third birthday, Jonathan appeared to skip romance and went straight to the practical. Octavia laughed it off. 'Anyone can buy fancy knickers. Not everyone is lucky enough to have a husband who can build a cupboard to keep them in.'

Since we'd had children, our walk on Christmas Day was simply a pressure cooker valve – a breather to let off steam about our families so that we could return with smiles on our faces. Today, more than ever, I'd be glad of the escape.

A beep on my mobile signalled Octavia's reply.

Jonathan deep in the doldrums and moaning about how much I've spent. Mum quoting gloomy figures from Daily Mail about job market. Kids high on sugar. Happy days! Can't wait to go for our walk – 4-ish?

Poor Octavia. I didn't know how she stood Jonathan and his penny-pinching. I'd pointed it out early on and we'd had one of our few proper rows about it, descending into a slanging match about me being born with a silver spoon in my mouth. All credit due to her though, she'd been the first to cheer me on when Scott and I shunned my dad's money and made a living doing up tatty old houses.

Was it really all for nothing?

Octavia

Jonathan usually loved choosing the Christmas tree. He would spend hours in the local garden centre, debating with the children until they found the perfect specimen, the one and only Norwegian spruce that could grace our lounge. Then he'd haul it into the right place, the exact spot between the fireplace and the dresser. Immi and Polly would decorate it according to Jonathan's rigid spacing and ornament eking-out rules, with Charlie chucking the baubles on willy-nilly.

But this year Jonathan had come up with 'I haven't got time/the girls don't want to go today/the trees will be cheaper nearer the day' until the one ritual I could delegate without guilt had plopped back onto my plate. The result was spindly and lacklustre. Instead of the usual good-natured banter over whether to have the fairy or the star on top, the kids had argued over who was going to hang up the bloody glass reindeers and who got stuck with the crappy old snowflakes. Resentment had sliced into my fantasies of a cheery household floating about singing angelic bursts of *Once in Royal David's City*, and lingered right through to Christmas Day itself.

Mum had arrived at eight o'clock that morning as though we would need five hours to prepare a roast lunch for six people. She stood in the kitchen hovering but not actually 'doing' until the hairs on my neck were quivering with irritation.

I managed to shoo her out to play Scrabble with Immi, which meant I could slosh industrial quantities of Chablis into my glass without copping the fourteen units a week speech. This year's project of knocking our lounge and dining room together to make one big living space was beginning to look like a mistake. Instead of being tucked away with the XBox, Polly and Charlie were right under Mum's nose. As Mum thought anything more hi-tech than a landline was the path to all evil, it was only a matter of time before she decided to deliver the 'Give a child a cardboard box and they'll be just as happy' speech.

Normally, Charlie would laugh and say, 'Oh Nanna, get real,' but this year, a huge bellow of 'Jesus Christ, we're not in the 1950s' came echoing through to the kitchen. A door slam followed.

I poked my head through the hatch and saw my mother rear up like a meerkat on its look-out mound, turning from Jonathan faffing about with the precise angle of the serviettes, to me, waiting to see how we were going to deal with – shock, horror – God's name being taken in vain on Christmas Day.

Jonathan rolled his eyes and went back to straightening the knives and forks that Polly had thrown down in a slap-dash manner. I tried Roberta's New Age bollocks of visualising lying in a hammock in Barbados, but discovered that only a hiss at the husband would do.

'Jonathan, do you think you could go and deal with Charlie, please, while I finish off lunch?' I probably sounded calm to the casual listener but sixteen years of marriage had taught him to recognise the meaningful '—CCCHHH' on the end of that sentence. With one last tweak of the table mats, he made his way upstairs.

I shouted through to Polly. 'Come and take through the cranberry sauce for me, love.'

No answer. I shouted again.

'In a minute.'

'No, now, we're nearly ready to sit down.'

'I'm just finishing this game.'

I bit back a bellow of 'Come now!' Never mind a flipping virgin birth, my kids doing what they were told the first time I asked them would be the true miracle of Christmas.

Instead of Polly appearing, Immi came into the kitchen instead. 'My tummy hurts. I don't want any lunch.'

Honestly, next year I'd just do beans on toast.

'It'll make you feel better if you have something to eat. I've made your favourite, cauliflower cheese.' I stroked her strawberry-blonde curls.

'I'm not hungry. I already ate all my selection box. Do you want to know what I had? I had a Curly Wurly, a Mars bar, a Milky Way, a Twix – I've got one stick of that left – and a packet of jelly babies.'

At this rate, we'd need an appointment with the emergency dentist. 'I thought Dad said you could only have one thing.'

'He did, but then when I asked him if I could eat the rest, he just went "hmm" and carried on reading his book, so I thought it was OK.'

I could feel a bit of a Jesus Christ incident coming on myself.

'I gave the Maltesers and Revels to Stan, though. I wasn't that greedy.'

'You shouldn't give chocolate to dogs. It's bad for them. Anyway, never mind.' I turned back to stirring the gravy, which had now gone all lumpy.

I took a deep breath and called through to the front room. 'Mum, it's ready. Can I pass you these things through the hatch?'

42

Mum scurried over and busied herself with the food, just as Jonathan reappeared.

'Charlie won't come down.' There was something pathetic in his tone, a waiting for me to get it sorted.

The food was getting cold, which made me want to have my own tantrum. It was definitely early-onset middle age – more bothered about chilly carrots than my son having a Yuletide meltdown. Not for the first time, I mourned the era of spending every holiday backpacking on a diet of beer and crisps. I trudged up the stairs, shouting 'Start serving' in the general direction of Mum and Jonathan in the hope that between them they might summon up the initiative required to get a few Brussels on plates without me.

'Go away.' Charlie was nose-down in his pillow.

'Please don't spoil the day, darling. I know Nanna's irritating. She irritates me as well and no doubt, when I'm old, you'll bin my false teeth so you can't hear what I'm saying either.'

'I hate Christmas.'

'So do I.' And I really meant it.

That made Charlie sit up. 'How can you hate Christmas?'

'How can you?' I smiled, trying not to think of my gravy getting a skin on it. 'Come on, love, help me out here.'

He got to his feet, torn between wanting a hug and wanting to be bolshie. 'OK. Sorry.'

I squeezed his hand, or rather the cuff of his sweatshirt. At fifteen, Charlie didn't seem to have hands any more. He scuffed down the stairs, still my little boy under that gangly mini-man.

In the dining room, I jollied everyone along, praying that Mum wouldn't choose right now to need an apology. 'Let's pull the crackers.' Polly snatched the fat end of the cracker from Immi, claiming ownership of some plastic earrings. Immi burst into tears and slid under the table, refusing to come out even when Polly handed them over.

As I slopped the chipolatas wrapped in bacon onto plates, I heard Stan throwing up his honeycomb centres in the kitchen. Season of festive fun, my worn-out old arse.

I wondered when I'd last enjoyed Christmas.

An image of peeling off wetsuits, dragging a windsurf up a deserted beach and huddling round a fire with a couple of beers and some prawns on skewers rushed into my mind. I could almost smell the Mediterranean maquis that grew along the seashore. My twenty-one-year-old self, with pink hair, toe rings and a penchant for batik, would be hard-pressed to recognise me now.

The age-old longing that I kept buried, occasionally bunging another layer of earth on top, caught me off-guard. I wondered if he ever thought about me.

Roberta

Christmas Day in the Green household was a day for singing twee Australian songs. This year, I clung to the ritual as proof that we were still a family, rooted in our customs and traditions. I closed my eyes as I sat in the passenger seat, marvelling at Scott who was blasting out 'Waltzing Matilda' as though he were off to Bondi Beach with no more on his mind than the state of the surf. Despite Alicia's entreaties, I couldn't join in.

When we arrived at the hotel, I prayed that I'd made a good choice this year. I wasn't sure I could face one of Scott's forensic investigations into why they'd run out of red cabbage today. Scott strode in, making himself known to the staff, booming a big Happy Christmas to all. Alicia was right behind, light on her feet in her silver sandals, as wispy and delicate as Adele was stocky and stout. Granddaughter and grandmother linked arms together, pointing out the tree covered in glittery hearts and crimson ribbons. I glanced around at the other families and wondered if any of their smiles camouflaged upset so intense that they could feel it trembling in their chests.

Staff in black and white uniforms offered us Buck's Fizz

at the door to the wood-panelled dining room. Scott picked two from the tray. As we sat down, he handed one to Alicia.

'She's under eighteen. She can't drink that in here,' I said.

'Lighten up. It's Christmas, for God's sake. Bloody British licensing laws. They're not going to chuck us out. It's only like a bit of lemonade and orange juice.'

Alicia looked at me, not knowing which way to jump. She'd been pretty subdued since my return from the police station and I hated her having to be the peacemaker, in the impossible position of trying to protect me without angering Scott. I put on a smile. 'I'm sure Daddy's right. Just don't draw attention to it.' She glanced round and took a big gulp.

Adele was cooing over the log fire. 'In all these years I've never got used to Christmas in the sunshine.' Off she went on her usual discussion about what it would mean to move back to Scotland now, but with all her brothers dead, and barely knowing her nieces and nephews, except that wee Caitlin who would keep coming out and staying for months on end . . .

Scott yawned and beckoned for some more drinks. Alicia started texting God knows who. Adele paused just long enough to order her meal then continued to reel off a never-ending list of relatives with respective geographical locations. 'My cousin Archie is still in Aberdeen, but his wife, Siobhan, she passed away in 1999. No, let me think. Not 1999. It must have been 2000, because it was the year Sydney had the Olympics . . .'

My will to live was seeping away by the time the scallops on pea puree arrived. Scott raised his glass in a toast. Alicia's glass was empty and two bright spots had appeared on her cheeks. I ordered her an orange juice. We drifted in and out of conversation, with Alicia quizzing Adele about whether you could tame a kangaroo while Scott quaffed the Châteauneuf he'd chosen.

Enormous platters of roast goose arrived. 'I wonder how Octavia's getting on cooking for her brood,' I said. 'It's such a luxury to have it all done for you.'

Scott looked over at me. 'She hasn't trained Jonathan right, has she? Unlike you, who's never cooked from day one.'

I put my mouth into a smile and kept my tone light. 'That's not true. I do cook, though I get a bit stressed if I'm catering for a lot of people or your business colleagues.'

Scott always liked to make out I was too idle to do anything myself, but the truth was he thought paying other people to clean, fix and garden was a sign that he'd arrived. He loved boasting that his wife didn't have time to work because 'managing the staff was a full-time job'. Despite Scott's dismissive words, cooking was the one area where I still retained a little control.

Adele was brewing up opposite me, no doubt ready with some comment about how she always makes double the amount and freezes half of it, but Scott hadn't finished.

'Come off it. When did you last cook a proper meal? Something that wasn't out of the freezer or the microwave?' He stuck a whole potato in his mouth and sat back with his arms folded.

Alicia frowned and put her fork down. 'Dad, that's not true. Mum was cooking fish pie the other night when you called the police on her. And she'd made that asparagus quiche she'd seen in a magazine.'

Adele jerked round to face Scott. 'Police? What police? Scotty?'

Scott ignored her. Everything in me tightened, ready for blast-off. Before I had time to think of a cover-up, if a cover-up were possible, Scott turned on Alicia. Bits of potato flew out of his mouth, sticking to his wine glass. 'If you hadn't gone out dressed like a little trollop then I wouldn't have got angry with your mother.'

I put out a calming hand. 'Anyway, that's all over and done with. We were both a bit silly. Come on, let's not spoil Christmas Day.'

I expected Alicia to back down and appease Scott as she usually did, but she surprised me. 'I'm not spoiling it, Dad is. I wasn't dressed like a trollop, was I, Mum?' Alicia said.

'I'm not going to discuss any of this now,' I said, making a conscious effort to keep my voice low.

The Buck's Fizz had unleashed a bravery in Alicia I'd never seen before. 'There was nothing wrong with what I was wearing. It's called fashion, Dad. You're always ruining everything. Keira's mother saw the police taking Mum away on Thursday night. All my class were asking me how many years she'd got and pretending to put handcuffs on me.' Her bony shoulders were hunched up around her ears.

'Why did the police take Roberta away?' Adele was wide-eyed. 'Scotty? You didn't tell me that.'

I was just working out which words I was going to put together to form an explanation that wouldn't wreck the whole day when Scott slammed down his knife and fork with such force it made the glasses chink together.

Scott scraped back his chair but didn't get up. 'Mum, shut up. It's none of your bloody business.' I had my hand on his arm to quieten him down, but it was too late. 'Don't you dare shush me. If you weren't such a shit mother, I'd never have called the police in the first place.'

The silence in the dining room dominoed from table to table until the only noise was the laughing and banter from the customers by the window. I steeled myself to look round. The Maître d' was bristling his way over.

'Everything all right, sir?'

'Yes. Fine.' Scott didn't sound contrite or conciliatory.

The Maître d' didn't go away. I was aware of the woman at the next table telling her children to be quiet and turning their heads away from us. I closed my eyes. I wanted to smile and pretend everything was OK. I looked down at my plate and picked up my fork. My stomach wouldn't co-operate. It had shut down, closed over like a pair of lift doors. Alicia was huddled in her chair, tension radiating from every pore.

Adele stepped in. 'Sorry for the noise. My son is a very passionate man and I think I may have spoken out of turn. That's families for you. We know how to push each other's buttons, don't we, Scotty?'

Scott mumbled something and the Maître d' offered a crisp, 'Very well, sir,' and clipped off again.

Nobody spoke. Not even Adele. Alicia sat opposite me with fat tears dropping onto her plate. I reached over for her hand. She gripped my fingers hard, like she used to when she was a toddler and a dog sniffed at her. 'I can't eat any more.'

Maybe it was the rasp in her voice. Or the whispers in the dining room. The heads craning round pretending to look for a waiter, but having a jolly good stare at the wife with the atrocious husband instead. Alicia's humiliation was tangible, her whole body rigid. We were supposed to protect her, not invite ridicule. I looked at Scott. His jaw was set, that familiar look of self-justification clamped around his features. A hot rush of emotion coursed through me. Then a surge of release as though I'd removed a pair of crippling shoes.

Just because I wanted our marriage to work didn't mean I could make it work.

I was never going to make it right. Never. I got quietly to my feet, fished in my bag and handed the BMW key to Alicia. 'Just pop out to the car for a minute, darling.'

Alicia hated being the centre of attention, and relief mingled with her confusion. She scuttled past Scott before he had time to argue. I looked at Adele, who was fiddling with her necklace and looking every one of her sixty-eight years. 'I'm sorry, Adele. We shouldn't have let you come over this year. We've had a bit of a tough time lately.'

I sucked myself in, clenching every muscle in my stomach in case I suddenly jellyfished onto the floor. There was only one chance to say this. I screwed up my eyes, then dived in. I forced out little more than a whisper.

'I'm leaving you.'

Scott sat back in his chair, hands in the air in disbelief. 'Don't be silly. Where are you going to go? Come and sit down.'

I couldn't say anything more. Too many eager faces were waiting for my next move. Yet another occasion when a random crowd would witness Scott 'having his say'. I'd add it to the list of sunny barbecues spoilt by a wine-fuelled argument with the host. Parties when Scott had decided to 'have a word' with a guest he deemed to be flirting with me. Meals where the chef's opinion on what made the perfect dish differed from Scott's. Enough of my life had been played out in public. I stared at the man I'd loved for so long.

Maybe I still loved him. Now I had to save myself. And Alicia.

He looked like he didn't believe me, as though he somehow thought he had the magic word, the clever spell to bring foolish Roberta back in line. My last glimpse of him was sitting there puzzled, as though he'd been showering me with compliments and I'd taken umbrage at nothing.

I turned round and concentrated all my energy on putting one foot in front of the other. I squeaked out a 'thank you' and a 'sorry' to the Maître d' at the door without stopping to hear his reply. Just a corridor to go. A courtyard with a Christmas tree. A patch of grass. Then the car. Alicia was standing by the passenger door as pale as an icicle in the sun. I pushed out the last words I could manage.

'I'm sorry, darling. I've left your father.'

Octavia

Christmas Day wasn't a day for unexpected visitors, so when the doorbell rang, I assumed it was carol singers and left Jonathan to deal with them while I organised the Christmas pud. I'd poured the brandy over it and Polly was about to take centre stage lighting it, when Jonathan shouted through to me.

'Roberta's here. And Alicia.' Jonathan didn't do gushing welcomes.

I came out into the hallway, squeezing past Jonathan and all the anoraks breeding away on the coat hooks. Jonathan clearly thought he'd covered the social niceties and disappeared back into the dining room. I hugged Roberta. 'Happy Christmas. Hello Alicia, darling. Come on in. Have you had a good day? You're early. I thought we were walking at four.'

Before she could reply, Polly shouted from the dining room. 'Mum! Mum! When are we going to light the pudding? Charlie says he's doing it, but I want to.'

'I'm coming. Just a sec.'

I turned back to Roberta. She was silent, flicking at the tassels of her scarf. My smile faded.

She stepped forward. 'I'm sorry to do this to you on Christmas Day. I know you've got your own issues to deal with.' She didn't get any more out. Just stood there, silent tears running down her face. Alicia was wary, her face buttoned-up and defensive. I did an inward sigh.

'Not more trouble with Scott?'

Roberta nodded.

Polly shouted again.

I took Roberta's arm. 'Oh God. Shit, just let me do the Christmas pud with Polly, then I'll be right with you. Come through.'

'It's OK. I'll sit in the kitchen. You finish lunch. We don't want to get in your way.' Roberta looked gaunt. I wanted to bring her in and warm her up with chunky soup and beef stew.

I ushered her down the hallway. 'Make yourself a cup of coffee. Alicia, there are some little chocolates on the side, lovey, help yourself.'

I dashed into the dining room and sat back down next to Polly. Jonathan raised his eyebrows. Turning away so Mum couldn't see, I pulled a 'yikes' face at him. As Polly snatched up the matches, I put my hand out for them. 'Here, let me show you.'

'I can do it. I'm not a baby.' She scraped away until the match snapped.

'Isn't Roberta coming in to say hello?' Mum asked.

'Not just yet. She didn't want to interrupt our lunch.' Roberta wouldn't need Mum's tuppence-worth today.

'It's very rude to leave her in the kitchen.'

I cut Mum off, leaving her pursing her lips and muttering about common courtesy. I turned back to Polly.

'Right, darling. Have another go. Strike it gently, but quickly.' I was itching to put my hand over hers and hurry her along, conscious of Roberta sitting next door with her life going up the Swanee while we were faffing about with the finer points of pyrotechnics.

Tongue out in concentration, Polly raked the match across the box until, to everyone's relief, it finally burst into flame. I pushed the pudding across to her. The brandy lit with a whoosh. Polly beamed. I glanced through the hatch at Roberta. I wondered if she wanted to stay the night. Jonathan had already given me the belt-tightening speech, as if I needed it. He wouldn't be sharing out his dinner too eagerly.

Out of the corner of my eye, I saw Polly lean forward to sniff the brandy that was licking about over the pudding in a purple haze. I managed to say 'Careful' before a flame burned its way up a length of her brown hair. She screamed. Jonathan grabbed a serviette and his glass of wine and belted round the table, sloshing and smothering. I shot out of my chair, patting at her with the edge of the tablecloth.

Polly started crying, 'My face, my face.'

The room smelt as though I'd let a pan of rice boil dry. Jonathan dashed into the kitchen, shouting at Roberta to get some ice out of the freezer. Immi came flying round and clung to me, shock pinching her face. I cuddled her while I inspected the damage.

A chunk of hair had burnt off about halfway up, the charred ends black against the pale brown. A red welt ran vertically up her cheek.

Jonathan raced back in with a bowl of iced water. Polly was shaking as we bathed her face. Jonathan held back her hair, shushing her gently. 'It's going to sting for a bit, but you'll be OK.'

'What about my hair? They'll all laugh at me at school.' Her little chest was heaving up and down.

'We were going to get it trimmed anyway. The hairdresser will sort it out.' I leaned towards Jonathan. 'Do you think she needs to go to hospital?'

I thought I'd whispered, but Polly wailed, 'Hospital? I don't want to go to hospital.'

Jonathan frowned. 'No, I don't think so. Let's see what it looks like in a few minutes.' He carried on holding Polly's hand and telling Immi not to worry. Charlie had already decided that Polly was being a drama queen.

Roberta's head appeared through the hatch. 'Is she OK?'

I nodded. 'I think the skin might blister a bit but it's not too bad. You'd better stay out there.'

Roberta nearly managed a smile. At the sight of anything worse than nettle rash, Roberta was a great one for fainting to the floor like a Victorian duchess.

While we held Polly's cheek in the water, I murmured to Jonathan that Roberta might need to stay the night.

'On Christmas Day?'

I must have looked incredulous that Roberta's whole world was going tits up and Jonathan was quibbling over a clash of diaries.

'Go and deal with them. I'll look after Polly,' he said, pulling her into a cuddle.

I called Alicia through and persuaded Charlie, with a bribe of cheesy footballs, to show her how to play Rugby League Live on the XBox. Alicia perched on the footstool, straight-backed. She always looked as though she was doing you a favour by sharing the air in the room. I could see why my children found her hard to warm to.

I grabbed a bottle of Shiraz and another of Chablis, and went to join Roberta. Wine cutbacks would have to start another day.

'What's happened now?' I poured us both a huge glass of wine.

'I've left him. I hope I've done the right thing.'

An uncharitable suspicion that she'd be back with him within the week stopped me dancing an immediate jig. Instead

I tried to take a neutral stance though I was dying to say, 'About bloody time! Arsehole! Hoo-raaaah!' Overt hostility to Scott had led to Roberta practically severing contact with her family. She'd drawn a definite line in the sand many years ago about how much criticism she would tolerate from me.

So I kept quiet as she told me bits about her day, including him thinking that a quick shag would sort everything out.

I hoped his balls had blown up.

She was just filling me in on the Maître d' hovering with intent when there was a knock on the door. Stan leapt up barking, nearly overturning the kitchen table.

Christ. I'd already had a jobless husband, a husbandless friend and a hairless child to contend with. I wondered what I was missing. I threw the door open.

Of course. The wifeless wanker.

'Octavia. Hello. Happy Christmas.' Scott had that honey-voiced thing going on. He was all charm, head tilted on one side, big white smile dazzling away.

'Hello.' I anchored my feet, wondering whether I would be able to stop him barging in.

'Where's Roberta?'

'She doesn't want to see you.' I concentrated on sounding matter-of-fact.

'Come on, I just need a quick word to sort things out.' He stepped forward slightly.

I stood firm, but my adrenaline was flowing. 'I'm sorry, Scott. I can't let you in. She's exhausted. She can't deal with you right now.'

He gave my shoulder a friendly little squeeze, as though he was going to produce such a winning argument I couldn't possibly refuse him.

I didn't move and I didn't reply.

Then the charm was gone. He leant over me, chest jutting, chin out.

'Christ, you piss me off. You always think you know best. Sticking your bloody beak in where it's not wanted. Telling me when I can see my wife. Just get her out here so I can talk to her.'

I had my hands on the wall barring the door. I concentrated my weight in my heels to stop my legs shaking. And then, praise the Lord, Jonathan arrived. 'Everything all right?'

I wasn't certain that Jonathan was the ideal peace negotiator, given that the two men had failed to bond at the hundreds of social occasions we'd shared over the years. Jonathan thought Scott was a knob and I was pretty sure that Scott had an equivalent anatomical description for Jonathan.

On the other hand, if Scott lost his temper, Jonathan's ability to stay calm might avoid bloodshed, given my tendency towards the hotheaded end of the spectrum.

'I need a little chat with Roberta.' Now he was using a completely different tone, as though he'd popped round to borrow the latest Ian Rankin.

'Sorry, mate. Go home and cool down. Talk about it tomorrow.'

'Johnny, just get her out here for a minute, will you?'

Jonathan hated people calling him Johnny. He put his hand on the door and made a slight movement to close it. 'Time to go. She's not going to speak to you today.'

Scott stood with his hands on his hips. Builder's hands. Great big shovels that could take the side of your face off with one swipe. He stepped forward to lean on the doorjamb.

Jonathan ushered me backwards. 'You go in, Octavia. Scott and I will sort this out.'

Lamb and slaughter sprang to mind, but I darted behind him. Jonathan put his hand on Scott's forearm. He must have heard me gulp. Scott shook him off but backed down the steps. 'I bet you two love this. A big drama in your sad little lives. It's pathetic. Forgot to say, I was really sorry to hear you got the push, Johnny, mate. Shame.'

Jonathan slammed the door shut, flicking the 'v's. I hugged him, weak with relief. He'd get another job. Scott would always be a wanker.

Roberta

The arrival of New Year's Eve made me want to take to my bed at eight o'clock until the need to look cheery about the coming year had passed. Octavia was impervious to my pleas to be left at home alone. I wasn't sure I could dig out the brave face she'd expect: every time I thought about Scott, I wanted to rush back home and double-check we couldn't resurrect all that love that I'd once thought could carry me anywhere.

But Octavia was determined to drag me to the party at Cher's, my irreverent and exuberant neighbour. Cher had recognised a kindred rebelliousness in Octavia when I'd introduced them. Whenever Cher had a 'bit of a knees-up', Octavia was always on the invitation list. Which, right now, was not working in my favour. Since Alicia and I were still living at Octavia's, waiting to be rehoused like tabby cats with one eye, doing our own thing was impossible.

I'd intended to move into a hotel straight after Christmas until I discovered that Scott had emptied our joint account. I kicked myself for not pre-empting it. I couldn't believe our relationship – all that passion, all that deep and sustained effort – would become distilled down to pure finances.

Instead of blowing the little money I had squirrelled away in my own bank account on a hotel, Octavia convinced me to use it to rent a flat in the New Year. But the longer Alicia and I squashed into Immi's bedroom, the more appealing patching things up with Scott appeared.

I hated myself for being so ungrateful. Octavia had tried to make me so welcome, jollying Jonathan along and giving meaningful stares to the kids. In a house already bursting at the seams, me wading in with several suitcases of belongings, hastily collected when I knew Scott was taking his mother to the airport, wasn't ideal. Nor was the bathroom situation. If I didn't get a bit more privacy for my ablutions soon, I'd be needing more than a bowl of prunes for breakfast. I wasn't sure what was worse: Jonathan hovering around clearing his throat outside their only loo because I'd inadvertently taken his 'slot', or coming back later to find the seat was warm.

I knew we'd put a strain on Octavia's festivities. I didn't want to ruin her New Year as well. She refused to go to Cher's without me. Cher herself had wasted no time in ringing to find out why she'd seen me going off in a police car. I didn't have the energy to invent something, so I'd given her a sanitised version of the truth. She was outraged on my behalf and told me that Scott was 'officially disinvited'. Eventually, I'd resigned myself to an evening of embarrassed shuffling while people fidgeted about for the right thing to say to a newly single woman.

Contrarily, even Jonathan was keen to party. Despite his oft-aired view that most of the people Scott and I mixed with were – in his words – 'up their own arses', he thought Cher's husband, Patri, was a 'top bloke'. Patri's family had moved from Sardinia to Britain in the fifties, set up a successful café-deli chain over the ensuing decades, and had now diversified into a huge import-export business. But Patri, despite his love for sunglasses inside and a good Barolo, still called a spade a spade. As a host, he was second to none in the generosity stakes, which seemed to eradicate most of Jonathan's chippiness about grand houses and the people who inhabited them.

Octavia adored Cher, even though she mocked her endlessly for being a footballer's wife. Although she pretended to disapprove, Octavia loved the whole extravagance of Cher's life, the cook, the housekeeper, the way Cher simply tipped her Pinot Grigio down the sink if she was in the mood for Chardonnay. Not for her a life of cling film and leftovers.

And if I'd ever thought I might be able to resist, Cher extending the invitation to Alicia made refusal impossible. Cher's granddaughter, Loretta, was sixteen and Alicia's epitome of cool, with her kohl-lined eyes, fake eyelashes and hair extensions right down to her behind. It was the first time Alicia's face had shown anything other than indifference or worry since we'd left the restaurant on Christmas Day. I had no doubt that as an only child, she was also looking forward to a bit of time away from Octavia's raucous trio, who were distinctly put out to be left at home with their grandmother.

So in the end, I put on the long jade dress Octavia had snatched up when we'd gone back to the house. I disguised the bags under my eyes with concealer and located a smile that threatened to wobble at any moment.

When the taxi drew up outside Casa Nostra – Patri's little Mafia joke – I stared back at my old home next door. The lights were on in the drawing room. I wondered whether Scott was there. He refused to tell me what he was doing as 'he was no longer married to me, it was none of my concern'. I just couldn't cut myself off like that. I couldn't imagine that a year from now we'd still be apart. Or that I'd never step through my front door again.

Alicia hooked her arm through mine. She looked over at

our house, all spaniel-eyed. Scott never had much patience with her: he thought I'd spoilt her and was always telling her to 'get real'. Alicia hadn't asked about Scott once. All her questions had been related to how soon we could leave Octavia's. I didn't blame her for hankering after the peace and quiet of home but I couldn't investigate her feelings right now, when I was barely holding myself together. Talk, yes. But now, no.

Octavia stepped in to distract us both. 'You look lovely tonight, Alicia. Your mum used to have a miniskirt like the one you're wearing. In fact, believe it or not, we both did.' The tension in her eased as Octavia went on to describe my leg warmer phase and penchant for putting my hair into hundreds of tiny plaits overnight so that the next morning I looked like I'd accidentally stuck my finger in a socket.

When we got to the front steps, Jonathan ushered me forward. I'd noticed before that black tie made men more chivalrous, and Jonathan was no exception. One of the Filipino staff – 'Patri's Fillies', as he called them with a cavalier disregard for political correctness – answered the door. Cher tottered across the marble foyer looking as though she was fresh from a performance in the Big Top. A feather boa curled round her neck and her long dress was slashed almost to the waist. Her taut face contrasted with a décolleté that had spent too many summers frying in baby oil on the Costa Smeralda.

'Happy New Year, everyone. Hi, Alicia. Go on up, Loretta's upstairs with a few friends. They're on the karaoke machine.'

I waited for Alicia to ask me to come with her but she gave me a little wave and headed off across the hallway, long limbs under her miniskirt like a baby giraffe.

Cher launched into a stage whisper. 'So glad you came, Roberta. I told that husband of yours to sling his hook. Us girlies have to stick together, don't we, ladies?'

I hoped Scott wasn't sitting on his own working his way through his collection of single malts. Perhaps he'd have gone out with the chaps from the rugby club. I hadn't spent a single New Year's Eve away from him since we met. I wasn't sure I wanted to start a new tradition now. I forced my thoughts away from next door.

Gold bangles jangled as Cher swept us into the drawing room. About ten other couples were already standing among clusters of red and silver balloons. Several Filipino maids were weaving about with platters of goat's cheese crostini and trays of Kir Royale. It felt so odd to be here without Scott, I almost baulked at the door. He was the one who dived into social situations, shaking hands and sweeping me into the centre of things. Octavia gave me a little wink and walked ahead. I braced myself for a chorus of 'Where's Scott?' but Cher had already rescued me on that front. Sometimes indiscreet friends were an advantage.

Patri came striding over, sunglasses balanced on his head, quite the ageing rock star with his velvet jacket and greying shoulder-length hair. 'All right, Octavia, Jonathan? Roberta, darling. You look gorgeous, not a day over twenty-one. A lot to celebrate in the coming year, then?' He took my hands in his.

'Celebrate?'

Frankly, I felt like throwing myself on the log fire that was crackling away behind me.

'Yeah, getting rid of that husband of yours. Never did like him. Couldn't understand what a classy girl like you saw in an oik like him. My granddad was a peasant, worked the fields. Me dad was a brickie, but we was brought up to treat women nice. You'll find someone who deserves you now.' He took a big drag on his cigar and blew a smoke ring upwards. He stopped a waitress. 'Here, have some bubbles.'

'He had his good points, Patri. It was as much my fault

as his.' I wondered if my desire to defend Scott would ever wear off. How many more people were going to come out of the woodwork now and say they'd hated him?

'Don't do yerself down, girl, I know what that Scott was like, his way or the highway. He should of recognised his good fortune when he had it. Anyway, cheers, doll. All the best to you.'

He raised his glass to me and off he went, slapping the blokes on the back and the women on the bottom.

I clinked glasses with Octavia and Jonathan, and tried to contain the gathering force of sadness wrenching its way up my chest. Jonathan, with a rare flash of empathy, tried to help me out. 'I know Scott had his moments, but he could be great company when he was in the right mood.'

Octavia couldn't quite contain herself. 'Yes, but the right mood had become rarer and rarer of late.'

I forced my lips into something like a smile and dabbed my little finger at the tears stinging my eyes.

Octavia shook her head. 'I'm not going to be nice to you in the interests of your mascara.' Before I could escape to the loo, the Lawsons from a couple of doors down spotted us. Michelle's two topics of conversation were the catchment areas for good senior schools and her IBS. On the upside, if we were locked into a discussion about too much or too little fibre, there would be less airtime for anyone to investigate the demise of my marriage. We were soon in a kissy-kissy bump-noses-and-cheeks fiasco that the British never mastered properly.

Michelle said, 'How *are* you?' as though I'd been through a gruelling operation to have an embarrassing lump removed and was on the road to recovery. After a cursory greeting, Michelle's husband, Simon, a forceful man who thought he was wittier than he was, turned to Jonathan to rant about government cuts in the health sector.

Before we became too engrossed in the merits of rice milk, Cher banged a huge brass gong and waved us through into the dining room, where an enormous oak table shone with crystal and silver. She searched me out and showed me to my seat. 'Roberta, I've put you next to Patri. He'll look after you.' It hadn't occurred to me that I wouldn't be next to Octavia. I resisted the urge to cling to her and make everyone swap places.

'Lovely, thanks.' I took another gulp of champagne and waved to Octavia as she took her seat down the other end of the table.

I kept my hands in my lap, staring at the pattern on the elaborate silver cutlery. I didn't want to look up in case people were whispering about me. I wasn't sure I could even pick up my wine glass without knocking everything over and shattering Cher's finest Waterford.

Michelle sat opposite me. As always, Patri – who loved a bit of pomp and ceremony – had had menus printed up. The waitress handed one to Michelle, who immediately called her back. 'Has the mushroom soup got cream in it? I can't eat venison. It's barbaric. Did Cher organise any alternatives? Butternut squash risotto? Rice doesn't agree with me. Could you see if they could make it with quinoa?' The poor girl backed out to the kitchen, promising to see what she could do.

My heart sank as Simon plonked himself next to me. 'Patri on the other side of you, is he? A rose between two thorns.' He looked over at Michelle. 'Alright, Miche? Better bring a packed lunch for you next time. Don't want you eating the wrong thing and farting us out of the room.'

Simon looked round at Patri and me for approval. Patri clicked his tongue and frowned. Michelle hissed back at him whilst I concentrated on buttering my roll.

He turned to me, nodding at the bread in my hand. 'Nice

to see a girl with an appetite. Better not overdo it, though. Being back on the market and all that. Don't want to get too chubby. Men like a bit of flesh, but not too much.'

I looked down at his stomach. It bulged out like a cushion between his braces. I slathered on a little more butter and ignored him, although I soon realised he was like a dog that creeps out from under the table to mount your leg as soon as the owners aren't looking.

'So. Approaching the New Year as a single girl, then.'

'It's early days. I'm still coming to terms with it.'

'Must be a bit lonely.'

Patri saved me by banging his spoon on a wine glass with a satisfying ching. 'Before I get too piddled, Cher and me would just like to welcome you all to our New Year's Eve dinner. I did too much waiting on tables when I was younger, so I'm not doing it any more. In this house you've got to help yourself, or ask one of the Fillies.' He pointed his cigar at the rows of wine on the sideboard. 'On the plus side, you can have anything you want. If you go home saying, "Christ, that was a dry old do," then you've only got yerself to blame. *Buon appetito!*'

Patri sat down, stubbing out his cigar on his side plate. 'It's me lucky night tonight, doll, sitting next to you.' He lowered his voice. 'You doing OK? Where you living?'

'I'm staying with Octavia at the moment. I discovered Christmas Day wasn't a terribly good time to look for a house to rent.'

Simon was practically dipping his chin into my soup to catch the conversation. He stuffed a large piece of bread into his mouth. 'Come and sleep in my spare room any time. You can pay me in blow jobs. Haha.'

He guffawed away, specks of olive ciabatta landing in wet blobs on my bare arms. I didn't dare look at his wife. I tried to think of a suitable response, if such a thing existed.

But Patri wasn't having any of it. 'Simon. Shut up. Have a bit of respect.' He'd put his spoon down and turned towards him, elbow on the table.

That familiar queasy feeling startèd to rise, panic that confrontation was on its way. I smiled, blocking Patri's view of Simon. I caught sight of Michelle's pursed lips out of the corner of my eye. 'It's fine, it was only a joke, Patri, come on.'

Simon patted my arm, not the slightest bit abashed. He drained his glass. 'Roberta knows how to have a bit of fun, don't you, sweetheart?'

Patri settled back in his chair, but his gold signet ring tapped out irritation on the surface of the table. I glanced over at Michelle. She touched her spoon to her lip before pushing the bowl away. It was going to be a long evening. I looked down the table for Octavia. She had her head thrown back, laughing at some new friend's joke. Even Jonathan looked jolly for once, though he usually cheered up when he was drinking other people's Pouilly Fumé rather than his own supermarket special.

By the time the main course arrived, my fragile brave face was cracking. Patri had devoted himself to listing Scott's shortcomings, waving his forefinger about to make his point.

'Never liked the way he spoke to my dog, *porco cane*. Never trust a bloke who drinks that bloody Mexican beer. *Madonna*, should've been doing a thank-you dance to the love gods that you was prepared to put up with him.'

That took him through seconds of venison and thirds of celeriac – or 'cheleriac', as Patri called it. There were moments when Patri was so accurate about Scott's failings – 'Only saw the good in himself, that one' – that I had to smile. I knew he meant well, but the communal need to lambast him at every opportunity made me feel a total idiot for marrying him in the first place. I was terrified that a laugh might turn into a sob at any moment. On the upside, Simon was finding himself fascinating elsewhere, recounting anecdotes about going on a deer shoot to some bored faces opposite. Michelle had sucked in half of her face with disapproval, but I couldn't decide whether that was related to Simon's hunting stories or whether her entire life was failing to live up to her expectations.

Just when I thought I might be able to guide Patri away from me and onto the other guests, the pecan pie arrived and he changed tack, sifting through his social network for replacement husbands. 'Maybe Sharky. Bit old for you, early fifties. Good bloke though. Spends his summers in Antibes. Got a nice pad in the Bahamas.' Now and again, he'd shout down the table to Cher. 'Oy, doll. Freddie got divorced yet from Queenie? How about him for our Roberta here?'

Then Cher would call him a daft old bugger and tell me to take no notice. 'Half of them are ex-cons, Roberta. Don't you be getting mixed up with them. You'll have to dig up the cash in the back garden before you can go to Waitrose.'

Then she cackled at her own joke while Octavia mouthed, 'Are you OK?' at me.

I decided to take some respite from smiling by escaping to Cher's downstairs cloakroom. It was like something out of a Parisian hotel with gilt mirrors, feathers and fairy lights. I killed a bit of time working my way through her range of creams, starting with the lavender hand balm and finishing with a rub of spider lily body lotion into my elbows and calves. Smelling like a florist's stall couldn't be worse than Patri's cigars. I examined the various perfumes and after-shaves. Cher's favourite, Poison, gave me a headache. Charlie reminded me of my teenage years. Issey Miyake Pour Homme. Very fresh.

No *homme* to buy it for.

I picked up a smoky purple bottle. Soul. Hugo Boss. Scott's

favourite. I sprayed some on my wrist. A picture of Scott getting dressed, clean-shaven, shirt open, flashed into my mind. I banged the bottle back down. I needed to stop feeling sorry for myself and get back to the party. Michelle was waiting as I came out. 'Sorry. Didn't realise I was holding everyone up.'

'How's it going, Roberta?'

'Fine. I feel a little strange on my own, but Patri and Simon are looking after me.'

'I suppose we'll have to keep an eye on our husbands now you're single. Simon doesn't like Sloaney brunettes anyway.'

I looked at her to see if she was joking, but her eyes were all squinty and suspicious. Everything about her was sharp and jutting, like an aggressive toothpick. Inappropriate jokes were obviously the uniting factor in the Lawsons' marriage.

Scott had always schmoozed Simon and Michelle for Simon's City connections. It dawned on me that I didn't have to toe the couple line any more. 'Don't worry. You're safe. I don't like fat bullfrogs.'

I click-clacked back across the foyer without waiting for her reply. I detoured to Octavia on the way back to my seat and whispered that I would slip off home after coffee. 'Don't do that. You've got to see New Year in. Anyway, Patri's given all the youngsters some sparklers and Chinese lanterns to set off. Alicia's having a ball. We'll leave straight after twelve. Come and sit with us.'

I glanced around at her company. All couples. One woman was telling everyone how amusing her husband was; another man was gently untangling his wife's hair from her necklace. Even Jonathan was resting his arm round Octavia's shoulders. I hadn't appreciated what a luxury it had been to have a husband at my side for all those years.

'I will in a moment, just going to find a cup of coffee.'

Octavia nodded vaguely and joined in a joke about men

69

and their inability to change loo rolls. I could have said I was off to trap a mountain gorilla in the back garden and she wouldn't have noticed. Compassion fatigue and red wine had set in.

Patri was holding forth about the merits of Sardinian cheese on the other side of the table and I couldn't face Simon on my own. I slipped into the hallway and out into the orangery. I loved that room. Cher was brilliant with plants. She was the only woman I knew who'd managed to grow an avocado tree from a stone. I bent down to admire her amaryllis. Shouts, laughter and the sound of Cher doing her Dolly Parton *Jolene, Jolene, Jolene* party piece drifted through from the dining room. I peered through the windows into the garden. Moonlit sky. Perfect night for romance.

I couldn't imagine kissing anyone other than Scott.

'Waiting for me, were you?'

I swung round. Simon.

'What's a gorgeous girl like you doing all on her own?'

'I was just going back to the party.' I started to move towards the door. He was heavy on his feet, staggering.

'Come here, give me a New Year's Eve kiss.'

He lunged towards me, managing to land his big fat lips on my bare shoulder. I could smell the wine on him. I pushed him away.

'No, stop it, Simon. Don't be silly. Get off.'

'Playing hard to get now? You girls knocking forty can't afford to be too choosy.'

He made a grab for my breasts. I shoved him off and he blundered into a shelf of spider plants. They went smashing to their death, earth and terracotta slithering across the floor. I snatched up the Yucca plant next to me and held it in front of me like a sword. I cursed my long dress, which kept catching on the heels of my stilettos.

'You don't know what you're missing. You frigid bitch.

Bet Scott was playing away if this is the sort of welcome he got at home.'

'Simon. Here's some free advice. Get lost. And never speak to me again.' Brave words that might have been more effective if my voice hadn't come out all tight and strangled.

He stepped towards me again, sweat shining on his forehead. 'You'll be begging me for it in a few months.'

I was debating between pushing the spiky Yucca in his face or hurling it at him and making a dash for the door when the whole orangery lit up, leaving us blinking like a pair of moles. I didn't have time to say anything before Patri marched in, grabbed Simon by his jacket and dragged him across the hall.

'*Porca miseria*. You prick. Get out. Get out now. And take that miserable bitch of a wife with you.'

Patri flung the front door open and hurled him out. Simon was concentrating too much on shouting 'Prick tease!' and not enough on the frosty steps outside. His behind caught the edge of them with a dull thump. Well-cushioned as it was, it would still have hurt. Patri was bellowing in the hall, not caring who heard, instructing one of the Fillies to find Michelle and get rid of her now. Or rather 'NOW!' Within moments, Patri was thrusting Michelle's cashmere wrap into her arms and propelling her outside. For a chap in his late sixties who'd be snapping his fingers for another glass of brandy on his deathbed, he didn't mess about.

He slammed the door. '*Bastardo*. Roberta, what can I say?' He spread his arms open wide. 'You're my guest, you come to my house and a guy, a friend, thinks he can have a go with you?'

My heart was slowing down. I wanted a hot flannel to scrub at my arms and chest where Simon's fat fingers had manhandled me. I used to be a person who could see the funny side of everything, always laughing when I shouldn't have been. 'I'm so sorry about the mess. Look at Cher's poor plants.'

'The plants? No one cares about the plants. Bloody bloke. He won't come here again. Tell me how I can make it up to you for having such stupid friends.'

'You don't have to make amends. He's not your responsibility. I can look after myself.' I pressed my fingers into my eyes. I didn't know whether that was true.

'No, I want to do something for you. What do you need?'

More than anything, I needed a house, but I didn't want to involve him in my life to that degree. I knew Patri, he wouldn't just keep an eye out for properties, he'd make it his life's mission. Scott was always telling me how we 'owed people dinner' or he 'owed them a favour'. I didn't want to owe anyone anything any more. But Patri wouldn't take no for an answer.

I glanced through the doorway to Octavia, hoping she might come to my rescue. But she was in full flow, recounting a story that required much flapping about of hands. No one would ever know she was worried sick about money.

I turned back to Patri, suddenly inspired. 'There is one thing you could do for me.' I explained about Jonathan's redundancy. 'He works really hard. He could fix or set up any computer systems you need.'

Patri nodded. His dark eyes narrowed. 'OK.'

I wanted to ask, 'OK what? OK you have something for him? OK you've heard me?' I was desperate to run over to tell Octavia some good news, but no hopes were better than false hopes.

Patri took my hand and led me back into the dining room. 'Come on. Nearly midnight. I'm going to get the kids down for the Chinese lanterns.'

Marvellous. That meant it would soon be time to go home.

Octavia hurried over to me. 'What was all that kerfuffle about? I didn't realise you were out there.'

'Tell you later. Let's watch these lanterns, then I'm definitely going to call it a night.'

We thronged out into the garden. Patri, Jonathan and the teenagers crowded round, all vying to take charge. Alicia was joking and laughing. One boy with a messy shock of blonde hair seemed to be paying her special attention. I listened hard. No swearing. Well-spoken. He took off his scarf and tied it round her neck. Her face lit up. Loneliness sucked me down somewhere dark.

The buzz of interest faded as the lanterns refused to light. Patri threw down his matchbox and dispatched various Fillies to find torches and lighters, the ratio of Italian to English increasing with his frustration. Octavia and I went to sit down by the fence. She turned her face to the sky, her words slurring.

'Whenever I see stars, I think of Xavi. There were so many of them in Corsica. I wonder if he can see what we can see. Prob'ly better cos they don't have all the light pollution. If he's there. Could be anywhere.' Her head lolled onto my shoulder. I couldn't believe that after nearly two decades, Octavia was still going on about Xavi. She hadn't mentioned him in ages. She should have whitewashed him from her memory after what he did.

'Sshhh. Jonathan's coming over.'

Octavia wasn't to be derailed. 'I still don't know what I did wrong. I loved him. Why do people leave if they love you?' She stabbed a drunken finger in my direction.

I had no answer for Octavia's romantic catastrophes from years ago. My own disaster was so fresh, oozing agony into the darkness. I was the last person to claim insights on relationships. I shivered, huddling up to her under her faux fur wrap, the cold of the wooden bench creeping into my thighs. Octavia didn't seem to need a response.

I caught a familiar sound on the other side of the fence. Throaty, lusty laughter. Not broken-hearted, brave-faced laughter.

Scott's laughter.

Octavia was swaying, slumped on the bench, her eyelids drooping. I was bolt upright, ears straining for voices.

One high-pitched one. One deep teasing one. The clunk of the cover from our outdoor hot tub. The gurgle of bubbles. Playful screams. Loud splashes. Giggles. Silence. More silence.

My stomach lurched. He knew I was here, next door. I realised I'd imagined that Scott would be devastated, plotting how to get me back. But that wasn't his style. Far easier to find someone else to impress with his big-man talk, and punish me into the bargain. After all these rollercoaster years, all the times I'd longed to walk away, I was still hoping there was a little ember of love left, waiting to be fanned. I reminded myself of Octavia's words: 'What man puts a woman he loves in a police cell?' She was right. He didn't deserve for me to miss him. But I did.

I wanted to pole-vault the fence and see what was happening. I wanted everyone to stop talking so that I could listen. My mind was searching, craving innocent explanations but coming up blank. A cheer went up as the first Chinese lantern struggled into the air, hovered over the summer house, skimmed the branches of the sycamore tree, then disappeared high into the sky, a tiny glow against the universe.

I hugged my arms around myself and offered up a wish for a time when my whole life didn't seem rotten from the inside out.

Octavia

January passed in a flash. After Jonathan had exhausted the job opportunities within a 10-mile radius of where we lived, I'd encouraged him to apply for jobs abroad. The more I thought about it, the more excited I became. The idea of exploring somewhere new made me want to rush to a map of the world and draw up a wish list of destinations. Italy. Barcelona. Paris. I'd love to introduce the children to a different culture and watch their minds expand: it frightened me that Immi thought Scotland was the capital of England but knew Jack Wills and Superdry were far more must-have than anything from Asda. When I was with Xavi, I'd dreamt of having bilingual children. Maybe I still could. And yet, despite my best efforts highlighting jobs in Tokyo, Bangkok and Kuala Lumpur, by the time Jonathan's birthday rolled around at the beginning of February, he was still fixated on jobs within half an hour's commuting distance.

Birthday cheer, then, was in short supply. Obviously, I'd known he was going to be thirty-nine for the last three hundred and sixty-four days – but that hadn't stopped me racing from the nursery to the supermarket for fillet steaks on the very eve I needed to cook them. We'd been living on an economy diet of lentils, chickpeas and turkey mince, so I was glad of an excuse to splash out. I'd just arrived home and was bunging the meat in a sherry and mustard marinade when Roberta turned up.

Post-marriage, we didn't do many unannounced visits. Though since she'd rented a ridiculously tiny flat in a fancy new development shortly after New Year – 'I'd rather have pristine and small than grotty and spacious' – she'd been round much more often. For a brief moment, I thought she'd popped round with a present for Jonathan. I glanced down, but there was no sign of the shiny gift bags Roberta couldn't live without. She was huddled into her mac and looked so pinched and miserable that I bundled her straight into the kitchen, batting away the children with a packet of HobNobs and a promise that tea would be ready soon.

As soon as the door was shut she told me, in a strained voice, that Scott was thinking of moving his new girlfriend, Shana, into her old house. 'I know I should be delighted, because it will stop him hassling me and telling me what a rubbish mother I am all the time. But I keep thinking about how special he'll be making her feel. All those little details he's so good at. Alicia told me she runs her own lingerie business and that Scott keeps raving about what a brilliant businesswoman she is.'

I couldn't see that Scott directing his attentions onto some other poor woman was anything other than a cause for cracking open the champagne and setting off the party poppers. I could hear the frustration in my voice as I said, 'When did he last make you feel special? I know he did all that dramatic crossing-continents and grand-gesture malarkey at the beginning but apart from the odd bunch of daffs he gets his secretary to send you, he hasn't been putting on the Ritz lately, has he? He'll soon turn nasty with this Shana floozy when he doesn't get his own way.'

Roberta sighed. 'Maybe if I'd insisted on having my own career instead of just renovating our houses, he might have had a little more respect for me.' Roberta sounded brittle, as though something inside her had tightened too far.

'You have had your own career. It was your input and your designs that made the houses so saleable. If you hadn't project-managed every detail, sorted out those bloody builders, architects and landscape gardeners, you'd never have made so much profit. Without you, he couldn't have built up his property business.'

Roberta was so smart in so many ways. I just couldn't comprehend why she had this blind spot when it came to Scott. I busied myself getting mushrooms out of the fridge so that she couldn't see my exasperated face. I tried to sound sympathetic. 'Scott didn't want you to go out to work. As far as I can remember, that hotel chain offered you a job revamping that place on New Road and he practically forbade you to do it.'

'I don't think he forbade me to do it, did he? I think he just thought the timing wasn't terribly good because Alicia was so young and it would be tricky finding the right childcare.'

Especially if your husband thought his part of the bargain stopped at the sperm donation stage.

'That's not how I recall it. Anyway, whatever the rights and wrongs, you can't escape the fact that Scott was a bully and you're better off without him.' I clenched my teeth and waited. Even when Scott was behaving like a total turd, Roberta had never liked me criticising him.

I wasn't sure that had changed.

Roberta swirled her coffee. 'That's just it. I don't think I am better off. We've been talking a lot lately, mainly about arrangements for Alicia but about us, too. It's almost like talking to the old Scotty, from years ago, before he got so aggressive. I do wonder if he ever dealt properly with the miscarriages.'

'No one wanted those little boys more than you, and you haven't got all bitter and twisted.' I was so cynical about Scott and his motivations that I couldn't find it in myself to be sorry for him.

'I know.' A pause. She looked away. 'He did say that if I wanted to come back, he would finish with this other woman.'

My head ached with the effort of not telling her to go and get her chakras realigned or her aura smoothed, or whichever one of her bollocky New Age therapies it would take to make her see sense. 'Woo-hoo, what a ringing endorsement. He might dump the other Sheila if you're prepared to forgive and forget. Not "I'll always love you and I'll be sitting here broken-hearted and experimenting with razor blades until you give me a second chance." He should be licking the floor in front of you, begging forgiveness.'

'We were happy most of the time. I know he could be difficult, but he was a good provider. He's got a girlfriend now, but he wasn't a philanderer.'

I shook some balsamic vinegar into the marinade and tried to sigh quietly. 'I think it's human nature to remember the good times and forget the bad ones. Can I give your rose-tinted specs a little polish? Half the time you couldn't even speak to your friends on the phone in case the spotlight wandered off him. Then there's the small matter of that little trip in the cop car. Plus the fact that as soon as you left him, he stopped you getting access to any money – money that you had helped him create – never mind that you still had his daughter to take care of.'

Roberta rested her head on one hand. 'I know. I did have that conversation with him. He admitted he'd been out of order, said he wasn't thinking straight when I left him. He's sorted out an allowance for me now, until we get things onto a more formal footing. That's if I don't go back.' Her voice was small, sinking down into her chest.

By contrast I thought my voice might start bellowing out of mine until the neighbours could hear. 'Why would you want to?'

'I never imagined being a single parent. I feel like I've let everyone down after insisting that I knew what I was doing, marrying Scott. I don't want Alicia growing up without a father. I keep hoping that she'll get closer to Scott as she gets older. That won't happen if he has a baby with this other woman.'

'But you also don't want Alicia growing up thinking that it's OK to let a bloke swear at her or lock her out when the mood takes him. If Alicia got together with someone who treated her like Scott treats you, you'd think you'd failed as a mother. And she's not growing up without a father. He sees her whenever he wants, doesn't he?'

Roberta was shrinking into herself, dwarfed by the collar on her coat. Hard to believe this was the woman who'd run the debating society at school. Who'd petitioned her MP about cuts in funding for the arts. Whose letters to *The Times* were legendary. Scott had worn her down over the years until she wouldn't recognise her own opinion if it took a chunk out of her arse. But maybe I was turning into Scott, haranguing her until she agreed with me, whether she thought I was right or not.

I was working out how to do a quick backpedal so she didn't feel the whole world was against her, when Jonathan came through. He looked amazed to see Roberta, even though he'd only been on the other side of the hatch. His face always took on a wary look when Roberta appeared, in case she might suddenly come and stay again for another ten days.

'Hiya. How are you? Things falling into place a bit better now?'

Roberta shrugged. 'We're fine, thanks.'

Jonathan glanced at me. 'Flat working out okay?'

Roberta nodded and his shoulders relaxed.

That was enough to convince Jonathan that no further investigation was needed. 'Is it nearly dinnertime? I'm looking forward to my birthday steak.'

Roberta gasped. 'Oh God, is it your birthday? Sorry. I'd better go.'

'You're all right. I can make myself a sandwich if you want to stay a bit longer.'

I was caught between not wanting to chuck Roberta out and feeling that for once, Jonathan did deserve to come top of the pile. He only managed to fight his way past the kids, and even the dog, about once a year.

Roberta took the hint when Jonathan fetched out a kilo of bargain-bucket margarine and started making an enormous doorstep, hoovering up a whole pack of ham. It took all my birthday goodwill not to start nagging. Instead of birthday sex, it would be birthday row if he sat down to my steak and declared he wasn't hungry.

I showed her out and we stood chatting on the threshold. Jonathan never understood how we saw each other so often, yet never ran out of things to say. I sucked her into a big hug. Her shoulder blades were so bony, she was in danger of slicing through my arteries.

'Maybe you need to think about finding a distraction yourself?' I said.

'Such as?'

Sometimes the woman was so slow. I laughed. 'How about a new man?'

'Oh God. I couldn't bear it. How would I meet anyone anyway?'

'The internet. At least you can see what they look like first, so you don't end up with some warthog.'

Roberta pulled a face. 'I can't think of anything worse.

80

Can you imagine if I actually had to have sex with someone new? All that fumbling and getting in a tangle with your underwear.'

'Don't be silly. The men you'll meet will have worked out the whole bra thing by now. I'd be more worried about whether they can still get it up. We could look on a website – what about that one they're always advertising on the radio – Just Clicked? You don't actually have to go out with anyone. We can just have a nosey and see what's available. Go on, it'll be a laugh.'

'Oh yes, an absolute hoot, for you, maybe.' But she didn't sound dead set against it.

Given that she was dithering over Scott again, there was no time to lose. 'Right. I'm going to come over tomorrow evening and we'll crack on with your new life. We can always give you a false name.'

'You can come over but I'm not going to let you match-make.'

'We'll see.'

As she headed to her car, her step had lightened slightly.

Roberta

When Octavia had an idea in her head, she was impossible to resist. Before she came over the following evening, I was determined that I wasn't going to let her bamboozle me into looking for a man online, but she breezed into my apartment with a bottle of fizz 'to celebrate a new beginning'.

Before I knew it, we were sitting at the tiny breakfast bar, poring over the pictures on the Just Clicked website. Octavia was drawn to the skinny guys, whereas I could never envisage going out with a man who could fit into my jeans. I preferred men who looked like they could take on a bear and win if the need ever arose. She liked dark, broody men, even though she'd ended up with Jonathan, who was gingerish. I leaned towards men at the Scandinavian end of the spectrum.

Octavia pointed to a man who epitomised the word 'ordinary'. 'He looks nice. Friendly eyes. Shirt's quite trendy.'

'Trendy? He looks like he buys his clothes from Topman. Bet he reads *Angling Weekly*. How about this one? He's rather attractive.'

'No. Too serial killer. Look how pale he is. Looks like he's been living in a cupboard under the stairs.' Octavia scrolled down. 'What about this one?'

'I'm not that desperate. Forehead like a skating rink. Too thin.' As we dismissed whole chunks of the male population on their hairline alone, I dreaded to think what they would say about me if I ever dared to put my picture out there into the brutal world of internet dating.

I trailed my finger down the page. 'Bet he's called Quentin.'

'Cuthbert.' Octavia laughed into her champagne.

'Cuthbert' was the name we used to give to any boy we didn't want to dance with at the school disco. 'Nick' was for the ones we liked. For a moment, it was like being fifteen again, judging a man on his haircut and shirt. If I'd messed up the first time around when I was approaching life optimistically and open-minded, I didn't rate my chances with bitter baggage, teenage daughter and a ring-fenced heart in tow. But Scott appeared to be getting on with his life, so I'd have to do the same. It might even do me good to meet someone new, someone I could be myself with, the self I was now. Not the self I was when I was twenty.

Octavia picked out a guy who looked Slavic, with high cheekbones and slightly protruding eyes.

'A bit amphibian-looking. Like his jacket though. And he's got attractive hands. OK, let's put him on the possibles list. He can be my middle-aged Nick,' I said.

'OK, let's choose one more, then we'll set up your profile.' Octavia filled our glasses again. 'What about him? He looks a bit Mediterranean. He's got gorgeous hair. Reminds me a bit of Xavi.'

'Everyone reminds you of Xavi. About time you blew out that ancient torch for him. Never let it be said that Octavia Shelton is fickle. I wonder where he ended up. Maybe he finally came back to Cocciu after all that travelling, married a girl in the village and is now a staid old man, out on his fishing boat at weekends.'

'Doubt it. I can't imagine a tiny island containing him for

the rest of his life.' Octavia's hard edges still softened when she talked about him.

'Do you ever think about contacting him? You must have Googled him at least?'

'Nope. It just seems so disloyal and a bit slippery-slopey. Even if I found him, what would I do? I've got the life I've got now. Anyway, I'm probably a distant shag he can barely remember.'

'Don't be stupid. You broke his heart. He absolutely adored you. If your dad hadn't died, you'd have gone travelling the world with him.'

Octavia threw up her hands. 'Can you imagine Mum if I'd have dropped out of university and gone tazzing off to New Zealand with Xavi? Mind you, might have learnt more there than wasting my time finishing off a stupid French degree. Not essential for running a nursery and teaching two-year-olds *Humpty Dumpty*. Anyway, do you want to include this bloke or not?' She drained her glass.

'Go on then, I'll have the Xavi lookalike in homage to that flame – or should I say that bonfire – you never quite managed to snuff out.' I dutifully wrote his name down.

'It would never have worked. He was far too wild for me.'

'Fibber. You were waxing lyrical about him on New Year's Eve. Anyway, back then, you were rather wild yourself.' I dug a couple of bottles out of the bijou wine rack and waved them at Octavia. She went with the Rioja.

'Maybe I was, but you've got to grow up eventually. You can't keep travelling aimlessly. I couldn't have dragged the kids all over the world. Xavi was just a mad fling before I found Mr Right.' Octavia sighed. 'Let's sign you up. I'm going to use Cuthbert as your password.'

I recognised Octavia's closing-down tactics. She was absurdly defensive about Jonathan. If I ever dared to point out that he didn't seem very exciting, she would get all snippy, saying he worked so hard to support three children, as though one child didn't require a moment of effort. It would be interesting to see if Jonathan became a powerhouse of football/rugby/netball match attendance now he didn't have work as an excuse. I didn't know how she stood all his fussing about, running his fingers along the banisters checking for dust.

Her calling him Mr Right brought out the devil in me.

'I bet Xavi would be on Facebook. You could have a quick peek without him even knowing.'

'Yes, I could, but I'm not going to. I'm very happy with my life, thank you. Let's fill in the questionnaire about personality.' Octavia immediately started laughing. 'God, this is sophisticated. Tick the boxes that apply to you. 'I like to converse at an intellectual level.' Big fat tick. 'I enjoy luxury.' Huge double tick. 'I get discouraged easily.' Think that's another tick.'

'I don't get discouraged easily.'

'You do at the moment. At the New Year's Eve party, you told me every time I spoke to you that you'd never meet anyone.'

'Pardon me for being a bit depressed. I'd only left Scott six days before.' No doubt Octavia would have led them all in the conga and a burst of the hokey-cokey.

Half a questionnaire later, with my imperfections glittering in cyberspace, I needed a break. 'Come on. Let's see if we can find Xavi.'

'We're supposed to be finding a man for you,' Octavia said, but her protest was weak.

I shuffled her out of the way, logged on to Facebook through Alicia's account, and typed in Xavier Santoni. No results.

'He's probably living in the Corsican mountains and working as a shepherd,' I said, preparing to click back onto my dreaded dating profile.

Octavia put her hand on my arm, 'Try just putting in Santoni – might bring up one of his rellies.'

I nudged her. 'I thought you weren't interested anyway.'

'You've only got yourself to blame. You're the one who's let the genie out of the bottle. I've spent years telling myself "Step away from Google".'

Forty-six results for Santoni. I scrolled down. She pointed to the screen.

'Click on that one. I think that's his cousin, Magali.'

I went into Magali's photos. We stared at the pictures, trying to ascertain whether they were taken in Cocciu or not.

Octavia squinted at the screen. 'That might be Xavi's mother. Or maybe Xavi's aunt. Ooh look, I bet that's Magali's daughter. She looks just like her. I think that's his parents' garden – I'm sure that's the view down the hill, where we saw those wild boar with their babies when you came to visit me.' Happy memories were lighting up her face in a way I rarely saw any more.

She then insisted on clicking on every Santoni who lived in Corsica, searching through their friends, looking into the crowds in party shots, peering at children for any resemblance to Xavi. I felt as though I'd taken a bit of fun and turned it into something desperate.

Eventually Octavia sighed. 'He's not there. Probably living in a yurt in Ulan Bator. Anyway, let's stick to the task in hand.' She pulled out her mobile phone to take my picture. She'd lost some of her playfulness. I knew I'd touched a nerve.

Xavi had been special in a way Jonathan wasn't.

Xavi had such energy, approached life with such gusto. He was the perfect match for Octavia's whirlwind of ideas, her zest for the zany. Though now I reflected on it, it was a long time since she'd made us wash our faces in the dew on the first of May for eternal youth, or read the Tarot cards.

Little by little, her quirkiness had descended into something more pedestrian. Maybe it was age. Maybe it was having three kids and a demanding job. Maybe it was Jonathan. I hoped I wasn't going to become one of those bitter women who saw faults in everyone's marriage because my own had imploded. I pulled a face at the camera.

'Stop it, or you'll only get the boss-eyed axe murderers emailing you.' Octavia was zooming in far too close for my liking.

'I won't date anyone, anyway.'

'Of course you will. When they start telling you how gorgeous you are, how you look like a young Audrey Hepburn and that they've got a holiday home in Andalucia, a yacht in Antibes and by the way, you're going for dinner at The Savoy, you'll be dying to go out with them. Anyway, you're not looking for a husband, just someone to go to the cinema with.'

'I've got you for that.' I nodded as Octavia showed me a photo that didn't make my complexion look like a piece of ageing Stilton.

'You're not going to meet a bloke toddling off to the Odeon with me to watch a rom-com, are you?'

'You sound more excited about this than me.'

'If I was in your position, I'd go absolutely wild. Fill my boots. Shag myself silly. You might get married again in a few years' time and be stuck with the same bloke for half a century.'

I heard something in Octavia's tone that made me swing round to look at her.

Envy.

Octavia

I had ignored the alumni newsletter from the Middleton School for Girls when it arrived before Christmas. I'd confounded everyone's low expectations by getting good A-levels, but two decades later, I still resented my time there. The biggest lesson I'd learnt was that I was pretty crap at conforming. If it hadn't been for my symbiotic relationship with Roberta – our uniting sense of humour, plus her need for a little rebellion and my need for someone who knew the system so I could work it to my advantage – I would probably have dropped out and gone to tech college instead.

So my enthusiasm when she rang to say she wanted to go to the school reunion was underwhelming. 'Who do you want to see? Old Bristles Birtwistle for a quick Latin test? Penelope Watson for a quick rundown on Daddy's new Bentley and Mummy's latest steed? I can't afford it, anyway.'

'I don't want to see anyone in particular. I've rung up and they said there are still a few last-minute tickets left. Might be a way of extending my social network away from all the friends I share with Scott. I'm finding sitting in every night quite tedious. Go on. I'll pay. Pleee-aaase.'

'I can't let you pay. You're already spending a fortune on

that shoebox you're living in.' I still couldn't understand why she'd chosen somewhere with a concierge, a lobby and water features, rather than useful features, like bedrooms and a garden.

'Scott's in a generous phase at the moment. He's agreed to cover the rent till we can sort out the finances. He's trying to keep me sweet so I don't start claiming half the business, I think.'

'And you're going to roll over?'

Roberta sighed impatiently.

'I just want a decent settlement so I can get on with my life. I'm not squandering thousands of pounds in lawyer's fees trying to prove how much money Scott has got. I've no doubt the lion's share will be in some obscure bank account on the other side of the world by now. Anyway, will you come with me?'

'Christ. I hated that school. You were the only good thing to come out of it.' Still, I was impressed that Roberta was thinking positive. And slightly ashamed that I was more inclined to go if it wasn't my £35 I was wasting. Because, as Jonathan never missed the chance to point out, there was no money to burn.

'You would never have set up a holistic nursery if the rigidity of school hadn't scarred you for life. It's your opportunity to go back and show them what you achieved.' Never mind interior design, Roberta should have carved out a career as a hostage negotiator.

'True. Though that's a perverse way to be thankful for years of detentions and lectures on being responsible,' I said.

'You did leave school over twenty years ago.'

I hesitated, knowing that I was going to give in. Anything to keep Roberta from going back to Scott. 'OK, then. I'm going to regret this.'

Once I'd agreed to go, I brushed away any discussion or

plans. Thinking about any of them – teachers or pupils – reminded me how stifled I'd felt through all my teenage years. Roberta saw my household as liberal compared with her dad's strict rules of staying at the table until everyone had finished breakfast and not coming downstairs in your nightie. She loved learning how to dressmake with my mum or watching TV in our dressing gowns all day, legs dangling over the arm of the settee.

But my parents weren't liberal, they were good solid working-class stock, with ambitions for me, hence the pushing and prodding of their only daughter into a scholarship at a school for the posh and privileged. I wasn't sure they could deem their experiment an unqualified success.

On the night of the reunion, Roberta picked me up. She arrived all gussied-up with a cloud of dark hair, white palazzo pants, a lacy blouse and high heels that would have made me look like I'd just finished my pole-dancing shift. I'd meant to spend a bit of time titivating myself but Jonathan was sulking about me going out without him, cottering about how we didn't have money to waste on 'fripperies' then still managing to be cross when I told him Roberta was paying.

He'd decided his best use of time was to review our pensions that evening. Producing the relevant documents from my 'bung-it-in-a-box' filing system resulted in a mere fifteen minutes for a makeover, hampered by a missing eyeliner sharpener and my one decent top gone AWOL. In the end, I'd gone for a pair of black trousers I wore for work, spent a precious five minutes taming my hair so it didn't stick out like a monkey puzzle tree, and chucked a dried-up mascara wand into my bag to do my make-up in the car.

'I'm a bit nervous,' Roberta said. 'I thought I was OK talking about Scott, but now I'm not sure.'

'Don't be silly. They'll all be looking at you and thinking what an idiot he was to let you get away. We'll have a laugh.'

Which was ironic coming from me, given that my dread was increasing with every junction we clocked up towards our leafy Sussex school.

Roberta seemed more excited than nervous. As we drew through the gates, she started pointing through the window. 'Look, that's Veronica. And Cinzia. Oh my God. Elfrida looks amazing. She's really glamorous. I don't remember her being like that at school.'

I wanted to be interested. But I felt just like I had then. The dumpy poor girl who had to dye her hair a kaleidoscope of colours to get noticed.

'How soon can we leave?'

Roberta yanked up the handbrake. 'What is it you say to your youngsters at nursery? The only difference between having a good time and a bad time is attitude?'

I rolled my eyes and stuck a foot out of the car. 'Come on, let's go and do our tally of how many have married an Etonian, how many have sons called Sebastian and daughters called Lucinda, and how many women actually used any of their education except to work out the dimensions of their new Poggenpohl kitchens.'

Roberta was looking at me as though I'd lost the plot. 'Into the fray, my dear.'

We'd only been back on the school turf for five minutes and she was already sounding like she was off to a game of lacrosse. We walked across the quadrangle towards the hall. Once inside, I scanned the parade of maxi dresses, high heels and froufrou bits of material, somewhere between a wrap and a cardigan which only very stylish people could wear without looking like they'd accidentally walked out with a dishcloth tucked in their bra strap. I trailed behind Roberta, watching how she held herself tall, doing the meet-and-greet with her trademark graciousness.

She fitted in. I still didn't.

I grabbed a couple of glasses of wine from a passing tray. Roberta beckoned me over. 'Do you remember Verity? She's employed at the Foreign Office, lived all over the world. She even spent time in Rome. Imagine being able to pop into the Sistine Chapel on a daily basis.'

I smiled. 'Hi Verity. I remember you. You were in my French class. Sounds like you made use of your languages. I've only ever used mine to order croissants.'

Verity put out her hand. 'I'm sorry, I didn't catch your name.'

'Octavia. Was Octavia Austin. Now Shelton.'

Verity's hand flew to her face. 'Oh my goodness. Octavia. Crikey. I didn't recognise you. You look so, er, normal. And married, too. I thought you'd have bright pink hair and be off touring with a rock band or saving orang-utans in Borneo.'

I thought I would be too.

'Nothing like that.'

Roberta stepped in. 'Octavia is hiding her light under a bushel. She set up a holistic nursery where the children are outside for at least eighty per cent of the day. It's quite brilliant.'

Verity worked hard to chase a baffled look off her face. 'What, even when it rains?'

'Yes. We put waterproofs and wellies on. Children, especially boys, learn by moving around. In my opinion.'

'Golly. How innovative.' But her eyes were already wandering round the room.

I stuck my nose in my glass, doing a hooded-eyed telepathic grump to Roberta. I was still smarting from the 'normal'. Of course, I didn't want to look insane, ridiculous or freakish, but maybe creative, eccentric or flamboyant. I looked down. Verity was right. In my black slacks, supermarket T-shirt and cardie, I looked like any other harassed mother on the school run.

Nothing about me suggested a history of skirts made out of curtains, underwear as outerwear, the leopard-skin drainpipes that were my signature until Charlie was born and I got too fat. Why should Verity be interested in me? The traits I prided myself on, the non-conforming, the original thought, the do-and-dare, had drizzled away, leaving behind a face – and a person – you'd be hard-pressed to remember the morning after.

Roberta took my arm. 'Let's go and look at the photos from our year.'

I was still muttering, 'Normal. Bloody normal.'

We trawled the school photos until we found the one of us in our final year. I'd got into terrible trouble because I'd puffed my cheeks out like a blowfish. My eyes were bright with mischief, my hair standing up in peroxide white spikes, the compromise I'd made when they'd threatened to expel me when I'd dyed it pink. I looked so full of life. Roberta was standing behind me, biting her lip with the effort of not laughing. She pointed to the picture. 'Oh my God. Look at you. You naughty thing. Do you remember how cross Mrs Metcalf was?'

Mrs Metcalf was so easy to imitate because she had a lisp and a strong northern accent. 'Ruining the photo for everyone, and the reputation of the school.'

Roberta laughed. A voice behind me said, 'I'd recognise that voice anywhere. You were such a brilliant mimic.'

I turned round to see Fliss Morris, who'd been head girl, golden girl, star woman of lacrosse, hockey and netball. But I'd still managed to snatch the lead from her when we auditioned for *Annie*. 'No pink hair any more though?'

Christ. Didn't realise no one would ever remember anything else about me. 'No. Just my middle-aged mousey brown.'

'Haha. Now you're going to tell me that you ended up married with two kids and became a school teacher.' She said it as though it was so unlikely, I almost told her I was an anthropologist just back from a study of the Inuits.

Instead I shrugged and said, 'Three kids. Nursery teacher.'

For someone who was supposedly well bred, Fliss made no attempt to disguise her hilarity. She kept shaking her head and spluttering, 'I can't believe it. You're offering me tremendous hope for my daughter. She's had her navel pierced and goodness knows how many earrings she's got. Maybe she'll rebel now and become traditional like you later on.'

Traditional. Sodding traditional.

As far as I was concerned that was in the same category as 'pleasant', 'nice' and 'agreeable'. Not compliments. I turned back to the photos. 'You've barely changed at all.' Anger made me want to say, 'Still the same tombstone teeth and snorty laugh.' Of course, I was 'traditional' now, so insulting random people I hadn't seen for twenty years was no longer an option.

Roberta had discovered some blonde woman I vaguely recognised and was comparing notes about divorces and internet dating. I was trying to escape Fliss before she could make me feel any worse about myself when Roberta waved at an elderly gentleman across the hall. Jesus. Mr Hardy, our old maths teacher. He should be dead by now. He made a beeline for us. I groaned as he walked over, back ramrod-straight, dapper.

'Roberta. How are you? Recognised you straightaway. Life treated you very well, I hope. Always interesting to see how people change. And Felicity. Still into athletics? County level? Jolly impressive indeed.' He turned to me. 'I don't think I taught you, did I? Face looks a little familiar.' He tapped the side of his head. 'Memory's not as good as it was.'

Resignation coursed through my stomach. 'I'm Octavia. Octavia Austin as was.'

The faded blue eyes flung open with surprise. 'Well, well, well. Octavia Austin.' Mr Hardy chuckled in the back of his throat. 'Quite a handful you were. I remember you handing in a maths book with an indescribably rude word written in every answer.'

'Was it "bollocks"?'

As soon as the words were out of my mouth, I blushed. Fliss giggled to my right. Mr Hardy jerked his torso back as though he'd expected me to unlearn the word over the years. He looked over his glasses.

'Yes, I believe it was.' He paused. 'I refused to let them suspend you over it. I thought you'd see it as a reward, not a punishment. I liked pupils with character. You had a lot of character. Such a vibrant girl. I imagine that algebra or no algebra, you've made your mark on life.'

I couldn't believe how many people it was possible to disappoint in one evening. In two decades I'd switched from a rebellious go-getter to a boring old trout going absolutely nowhere.

Roberta

Scott had torched my faith in my ability to sift the wheat from the chaff so thoroughly that I asked Octavia to choose from the astonishing number of men who'd responded to my profile on Just Clicked. I'd spent the last week and a half trying to wriggle out of going on a date but Octavia was having none of it. I'd only agreed to tonight because Scott was on a flight back from Australia and it was the last time there would be no chance of him walking into the restaurant where we were meeting.

First impressions told me Octavia had picked well. 'Jake' was there when I arrived, sitting at the front of the little Mediterranean bistro, looking out for me. Tick. He stood up the second I opened the door and mouthed 'Roberta?', then marched straight over to me. Tick. Sandy hair and not as tall as Scott but still close to six foot. I was glad I hadn't called to cancel. It had been touch and go while I was getting ready, so nervous that I'd flicked mascara everywhere and had to start again. I regretted looking at my fancy tea-rose body lotion and deciding he wouldn't merit it. I'd picked up Alicia's coconut body butter instead and now smelt as though I'd slathered myself in sun cream.

He shook my hand. Warm, soft, just the right amount of grip. Tick. A bit slighter than I'd imagined, but everyone was slight compared to Scott.

'I'm Jake. Lovely to meet you.'

Not 'How do you do?' Small cross. But then Octavia maintained that only the Queen, my parents and I ever said that any more. He guided me into my seat at a table by the window. The tight knot of trepidation in my stomach loosened as he spoke.

'Let's order some drinks. What would you like?'

I set a little trap. 'I'd like some white wine, please.'

He picked up the wine list. 'What do you fancy? Sancerre? Or there's a nice New Zealand Sauvignon Blanc here?'

Tick. Not a pitcher-of-house-wine sort of man. By the time he ordered the drinks – polite and respectful to the waitress – I was beginning to notice many good things about him. Friendly blue eyes. Good shirt. An endearing way of pausing, a sort of verbal standing back, waiting for you to speak. A total contrast to Scott's monopolising of the microphone with his opinions, wants and decrees. I tried to see his feet. I knew I'd have to make some compromises, but I had a thing about horrid shoes.

I glanced around the restaurant. Enough booths, dividers and low-level Latino music that we could have a conversation without the couple next to us knowing it was a first date. I'd anticipated being far too emotionally desiccated to be able to flirt. At best, I thought I would simply practise holding an intelligent conversation where the other person didn't automatically assume that my views were ridiculous. But as we ate our starters, I found myself leaning forward, staring into his eyes. After the Simon debacle, I was more careful than ever about exposing any flesh, but halfway through the stuffed peppers, I regretted my strait-laced tunic. I didn't want him to go back to his friends and tell them

97

that he must have ticked the box for nun by mistake. I surreptitiously nudged my breasts upwards. Crikey, I'd be going in for 'coffee' next. Surely I couldn't possibly meet the right man straightaway. At the very least I'd expected to suffer a few no-hopers – at least one fifteen years older than his photo, one toupee and one with a compulsive ex-wife disorder.

But Jake was either a great actor or a great guy. 'How did you get to be single, then, Roberta?'

'Too many years with the wrong man. Too domineering, really. I finally saw him for what he was.'

'How long were you with him?'

'Nearly nineteen years. Married fourteen.'

'You can be excused for a lapse of judgment. You must have been barely more than a teenager when you met him. I met my wife when I was in my late twenties and I still didn't spot the warning signs.' He broke off some bread, buttering the pieces individually, rather than treating it like a bacon buttie.

I was all for a man explaining away my mistakes rather than highlighting them. He had such a relaxed way about him. I loved the fact that he was interested in my opinions, encouraging me along with 'That's a really good point,' 'I hadn't thought of it like that,' 'Gosh. I don't often meet women as intelligent as you.'

I didn't feel intelligent, though. If I'd had half a brain, I'd have conceded that, years ago, my dad had a point about Scott. If nothing else, I was 'far too young to throw away all that education and get married without living a bit first'.

Somewhere into the main course, Jake shook his head. 'I don't know why you keep saying all these things about yourself. If I believed you, which I don't, you're a hopeless cook, a terrible mother, a rubbish driver, a lazy wife, an unfit blob. When you look deep into your heart, is that what you really think?'

I popped another piece of lamb in my mouth so I didn't have to answer immediately. When I did attempt to respond, a big gush of tears flooded my eyes. I tried to make a joke. 'I don't feel that I've excelled at much so far.' It was too late. There was no hiding my tears. I put my cutlery down. 'Excuse me.'

I ran to the Ladies and darted into a cubicle. I snatched up some loo paper to stop my tears running onto the silk of my tunic. I wasn't ready for this. Not at all. Fine for Octavia to say it was time to get back on the horse, or whatever vile expression she'd used. I'd make my excuses and leave. Stupid, stupid me. I splashed my face with cold water and walked back out, still doing feeble little sobs. If I ever went on another date in my life, I was not going to drink.

Jake was standing outside. He put out his hand. 'Hey. Sorry. My ex always said my timing was terrible.'

'Don't be nice to me. Just don't. Oh God. I think I'd better go.'

'No, don't do that. Unless this is all a front and you're trying to give me the slip. I bet you've just texted your friend to say, "Phone me with an emergency in five minutes." If that phone goes, I'm going to be very suspicious.' He handed me an ironed handkerchief.

I adored a well-timed white handkerchief over a red rose any day.

'Look, you don't have to be kind to me. You don't know me. I'm sure acting as a shoulder to cry on isn't your idea of a jolly evening. Let me settle the bill.'

'Let's finish eating. Look on the bright side. I've seen you cry and I still like you.' Even through my tears, it struck me that I could get used to a man being so straightforward, nothing to second-guess.

He steered me back to the table. I sat down and picked up my fork.

Jake smiled. 'I'm going to talk about myself for a bit, until you either fall asleep or decide that you can speak again.'

He told me he was passionate about skiing. Even though I'd loved it at school, I hadn't been since I met Scott because he thought it was a stupid sport. Jake had one teenage son to whom he was very close. He'd been divorced for six months and had had some horrors of dates. 'I met one French girl who only waited until after the first glass of wine to ask if I could help her with her debts and pay her rent. I met another woman who wanted me to go to a party with her to make her ex-husband jealous. And a real nutcase who talked about Ben all night, how sweet he was, how much she loved him. I thought it was her son but then discovered it was her horse.'

'So am I going to be your blubbing neurotic story?'

Jake laughed. 'No. You're going to be my "you won't believe what a gorgeous girl I met" story.'

For the first time since I'd left Scott, I could imagine touching another man.

I finished my lamb and felt confident enough to stay for coffee. I had moments when I forgot we didn't know each other at all. I felt like me, the proper me, the one with real opinions that came from deep-seated belief. Not the one I'd become with Scott, the woman who often held a sentence for a nanosecond before letting it roll out, mentally weighing up whether it was OK to be released, whether a simple observation would lead to an unholy row later.

'So what's next for you?' Jake ordered more coffee. I didn't want the evening to end either, even if it meant I'd be bouncing off the walls.

'What do you mean, what's next?'

'Divorce always brings some kind of change of direction. What's going to be yours?'

'Gosh. We're in the early stages of negotiating our divorce, so I haven't dared dig that deep yet. I don't know.'

'I bet you do know. If you're really honest with yourself, there'll be something there that you didn't do because of your marriage, that now you could do. Mine was cooking. My ex hated me wasting time in the kitchen, thought it was an excuse not to talk to her.'

I leant back. Part of me felt under pressure to show a bit of depth, to have a dream worthy of his interest.

I did have a dream.

It was just that whenever I'd suggested it to Scott, he had flicked it away as though I was some cute Barbie doll toying with a ridiculous notion.

'I don't want to sound pretentious.'

'You don't want to sound as though you've given up on change, ambition or thinking things could be different, either.' But Jake smiled as though he was the sort of person to encourage rather than belittle me.

So I told him. I told him about wanting to set up my own interior design business, focusing on transforming people's lives by encouraging them to let go of possessions and traditions in their homes that they'd always clung to out of habit, guilt, duty. I waited for him to do what Scott did – wrinkle his nose and tell me that was New Age bullshit and that I'd never make any money.

He didn't. He asked me question after question, about my theories on possessions, on whether I was taking items from my marital home or starting afresh, and even invited me to use his home as a guinea pig. It was only when the waiter started sweeping up behind the bar that Jake gestured for the bill. I reached for my bag but he put out a restraining hand.

'No. This is mine. No arguments. You can get it another time.' He raised his eyebrows in a question.

A little burst of warmth spread through me as I nodded. All those years I'd spent curling my eyelashes and trimming my cuticles, when bursting into tears was all it took.

And he was wearing Timberlands.

Octavia

I was going to win Crap Fair-weather Friend of the Year, but I'd begun to dread Roberta phoning. Her favourite time to call was seven o'clock in the evening. As Alicia chilled out in front of the telly, our daily conversation appeared to be her main source of entertainment. She'd come on the phone, her voice despondent and flat, so I didn't feel I could say, 'Sorry, but I'm trying to listen to Polly's reading for assembly, check Charlie's chemistry homework, make a spaghetti bolognese and decipher Jonathan's latest job rejection.'

Instead, I wandered about the kitchen with the receiver wedged on my shoulder, stirring with one hand and waving away the kids with the other. They thought a phone call was the perfect opportunity to start mouthing incomprehensible messages or stuff themselves with biscuits.

That evening, though, her voice was different. Almost giddy. She'd texted the previous evening to let me know that she was home from her date, but no details. As soon as we started talking about Jake though, I could tell that the boy had made quite an impression. Since she'd split up with Scott, Roberta had developed a hardness, as though just surviving meant that she had no room left to cut anyone any slack.

But instead of launching into a list of ten things she didn't like about him to make me laugh, she sounded all gooey and said, 'He was lovely. I really liked him.'

I kept butting in with all the things I wanted to know. 'What did he look like? Better or worse than the picture? Was he posh?'

'Better than his photo. Very kind eyes. Not Eton-posh, but well-spoken. Maybe a bit regional, now I come to think of it. Southern somewhere. Even Dad might have liked him.'

'That good? Christ.' Scott had horrified Roberta's father so much with his backslapping and matey chat that he'd begged me – the girl he proclaimed 'an unruly influence' on his daughter – to make Roberta see sense. For once in my life I agreed with him, but our combined disapproval had done nothing to dissuade her.

'Does he own his own house? What car has he got?' I pulled the washing out of the machine and starting draping pants and socks over radiators. Jonathan had declared the tumble dryer out of bounds until he got a job.

'I didn't ask what car he drove. I think he lives over by the park, but I don't know whether it's a house or a flat.'

'Bloody hell, Roberta, you're out of practice. You're not asking the right questions. I think I'd better meet the guy.'

'I've had all the wealth. It didn't make me happy.'

'I know, but believe me, counting the pennies isn't a great relationship-enhancer either. You must know what he does for a living?' Immi came in, making starving-to-death signs at me. I turned my back on her and she wandered off again.

'Of course, it was on his profile. He runs a printing business.'

'So did you find out whether he was in his back bedroom with a John Bull set or whether he owns a massive factory?'

'I'm not entirely sure I care. He seemed like a genuine gentleman. He paid for dinner.'

Born into a family where weekends involved theatre premieres, exhibitions and opera, Roberta wasn't someone destined to slum it. At school she loved coming to mine, sleeping in the shabby little attic bedroom I hated, relishing Mum's Angel Delight and chocolate mini rolls.

Because it wasn't her real life.

In the sixth form, she only went out with blokes who had cars and wined and dined her. I considered myself lucky to get a Fanta down the park and a grope behind the bowling shed.

'So?'

'So, what?'

'Did you kiss him?'

'I did.'

'Well? Come on, tell me the gory details, I'm living vicariously here.' I could still remember my first kiss with Xavi, on his father's boat.

'It was nice.'

'Just nice? Or fireworky good?'

'God, I don't know. It's so long since I've kissed anyone other than Scott. It felt a bit odd. I thought it would be more embarrassing but I'd had a few glasses of wine and it felt right. He was a really good kisser.' Roberta sounded dreamy, as though her sharpness had taken a dunking in Lenor.

'Are you meeting him again?'

'He asked to see me again tonight.'

I gasped. 'Oh my God. Last night and tonight? Don't tell me he's been texting you all day?'

'Not all day. Once or twice. Just, really enjoyed last night, looking forward to seeing you.'

'He sounds keen. Jonathan only texts me to tell me to transfer some money into his current account. Where are you going tonight?'

'He's cooking me dinner.' She giggled.

'Chez lui? Sounds like the big seduction scene. Make sure you pack the condoms.'

'I'm not going to sleep with him.' She sounded horrified. 'I don't think I've made the mental switch from being married to Scott yet.'

Roberta's prudishness was like something out of *Pride and Prejudice*. 'What's that got to do with anything? Scott's busy twanging the G-strings of that woman with the lingerie business, isn't he?'

'I do know that. But I'm not Scott. I've never slept with anyone on a second date.'

Christ. I often hadn't bothered with a second date because I'd slept with them on the first. 'You're thirty-nine. You've had a child. You don't have to pretend to be a virgin any more.'

'He might go off me if I sleep with him.'

I slammed the washing machine shut. 'Why should he? Scott never had any complaints in that department. Surely men our age realise that women don't think that they've found a new husband just because they've had sex?'

'I'm not so sure. The whole idea terrifies me.'

Roberta was one of the few women I knew who could not only wear a bikini but turned heads in one. 'He should be so lucky. You're gorgeous. Just be grateful that you haven't got boobs that you can tuck into the top of your pants. Ring me tomorrow and let me know how it goes.'

I put the phone down feeling unsexy and past it. Nothing on my body was where it should be any more. Everything hung rather than sat. And though I kept telling myself to 'move on', I was still smarting from the whole school reunion debacle. Even without multi-coloured hair, people should have been able to recognise me. No one had looked at Roberta and wondered which faded face she was. Then, my USP was my rebellion, whereas hers had always been her glamour.

106

Sure, she'd sprinkled glitter in her hair, stuck stars on her face and worn a Lycra cat suit when we went to parties from mine. But then, as now, she'd only ever drawn attention to herself for her beauty, not her daring.

I didn't have beauty to begin with. Now I didn't have daring either.

I chucked some fish fingers in the oven. That just about summed my life up: back in Corsica, I'd caught sea bass and grilled it on an open fire.

Xavi wouldn't have let me become this excuse for an adventurer, this person who went to Brighton for the day, tried on silver Doc Martens and red patent platforms, but then bought a square-toed black court from the M&S Footglove range.

I struggled to remember the last time I'd felt like I was a prize to be treasured. In the early days, Jonathan had admired my ballsiness and I'd liked having him as a safe platform to springboard from. Lately he was always telling me to 'rein it in', whatever 'it' was.

Xavi had made me feel I was the bravest girl alive because I was always ready to grab my microscopic rucksack and head off without needing to know where I would sleep that night. I bet Xavi didn't take £5-worth of five pences to the bank on a regular basis like Jonathan.

I stuck the food on trays and let the kids eat in front of the telly for once. I pretended I needed to get some work done in the kitchen. In reality, the urge to know if Xavi had a sensible haircut and a steady job was consuming me. I'd resisted the lure of Google all these years, afraid that the mere typing of his name might make me hanker after things that a married woman with three children shouldn't even be thinking about. But since the evening with Roberta, every time life slowed down long enough for me to daydream, Xavi was there, with that pent-up energy, ready to be diverted into an escapade.

I had to know. With one click of the mouse, I smashed down the carefully constructed barricades that had kept my memories of Xavi pinned back in the distant past.

A wash of relief ran through me, the adrenaline of admitting that he was still there, still in my mind and my heart.

Google. Xavier Santoni.

Quite a few came up, but none in Corsica. My search spread to France and the rest of Europe, and then beyond. Squinting into tiny pictures, staring at middle-aged men, mentally trying to age those high cheek bones, those brown eyes simultaneously wary and mischievous, that taut way he had of holding himself as though someone might jump out from behind Cocciu's medieval crannies.

I lost a large part of the evening to Google Earth, zooming in on every inch of Cocciu. I started at the boarding school where I taught English for a year when I was twenty. From what I saw on screen, it hadn't changed much. I hovered on his parents' house, magnifying the Corsican coastline, kidding myself that I recognised particular beaches. Every time anyone came into the kitchen I banged the laptop shut, muttering about accounts that needed finishing.

It was all fruitless. It hacked me off that I could look at pictures from the bloody Hubble telescope in space, but couldn't find a single reference to the man who was lodged in the corner of my heart that was forever *Corse*. I was pathetic. So little excitement in my life that my heart was all a-flutter at the idea of finding a *photo* of a man I loved two decades ago. I deleted my search history.

Now I just needed a Control + H for my feelings.

Roberta

I drew up outside Jake's house. I was early so I texted Alicia to say I was thinking of her and sent my love. I hated her staying at Scott's for two nights a week but it was the only way he'd forge any kind of relationship with her. It was his first evening back from Australia after a fortnight away but she still made a fuss about going. I hoped it stemmed from a misguided desire to protect my feelings rather than because she really didn't want to see him. I'd spoken to her when she'd arrived at his after school though, and she'd been very guarded. I could hear Scott grumbling in the background and she'd been quick to get off the phone. Hopefully he'd just been impatient to spend some time with her.

I was just getting out of the car when my mobile rang.

'Hi Mum.' Alicia's voice sounded small and distant.

'Hello darling. Are you OK? You sounded a little sad earlier.'

'I'm good. Shana's here.'

A feral spike of jealousy shot through me. 'Is she kind to you?'

'She's OK. She's only twenty-six and she thinks she knows it all. Like, she has all these opinions about music and keeps trying to rap. Dad thinks it's really funny and encourages her, then joins in himself. It's cringey. And they're all over each other.'

I tussled. I knew I should fetch her and bring her home. But I wanted to spend the evening with Jake. I'd taken responsibility for Alicia the whole time Scott had been in Australia, living in that tiny apartment without a second to myself. Maybe I was too selfish to be a mother. Maybe Scott had been right.

I sighed inside. 'Do you want me to pick you up?'

'No. It's all right. I'm going to a party with some friends from school.'

'Lucy and Daniela?'

'No. Some girls in my class. You don't know them. One of their brothers is picking me up. He's passed his test.'

'Did Daddy say that was all right?'

'He doesn't care. Better for him if I go out, then he and Shana can have sex.'

I didn't quite know how to deal with that one. I wished I were more like Octavia. She wouldn't let that comment drop into a vacuum. Goodness knows what warped view of relationships Alicia had. 'Be careful. I'd rather Daddy ordered you a taxi.'

'Mum. It's all organised. I've got to go with him now, otherwise they'll think I'm pathetic and spoilt.'

I felt a surge of fury that Scott wasn't worrying about whether Alicia would get home in one piece, out on the town with God knows who. I should have insisted on a better school for Alicia rather than the local comprehensive, which Scott chose because he didn't agree with all that 'selective shit' – 'Sink or swim, Robster, sink or swim.'

Too late for all that.

'Make sure you wear your seatbelt. Don't get in the car with him if he's been drinking, will you?'

110

Jake was waving at me from his doorstep. I gestured that I'd be two minutes.

'I am fourteen, Mum. I'm old enough to know what I'm doing.'

I hoped that Scott was going to insist on her coming home at a reasonable time. She said goodbye and rang off. It never occurred to her to ask where I was. I applauded the selfishness of teenagers.

I walked up Jake's drive a little less joyous than I had been ten minutes earlier. At least I could tell Octavia that he had a house, 1930s, detached, complete with drive and BMW 4x4.

So not a pauper then.

The guilt Alicia had sprinkled over me seemed shamefully short-lived when Jake took my hand and kissed me on both cheeks. 'Come in, I'm so pleased you came. I thought you might blow me out.'

He had a confidence about him that settled me rather than put me on my guard. The house smelt of ginger and cinnamon. A man who hadn't popped to Waitrose for ready-made lasagne. He led me into the sitting room. 'Here, have a seat, I'll get you some wine. White, isn't it? Or would you prefer some bubbles?'

'A drop of white would be lovely. I've got to drive.'

'Let's see how it goes. I can always call you a cab. Excuse me one second while I get the drinks.'

I nodded and breathed out slowly. I felt nervy, like I used to before I was married, when Scott and I were about to be reunited after several months apart. I didn't want to think about him now, so I forced myself to concentrate on examining the sitting room. Very masculine – lots of dark leather, brown curtains, no ornaments. Open fire and big comfy sofas. Not the trendy sofas Scott had insisted on, which had all the comfort factor of a Ryvita.

I could have worked wonders on softening the room. Wallpapered the chimney breast with some of that gorgeous poppy-print paper I'd seen in John Lewis. Creamy paint for the walls to give it a nice warm lift. A cosy shaggy rug, red curtains and cushions to bring it all together. I decided it was a little early to offer interior design tips in case he thought I wanted to move in.

There was nothing to suggest there had been a woman around lately. I made a mental note to find out whether there'd been anyone serious since the wife.

Jake came back in from the kitchen with drinks and nibbles. I settled back into the leather armchair, trying to put my mouth into a relaxed shape.

'Hope you like my cooking. My son thinks it's OK, but then his mum doesn't spend much time in the kitchen so he finds it a relief to come here and get some decent food. I've made Moroccan chicken – I should've asked before, you're not allergic to nuts, are you?'

'No, sounds lovely, thank you.'

'God, this is weird, isn't it? Sitting around being polite. I wish we could fast-forward to a time when we're really easy with each other and I'm not sitting there thinking, shit, I want to say some nice things to her, but I can't because then she'll think I'm a stalking loony and get scared off.'

I smiled over my glass. Jake's ability to admit to feeling vulnerable was ridiculously attractive. I nodded at his bookshelf. 'You like reading then?'

'My wife used to get infuriated because I preferred reading to watching telly. She said it was another example of my selfishness, that I liked to shut myself away rather than share experiences.'

'I can't fall asleep without reading.' I felt myself blush at the mere mention of anything to do with bedtime. But Jake didn't laugh at me: we embarked on a lovely discussion about

112

authors, directors and playwrights that Scott would have dismissed with a 'Let me know when Sylvester Stallone's got a new movie out.'

Eventually Jake stood up. 'Let's eat. I've set up in the kitchen. I find the dining room a bit Buckingham Palace, shouting down the table when there's just two people.'

'Can I just pop to your loo?' I still hadn't quite got my nerves under control. I opened the door he pointed to and gave myself a stern glare in the mirror. I reminded myself that it was only a dinner; a chat with someone I didn't know very well. No need to go on the defensive just yet. I looked around. Loo seat down. Marvellous. I lifted it up. Vague smell of bleach. Hallelujah. When I washed my hands, the towel was crisp and dry. Mr Muscle and air freshener on the windowsill. Fabulous. I thought of Octavia's words. 'Treat it as a bit of fun. Don't start getting all tight-arsed and uppity with him.' God knows how serious I'd have been if I hadn't had Octavia teasing me all of my life. Unlike her, the 'go with the flow' gene didn't feature in my family.

I headed into the kitchen. Jake was stirring away at the stove. The table was set with candles, proper cloth napkins, side plates. The kitchen was dated – country cottage rather than the granite and stainless steel I was used to – but the pine carvers looked far cosier than the chrome bar stools round my breakfast bar.

Jake dished up, chatting about his son, Angus, pointing out a photo of him holding a big silver cup. 'He's a great tennis player. I can't beat him any more. Thrashes me completely.'

'Does he know you're dating again?'

'God, yes. He's desperate for me to get a girlfriend. I'm sure he thinks that if I'm having sex I won't notice what he's up to himself.' There was a pause. If it had been a cartoon, he would have clapped his hand over his mouth. As it was, he screwed his eyes up and said, 'I can't believe I just said that. Out loud.'

I shrugged. Given that I'd been wondering all evening what Jake looked like with his clothes off, I was struggling to look shocked. He carried on serving coconut rice. He looked straight at me, his blue eyes wary.

'I'm sorry, that was really crass of me.' He gave me a sheepish smile that made him look like a cheeky teenager himself. 'You are rather gorgeous. I guess it was on my mind. Of course, that's not the only thing I like about you.'

'Thanks.' I squirmed in the silence that followed. 'Tell me about your job.' My body wasn't so keen to abandon the topic, fizzing away with zingy little darts of thrill.

Over dinner, Jake explained about his high-pressured printing business, how his best customers were pharmaceutical companies, property developers and estate agents. I didn't bother to mention Scott was a property developer.

In fact, I didn't mention him at all.

Instead, I kept noticing more things I liked about Jake. His long eyelashes. His neat nose. His easy laugh. The chicken was wonderful, but I was an ungrateful audience as he could have served me a Cup-a-Soup and I would have barely noticed. Now I listened carefully, I could hear the slight West Country inflection in his voice. Scott's Australian accent never bothered me but I'd always considered anything west of Berkshire as verging on the provincial. But there was nothing country bumpkin about Jake. Just lilting sexiness.

He nodded towards the wine bottle. 'Taxi?' I nodded back, chasing away the thought that I might surprise myself and stay over. No sex. I wasn't ready for that, but I definitely wanted to investigate what was under that green shirt rather more closely. He grinned, and I saw his whole body relax.

'Brilliant. That makes me feel as though you haven't got

the meter ticking on how long you can stay. Takes the pressure off having to be super-entertaining to keep you here.'

'Do you want to keep me here?' The wine was making me brave.

'Stop fishing. I think you know the answer to that.'

He stood up to clear the plates and stroked my hair as he walked past. I almost heard the surge of blood as my heart speeded up.

'Dessert? I've made some tiramisu. Or do you want a break and we'll have some later?'

'Later, if that's OK.' I just wanted to kiss him. Forget pudding. I was going to need a paper bag to blow into shortly.

'Let's go through then and enjoy the fire.'

He gestured for me to lead the way.

'You're tall, aren't you?' he said, as we walked into the sitting room.

'For a woman, I suppose. I'm not taller than you, though.'

He swung round. 'No. Let's see. Your shoulders are about two inches lower than mine. So I suppose if I bent forward very slightly and you lifted your chin a fraction . . .' He tilted my face upwards and then, gently, gently put his lips on mine until I felt my legs start to tremble.

The fire was scorching into the backs of my jeans. That kiss merited a little singed skin. My limbs felt as though vital supporting bones had been removed.

'Let's sit down. It's getting a bit hot over here.' He took my hand.

We ended up lying on the sofa, nose to nose, talking the nonsense that you can only get away with at the beginning. He was tracing patterns on my neck, occasionally stretching up to kiss me. When he did, my whole body seemed to melt, disintegrating into the sofa until my head whirled and I was only aware of his solid body next to mine.

I felt so adolescent, necking on the sofa, as though we'd

have to smooth our clothes into place when our parents turned up. With a sure touch, Jake unbuttoned my blouse and unhooked my bra, lifting his head long enough to see whether or not I objected before kissing my breasts. I tensed.

Although I knew it was stupid, I still felt unfaithful to Scott.

I forced away the guilt and focused on the glorious sensations Jake was creating in me. I'd just pulled Jake's shirt out of his trousers and was discovering his smooth chest when the sitting room door was flung open.

Being a male household, there were no cushions to grab. The best I could do was to cover my breasts with my arms. Jake leapt up, tucking his shirt in. 'Angus! I didn't know you were coming back tonight.'

Angus stood in the doorway, hand over his eyes in a comedy fashion. He was every bit his father's son, a blonder version, more tousled and angular. 'Obviously. Sorry. I texted you to say Mum couldn't take me to school tomorrow cos she's got to leave early for work, so I'd be staying here.'

Jake gathered himself. 'My phone was switched off. Right. Give us five minutes and then I'll introduce you.' There was an undercurrent of amusement in his sternness.

'Sure.'

Angus put up a hand to me and sauntered off. I heard the fridge opening and closing and the clatter of plates.

I couldn't look at Jake. I started snatching up my bra and shirt and buckling my belt. Jake put his hand on my arm. 'Hey. Don't rush off. I wanted him to meet you. Not like this, but he'll be fine about it. I'm really sorry.'

'No, look, I'm going to get going. I can't sit here and make polite conversation with Angus when he's just seen me half-naked.' I wanted to run away.

Jake grinned. 'I'm sure seeing your breasts will be the highlight of his young life.'

My ability to laugh at myself was not amongst my most pronounced character traits. 'No. I can't face it. I'll fetch the car in the morning.'

He reached out for me. 'Come here, don't get upset. It was just unfortunate. No one's fault.' He looked as though I was creating a drama out of nothing. I'd like to have seen his face if Alicia had walked in when he had his pants down.

I shrugged him off and rang for a taxi. 'Thanks for dinner. It was lovely.'

I marched out into the hallway, picked up my coat, and dashed past the kitchen where Angus was eating tiramisu straight out of the bowl. I gave a bemused Jake a peck on the cheek and plunged out into the cold to wait for the taxi, banging the door behind me.

I almost ran down the garden path, vacillating between feeling that I'd shown myself in a poor light and anger that Jake hadn't double-checked arrangements thoroughly. Upset lodged in my throat. No taxi in sight. Within seconds I heard the front door open. I didn't turn round.

Big warm arms went round my back.

'Roberta. This is life with children. Yes, it's embarrassing. No, it's not an ideal way to introduce you to Angus. You don't have to fall apart over it, though. We're not the only couple who've met, liked each other and got a bit frisky on the sofa and been disturbed by unreliable offspring.'

I turned round. 'This is so hard for me. I haven't been out with anyone new since I was twenty. I don't know whether I can cope with all these complications.'

'Angus is not a complication. He's a teenage boy who came home when I wasn't expecting him. He's not a toddler I've got to look after every minute of the day. But he is my son and I'm not going to ban him from coming home. I will leave my phone on next time though.' The intonation in 'next time' held a mixture of hope and enquiry.

The lights of the cab swept up the road. My tantrum drained away. At my age, it was unrealistic to expect someone as lovely as Jake not to have any baggage. 'Sorry for getting it all out of perspective.'

Jake gave me a quick kiss. He opened the car door. 'Sorry we were interrupted.'

'Me too.' I sat back in the cab and touched my lips. Maybe there was life beyond Scott after all.

Octavia

Roberta arrived at nursery at lunchtime with a wonderful bag of picnicky goodies. I waved her in, shoving the photos I'd been sorting through into my desk. I'd spent the morning alternating between double-checking that Xavi hadn't suddenly joined Facebook and peering at pictures of my twenty-year-old self, wondering when I'd become this woman no one recognised. When I was young I'd never considered myself pretty, but now I looked again there was a certain elfin attractiveness about me that I hadn't appreciated.

Roberta couldn't have picked a better day to tip up. I was bruised from a row with Jonathan the night before and I needed someone to tell me how right I was, even if I was wrong. 'Thank God you're here. Brighten my day.'

'Is there something vexatious to your soul?' Roberta raised her eyebrows. It was a standing joke ever since we'd been forced to learn *Desiderata* at school.

'Yes, I think we can safely say the universe is not unfolding as it should.'

I filled her in on my discussion with Jonathan over whether I should go to the annual conference for nursery managers. Usually I moaned like hell at the prospect of a weekend in a soulless business hotel in the company of people who used too many hand signals and exaggerated facial expressions.

This year though, I really fancied a break, any break, from Jonathan's long face. As soon as he raised his eyebrows and said 'I don't think we can afford for you to go,' I craved that weekend away.

I became obsessed with the chance to lie on a bed for five minutes without anyone wanting me, the opportunity to stay up late, drink too much cheap Shiraz and tell embarrassing secrets to people I'd never met before.

And feed my addiction to Googling Xavi.

'Maybe you'll be able to afford to go next year? It's not the end of the world, is it?' Roberta said.

This from a woman whose idea of economising was ordering groceries from Waitrose rather than Abel & Cole.

'No. It's not.'

Compared to Roberta's traumas, it wasn't. But it still mattered to me.

'I'd have preferred it if Jonathan hadn't then made his point by highlighting the things on my shopping list that we don't need. Why would we need Brie rather than pre-fab squares of cheese? Squash when we can drink tap water? Christ, when he went shopping last, we ended up with plastic ham, 'value' toilet paper that took the skin off my arse, and long-life-never-seen-an-orange juice.'

Roberta's face was a picture. Her father used to wave away every restaurant bill without looking at it. He just handed over a credit card and said, 'I trust you.'

Roberta looked pained. 'What sort of man spends time reading supermarket lists, deciding what's in and what's out?'

'Particularly when he could be walking Stan or fixing the blind in Polly's room. But the real reason I'm so hacked off is because a new MacBook Pro arrived at the crack of dawn this morning. Clearly blueberries to help me live a long time are out, but high performance graphics rock on.'

Roberta shuddered. 'How selfish.'

Even though Jonathan's excuse that he needed a better computer for his job applications had done nothing to calm me down, it was a testament to the contrariness of human nature that I didn't want Roberta slagging off Jonathan. Especially when Scott's faults could be seen from outer space.

'Anyway, how did it go with Jake?' I poked into the bag. 'Brilliant, vegetarian sushi. Well remembered.'

Roberta unwrapped her crayfish sandwich and told me about Angus walking in. I laughed until I snorted red cabbage across my spreadsheets.

'Only you could get the arse-ache about that. He hadn't arranged it. Talk about a bloody drama queen. Jesus, girl. How was he this morning? Did you see him when you went to pick up the car?'

Roberta swigged her super-healthy juice. She looked a bit shamefaced. 'I was too mortified to ring the bell in case Angus answered.'

I rolled my eyes. 'Bloody hell. You're worse than a teenager yourself. Jake sounds lovely, far more tolerant than you should reasonably be able to expect. Like Angus is going to remember your knockers. He's probably wanking away to giant Playboy H-cups in his room every night.'

Even Roberta had the good grace to laugh at that. 'Do you think I should telephone Jake?'

'Yes. As soon as you leave me. Before he finds someone on Just Clicked who's not as mad as you are.'

Roberta's serious face made me soften. 'Or as gorgeous and funny.'

Once she'd licked the last spoonful of yoghurt, she couldn't wait to disappear. Now she'd got the dating bug, she was a woman with a mission. I leaned on the windowsill and watched her on the phone in the car. She had an elbow on the steering wheel and was smoothing her eyebrows with her free hand, her equivalent of nail-biting. Her face was solemn and then, suddenly, she smiled. Good old Jake. He was obviously very forgiving. After all those years with Scott, it was her turn for a good guy.

I shouldn't be jealous of her. Really I shouldn't.

Roberta

I was in danger of becoming an estate agent stalker, constantly pestering young men with pungent aftershave about whether they'd heard of any houses coming onto the market. After two and a half months of living in an open-plan rabbit hutch, I was desperate for a proper home again, rather than a rented shell. I'd been seeing Jake for five weeks and felt ridiculously thrilled the first time he called me his 'girlfriend'. On good days, I was beginning to see buying a new house as an exciting beginning rather than a depressing symbol of my failure. I just needed a bit of luck to find somewhere decent.

I had trailed in and out of stacks of dreary homes, usually with Octavia knocking on walls to show how flimsy new-build houses were. She kept trying to persuade me into something with a 'bit more character'. I was adamant I wanted something modern and maintenance-free. In the end, I stopped taking her with me. I couldn't think properly with 'a strong wind and this will blow over' clouding my judgment.

Gloriously, one of the estate agents had phoned me first thing Monday morning. By early afternoon, I had seen a brand-new house I wanted to buy, the first one that didn't make me feel that I was going to be slightly dissatisfied for the rest of my life. It didn't have the boot room, conservatory or gym that I'd taken for granted previously, but it had three double bedrooms and three bathrooms and as Octavia pointed out, no one's heart would be bleeding for me too much. Thankfully, there was no chain. The estate agent assured me that I could complete within a month.

I phoned Jake as soon as I'd finished looking round. He was at the airport on his way to a print conference in Germany.

'Sounds fantastic. Are you going to let me see it?' He was shouting over the noise of announcements in the background.

I surprised myself. I wanted him to love it as much as me. 'Of course, if you'd like to. Don't put me off it, though. I think it's perfect.'

'I wouldn't dream of it. Just interested to see what the next big thing in interior design chooses for her own house. Try and set up something for Friday when I get back.'

I smiled. I loved it that he believed in me. I heard the check-in girl ask him to put his luggage on the scales. We said a quick goodbye. I was surprised to feel more alone than I had for ages. Since the 'Angus evening', we'd seen each other regularly. Very occasionally, I'd invited him over to my apartment when Alicia wasn't there, but the bed winking away in the corner of the sitting room put me on edge. I hadn't let him stay over yet and despite a series of invitations, I hadn't stayed at his either. If he minded, he'd been too well-mannered to force the issue.

Some mornings, he'd pop out of work for half an hour and we'd meet for coffee, hold hands and each other's gazes while the minutes flew past. We spoke every day, several times a day. I'd got used to having someone around, someone whose voice lifted on the other end of the line when he realised who it was.

He'd even organised a surprise trip to London's Design

Museum, where he'd let me wander at my own pace. Unlike Scott, he didn't seem to consider doing something that interested me rather than him a huge sacrifice. Over afternoon tea at the Dorchester, he encouraged me to believe that setting up my own business as a hands-on interior designer wasn't beyond my reach.

Every time I saw him, he drip-fed little nuggets of encouragement. 'You've got an amazing sense of colour.' 'I know you could work out what to do with this space.'

Eventually I felt brave enough to contact the new business adviser at the bank. I'd never dealt with start-up finance before – that was Scott's department – but Jake was a godsend. Without taking over, he talked me through various drafts of business plans until my panic subsided. It was going to be a long few days without him.

It was three o'clock when I pulled into the underground car park at the apartments. I heard a text arrive. Jake was sweet like that. He'd probably read my mood. I stared at the phone and my stomach tightened.

Can we meet? Need to talk. Woof.

An old joke from happier times. Scott. Scottie Dog. Woof. What did he need to talk about? We'd almost settled the money. He was going to buy me out of Watermill Drive and give me a lump sum towards my new house. His monthly payments were generous so my mortgage wouldn't be too much of an issue as long as I was careful. Maybe he was going to try a last-minute shafting. I glared at the phone looking for a hidden message. Woof was friendly. No kisses though, but then I supposed kissing days were over. Still, an improvement from recent texts questioning my abilities as a mother and wife.

I took the lift up to my apartment on the third floor, a big cloud rolling across my house-hunting high. I needed to play Scott carefully. He was quite capable of scuppering my plans for sport. Perhaps he wanted to discuss how he could improve his relationship with Alicia. She still hated staying with him.

I washed my hands and picked up a towel I must have missed in my morning bathroom blitz. I hung up some coats on the back of Alicia's bedroom door, a tiny box room that she hated. She'd ignored my request to make her bed. I discovered Alicia's sports bag tangled up in the duvet and sighed. She had a swimming gala the following day and was staying at Scott's that night.

No time like the present. I'd take her kit over, find out what Scott wanted and meet Shana, who, like it or not, was going to be part of Alicia's life. I didn't bother to text – I wasn't going to ask permission to go back to the house that, for now, I still partly owned, even if Shana had installed herself there on a permanent basis. I topped up my lipstick and put on another coat of mascara.

The car practically drove itself to Watermill Drive. The cherry blossom was out. When we moved there nine years ago, I thought I'd arrived. Proved everyone who believed I'd married a loser wrong. Even my dad had had to concede that Scott had done well to go from penniless surfer boy to mansion owner in a decade. Maybe Shana thought she was over the finishing line now.

I punched in the gate code and let myself in. With any luck, Shana would be staring at the CCTV monitor and wondering who the hell I was. I parked right in front of the pillared entrance and rang the bell. I sucked in my stomach, feeling a zigzag of adrenaline buzz through my body.

The blonde woman who opened the front door was wearing jeans and a vest top. Octavia would have christened her 'Miss Minus Mammaries'.

'Hello, I'm Roberta, Scott's wife. I just wanted a quick word with him.' I only used 'ex-wife' when it suited me. Even to me, my voice sounded over-the-top posh.

'Hello. I'm Shana. Pleased to meet you.' She held out her hand. Nasty little nails, all stubby and spade-like. I'd been expecting some sharp-suited mega-brain, fresh from closing a deal for ten thousand push-up bras while her bank manager held on the other line.

Instead, she looked as though I'd disturbed her while she was emptying the bins.

She hesitated. 'I'll get Scott for you. He's in the office in the garden.' She beckoned me in. 'Do you want to wait in the kitchen?'

I wanted to say, 'I'll wait in the flipping master bedroom if it suits me,' but instead I smiled and said, 'Thanks, but I'll pop out to the office.' Panic flashed across her face. Scott had obviously found a new target for his tempers. 'It's OK, he texted me. He wants to see me.'

I didn't wait for her to lead me into the kitchen. I marched on through, trying to shake off the feeling that I had burst into a stranger's house. The hallway smelt as though they'd been cooking fish. In the kitchen, a pile of dirty cereal bowls stood by the sink. A bunch of roses drooped in a vase. My wonderful Poole pottery vase. My black granite work surfaces were all smeary.

Shana trailed behind me. I reached up above the French windows for the key.

'We don't keep the key there any more. I'm paranoid about security in a house this size.' She reached into a drawer, searching under a jumble of phone chargers and computer leads. Tidying up didn't seem to be her priority.

That wouldn't work for Scott, not at all.

I managed not to snatch the key from her. She followed me out into the garden, her ugly Birkenstocks scuffing down the steps behind me.

I knocked on the door of Scott's office, then poked my head round. 'Hello there, Woof.' I was friendlier than I would have been without an audience. Out of the corner of my eye, I saw Shana's head crook with curiosity. 'Woof' was a low blow.

Scott jumped to his feet. 'Robbie!'

He was all 'hail-fellow-well-met' as though the only words that had ever passed his lips were those of tenderness and love. He glanced over to Shana. 'Hey, Shanie, just got a few things to talk about with Robbie. Can you get us some coffee, babe?'

Shana reminded me of a child denied a pudding. I turned to her, suddenly feeling sorry for her. She was too young to be dealing with Scott's mind games. 'Not for me, thanks, I'm not staying. Just came by to drop off Alicia's swimming stuff.' I held the bag up.

Scott scowled. 'Just me, then, not too much milk.' He had an amazing ability to roll dismissal and disrespect into civilised-sounding sentences. Shana nodded and slunk off up the garden.

Scott pushed back his swivel chair. 'Couldn't keep away from me then, Robster?'

I hated it when Scott called me that. He never called anyone by their proper name. My father would be delighted not to have to suffer 'Little Fella' or 'Davey-boy' again.

'You wanted to talk to me.' I kept my voice steady and firm. He was one of the few men I knew who looked good in lilac. He'd let his hair grow a little, casual and carefree, the way he was when I first met him. I reminded myself that the boyish grin soon clouded over when he didn't get his own way.

'Yeah. The thing is, I think we've both said a lot of stuff we didn't mean. We need to clear the air, make a bit of a new start. For Ali's sake. I think she blames me for how things have ended up.'

In the interests of peace, I decided not to say, 'Are you

surprised?' I'd make the most of Scott being in charming mode. He was confident, as usual, that I'd rush to fit in with him.

'What were you thinking?'

'Can I take you to dinner?'

'Won't Shana mind?' I glanced over my shoulder. No sign of her plodding along with Scott's coffee. If she had any sense, she'd have packed her rucksack and left.

'I'll deal with her.' Same old Scott, brooking no argument.

My desire to get us onto a footing where we could have a constructive conversation battled against my determination to stand up to him. 'You *are* living with her, right? Isn't she going to mind you wining and dining your not yet ex-wife?'

Scott laughed. 'Nah, she won't mind.'

'Why do you want to go for dinner? What is there to say? Except that we messed up?' My voice was clinging to my throat, struggling to get out. A faraway prickle of tears was starting to gather.

'There are a few things I want to discuss. Don't tell me you've already hooked up with someone else?' His voice had taken on a steely edge, the tone that usually preceded a row.

'God, no. You're a tough act to follow.' I clenched my teeth in case I suddenly blurted out 'Jake'. My fragile new confidence wasn't up to a full-on jealous onslaught from Scott.

'Dinner it is, then. Got a lot on at the moment, so let's say this Friday. Eight o'clock, Chez François. I'll send my driver to pick you up.'

'No, it's OK, I'll get a cab.'

'Babe. My driver. No arguments. No wife of mine is going to hang around street corners trying to find a taxi.'

'I'm still your wife then, am I?' I was glad Octavia couldn't see me pandering to his ego. I couldn't seem to snap that last little thread attaching me to him.

'Maybe for longer than you think.' Scott started jabbing away at his Blackberry. 'See you Friday.'

I crossed Shana coming down the path with coffee in a cup. Scott only liked the big white Villeroy and Boch mugs. I picked up my Poole Pottery vase on my way out. The red would be perfect in my new house.

It wasn't until I reached the car that I realised that I'd double-booked Scott with Jake's arrival back from Germany.

Octavia

Jonathan's job interview post-mortem varied. Depending on the day, he'd come back saying, 'I've got a good feeling about this one. There were only two other candidates and the recruitment guy seemed to think I was the preferred candidate. It's about time something went my way.' For the first few times, I'd get excited along with him, imagining how I'd pop out for a bottle of champagne and tell him I knew he'd do it all along.

Being the favourite, however, often seemed to shrivel up under a banner of 'The chemistry wasn't quite right', 'They felt my skill set was too sophisticated for what they were looking for' or 'The position was too junior, I'd have been running the show within months'. Now I'd dropped my expectations, saving my energy for the post-rejection mop-up.

Far worse was when the interviewers 'looked as though they were barely old enough to wipe their own arses'. Jonathan would treat me to a step-by-step account of every question, every objection, how he put them right, and then conclude that they were frightened of the competition and couldn't possibly bring him on board because they'd all be out of a job once his brilliance swept them aside.

When Jonathan had been made redundant nearly three months ago, I'd felt a glimmer of excitement that we might be able to make a new start abroad. But as one job rejection followed another, I understood that the days – before Charlie made his unexpected appearance – of Jonathan ruffling my hair and going along with my madcap ideas were over. Now, three kids later, we appeared to be in responsibility lockdown. Our duty was to feed them into one end of the school sausage machine in order to produce neat little packages conforming to the norm. Hence, 'a secure job within a 30-mile radius with a good pension' was a much greater priority than 'rushing off to the other side of the world without thinking things through'.

Unfortunately, thinking things through to the nth degree that Jonathan required was the enemy of inspiration, of spontaneity, of living with joy in your heart and adventure in your soul. When Jonathan and my mother had propelled me into marriage 'for the good of the baby', I was naïve enough to think that my gallivanting spirit would somehow rub off on him. Instead, his stick-in-the-mudness had turned out to be the stronger influence.

As finances dwindled, my little dream of bohemian kids in an orange grove in Spain or metro-savvy Francophiles hanging out in Montmartre expired like a pork chop past its sell-by date. I stopped thinking about Thailand and started thinking about re-mortgaging. On some days, even selling. Roberta told me she'd put in a good word for Jonathan with Patri, but we never heard anything. I didn't feel I could hassle Roberta when she had so much to sort out herself. But just when I'd given up on that as a possible lead, Patri phoned him up for an interview.

The day they set coincided with a time when the sky was dark, the future was black and Jonathan was on the scrap heap. If Angel Gabriel himself had burst through the door tooting on a trumpet, Jonathan would only have been able to see the grubby mark on his white tunic. Even as he shrugged into his jacket, he was telling me that Patri was only doing it as a favour to Roberta and that there probably wasn't a job to be had anyway. 'It's going to be a right waste of time. I might call and cancel.'

'Don't do that. Just go with an open mind. It might lead to something else. Maybe not now, but he could be a useful contact.'

'I've got lots of useful contacts.'

'Isn't the whole point that you never know what might lead to work? Don't they always say it's who you know?'

'I know lots of people and it hasn't got me anywhere yet, has it?'

My temper was creeping up. A row wasn't going to put him in the right frame of mind for gratuitous charm and sparkling responses. I hauled my irritation in. 'I know it's frustrating, but Roberta has given you a good press.'

'I don't need charity. I need a proper job.'

I took a deep breath and waved him off, smiling broadly as an antidote to his downturned, downtrodden, just plain down everything. Then I took myself off to work, finding a perverse pleasure in hunting for earthworms outside in the rain with a bunch of four-year-olds.

We were just admiring the way a big fat worm was burrowing back into the soil when one of the nursery assistants called me to the phone. 'It's Jonathan. He says it's urgent.'

I grudgingly headed inside to the office, instructing the children to see whether they could catch an earwig before I got back.

My hopes weren't high; usually Jonathan's idea of urgent was the internet connection going down. 'Hello?'

'I've done it!'

'Done what?'

'Got a job!'

'What? With Patri? That's fantastic.' Relief trickled through me. No more black cloud lurking on the sofa or standing sulkily in the kitchen watching me unload the dishwasher. No more supporting role as bolsterer of job-hunt ego. No more bloody 'value' tea bags that tasted like stewed cockroaches.

'Guess what? He wants me to set up his company's entire computer system in Sardinia.'

'Can you do that from here?'

'That's the best bit. I'm going out next week to do an initial recce for a few days. When I've worked out what needs doing, he's going to pay for us both to go out there for a little break. It's high time you had a treat, I know the last few months haven't been easy. We should go without the children. Let's see if your mother can look after them. I'll be at work in the day but we can explore in the evenings. It should be quite sunny if we wait until spring.'

I didn't think Jonathan and I had spent more than an afternoon on our own since the kids were born. I hoped we wouldn't realise we were that couple, gazing awkwardly round the restaurant, wondering what everyone else is talking about. I guessed we'd find out. I wasn't sure I had much to report apart from erratic but frequent internet trawling for an old boyfriend and a concern that the seal on the washing machine was about to go.

Then I had another thought. I was shocked how thrilling I found it. Sardinia was just a short ferry ride from another island.

Corsica.

Roberta

The five days Jake had been away seemed to last forever. I arrived at Gatwick to pick him up ages before the plane landed, scanning the crowd for his straw-coloured hair. I kept getting little flashbacks to meeting Scott when he came back from Australia, desperate for the moment when he would fold me into his arms and the weeks of separation would melt away. I still couldn't believe that huge love had dissipated into something wretched and painful.

Everyone had known it wouldn't last except stupid, obstinate me.

I elbowed aside the sadness that had dogged me since Christmas. I no longer wanted to spend my days curled up in a foetal ball but I still had moments of acute despair that only Jake could dispel. I craned my neck looking for him. My heart kept lifting then settling every time a man of his build came through the door. When he did finally appear, he looked relaxed and happy, not ready to explode about slow baggage handling, queues at passport control or any of the other things Scott took so personally.

He pulled me to a spot just out of the main traffic and hugged me. He smelt minty. I wanted to be one of those women who leaps into her lover's arms regardless of everyone else around but after a brief peck on the lips, my buttoned-up self won the day.

'I've missed you.' Jake made it seem so straightforward to say simple things.

I squeezed his hand. 'I've bought sandwiches. I wasn't sure what you'd like, so I got a selection.'

In my mind's eye, I saw Octavia teasing me. 'He says he misses you and you say prawn mayonnaise or cheese and pickle?' Even I could see how she'd find that funny.

'You're a sweetheart. I'd like to get out of the airport, though. Shall we drive back to mine and go for a picnic by the golf course?'

I hesitated. I suddenly felt shy. 'I wondered if you would like to pop in to see my new house first? I need to measure up for some curtains. I can reschedule if you don't fancy it.'

'I'd love to.'

I adored Jake's ability to go with the flow. We held hands to the car. Scott hadn't been much of a hand-holder. He saved getting physical for sex. Jake threw his suitcase in the boot then climbed in, making no attempt to look round to see if there was anything behind me. Reversing out of parking spaces appeared to be yet another thing I could do without Scott.

Jake whistled when he drew up outside my new house. 'Wow. I didn't realise it was overlooking the green. What a great location. And close to the station for when you get design commissions in London.'

I was delighted that he liked it, but surprised myself by enjoying his approval rather than *needing* it. Maybe the pre-Scott me, the woman I remembered from the distant past, who could offer an opinion without adding "Or maybe that's just me", was making a comeback. About time.

The estate agent, however, decided that Jake was the one

to woo and clicked around the house, pointing out the under-floor heating, the integral smart TV, the electric doors to the garage. Even when he detailed the wiring system and burglar alarm, Jake nodded politely. It was so relaxing to be with someone I didn't have to watch like a hawk, ready to intervene. I couldn't imagine having to apologise for him. I measured up the sitting room curtains, then headed into the kitchen.

Jake opened the wine fridge. 'Very swish. I can imagine a lazy sunny Sunday outside with the Chablis cooling nicely in here.' Then he blushed. 'If you invite me, of course.'

The fact that he could even think several months ahead to the summer shot out another little root of trust in my soul. 'Let me show you upstairs.' It was my turn to colour up. It was time to get the whole bedroom business out of the way so I didn't feel as though there was an unspoken 'nudge, nudge, wink, wink' every time upstairs, beds or taking off clothes were mentioned.

The estate agent muttered something about checking the meters in the garage. After Jake had admired the wet room and the guest suite, we wandered into the master bedroom. I leaned out over the Juliet balcony with its view over the green.

He stood behind me and put his arms round my waist. 'Can I christen this room with you?' It was the first time Jake had made a direct reference to sleeping together. A charge of desire shot through me.

'Maybe.'

He pulled me round to face him and brushed my lips with his. 'Let me know when you're ready to hear all the things I want to say to you.'

I giggled, but something was dancing deep inside me. I had little images of us poring over the *Sunday Times* in bed at the weekend and lazy brunches at the pale wooden dining table I'd spotted in town. Then a picture of Scott picking up

Alicia and seeing Jake's car burst in on my thoughts. I jerked away and headed back downstairs. 'Come on, it's nearly half past two. Let's go and get lunch.'

As soon as we got into the car, my euphoria at my wonderful house and a gorgeous man who appeared to like me a lot ebbed away. I clearly had some way to go before I could say whatever I wanted to without fearing the response, because I kept putting off telling Jake that I was meeting Scott later and wouldn't be able to stay for the evening. He was oblivious to my sudden silence, chatting about the interior design brochures he'd collected for me at the exhibition. I couldn't concentrate on German kitchens and new gadgets. I should have cancelled Scott, not Jake, but I wanted to have one last conversation, to seek out the final proof that all that love really had withered away.

I didn't know how to explain that.

In the end, as soon as we arrived at Jake's, I blurted out that I would need to go home about 6.30. He looked at me, surprised and disappointed, but I let the questions hang, busying myself with putting the picnic in a rucksack.

We walked along the golf course, darting across the fairway between golfers and meandering through the woods. I'd borrowed a pair of Jake's wellies and an anorak. I didn't know whether to be affronted when he told me that it was the sexiest he'd ever seen me.

He laughed. 'Just take the compliment for what it is. You look beautiful, really natural, like a girl from a yoghurt advert or something.'

Jake leaned against a tree and put his arms around me. 'I like you wearing my clothes. I loved seeing your house. It makes me feel as though you could become a very important part of my life.'

I kissed him so I didn't have to reply. In a remarkably short time Jake had infiltrated my daily life with good morning texts and goodnight phone calls. And still Scott hovered on the edges of my mind. Logically I knew that we could never go back to each other, but the shame of not trying hard enough persisted. Sleeping with Jake would be the final confirmation that I'd failed and my marriage was defunct.

Until now, I'd shied away.

But there, on the golf course, my reservations were dissolving. Jake's face was cold but his mouth was warm. Swaddled in all that anorak, I still felt his pelvis pressing into me and mine returning the greeting. He smelt of shampoo.

'Let's go home before we give some old golfer a heart attack. I promise that Angus isn't around. He's in the Lake District on a school trip.'

I nodded. Scott always moaned that I could never live for the moment – 'carpe diem, Robster, carpe diem' – so I managed not to say, 'What about the picnic?'

We strode out for his house, stopping to kiss, hungry and impatient. I waited to feel shy as we got to the house but sex was the one area in which I'd retained some self-esteem. Even when Scott hated me, he still wanted me. Jake tugged off my wellies, threw my anorak onto the floor and half-carried me, half-dragged me into his bedroom. I only had time to register that the room was bare except for a huge sleigh bed before he drew me to him and eased my clothes over my head, nimble hands undoing my belt, then his.

'Come on. Don't get cold.' He flipped the duvet back and we snuggled together for a moment, tongues teasing each other. Jake's hands were all over me, stroking gently, then harder. He did an exaggerated breath out and smiled. 'You OK?'

I didn't answer. The time for talking was long gone. I just took off my underwear, then eased off his boxers. He pulled me towards him and slipped inside me with a moan. I strained against him. He bit his lip, tiny sighs escaping. Scott always fought me, giving me instructions and making demands, even in bed. Jake was happy to take what came his way, his eyes holding me with a look that made me want to stay locked in that moment forever.

As the pace increased, he was struggling to hold back, his breathing became jagged and I adored the sense of power it gave me. He had the wary look of a man who's not sure how much longer he can last. I was desperate not to have that 'No, it's fine, no, don't worry, it'll be my turn next time' conversation so I pushed my pelvis hard into his, arching my back and gripping his shoulders until I experienced sensations that were so primeval, I had to work hard not to cry out.

Jake rolled onto his side. He swept my hair out of the way and kissed me. 'You know I'm falling in love with you? You should come with a health warning.'

Without replying, I tucked away that fragment of conversation for later, to revisit when I could think straight. It was a long time since my emotions had felt so uncomplicated. Just pure happiness, without an underlying layer of defence. We lay there, tracing each other's faces, stroking and murmuring until we must have dropped off. When I woke up, it was pitch black outside. I snuggled into Jake. It was funny how I fitted into him so well after years of shaping myself to another body.

Damn. Scott.

I wriggled my arm free to look at my watch. Seven-fifteen. I leapt up. Jake jerked his head up. 'Where are you going?'

'It's quarter past seven. I'm late.' Scott hated to be kept waiting. There was no way I'd get back in time for Scott's driver to pick me up. I scrabbled into my clothes, snatched up my phone and nipped into the bathroom.

My heart was thumping as Scott answered.

'I'm really sorry. I'm running horribly late. Would you mind if we go to the Red Garden instead? It's just round the corner from my apartment building.'

I was trying to keep my voice low so Jake wouldn't hear me. Scott detested last-minute changes that weren't his own, but after an initial disgruntled snort, he offered to meet me at home and rang off quite cheery.

I went back in to say goodbye to Jake. He was sitting on the edge of the bed. His face had taken on a set look. The closeness of the last few hours had suddenly become a sea. 'Where are you going tonight?'

'Back home, then out for a quick supper. Something has come up that I need to sort out.'

'Something to do with Alicia?'

'I didn't say that.'

'You didn't say anything. I assumed that it had to be Alicia, otherwise why would you cancel our evening tonight?' Jake pulled on his boxers and stood up. 'I'm not the enemy. You make love to me like you really want me but won't tell me where you are going? Help me out here.'

'I'm having supper with my husband. Ex-husband. I need to discuss some things with him.'

Jake shrugged. 'So why not say that? Do I like it? No. Does that mean you shouldn't do it? No. But I'd like to think we could be honest with each other.'

He reached out for me but I was frantic about being late. Scott would be inspecting me with a microscope; I needed a shower at least. I gave him a quick hug. 'Sorry. Should have explained. I don't know why I didn't. Let's speak tomorrow.'

I ran out to the car, leaving Jake doing up his trousers and shaking his head.

Octavia

Jonathan managed to make going to Sardinia sound as though he'd been conscripted to do some rock-smashing in the mountains of Uzbekistan rather than trot off to the Costa Smeralda to do the work he was passionate about, next to beaches of pale sand and marinas full of squillion-dollar yachts.

I spent the week before he left fielding questions such as 'Do I need water purification tablets?' and 'Will I need zinc cream for my nose?' By the time we got to 'I'd better take some Imodium in case I get a trotty-botty,' I was on countdown. Jonathan's interest in his bowels was top of the 'traits least likely to get you a shag' stakes, closely followed by his tendency to assume that every dry patch of skin was cancer. The children sucked up my microscopic supply of nursing patience. I had none left over for adults.

The night before he left though, I was surprised to find myself a bit unsettled. The sporadic weekends away with Roberta, which had characterised the early part of our marriage, had faded as meagre finances and the arrival of children squeezed them from our routine. Now, Jonathan and I were so rarely apart at night, I couldn't imagine sleeping in the bed on my own. With his suitcase packed, passport found and cheese sandwiches for the journey in the fridge, I felt a little surge of affection when he held out his hand to me and announced that he thought we should have an early night.

I sped into the bathroom, ran a razor over my armpits, cleaned my teeth and pinched a squirt of the Calvin Klein I'd given him for Christmas. I wondered about leaving my bra on. Even the dog looked at me in a strange way when he saw me naked, as though he wasn't quite sure whether I was human or cow. The pert breasts I'd been so proud of at twenty – my one decent physical attribute – were now hanging from my chest like rock climbers dangling desperately from a fraying rope. I scowled at myself in the mirror, slung my bra into the laundry basket and scuttled back across the landing, propping up my boobs-cum-emergency-torpedoes with my arm.

In the event, I could have tied them in a bow for all Jonathan cared. He was flat out, buttoned up to the neck in his stripy pyjamas. *Scientific Computing World* magazine was snarled up in the duvet. I slid into bed. It was hard to believe that Jonathan had once insisted on working diligently through *Sex 365: A Position for Every Day*. The split condom that had resulted in Charlie had happened when we'd tried the Saucy Samba. Now I'd be lucky to get a Two-minute Tango.

I sank back into the pillow full of self-loathing. Bastard breastfeeding. No one tells you that it'll knacker your breasts for life, leaving your husband more riveted by a feature on spambots than a good old-fashioned rumble with the wife.

The next morning I was still feeling like the girl at the disco who'd failed to get a dance. Jonathan seemed oblivious, even when I'd huffed and puffed about him being so worn out sitting around all day.

He looked bemused and said, 'No rest for the wicked,' like a voice recognition service with a limited repertoire.

I'd meant to get up, cook him breakfast and slip a couple of 'we'll miss you' notes in his suitcase for him to find when he was away. After he turned my paltry medicine chest upside down looking for pile cream 'just in case', I would have been hard-pressed to care if he was off to a war zone. By the time Patri's chauffeur turned up, my irritation was thumping about like a mouse trapped in a tin and I let the children lead the way in seeing him off. Immi waved goodbye with Stan's paw. I managed a quick hug and a dried haddock touch of the lips.

By then, Jonathan had the sweet scent of work driving him forward, so he probably wouldn't have noticed if Stan had given him a big slobbery kiss instead of me.

Roberta

I burst into the foyer of the apartment building. Scott was sitting with his feet propped up on a little table, fiddling with his phone. He reminded me of a cat flicking its tail, deciding whether to pounce or to relax back into sleep. He'd never been early in his whole life, and here he was ten minutes before schedule. I couldn't go out with my ex-husband smelling of another man. I ran up to him. 'Sorry about changing the arrangements at such short notice. I'm going to dash up for a shower and I'll be right down.'

He stood up. I backed away. 'You don't need a shower, you look awesome. Let's go straight out for dinner. There's loads I want to talk to you about.'

'No, no. I've been doing some serious walking this afternoon. I must reek.'

'OK. I'll come up with you. I'd like to see what it is I'm paying for.'

I tried to get rid of him. 'Why don't you have a drink at the restaurant while I get changed and I'll meet you there in a few minutes?'

'I'm not going to sit there like Norman No Mates. Don't forget I've seen it all before.'

I don't know what face I put on, but he laughed.

'Come on, Robbie. Alicia tells me that you've bagged yourself quite the city centre pied-à-terre. Might give me some ideas for that land I've got on option over on West Street. I'll watch the news while you make yourself beautiful.'

He took my arm and walked me to the lift. I didn't know where to look. I knew he would be taking it all in, the mud on my trousers, my bed hair. My bra strap was twisted. I could feel it digging into my shoulder. I tried to look nonchalant. I could hear myself swallowing. He leaned against the lift wall, staring at me.

'You did get muddy today.'

The bald statement made me nervous. 'I went walking, we got lost, that's why I was late.' We. Damn. Too late.

'We who?'

'I was with some friends, new friends. It's my New Year's resolution to get more fresh air. It was such a lovely spring day. It can get a bit claustrophobic here.' I hoped I'd made it sound as though I was in the company of the local ramblers group.

'Friend or friends?'

'Does it matter?'

He frowned. I pushed down the flutter of unease. I didn't have to be what he wanted any more.

Scott stepped out of the lift first. 'It matters to me.' His words hung between us, gentle, caressing, almost vulnerable. He sounded like he did when we first met, before I was a done deal. Intensity mixed with sensuality. Scott shone a spotlight on you and made you feel a star.

When we reached the apartment, I fumbled with the keys. Scott took them from me and opened the door. He whistled as he took in the chrome kitchen and plasma TV. 'This is all very hi-tech.'

'Most of the places for rent are complete dumps. I had to

find somewhere Alicia could be happy in. It's a real squash for both of us but at least it's clean and modern.'

'It was your choice.'

Hobson's choice, maybe. I ignored the comment.

I handed Scott the TV remote, passed him a beer out of the fridge and closed my laptop, but not before my stomach had done a little flip of pleasure at the sight of an email from Jake with 'Tonight' in the subject line.

'Make yourself at home.' I dived into the bathroom. As I plunged under the shower, I shut my eyes and thought of Jake, with a spike of longing. I hoped he wasn't furious with me. Once I'd scrubbed away every last trace of him and brushed my teeth, I looked round for my clean underwear. Which I hadn't brought through. I dithered. Underwear I'd worn for Jake, or wrap myself in a towel and fetch some? Ridiculous to come over all coy now with the man who'd seen every lump and bump for the last nineteen years.

I shuffled out like a self-conscious teenager towards the wardrobe in the corner of my kitchen/bedroom/sitting room. Scott looked up from the rugby game he was watching. 'Sight for sore eyes. You've lost a bit of weight. You look good, babe. I like you better skinny.'

Dignity forbade me to answer 'I forgot my pants', but I didn't want him thinking I was doing a striptease for his benefit. 'Won't be a moment. Just need to get dressed.'

'What're you going to wear for me?'

'None of your business' was the first answer that sprang to mind. Scott always liked a say in my clothes. He hated anything baggy or unfeminine. I'd rather enjoyed wearing palazzo pants since we split up. They suited my tall frame. I didn't want him to think I was trying to please him but it would be easier to have a discussion about Alicia if he was in a receptive frame of mind. Frankly, with so much to resolve, if a frilly blouse was going to smooth the way, then who was I to argue?

Scott came over to join me. Too late, I remembered Jake's trench coat hanging in the wardrobe, which I'd promised to repair the hem on. I snatched up my green dress and slammed the door shut.

I practically barged him out of the way, losing the towel on my top half as I moved.

'Oopsy daisy.' Scott cupped his hand under my breast. 'You always did have nice boobs.'

I pulled up the towel. 'Stop it. Just give me five minutes to sort myself out.' But somewhere was a spark of satisfaction that he still fancied me. At least I had more to put in a bra than Shana. I grabbed some underwear out of a drawer and turned towards the bathroom.

Scott put his hand on my shoulder. I didn't look round. Just stood there, guilt, need, shame and sadness whirling around without a coherent strategy between them. He put his arms round me from the back and leaned forward so his mouth was by my ear. 'You're beautiful.' One hand crept round over my breasts. The other pulled me round to face him. I clutched the towel, my arm up as a barrier. I was shivering. All the hairs were up on my arms.

I tried to pull away but something in me wasn't fully committed to escape.

Scott didn't ask twice. He pushed the towel to one side and ran his hand over my buttocks, his mouth hard on mine. The caresses, the kissing, the pressure of his hands and mouth were all part of a well-orchestrated dance that we no longer needed to rehearse. I recognised the dominance and ownership inherent in every gesture.

The opposite of the unselfish tenderness I'd experienced from Jake.

An unselfish tenderness I'd like to experience again.

I stepped back. Scott carried on unzipping his flies. 'What?'

'I can't do this. It just complicates everything. I don't want to be half in a marriage and half out.'

Scott put his hand on his hips. 'You weren't thinking that a moment ago.'

'You're living with Shana.'

'Come on. That's just sex. You know that.' His voice had taken on a mellow tone. He held out his hand to me. 'Sit down for a minute. No funny business, I promise.'

I covered myself up and perched on the edge of the bed. I studied him, trying to work out where it had all gone wrong. Once, he'd made me believe that love could overcome everything. Now, he just intimidated me. How had the self-assured girl he'd put on a pedestal become me? Tears gathered at the corner of my eyes.

'Robbie. I've missed you. I've made some mistakes, acted like a total dickhead.'

In my mind, I heard Octavia's voice echoing, 'You're right about that.'

'We've let this go too far.' He gestured. 'What are we doing? You staying here with barely room to swing a cat. Sleeping, eating and living in one room. Me rattling about in that big old place. I think we should try again.'

I waited for him to burst out laughing, to do his 'Had you going there' routine. But he looked so earnest. I knew this man. I'd battled for him. I'd put him above my friends and family. I had a daughter with him.

Maybe I was a fool to think I could ever leave him.

Scott tried to take me in his arms. 'Come back to me. Things will be different. I promise.'

I leaned into him, his familiar contours slotting into mine. I closed my eyes and imagined moving back in with Scott, returning to my old life. I'd hoped for a happy little fillip of excitement at the thought, a sense of righting disequilibrium. Instead dismay consumed me. I pulled away.

'We can't go back now. We haven't resolved anything. All our problems are still there, but more besides.'

'Like what?'

'Alicia knows how bad things are between us. She's been caught in the middle. She saw me go off to the police station. She – and I – know you started a relationship with Shana the second we were out of the door. We can't just brush it all under the carpet.' My voice started to crack.

Scott shook his head. 'You're wrong. We're meant to be together. You always said that.'

I got up and opened the window. I felt as though I was suffocating. 'Let me put some clothes on.'

'Why don't I get undressed instead? I'll show you how much I love you.'

'Sex is not love, Scott.'

'What? You coming over all nun-on-the-run now? A minute ago it seemed like you were up for it.'

'Scott. This is not about sex. Really it's not. The sex has never been an issue. I do love you, I always have done, but I can't live with you any more. How can I trust you again?'

Scott held his hands up. 'Come on, doll. Maybe I over-reacted a bit. I'd been under a lot of pressure at work, you know what things have been like in the property business, the site that got flooded up in Queensland, the subsidence at that development in Kent. Cut me a bit of slack.'

'Most husbands don't think, "Things are a little tricky at work, let's call the cops on my wife."'

Scott's lips clamped together. Before he could reply with a vicious litany of my failings, I shot into the bathroom with my clothes. I tried to organise my thoughts as my bra took on a life of its own, tangling around my limbs like honeysuckle. I ran my wrists under the cold tap, pulled my dress over my head and walked back into the room.

150

'We're always going to be attached to each other in some way. We've got Alicia and there's been a tremendous amount of history, good and bad.' I swallowed, wondering, for the umpteenth time, if I'd managed to produce a big noisy family, whether we would have been more united, the dynamic between Scott and me less intense. 'But the truth is, you don't like me very much, or at least, you don't behave like you do.'

'Wrong. I love you.'

'You do not love me, Scott.' I registered a jolt as I realised, after all these years, that it was true. 'You like parading me in front of your business colleagues, but love me, for me, for what and who I am, no. Definitely not.'

Scott screwed up his face. 'That's just not true. Christ, I spent four years flying backwards and forwards from Australia so often, I never got over my jet lag. Why would I have done that if I didn't love you? I moved halfway across the world to be with you.'

'That was fifteen years ago now. And you've been a little bit angry about it ever since. I'm not blaming you, I just don't think you've ever settled properly. Maybe living in a suburban environment doesn't suit you after growing up with so much space. Maybe you feel it's my "fault" that we couldn't have any more children. But whatever resentment you've got going on, I'm at the root of it.'

Scott kept shaking his head as though I was deranged, embarking on a random argument. 'Of course, I would have liked more kids, but I got used to that over time. No, the thing that's really finished me off is that I've never been good enough for you. Your school friends practically falling on the floor that you'd married a penniless Australian. Your father going on about business etiquette and me not under-standing how "it's done over here" when he was a bloody accountant, a flaming PAYE. Your mother's disappointment

151

every time I forgot to pull out a chair or open the fucking door like she'd lost the use of her own arms.'

I felt as though my marriage were a fluffy little feather on my hand, waiting for the faintest puff of air to blow it away forever. Fear of drawing a final, terminal line under the great love that had consumed me for most of my adult life was fighting to triumph over the certainty that going back to Scott would mean subjugating myself to his moods forever. I'd have to forget any notion of running my own business. And Jake.

'I'm sorry you feel like that.' I patted his arm. 'Anyway, I'd like to think that we can move on. It will help Alicia if she sees that we can be civil to each other.'

'So you're not coming back?' An accusation, not a request for information.

My shoulders sagged. I paused. My lips were dry. 'I'd love to if I thought we could make it work. But we can't, Scott. Even you can't have enjoyed the last few years much.'

'That's typical you, isn't it? No bloody backbone. Gets a bit hairy and you're off.'

'I disagree. Many women would have left you before I did.'

'Well, it suited you, didn't it? Living the life of Riley whilst I worked my bollocks off. Hanging out with that tightwad friend of yours while she scrounged off you.'

I crossed my arms. 'Octavia pays her way. And I was working just as hard as you except that I wasn't being paid. If you remember, I wanted to set up an interior design business but you wouldn't let me.'

'Who would have employed you? Anyway, I needed you to sort out our properties.'

'Bloody hell, Scott, I have got a degree, I'm sure someone might have given me a chance.'

'Change the record. We all know, everyone in the universe knows, that Roberta Clever Clogs Green has a degree. In creative arts. You make it sound like you're a fricking brain surgeon.'

'I'm not trying to score points. I don't want Alicia growing up thinking that it's normal to live like we did.'

'What do you mean by that?'

'That it's OK to have a man shouting in her face if she disagrees, being rude to her friends, making her have sex even when she doesn't want to.'

'When have you ever had sex when you didn't want to?'

I put my head in my hands. 'This is NOT about sex. This is about you never considering that what I have to say, what I think, what I feel, is important. It's about you getting your own way or turning nasty if you don't.'

'You're insane. You've had everything you want and it still wasn't bloody enough. Little Miss Marvellous, poor little rich girl. You'd better go whining to Daddy about meanie-beanie Scott making you unhappy.' He did up his flies and yanked his belt tight.

I let my breath out. 'I knew you'd react like this, which is why we are where we are.' I held my hand out to him. 'I don't think I am Miss Marvellous, for the record. I feel like a monumental failure.'

He flicked my hand away. 'Piss off with your hairshirt and self-flagellation bollocks. You're not even as beautiful as you think. Top lip's getting a bit dark.' Scott mimed stroking a moustache, which made me want to rush to my magnifying mirror.

I had risked something special, something kind and honest and wholesome with Jake for this child, this petulant brat, who could not take responsibility for his actions. Never had. Never would. I took a breath. 'I'd like you to leave now.'

'I'm fucking paying for this flat, I'll leave when I want.'

'In that case, I'm going to sit downstairs in the foyer until you go.'

This was the last time Scott was going to call the shots. No more pleading. No more begging. No more Scott, full stop.

I grabbed my bag, slipped my feet into some ballerina pumps and walked out. Halfway along the landing, adrenaline started to pump round my body, pushing itself into my legs, quickening my pace. I ran to the lift. I glanced back over my shoulder. No sign of him. I stabbed at the call button.

I didn't want to hear what Scott had to say now he'd had time to think. I didn't need any more insults to replay over the next few weeks and wonder whether they were true. The lift arrived and I punched the button for the ground floor, willing the doors to shut, leaning back in relief as I started to descend. My feet echoed across the tiled entrance floor at a slow, deliberate pace, the poised Roberta for the outside world. I nodded to the concierge and pretended to study the 'Fountain Apartments Community Noticeboard'.

Leaflets about non-surgical facelifts and cellulite reduction jostled for space among adverts for semi-permanent make-up and fitness boot camps. I was still getting used to the fact that Jake barely commented on what people looked like. Not even me. I hadn't yet worked out if that was liberating or insulting.

Still no Scott. The bastard. I imagined him sitting up there, feet on the sofa, helping himself to another beer. I'd call his bluff and go back to Jake's.

I texted Jake: *Scott about to go. Usual awkward self. Sorry for leaving early. Is it too late for me to come back? xxx.*

Ten minutes passed. No reply. Perhaps Jake had gone out. I couldn't expect him to sit around for me. I was debating calling Octavia when Scott emerged from the lift. I tensed, ready to rush over and calm him down before we gave the concierge an evening to remember.

But Scott strolled across the foyer, raised his hand and said, 'Lots to think about, Robbie. Sorry we had to give dinner a miss. We'll talk again soon.' He winked and sauntered out, as though it was the first sunny day of spring and he was off to the newsagent's to pick up a paper.

Nineteen years, and I was still no closer to second-guessing that man.

Octavia

A couple of days after Jonathan left for Sardinia, Roberta called to see if she could come over for the evening. All our meetings recently had been like a news flash, a smash and grab of the latest upsets in Roberta's life. With Jonathan away and the girls in bed early, I'd finally be able to ask her opinion about why on earth I'd suddenly developed a weird obsession with Xavi.

Roberta was late, which was unusual for her. I kept peering out into the street, looking for her taxi. I couldn't wait to start bouncing from subject to subject without explanation or preamble. Unlike Jonathan, who looked bewildered when I changed the subject without holding up a 'I am now moving on to a different topic' sign, Roberta had no problem shifting from the children's misdemeanours to my mother's arthritis, my blocked drains and any other tangent I cared to pluck out of the air. Jonathan's inability to remember the basics about people he knew, let alone ones he didn't, sucked the energy out of my storytelling.

When Roberta finally arrived half an hour late, I threw my arms round her and hugged her tight.

She seemed impatient to shake me off. 'Sorry I'm late. I've had a bit of a day.'

I stuck my head round the lounge door to check Charlie wasn't viewing anything on the computer that involved bare bottoms, then hustled her into the kitchen and poured the wine. 'So what's been going on?'

I did a double take when I sat down. It had to be at least ten years since I'd seen Roberta without any make-up. I'd always envied her perfect alabaster skin. Mine needed green-tinted cream to tone down my just-been-pitchforking-bales-of-hay complexion. Today it was Roberta's turn to look blotchy and harassed. She took a large swig of wine. 'I can't get hold of Jake. He won't answer my calls or emails. I drove past his house and he was there, so I know he's ignoring me.'

'Why would he do that? Have you fallen out?'

'I've been really stupid.' She turned to stroke Stan instead of looking at me. Normally, she didn't go near him because he made her hands smell. I knew what 'stupid' was. I picked up my glass and swirled it.

She looked sideways at me. 'You're going to be furious with me.'

'You're not going back to Scott?' I concentrated on sliding rather than slamming my glass onto the table.

'No. Definitely not.'

I relaxed. Roberta carried on scratching Stan's ears.

'What then?' I sounded snappier than I'd intended. Roberta's head jerked up at my tone, so I smiled and said, 'What have you done now?'

Roberta filled me in on Jake, their 'fantastic, generous sex, really good for a first time'. Listening to her, I felt about as desirable as a granny in winceyette bloomers. I was too ashamed to tell Roberta that Jonathan had fallen asleep before I'd even got into bed. When she told me that she'd ended up snogging Scott, my first reaction was 'big deal', quickly followed by mute amazement that Roberta would want to be in the same room as him, let alone swap spit.

'You'll think I'm pathetic, but I got all confused. I don't think I'd accepted that it was over. But now I know I don't want him.'

I shrugged. 'That's a step forward at least.'

She told me about the email Jake had sent. 'I only got the chance to read it after Scott left. It was so sweet, telling me that he knew sleeping with him was a big step and he wanted me to know that he didn't take it lightly. Then he said he was embarrassed to admit that he was feeling quite jealous but that I shouldn't take any notice because intellectually he knew that I needed to build a working relationship with Scott.'

'So what's the problem? He gets that you need to be friends with your ex. Jake doesn't need to know that you decided to give Scott a pity snog, for reasons known only to yourself.'

'Even though I haven't told him that Scott tried it on, he won't answer the phone to me. I don't understand it. He sends a grown-up email, then acts oddly.'

I raised my eyebrows. 'You think *he's* odd?'

Roberta got that belligerent look on her face. 'OK, I know you wouldn't have done it because you're too damn sensible.'

'It's not about being sensible. I wouldn't have put myself in a position of giving a bully a second chance.'

'Scott's not really a bully. He has exceptionally clear ideas about how he wants to live and how he expects people to behave.'

'He *is* a bully. When are you going to stop sticking up for him? We all have clear ideas about how we want people to behave and we're often disappointed, but we don't start bunging people in cells or making them frightened to disagree with us. You're confusing love with obedience.' Frustration was making my voice rise. Roberta deserved so much better, if only she could see it. 'It just makes me really sad that even though you're planning to divorce him, he's still dominating your life.'

'I'm not going to let that happen any more.' Her voice was hesitant. 'Do you think you could phone Jake for me? Just to check his mobile is working and I'm right that he is deliberately ignoring me?'

'What will I say? My friend fancies you, but she's too shy to speak?'

Roberta shrugged. 'Just make out it's the wrong number. It would be far too excruciating to admit you were phoning on my behalf.'

'I'll say I'm looking for Stan,' I said, nodding towards the dog. Even Roberta grinned at that.

My own heart was thumping when Jake answered. Roberta's eyes were on stalks. He sounded suspicious and irritated when I asked if Stan was there. Roberta was straining to hear his voice.

I took a second to look her in the eye. 'He's there all right.'

'Did he sound as though he was at home? Was there any noise in the background?'

I couldn't give a precise location on the basis of a twenty-second phone call.

Roberta kept throwing her hands up. 'I do not understand men. I suppose I can go round there and try and sort it out tomorrow.'

For the rest of the evening Roberta dutifully asked me about the children, Jonathan and how the business was going, but I could see that every ounce of her wanted to jump in a cab and wing it round to Jake's. Even when I burst out with the fact that I had been scouring internet continents for news of Xavi, she just shook her head.

'Will it make you feel better if you find him? You're not

about to up sticks and go and live on a barge. Believe me, it's no fun out here on the other side.'

The big thing I wanted to discuss with her – the fact that I couldn't stop thinking about Xavi or fantasising about seeing him again – just fell away. Until Roberta took the lid off Pandora's box by encouraging me to look for him, I'd been bumbling along with Jonathan, accepting that middle-aged marriage wasn't a thrill a minute but not really questioning my lot.

But now I wanted to question everything.

Why we were living in a conservative little town when we could have moved anywhere in the world. Why Jonathan's stance on everything was always the one that entailed the least amount of joy. And why, after all these years, the need to know where Xavi was didn't so much bubble as rage within me, forcing out a longing that I didn't know I was even capable of.

Just for once, I would have liked Roberta to focus her big brain on my 'issues' and come up with a half-decent explanation about why a busy mother of three was obsessing over a curly-haired ne'er-do-well from years ago.

But the bald truth was that, as far as Roberta was concerned, I was married. A warm body in bed and someone to check the tyres on the car meant I didn't have any issues.

Roberta rubbed her eyes and picked up her handbag. 'I'd better make a move.'

'You're not going to do a midnight raid at Jake's house, are you?'

She huffed. 'How well you know me. No. I'm going straight home.'

As I shut the door, I realised that Jonathan hadn't phoned to say goodnight.

Roberta

Octavia had confirmed it. Jake was ignoring me. He'd told me he was falling in love with me, so why would he suddenly start acting like a total bastard? I'd obviously upset him and I needed to find out how. The Rioja that Octavia and I had consumed convinced me of the wisdom, no, the absolute necessity, of emailing Jake and resolving it with him, once and for all. Pride be damned. I logged on and wrote:

Dear Jake,
  I am sorry if I have done something to upset you. I am very fond of you and think we could have something special together. Please, please contact me – even if it's just to finish with me face to face! I can't bear not knowing.
  Yours, Roberta

I got an immediate reply in my inbox.

Dear Roberta, I trust you will find this forwarded email self-explanatory. Jake

Hi there Jake,

It's 9.30 and I felt you should know that I've just spent the last forty-five minutes in bed with my wife, here in her flat. I agree with you that sex with her is 'extraordinary' but I wouldn't advise you to get too involved as I don't think she's ready to move on yet. We've made some mistakes in our marriage, but we are both ready to try again, which I think, mate, means you are out of the picture.

All the best
Scott Green

Octavia

Jonathan's week in Sardinia flew past in a happy rebellion of letting Stan lick the plates in the dishwasher and lingering in hot wasteful baths instead of sticking to Jonathan's four-minute shower rule. However, I didn't want him to think we hadn't missed him so Immi and I made a 'welcome home' banner and I'd got the champagne chilling. Even if absence didn't make the heart grow fonder, it would still give us something new to talk about. Sadly, my big sexy welcome-home kiss shrivelled up like an old parsnip at the back of the fridge when he shoved his briefcase at me and started grumping about our recycling bins not being emptied before he'd even got in the door.

I clung onto my fantasy. 'Champagne?'

'Are we celebrating something?'

'Yes. You coming home. You getting a job. The beginning of April and end of winter. Not having to sell the house.'

Jonathan yawned. 'Let's save it for another day. I'm knackered. I won't be up for long. Tea would be great.'

I put the kettle on, took one glass out of the cupboard and popped the champagne. I raised my glass to him, daring him to mutter about me getting 'expensive tastes'.

'Welcome back.'

Before I'd put the foil and wire in the bin, Jonathan had put a teaspoon in the top. The mood I was in, I wouldn't be needing that teaspoon. I forced myself to ask him how his week had been.

'You should see their computer system. I'm going to have so much fun working there. Talk about all the gear but no idea. State-of-the-art doesn't describe it, but it might as well be a bloody Amstrad for all the use they're getting out of it.'

Off he went, launching into a blow-by-blow account of the computer system, the hitches, the potential problems he foresaw, with barely a flicker of interest in life on the home front. I'd be flattered if he could muster up even half as much passion for me.

Over dinner, I tried to steer him onto the bit about Sardinia that interested me: if I went out with him on his next trip, would I be staying in a quaint fishing village with black-clad women making lace tablecloths, or would we be in a concrete jungle with computer sheds for company? Jonathan had obviously been so starved of the work drug that even when he tried to answer, he drifted back into a description of the work challenges ahead.

'So would it be worth me coming out?'

'I'd be working long days.'

I watched him rinse every last little grain of couscous off his plate. I poured my third glass of champagne. 'I'm overwhelmed by your enthusiasm. Don't you fancy a few days away without the children?'

'Yes, but I don't want you nagging me because I can't spend much time with you.' Jonathan slipped off his shoes and started spreading out old newspaper. I stared. He'd been home precisely one hour and twenty-five minutes. He pulled out the shoe polish box, tutting at the carnage within.

'I won't nag.' On the other hand, I might explode like a

bottle of lemonade with a Mento in it if he carried on paying more attention to his bloody scuff marks than my need for a change of scenery. I kept my voice neutral. 'I thought Patri had offered to pay for me to go out with you.'

Jonathan peered at the toe of his shoe as though a sergeant major's inspection was imminent. 'He did, but it's a bit soon to be asking for special favours.'

Slow circular movements with the polish brush. I waited for a glimmer of momentum, an offer to sort it out at some point. But just a frown as Jonathan got to work with the duster.

'Will you ask him at a later date?'

Jonathan nodded vaguely. More peering and buffing. Until now, Jonathan's absorption in work never bothered me. In some ways it was ideal. I wasn't cut out for a needy, jealous man who wanted my constant attention. I'd been able to dedicate myself to building up the nursery business and to bringing up the children relatively unconstrained by Jonathan's need to rotate the apples in the fruit bowl according to age.

While he was working methodically through his computer codes, we were making pancakes, sowing wildflower gardens for bees and teaching Stan tricks. Jonathan came into his own when precise explanations of military strategy were required. Or when science homework needed a bicarbonate of soda and vinegar volcano.

Over time the whole family appreciated that his obsession with computers left less opportunity for him to discover family misdemeanours such as the purple nail varnish on Polly's carpet and Immi's autograph on the lounge window-sill. Jonathan had his tidy, organised domain and I had my chaotic but entirely normal family world. I hoped they could overlap, that we could co-exist in each other's lives without the need for elaborate breathing apparatus.

Jonathan put his shoes down and straightened out the laces.

'Who's used all the whitener? I need that for my trainers.'

'I don't know. One of the kids, I suppose.' I couldn't stand it when Jonathan went shining along with glow-white trainers.

'Honestly. Those kids do exactly what they want. It's about time they started helping out and picking up after themselves.'

'Sorry if the family home offends you and the kids don't quite fit into your narrow little parameters. For the record, I'm far more interested in them having creative minds and broad horizons than whether they straighten the bloody towels or eat their crusts.' The champagne was opening a door on my honesty that should probably have remained closed. I wondered why he didn't trot off back to Sardinia.

Jonathan shrugged and took his trainers over to the sink, where he scrubbed at them with a nailbrush and washing-up liquid. I used to love the way he brought order to my world. He used to love the way I brought excitement to his. 'My little adventure,' he called me. I wondered when we'd got entrenched into opposing rather than united camps.

What we needed was some time away together without someone begging for help with physics homework the second we began a conversation. Sunny Sardinia would be just the ticket.

Roberta

I took Octavia's advice, forced myself to let the dust settle for a bit, then went round to see Jake. I chose a Monday, ten days after the whole Scott debacle, when I knew Angus was at tennis. I clung onto the hope that he might give me a chance if we spoke face to face. He opened the door, unsmiling and unreadable.

'Can I explain? I didn't sleep with Scott.'

'But you were in the bedroom with him?' He folded his arms.

My mind was moving slowly. It took me a moment to realise that instead of inviting me in, he was actually blocking the door. 'I was, but it wasn't like that. As you know, my sitting room *is* my bedroom.'

'I've managed to be there several times and not go anywhere near your bed. Did you have sex?'

'No, of course not.'

That one-hundred-per-cent categorical denial eluded me.

'But somewhere close?'

I could see what I had hoped for, what he had hoped for, shattering down the middle and falling to the ground like a building earmarked for demolition. Still, I couldn't lie. I shifted my feet on the doormat.

'I was confused. Maybe I wasn't ready to sleep with you. He wanted me back. I wanted to be sure that I was doing the right thing.'

'Answer the question. Did you get physical with him?'

'Yes, but—'

He took a step back. Hand on the door. A door that was shutting.

'Jake, I can explain. I know I was silly, I shouldn't have let him come into the flat in the first place. I only kissed him.' I tried to take his hand but he snatched it away.

'For old times' sake? Even though you'd just made love to me after waiting for so long? I thought it meant something to you. Sorry, but this isn't going to work for me. I had one wife who disappeared with an ex-boyfriend she'd seen on and off throughout our marriage. I'm not getting involved with someone else who's got an understudy in the wings.'

'Jake, please, listen, I made a mistake. I want to be with you. Scott and I are getting divorced.'

'I can't be your experiment. I had too many years of looking over my shoulder. I promised myself I would never get into that situation again. I've got to go now.' He glared at me with those intense eyes. Something softened fleetingly, then he shut the door in my face. I debated ringing the bell or calling through the letterbox like a desperado from the cast of *EastEnders*. I harboured a tiny hope that if I stood there long enough, he'd reconsider and come back out. Despair finally propelled me back to the car, where I wept onto the steering wheel until a woman en route to the park with her granddaughter knocked on the window to see if I was OK.

Over the following days, I emailed Jake with various out-pourings of apologies and excuses. He ignored me. Whatever kindness and compassion he possessed was clearly matched by an equal reserve of self-defence and resolve.

Mea culpa. I had no choice but to forget him.

When I got into bed at night, images of Jake rolled across my mind. His mannerism of fiddling with his watchstrap. The way he looked into the distance while he thought about what to say. His calmness, as though there wasn't a single problem in the world that was insurmountable.

Except getting physical with my husband, of course.

I lay chasing thought after thought, writing letters in my head, only to dismiss them in the morning. I drove past his house so often it was astonishing that I hadn't appeared on *Crimewatch*.

Like an alcoholic endeavouring to feel better by drinking a bottle of vodka for breakfast, I attacked the dating game with vengeance. My flimsy attempt at self-help was to find a new love to block out Jake and Scott. Internet dating websites knew more about me than Octavia did. The questionnaires felt like a multiple-choice where I was constantly ticking the wrong answer.

Did 'yes' to 'I read all of the warning literature before taking any medication' make me sound like a responsible adult or a dull killjoy? Was anyone in their right mind going to pick me if I ticked 'I am sometimes tempted to make fun of people behind their backs'?

Luckily, there wasn't a box for 'Sometimes my best friend and I giggle about other people's foibles and laugh until wine comes out of our noses.'

Would 'I often carry the conversation to a higher level' get me an articulate professional who could name five members of the Cabinet, or a super-intellectual prig with radical views on global poverty and melting ice caps? The four main emotions I'd felt in the last month? That was easy. Depressed, unable to cope, lonely and fearful of the future. I ticked optimistic, calm, energetic and happy-go-lucky.

I was trying to find a boyfriend, not someone to help me stockpile sleeping tablets.

My social life was quickly becoming more virtual than real, consisting of winking, icebreaking and deleting the men who wanted to know my favourite sexual position in their second email. The number of people winking at me could make or break my whole day. I agreed to go out with a man called Rupert, who didn't mention sex in his emails, worked as a vet and listed reading, jogging and eating out as his hobbies.

'Vet is good. Bit of a knobby name, though,' Octavia said. I swore she reflected her dislike for her own name onto other people.

I refused to bite. 'The rest of him sounds all right. Anyway, nothing ventured . . .'

Octavia was giving me the 'You need to get used to living on your own' speech more and more frequently, which only intensified my desire to be part of a 'normal' couple again. Everyone who told me I needed to be single for a while had a husband. They didn't have to wake up on a Sunday and think about how to fill the fourteen hours before bedtime. They could cook a family-sized casserole and not have to eat it for six days in a row. They could go to the school ball, a dinner party, Burns night, without a discussion about where 'the odd one out' should sit.

They didn't even have to like their husbands. They just had to have one.

So I repeated my 'open mind' mantra as I walked down to Café Rouge in the early April sunshine to meet Rupert. I spotted him straightaway, leaning back in his chair, hands behind his head. Heavier-set than he looked in his pictures. A bit of a gut hanging over his trousers. A pink flowery shirt that hit the Brit-on-holiday-in-Barbados look rather than the suave man at ease with his sexuality. He did look jolly and friendly though.

'Rupert?'

He jumped up. 'Roberta. Hell-o.' Did he wink? Surely not. No one over the age of fourteen winks. Maybe he'd spent too long on dating sites and was carrying it over into real life. He managed to shake my hand and pull me towards him slightly until I was stuck in that no-man's-land, just off balance, not knowing whether he was going to kiss me on the cheek or not. He stepped back without letting go of my hand until I felt like a cow he was sizing up. I sat down without being asked.

He plonked himself down opposite me, resting his chin on his hands in a 'you have my full attention' way. His eyes were bright and round like the rest of him. 'So, Roberta.'

Years of my father and his 'manners maketh man' stopped me saying, 'So *what*?' I smiled. No one was at their best when they were nervous.

'Shall we get a coffee?' I said.

'You don't want a drink?'

'It's a bit early in the day for that. I have to pick my daughter up later.'

'You won't mind if I do?' he asked, ordering a glass of Shiraz.

'Right then, Roberta, tell me all about yourself.' He leaned forward as though he was about to start making notes.

I gave myself a mental pat on the back. I wasn't going to repeat that mistake and end up weeping in the loo in an unhinged manner.

'You first.'

'Feisty. I like that.' He made a tiger-scratching gesture and a growling noise.

My facial muscles were finding it harder to move upwards but I was going to give him a chance.

He settled back in his chair. 'I'm a vet, as you know, deal mainly with cattle, horses, pigs, farm animals.'

171

At least I could tell my friends that without having to add a caveat emptor. Not a car salesman. Not someone who experiments on monkeys. Not a sex therapist.

He took me through a James Herriot A to Z of what his job involved. 'Of course my real love is dogs but my first placement when I was training was on a farm and I never managed to get back to domestic animals.' He scrabbled into his jacket and pulled out his wallet. He waved a photo under my nose. 'Look, these are my dogs, Boo-Boo and Remy.'

I stared at the photo of two rat-like dogs with enormous ears. They looked like something out of *Gremlins*. It was more excruciating than being presented with an ugly baby and searching for a compliment. I opened my mouth a few times before I found some words. 'What breed are they?' I tried to keep my voice light.

'Long-haired chihuahuas. They sleep on my bed. Boo-Boo likes to lie with her face on my pillow.'

Waking up with Bat Ears was not part of any plan for my future.

'Aren't they sweet? Remy likes to sit on my knee when I'm watching TV. He gets jealous if I cuddle up to anyone else.' Another wink. He motioned to the waitress for another glass of wine. I hadn't even finished my coffee.

I groped round for something to say. 'Have you got any other pets?'

As though two batty dogs weren't bad enough.

Rupert then treated me to a description of his cat, Fleecy, how she liked to sit on the arm of the sofa and started purring when *The Simpsons* came on. I never did understand cartoons for adults. He gave a demonstration of how he tickled her stomach and how her little paws curled over just so, until I thought that someone must be concealed behind the cheese plant taking a video, which would do the rounds on *Gotcha!*-type programmes forever more. I nodded away, smiling as though I was practising to be a ventriloquist, my brain racing to find an exit strategy.

Rupert suddenly grabbed my hand, spilling my cappuccino. 'It's so wonderful to meet another animal lover. I was so happy when I saw that you ran a rescue home for abandoned pets.'

'I've never owned a pet, apart from a hamster.' I didn't mention that I'd bequeathed it to Octavia because I'd been too scared to take it out of the cage in case it bit me.

He snatched his hand back. 'I thought you ran a rescue home? The border collie breeder?'

'Sorry. No. Think you've confused me with someone else.'

Rupert pulled out his Blackberry, muttering to himself. 'Must have been Amanda. Maybe Shelley. Perhaps it was Tricia.' He scrolled down his emails. He looked up triumphantly. 'Robyn, it was. Robyn Grant. That's it. She loved collies. I'm sorry. I got you muddled up. You know, Roberta Green, Robyn Grant, easy mistake.' He slammed his Blackberry down. 'Anyway, doesn't mean we can't have a nice time.'

I think he was aiming for a seductive look, but he flicked his eyelids up as though he was attempting to dislodge a mosquito.

'Actually, I think I should be going. I have to fetch my daughter.'

'Already?' He sounded distracted, as though he was still struggling to recall the finer details of the superior Lassie girl. He motioned for the bill.

'Sorry. I can't be late.' I was putting on my jacket when he said, 'Shall we go halves? That's seven pounds ninety each.'

I couldn't bring myself to point out that I'd had a coffee and he'd had two large glasses of wine. I put down a ten-pound note and watched as he counted out six pound coins.

'Can I see you again?'

Even then I hesitated. If I stayed much longer I'd probably end up sleeping with him on the grounds that I was too mortified to say no.

I swung my bag onto my shoulder. 'I've got a lot on at the moment. I'll email you when I'm free.'

Rupert's face took on a dark hue. 'You're blowing me out, aren't you?'

'I think you'd be better off with someone who likes animals a bit more than me.'

'You *are* blowing me out.'

No such thing as a graceful exit. Nearby heads were starting to swing round to observe the spectacle. Without looking at him, I said, 'I'm not, I just need to go and get my daughter,' and strode towards the door.

Rupert trotted after me, tugging at my arm. 'That's just an excuse. Why do you want to go now? You've only been here a little while. What's the matter with you? Six of the girls I've met up with want to see me again. I've even had sex with three of them.'

I escaped onto the pavement. I dredged up the strength to be rude. 'I'm sorry, I must go, right now, otherwise I'm going to be late.'

I marched off, ignoring his shouts of 'Wait a minute!' I walked so fast that the soles of my feet were rubbing and burning. As I stomped along, I rehearsed how I would make Octavia laugh with the latest fiasco but midway through describing Rupert, Boo-Boo the dog and Fleecy the cat, the familiar sense of humiliation and desperation swelled up. How Scott would hoot if he knew that I was spending my Sunday afternoons meeting chubby chihuahua lovers. I stormed through the apartment foyer, head down, grateful that the concierge was on the phone so that I didn't have to exchange pleasantries.

I jumped in the shower, washing away Rupert's sweaty handshake and saying, 'I will not think about Jake' out loud. I swaddled myself in a towel and picked up my latest interiors magazine, but my laptop was calling to me. Maybe, just maybe, the one to erase all memories of Jake had winked at me. My inbox was cluttered with messages.

I scrolled down. I clicked on Jordi, who listed his interests as Gaudi architecture, watercolour painting and poetry. I liked the sound of him but his second email put me off when he said that he wasn't interested in connecting with anyone who didn't have a proper appreciation of Philip Larkin's poetry.

I eliminated Mark, who listed his hobbies as 'chillaxing' and playing on the XBox. I could go to Octavia's to see Charlie lose himself in mindless killing sprees, mouth hanging open, eyes slightly manic. I deleted Natale, an Italo-American who had sunbathing naked topping his list of hobbies. Winningly, he wrote that I could call him Christmas if I liked that better, as 'Natale was the Italian word for Christmas'.

'Dad, this is my boyfriend, Christmas.' No. Definitely not.

I binned the Elvis fan – 'The King' – complete with curly quiff. I was not about to be seen on the town with anyone in blue suede shoes.

I sifted through the variety of sales pitches by middle-aged men – a picture of a giant sunflower one of them had grown from seed, photos of men holding pint glasses and flexing their biceps in vest T-shirts, one with a snake around his thick neck. Most hideous of all was the one who had headed his email SECOND CHANCE and then proceeded to tell me how his failed marriage had taught him the importance of regular sex, that old chestnut. I clicked on 'shut down'.

The only second chance I wanted was with Jake.

Octavia

By mid-April, Jonathan had disappeared off to Sardinia again for another ten days. Charlie was too busy getting up to no good with girls in his bedroom to notice. Polly and Immi missed Jonathan more and kept asking to phone Daddy. On the few occasions I let them ring him on his mobile, Jonathan would allow a couple of minutes' conversation about Immi winning the class tables challenge or Polly playing the Tin Man in *The Wizard of Oz* before turning the conversation to how expensive it was to call a mobile abroad.

The question 'Do you want to speak to Mum?' always provoked the same response – he'd call from the office phone later. Sometimes he did, but far more often I got a text telling me that there was some emergency, the server was down, there was a glitch in the system and we'd have to speak tomorrow.

I was so used to Jonathan giving me a list of things to do – check that we were on the best electricity tariff, flog his old *Everyday Practical Electronics* magazines on eBay, make sure I put Immi's blazer into the second uniform sale – that I felt guilty if I flumped down with a boxed set of *Breaking*

Bad and a giant bag of tortilla chips. Or spent yet another evening sifting through the Santonis on LinkedIn.

Gradually though, the whole house relaxed. Without Jonathan pinning up Immi's vocabulary on the fridge so that he could test her on 'onomatopoeia' and 'alliteration' before she'd even managed to shovel in a spoonful of Rice Krispies, she panicked less and appeared to be doing better at school. I probably fell into the lackadaisical mother camp, but I couldn't give a monkey about whether Immi would ever spell 'accommodate' properly. I loved her *joie de vivre* far more than anything we could slap an academic label on.

Now Jonathan wasn't micromanaging every axe blow and sponge wipe, Charlie was chopping wood and cleaning the car with something close to enthusiasm, if not efficiency. Polly shared Jonathan's passion for computers. But even she recognised that no Jonathan at mealtimes meant more chit-chat about our lives and less about the importance of putting screwdrivers back in their right place.

In a short space of time, we'd all wriggled round to fill the gap that Jonathan had left. If he wasn't careful, the waves would close over him.

Despite all the years I'd had to accustom myself to Jonathan's pernickety ways, I still yearned to recapture the way we'd complemented each other in that brief six months before I got pregnant. We'd travelled brilliantly together. I'd have the idea about where to go and he'd put it into practice in a way that meant we didn't have a thirteen-hour wait at a ferry port. What we lost in spontaneity, we made up for in extra bedroom time. We just needed some child-free opportunities to recreate that. So despite his stonewalling, I pressed ahead with my plans for Sardinia. Every time we spoke, I made a point of asking, 'Have you had any contact with Patri today?' 'Would you like me to give him a ring if you're too busy?' I was definitely going. Once we stepped out of our Mum and Dad shoes, he'd thank me.

The fear of unveiling my flabby white limbs at a chic Mediterranean resort spurred me into hula-hooping on the Wii every morning before work. I hadn't managed to shift much blubber but I did work up quite an appetite for Parma ham and mozzarella focaccia that only the Italian deli round the corner from work could satisfy. One morning I stood gazing at the huge map of Italy behind the counter, when a hearty slap sent a sharp tingle down my arm.

'Octavia. How are you? Managing OK without that husband of yours now we steal him away? Very clever man. Very clever.' Patri stood grinning, his white shirt and linen jacket lending an elegant charm to his handsome, well-worn face.

'The kids find it hard without him. I do as well, a bit. But he's loving it. He says it's beautiful out there.'

'We try not to send him so often. I ask your patience for the next few months. Why don't you go out and join him? I am always telling him, take Octavia. You rent hotel, apartment, whatever you want.' He patted his wallet. 'Jonathan will make me money. I can afford to keep his wife happy.' He winked. 'If it is like my house, the woman is in charge of holidays, parties and friends.' He handed me a business card. 'Call my secretary. You can use one of the company cars when you are there.'

Jonathan was obviously taking his responsibility not to mix work with pleasure far too seriously. Luckily he'd married me to save him from himself. I didn't need a second invitation.

Roberta

Even though it was a month since Jake finished with me, my obsession with him showed no signs of diminishing. I'd stopped fooling myself that the only place that sold my favourite herbal tea was the Co-op on his road on the other side of town. I reluctantly accepted I would drive past his house at least once a day, plus study his photo on his company's website at least five times.

Now and again, I'd have a flurry of internet dating. Sometimes I'd meet a decent man whom I would convince myself I liked until he texted to ask me out again and I found myself spouting lies about work/holiday/daughter commitments to avoid him.

The commitment to my daughter wasn't a complete lie as, increasingly, living with Alicia was presenting a challenge. Initially, I'd admired the way she'd handled our separation. Over the last few weeks though, she often blanked me out with a sulky silence or created a tense atmosphere in the apartment by scuffing about and answering with a minimum of monosyllables. It was impossible to see how I would know if anything was bothering her when a simple question about dinner preferences appeared to require the deployment of an

Enigma machine. To my shame, I'd begun to feel relieved when she was at school and I could concentrate on organising house surveys and finalising plans for my interior design business.

One morning I sat down on the sofa to read through the house files in readiness to exchange, when my hand came into contact with something soggy wedged between the leather seats. I pulled it out. A used condom. I dropped it with a squeak of disgust. Where on earth had that come from? Had it always been there? I ran to wash my hands then returned to examine it from a distance. Not dried-up. I could still see the fluid inside. Then again, it was rubber. Might not dry up for a hundred years. Surely it hadn't been there since the previous tenants? Scott? Had he left it there as some disgusting joke?

Alicia.

Alicia endlessly encouraging me to go out: over to Octavia's, to the tennis club, for dinner with Nicole and Brenda. I'd bought into her argument that she found it easier to study when she had the place to herself. The sick feeling I had when I realised Scott had emailed Jake came back multiplied by five hundred. My fourteen-year-old daughter was having sex. I'd been so self-absorbed that I hadn't noticed. Or hadn't cared.

No. I had cared.

Just not enough to see beyond myself, my hurt, my disasters, to look at how Alicia was managing.

I got up. I unravelled enough loo paper to reach to the moon and swept the condom into the bin. I'd been so worried about finding a new boyfriend that I'd completely neglected to monitor the fact that my baby – because she was still a baby – was embarking on something adult to fill the space left behind by her smashed-up childhood. My daughter, with barely enough bosom to fill a bra, was already acting like a mini-Lolita. Scott would consider himself vindicated: I was a useless mother.

I reached for my mobile. Scott or Octavia? I would have to kill Scott if he found anything remotely amusing about it. I phoned Octavia.

'You've got your gravel voice on. What's happened?'

I took her through it. She did laugh when she heard I'd put my hand on a condom, but I didn't feel the need to nip down to the garden shed for sharp implements because I knew she was on my side.

'You should be thankful that she's smart enough to use condoms. God knows whether Charlie would be sensible enough. Fourteen is really young, but we were all having sex at sixteen, so allowing for a couple of decades' shift in culture, is it that bad?'

'I wasn't having sex at sixteen.' I couldn't even get it right at thirty-nine.

'All right, apart from you, the Ice Maiden. The rest of us were.'

I took a strange comfort from the fact that there was no chance of me completely losing my sense of humour while Octavia was around. 'There's a huge difference between sixteen and fourteen. I never imagined that Alicia would be one of the early ones.'

'Do you want me to talk to her?'

Octavia's brand of practicality and her ability to relate to children would be far better than my hysterical 'How could you?' But I'd spent my whole life relying on Octavia. I needed to stop using her as a crash mat or battering ram as the occasion dictated.

'I'm going to deal with this one myself, darling. Thanks for the offer though. If I get myself in a pickle, I might reconsider.'

'You won't. You're stronger than you think.'

I wondered if I detected a note of hurt in her voice that I didn't want to involve her.

As I sat in the car waiting for Alicia to come out of school, I had plenty of time to think about what I was going to say.

My heart sank as she came into view. No sign of her best friends, Lucy and Daniela. I didn't know the two girls she was with. The blonde one was wearing too much make-up. Thick foundation, too dark for her young skin. The brown-haired girl had hard eyes ringed by thick kohl. They both looked older than Alicia. All three of them had their skirts folded up at the waistband so the tiniest breath of wind would expose their knickers – or G-strings – for all to see.

With a sick twist to my heart, I could quite see how some boy thought she was ready for sex.

Alicia walked by on the other side of the road, laughing in a way that didn't seem natural for her, loud and raucous. She shrieked down the street to a boy, who replied with his middle finger, much to the amusement of the ugly sisters she was with. My hands were leaving sweaty patches on the steering wheel. To my shame, I didn't even know where she went after school. I'd assumed that she went for a Coke with Lucy and Daniela or a little browse in Primark. I'd been so caught up in my own dramas, I'd never thought to check.

I knew that your mother shouting 'coo-ee' from the other side of the road was social death, so I decided to ring her. I watched her fumble in her bag then shake her head when she saw my name. She said something to the other girls, who shrugged and sat down on a nearby wall.

I tried to keep my tone light and went for the 'just passing, thought we might go for an early supper, get out of the apartment' approach.

'I'm on my way into town with some friends.'

'Perhaps they'd like to join us,' I said, praying that they wouldn't.

Alicia sighed. 'No, they so wouldn't.'

I tried not to sound desperate. 'I need to talk to you.'

I heard her shift a little, moving from irritated to curious. It hadn't occurred to her yet that she was the principal topic.

'What about?'

'Come for supper and find out. I'm parked just over the road.'

She called out to her friends, who swung their backpacks onto their shoulders and slouched off down the road. I waved to Alicia from the car. She managed a tight little smile as she crossed over to me. As she got in, her whole demeanour lightened as though she'd stepped off the stage and into the wings where she could stop playing her part.

'Can we go to Frederico's? We haven't been there for ages.'

On the drive there, we chatted more than we had in ages: about the swimming competitions she was entering, her new music teacher, how she found herself enjoying physics more than she thought. I was itching to ask who the two tarty-looking girls were, but I thought I'd start with the essentials such as who my daughter was having sex with. Once we were settled and her favourite bruschetta had arrived, she put her head on one side, a mannerism that had Scott stamped all over it, and said, 'So, what was the big hurry to speak to me? Have you finally got the house?'

'We exchange tomorrow. With a bit of luck, we could move in by the end of April. It's the perfect home for us. If you like, we can choose a new duvet for your bedroom.'

'So you're not going back to Dad then?'

'No, I'm not.' I'd expected her to plead his case, but the absolute conviction in my voice seemed to please her.

'I don't think you made him happy, did you?'

I made a show of chewing on an olive and removing the pit to give myself time to absorb the unfairness of the observation. Focus. It was a triumph that we were having this conversation, given how sparse our recent exchanges had been.

I didn't need to be right, only do what was right.

'No. I didn't make him happy. And vice-versa. But it's not your father I want to discuss. It's you I'm worried about.'

A wash of apprehension flashed across Alicia's face. 'Me? I'm fine.'

'I'm a little concerned that you might be involved with a boy.'

I knew straightaway that my hunch had been spot-on. From the base of her neck, Alicia's pale skin took on a deep pink tinge that spread upwards.

'What boy?' She became engrossed in chasing little pieces of tomato and onion around the plate.

'That I don't know. I was hoping you would enlighten me.'

'I'm not involved with anyone.'

'So who are you having sex with?'

Alicia's head jerked up. 'I'm not having sex.' Her eyes began to fill.

I bit back my desire to shout, 'Stop lying.' From somewhere, I managed to dredge up, 'I'm not cross. But I really don't want you getting tangled up in something that you aren't emotionally mature enough for.'

Octavia would have come out with a line like that.

'I'm not having sex. I haven't even got a boyfriend.'

I'd heard her deny eating the last piece of cheesecake more convincingly.

'Alicia. I found a condom in the apartment. It can only have been yours.'

185

Alicia seemed to shrink into herself, the layers of defiant teenager peeling away until she looked frightened and confused, the way she had when she was about seven at parties where pop music fried your ability to think, and kids high on slushy blue drinks were catapulting off bouncy castles.

A waitress with no sense of timing chose that moment to do the 'Any more drinks? Any sauces? Any tap water?' I waved her away and reached over for Alicia's hand. She hesitated, then gripped my fingers.

'Sorry.'

The tears were in full flow now, as though someone had lifted the valve on a pressure cooker after months of simmering grief. I only managed to stem my own weeping with the stern thought that if I hadn't let my emotions hang out for all to see, Alicia might have been able to burden me with a few of hers.

I took a large mouthful of my salade niçoise to give me time to bring my quivering chin under control. 'You don't need to be sorry. Though I do need to know what's been going on. Who are you sleeping with?'

Alicia pressed her napkin to her eyes. 'Buzz.'

I waited. And while I waited I had the mean-spirited thought that someone called Buzz, who no doubt had tramlines shaved into his hair and trousers halfway down his underpants, shouldn't be allowed anywhere near Alicia Charlotte Louisa Deauville Green.

'He's at the tech college. Anyway, he's dumped me. Said I was frigid.'

Apparently not that frigid. How could a fourteen-year-old be called frigid? 'I bet he doesn't even know what the word means.' And certainly couldn't spell it. 'Are you sure you're not pregnant?' As I said it, I tried to recall boxes of tampons in the bathroom.

'I'm not that stupid, Mum.'

'I don't think you are stupid. I just want to help you make some good decisions, and having a baby now wouldn't help.'

Mini-adult again. 'We were always really careful.'

Always. Always. How flipping often was always?

Somewhere over her tropical pizza with its childish pieces of pineapple, I knitted together the story of how her new best friends, Sinead and Jaqs, had adopted her after she dropped out of the Gifted and Talented maths class. I resolved to deal with that unknown gem at a later date. Part of her acceptance into the group was to date Jaq's brother, Buzz.

'I didn't even particularly like him, Mum. I did a bit at first, because he was always telling me I was beautiful, but then he kept wanting to have sex with me. I didn't want to but Jaqs and Sinead said that I was Little Miss Prissy. They kept going on about how many guys they'd slept with.'

'When did you first sleep with him?'

'That night I went to the party, when I was staying at Dad's and you were out somewhere and Buzz came to pick me up in the car.'

I vaguely remembered reiterating the importance of seat-belts and not letting him drink and drive. Completely forgot to mention the necessity of making sure he kept his penis tucked in his pants.

The truth was I hadn't investigated too much because I'd abdicated responsibility to Scott and I didn't want anything to spoil my evening with Jake. Round and round we went, with Alicia finally coming clean. Detail after sordid detail rained down on me: how they sometimes had sex in the flat when they knew I'd be out, how Buzz had told everyone she had pubic lice, how the boys were pretending to ride bikes every time she walked past.

I had brushed away her sullenness as 'being a teenager' rather than my teenager, in desperate need of help.

I stirred my caffè macchiato. 'I'm sorry. I wasn't there when you needed me. I won't ever, ever let that happen again.'

After some persuasion she agreed to be tested for STDs, so she – and I – could start life again with a clean slate. It was ironic that I'd spent my life living up to my mother's refrain, 'We are not a family that fails'.

No. Not a family that fails. Just a mother that fails.

Octavia

Despite my pincer movements, after a mere week back home, Jonathan had managed to go away for four days without me again. In the beginning, although I moaned like buggery, I still relished the mini-breaks from his nit-picking. Now the slog of single motherhood was taking the gloss off my guilty pleasure at chucking everything in the tumble dryer without looking outside to see if I could hang it out. I was so knackered that the only thing I still had energy for was my unsuccessful search for Xavi.

I never thought Jonathan did much to help with the kids but it turned out that just having another grown-up body in the house to keep an eye on the younger two, even a body absorbed in emails, gave me freedom. Even though Charlie was now sixteen, he was hardly ever here and couldn't be relied on to look after the girls. Suddenly, there was no popping out for a drink, no late evening supermarket shop, not even an hour at Zumba without organising a babysitter.

I tried not to moan to Roberta, especially as she'd just dealt with the whole sex-with-the-local-ruffian episode entirely on her own. In fact, my opportunity to talk to

Roberta about anything had shrunk dramatically. I missed her. She was either swallowed up in what she called 'mood boards' for the house, sourcing little swatches of material from Osborne & Little, or going to the Geffrye Museum to show Alicia how interior design had changed over the decades.

I thought all the cultural trips were the quickest way to get a fourteen-year-old searching for thrills with her pants around her ankles and feet on the windscreen, but Roberta had always existed on a higher intellectual plain.

I hadn't seen her for well over a week when she invited me to go out for a drink the night before she completed on her new house. A change of scenery would justify the cost of a babysitter. I was just about to suggest the little cellar bar on the edge of town when she informed me that we were going to The Clam with a couple of her new tennis friends whom I would 'adore'.

I squashed down the unpleasant thought that I was the last one to be invited.

I'd never been to The Clam before. I peered through the window. Half-empty. Lots of chrome. Abstract art. I pushed the door open. The heat, smoke and the sort of slicing music that Charlie liked hit me. I saw Roberta immediately, perched on a high bar stool.

As always, she outshone everyone else at the table, not just because of her dark hair framing her pale skin. She had a presence, a reserve about her that polarised women and challenged men.

I walked over, regretting that I'd agreed to come. Roberta got up to hug me and her friends shuffled round to make room at the silly little table that was so small it could barely hold four drinks. She introduced me to her friends, Brenda and Nicole.

Nicole stuck her hand out. 'Pleased to meet you.'

Something a bit rough in her accent. Something a lot glamorous in her appearance.

I immediately felt frumpy. Nicole had the nails, the highlighted hair, the single-stone necklace that matched her blouse, sitting in precisely the right place above her smooth and ample cleavage. 'I've heard so much about you.' She did some funny little giggle, as though she'd heard that I had an embarrassing hobby like collecting vibrators.

Brenda barely stopped her conversation with Roberta long enough to say hello. She clearly found it an effort to lift her eyelids in my direction, though that might have been down to the weight of her mascara. Maybe going through life with an old granny's name required an extra lashing of Maybelline to ensure that people didn't mistake you for someone who sat farting in an armchair all day.

'What can I get you to drink?' Roberta asked.

'A small glass of wine, please. I'm driving.'

'Driving?'

'Yes. I've got an open day for new parents tomorrow.'

Roberta got up to fetch my drink, saying to Brenda and Nicole, 'Octavia runs a nursery.'

Nicole laughed. 'You must be patient. I've got a three-year-old and a six-month-old and that's enough for me.'

'I think my children get a raw deal. I'm a right grumpy cow by the time I get home. Who's looking after your children tonight?' I asked, just to be polite.

That innocent question launched a diatribe about how difficult it was to find the right nanny and how she'd even been called back from tennis the other week because the three-year-old was having such a tantrum. Blessums.

Brenda sipped her wine and stared round the room, not even pretending to listen. I tried to remember any friends of Roberta's I had warmed to over the years. She was far more tolerant of people than I was. She had time for women who screwed up their faces in puzzlement the second you mentioned politics and who really did give a shit what the Oscar nominees wore on the red carpet.

Roberta came back, passing me the wine and interrupting the 'Turkish nannies are worse than Polish ones' speech. I bet Nicole couldn't even pinpoint Istanbul on a map. Roberta said, 'Nicole's just about to go back to work.'

She smiled. 'Yep. Ex-husband has been made redundant, so it's back to the grindstone. Quite looking forward to it in a way. Use the brain again.'

'What do you do?' I asked, wondering what someone whose conversation was so shallow could possibly be qualified for.

'I'm a radiologist. Specialise in uterine diseases.'

'Wow. That's a responsible job.' I hoped my mouth hadn't flung open. 'We know where to come to get checked out when we've slept with someone dodgy.'

Roberta shot me a warning look. 'Trust you to lower the tone.'

For some reason Roberta's words stung, as though I was letting her down in front of her new friends. Nicole laughed. 'Judging by the standard of men I meet, not much chance of sleeping with anyone at all.' Roberta nodded in agreement but her face clouded for a moment. She didn't talk about him much any more, but I knew she was still moping about Jake. All this falling in love with the first one that came along was a bit too Disney for me. Roberta needed to learn to be a bit more shag-and-go, though I guess that was easy for me to say when I hadn't put myself out there for two decades.

I raised my glass to her. 'Congratulations on the new house. I hope it's the start of wonderful things to come.' We all raised our glasses, then Brenda suddenly jerked into life like a malevolent puppet desperate for a moment in the

192

limelight. 'I'm toying with the idea of going back to work as well.'

I waited just long enough to appear disinterested before asking the obvious question.

Her eyelashes creaked up with satisfaction. 'I'm a divorce solicitor.'

'Plenty of work for you I imagine, then.'

Brenda stretched her lips into a smile. 'I might ease in with a couple of cases a week. I negotiated rather a good package for myself when I left the ex, so it's more to keep my hand in rather than for financial reasons.'

People who worked to keep their hand in pissed me off. I'd have loved the opportunity to 'keep my hand in' rather than work my tattered old arse off to keep hold of my mediocre terraced house and my ancient Volvo. The feeling of failing to fulfil my potential, stirred up by that bloody school reunion, bubbled up again. I lapsed into silence.

Nicole tried to rescue me. 'So, do you play tennis, Octavia?'

'No, I hate exercise. Roberta's always been sporty, first-team netball, hockey and cross country at school, but I only like dancing. And sex.'

Roberta tutted in embarrassment. 'Honestly. You've got sex on the brain. Anyway, you like hiking as well. You were always roughing it up mountains when we were younger. Octavia is the most adventurous person I know.'

'The closest I get to an adventure now is driving the kids to school in the snow.'

Recently I'd started popping into a trekking shop round the corner from the nursery to look at the backpacks and boots. I pretended I was off on a trip, somewhere challenging and daunting, somewhere I'd never been before, where I'd need guts and determination and grit. On wet grey lunchtimes, when I had the accounts to sort out in the afternoon, I

193

understood how people walked out of their lives and kept going until there was no turning back.

'I treat exercise like a job. I know that five days a week at nine o'clock, I'm going to play tennis or go to the gym, and I don't let anything interfere. The builders, plumber and car valet just have to fit round that,' Brenda said, with a little glance at her tanned biceps in a halter neck, even though it was really chilly outside. The way she said it made her sound as though she set aside an hour a day to work at a soup kitchen for the homeless.

Roberta did at least send me a little eye roll. 'Octavia does work and she has got three kids. It's a bit harder to fit it all in if you have to leave by 7.30 and go straight from work to school pickup.'

'Yeah, but we're doing it all on our own, no husbands to help out.' Brenda's mouth would have scrunched up if Botox hadn't ruined her ability to crinkle. She didn't interest me enough to get into a whose-life-was-hardest discussion.

Nicole stroked the fur on her gilet collar and said, 'I don't know what I'd do without my nanny. My husband never did much anyway. And I don't have to put my fancy underwear on for her.'

I wondered how Roberta could stand this puerile shit. The conversation turned to handbags – to Radley or not to Radley appeared to be the question. 'Did you see that gorgeous white Valentino bag that Angelina Jolie had? I went straight onto eBay to see if I could get one. Starting bids were £800,' Nicole said.

'Why would you spend £800 on a handbag? Do you get £800-worth of pleasure out of it, more than you would out of one that cost £70?' I glanced down at my black canvas sack.

Nicole giggled. 'I love knowing I've got something someone else hasn't. My ex-husband used to keep buying me handbags because he knew he'd get more sex. If he bought me Prada, he was definitely on for a blow job.'

I marvelled at how high-maintenance some women were. The thing that really blew my mind was that they managed to hook up with men who pandered to their silly whims. Jonathan would only have to come to parents' evening for me to crack open the frilly undies.

I shivered as the door opened and a blast of icy wind swirled around us. A group of rugby-player types came in, play-pushing and calling each other by nicknames.

'Oy, Wrighty, you getting them in?'

'It's Tealeaf's turn.'

'Sonic Six Pints bought the last lot.'

I must have drifted out of the handbag debate and been gawking more than was permissible for a happily married woman because 'Beaufort' suddenly walked over to me, a man-mountain of a prop with a neck like an oak tree.

He bent down and murmured in my ear. 'You look bored out of your tiny mind. You want to come and drink beer with the lads? We can't promise not to swear though.'

It was so long since any bloke, even one who looked like a distant relative of the African bush elephant, had noticed me that I blushed so hard I could feel my head sweat. The other three immediately stopped their conversation.

'No, I'm fine, I was just thinking about nicknames and how girls don't really use them.'

'If you play rugby, you gotta have a nickname. You don't get to pick. The boys give you one. See the one with the longish blonde hair? He's known as Airbag cos he's always bumping into everyone. That one with the red shirt is Brick, because he's built like the proverbial.'

Roberta and her friends were making goggle eyes at me, waiting for me to get rid of him. But linguistically, it was the most interesting conversation of the night. Beaufort didn't look like he had a degree in biochemistry but there was a certain mammalian charm about him. I waited for him to realise that I was a five-foot-two dumpling wearing last year's maxi dress and that just feet away from me, he could pick up this year's models, sleek and slimline. He barely looked in their direction.

'Why don't you come and meet the boys?'

'I was just about to go.'

'Come on, I'll buy you a drink. What are you having? Cocktail? What is it you girls like? Them mojitos?'

The three women looked agog. Maybe they were amazed he'd picked me over them, maybe they couldn't believe I was going to hang out with a bunch of drunken rugger buggers rather than a group of civilised girlies.

I slid off my stool. 'Why don't you all come with me?'

Brenda looked as though I'd just asked her to eat a witchetty grub. Roberta said, 'You go. I'll pop over when I've finished my drink.'

Typical Roberta. Fobber-offer extraordinaire. She could never say a direct 'no' to anyone.

Beaufort nodded over to his mates. 'We don't bite, you know.' But the others stayed rooted to their stools like a trio of gnomes minus the fishing rods. I allowed Beaufort to drag me over to his friends, expecting them to look over my head and direct their energy into enticing Roberta over.

Beaufort leaned down to me. 'They friends of yours? You looked like you'd rather be at home watching Corrie.'

'They were talking about fashion. And, as you can see, I'm not very interested in fashion.'

Beaufort shrugged and indicated his jeans and T-shirt. 'S'just something to stop you going out stark bollock naked, isn't it?'

I couldn't take my eyes off his neck. He reminded me of the wrestlers Dad and I used to watch on TV, snuggled up on the settee together. He'd always said that his daughter was the best of both worlds, 'not afraid to cuddle her old dad but tough enough to invade small countries'. He'd have been disappointed that I'd ended up with such a humdrum life. Before I could get maudlin, a gaggle of Beaufort's friends gathered round, pint glasses in hand, jostling to be top dog with the witty repartee.

'So what's your name then?'

I waited for the inevitable comment. 'You got seven brothers and sisters then?' Then everyone started introducing themselves, arguing over the origins of their nicknames.

'Butter – cos he's always dropping the ball.'

'No, it's cos I spread myself round the pitch easily.'

The one they all agreed on was Beaufort. 'You ain't never heard wind like it.'

As Beaufort came back with my mojito, they were all doing impressions of his farting and moaning about how no one wanted to share a room with him on a rugby tour. He didn't look the slightest bit ashamed. 'Lying bastards they are, all of them.'

After a few minutes I stopped worrying about abandoning the others and got on with enjoying myself. After tiptoeing around Jonathan's unemployed ego and trying to fit in with Roberta's nail-filing friends, it was liberating to swear and take the piss, brutal and near-the-knuckle, without having to ring and apologise the next day. I was the centre of attention, the quick-witted me rather than the nagbag who shouted at everyone for leaving towels on the bathroom floor. I felt twenty years younger and two stone slimmer, giddy, as though I was about to interrail off to an unplanned summer.

Butter gave me the biggest compliment. 'You can come on rugby tour, you can. Be our lucky mascot. Everyone will be fighting to share a room with you. Don't tell the missus though. She only lets me go if she thinks I'm sharing with

Beaufort cos she knows no woman in their right mind would ever go in a room he's been biffing in.'

Every now and then I caught Roberta's eye and beckoned her over. She kept wrinkling her nose and shaking her head, while the other two muttered to each other.

I looked at my watch. Eleven-thirty. I needed to go home. The babysitter cranked up an extra two pounds an hour at midnight. To a chorus of disapproval, I said goodbye. Beaufort leant down. 'Can I see you again?'

I hesitated. I couldn't remember the last time a man had shown any interest in me. I hadn't thought of myself as sexy in a million years. I showed him my wedding ring. 'Sorry. Would have loved to.'

He shrugged. 'All the beautiful girls are always taken. Too bad for me. Let me know if you ever come back on the market. East Park Rugby Club. You'll remember my name, won't you?'

'Couldn't forget it. Thanks so much, I've had a great time. You rescued me from death by a thousand handbags.'

His face changed as he looked past me. 'Your friend.'

I turned round. Roberta stood right behind me. She'd obviously overheard the last part of our conversation. She frowned and said, 'Are you coming? We were going to pop down to the Spice King for a curry.'

'No, I'm sorry. I promised the babysitter I'd be home by midnight. I'll walk out with you.'

Roberta sighed. I had been pretty rude. But I liked to choose my friends, not have them chosen for me. Roberta would get over it. I'd sat through loads of evenings when some gorgeous bloke had chatted her up while I got stuck with the Quasimodo mate. At least she'd had her own little posse to talk to.

To shouts and catcalls, we trooped out. Nicole hugged me and gushed a goodbye. Brenda barely acknowledged I was leaving.

And neither did Roberta.

Roberta

My housewarming lunch on the May Bank Holiday with more guests than I'd expected to say yes had me flapping about like a teenager off to the Prom. I wanted to be that woman who sashayed up to the door, hair loosely pinned in place by a pencil, glass of bubbly in hand, waving people through with a 'take us as you find us' attitude.

Instead I was polishing glasses, decanting hummus from its plastic pot into elegant bowls, and fussing over candles in the loo. I had hoped to portray a woman on the cusp of a new beginning after challenging times, not have all the wives whispering 'Poor Roberta' behind their hands and urging their husbands to offer to mow my lawn when summer came.

I had debated inviting Jake on the outside chance that he had forgiven me. After Patri's New Year do, the idea of being at a party, even my own, without a man in tow made me feel like a snail that had lost its shell. But ultimately, I lacked the appetite for fresh humiliation. In the end, I decided I could always lock myself in the downstairs cloakroom and admire my newly painted walls, a stony-grey that I loved so much I kept stroking it every time I went in.

Alicia was the most excited I'd seen her in ages. She had

an astonishing aptitude for colour and style, and I'd left the beautifying of the sitting room to her. I'd let her invite four of her own friends and, with an effort that could probably have diverted raging flood water, managed to avoid saying, 'Not Jaqs or Sinead.' My heart smiled at the familiar sound of Lucy and Daniela, and I wasn't too unhappy at Patri's granddaughter, Loretta, once I got over her pierced nose.

Alicia hesitated at the fourth person. 'You might say no to this.'

I tried my new Octavia-like approach. 'Try me. I might not.'

'Could I invite Connor? Loretta's friend, the blonde boy from New Year's Eve.'

The relief that it wasn't Buzz or his hateful sister made me far more enthusiastic at inviting another young male into Alicia's life. 'Of course. No monkey business though.'

She rewarded me with a roll of the eyes and a 'Muuuu-uuum', but there was an underlying warmth there that made me feel we'd forged a new bond, a linear mother-daughter link, independent of the family three-way triangle with all its issues. If I only focused on the excess of black eyeliner, the rebellion against daily showering and a horrible habit of including 'like' in every sentence, Alicia seemed a pretty normal teenager. She was definitely a little less angry and a little more chatty. I'd even been allowed to look at a couple of text conversations where she'd told the horrible Jaqs to leave her alone. Gradually, the sleepless nights obsessing about her losing her virginity were becoming fewer.

I banished that train of thought as the first people started arriving from the tennis club. Nerves made me gush disproportionately over bottles of Frascati and bunches of daffodils. Alicia was far more sophisticated, taking jackets and offering drinks.

No sign of Octavia. She was supposed to have come early to troubleshoot any last-minute jitters, though given how offhand she'd been at The Clam, I'd been quite happy pottering about on my own. Octavia thought excess wine compensated for all party shortcomings, whereas I liked to fiddle with vases, candles and lighting. Eventually, she burst through the front door muttering apologies and glaring at Jonathan. He'd arrived back from Sardinia that morning and was sporting a pale green shirt that had 'bought in Italy' stamped all over it. He actually looked quite handsome. In comparison, Octavia looked milk-bottle pale. She snapped at Jonathan to hand me the bottle of champagne he had tucked under his arm.

'Shall I open it?' He managed to sound like the perfect party guest but I was confident that I'd find it hidden behind a curtain to ensure that he consumed at least £15-worth of his precious Veuve Clicquot.

'Would you? Thanks.'

He trotted off to the kitchen. I turned to Octavia. 'Are you OK?'

'Sorry we're late. I ate some scallops past their sell-by date and paid the price puking up these last couple of days. I've only just started to feel better today.'

I tutted at her. Octavia thought mould on any food was an added extra rather than a 'Do not trespass here' sign. 'Thanks for making the effort to come then. You're the one who's got me this far.'

'Don't be silly. I wouldn't have finished university if it wasn't for you. So far we've had our disasters at different times.'

'Are you sure you should be here? You do look rather washed-out.'

Octavia pulled a face. 'I'm fine, though I'd better go easy on the booze. Anyway, I couldn't stand a day at home with Jonathan on my own. He's really beginning to annoy me. He's just told me he's off to Sardinia again this Thursday.'

201

Every time I saw Octavia, she seemed to be more and more fed up with him. Although she was the last person I'd expected to marry young, I'd been in favour of her tying the knot with Jonathan when she got pregnant with Charlie. I thought Jonathan would be a reasonable father and at the time, he seemed the perfect complement for her excesses, especially in the turbulent years following her father's death and Xavi's disappearance. And whatever she said about being happy to bring up the baby on her own, the prospect sounded terrifying to me. As Jonathan had aged though, his steadying influence had become pure killjoy.

But I didn't want to encourage her discontent. 'I don't suppose it's all fun though. He must be working hard, knowing Patri. He always wants his pound of flesh.'

Octavia sighed. 'I know, but at least he gets the evenings to himself. I'm juggling fifty thousand things while he's sipping bloody Prosecco and snuffling up spaghetti.'

The one thing I adored about being single, that made me want to spin around with my arms out, was not having any expectations of anyone else. Knowing that there was no one to rely on, ergo no one to disappoint me, obliterated so much resentment. No inappropriate birthday present to feel hurt about, no huffing and puffing when relatives came for Sunday lunch, no automatic assumption that all tedious tasks from sorting the car insurance to dealing with the wasp nest were mine.

No one to tell me what to think.

I smiled. 'Couldn't you go to Sardinia with Jonathan?'

'I'm gagging to. Patri's given me an open invitation. If it was up to me I'd be on the first plane out there. There's just the small matter of the kids. I had hoped my mother would have them but she's so busy with her golf and old biddy lunches, I haven't dared ask her. I think she finds them a bit of a handful as well, now they're older.'

'I'd have the children.'

'It's really tempting, thanks. I'll have a think about it. It would be hard work getting them all to their different schools.'

'I'd manage.'

'I'd have to persuade Jonathan. You know how he struggles with flexible thinking. He'll need time to get his head round the fact that his wife might be in the same space as his work.'

Just then Brenda came down the hallway. 'Big happiness in your new home,' she said, scooping me into an excited hug. She handed me a magnum of champagne. 'Hair of the dog. Only just recovered from the hangover after your little party the other night. You've worked wonders on the sitting room. The mirror looks great over the fireplace.'

I felt Octavia shift beside me. 'Not really a party, was it?' I said. 'More of an impromptu get-together for a bunch of singletons. Brenda, you remember Octavia from the evening at The Clam?'

Brenda said 'Hi' and smiled vaguely. Octavia nodded.

'Brenda helped me with the mirror. Took us ages to put up because we didn't have the right Rawlplugs or a decent drill.'

Octavia managed a smile that even a high-speed shutter couldn't have captured. 'You should have called me. I'd have come over with Jonathan's tool box.'

'I know, but I always feel you have so much on your hands with the children. And you've helped me out so much already.'

Octavia wouldn't understand that I wanted to work things out for myself now instead of letting her take over. It was easier to have a go at new challenges in front of people who hadn't already pigeonholed me into the 'good at shopping, going to the beauticians and faffing about with cushions' slot.

But she wasn't in a mood to be placated. She disappeared off to fetch a drink, leaving Brenda to fill me in on the latest doomed marriage down at the tennis club.

While I was making 'ooh' faces at Brenda, my eyes were straining through the doorway to the kitchen, scanning for Octavia. She was standing by my wine fridge, looking so prickly that she resembled a human holly bush, her eyes flicking over the guests. Octavia was usually the one who raced around with olives and crisps, at ease with everyone from vicars and high court judges to monosyllabic teenagers and the least appealing toddlers. She had an ability to remember people's names, where they went on holiday, children's schools, recalling them at impressive moments, months, often years after she'd met them.

I glanced over to Jonathan. He had his head back, laughing that whistling laugh of his. He normally shuffled about at parties talking about how long it took your liver to regenerate after drinking until we were all praying he'd go and sip mineral water in a darkened room. It was almost like they'd swapped places for the day.

I introduced Brenda to one of my old neighbours and started making my way to Octavia when Alicia beckoned me over. She was standing with a friendly-looking blonde boy. 'Mum, this is Connor.'

He gave me a firm handshake and looked me in the eye. 'Pleased to meet you. I was just telling Alicia that my school team often plays tennis at the club round the corner. They have some great barbecue parties. Perhaps you'd both like to come one evening.'

I wanted to phone his mother there and then and tell her she should congratulate herself on doing such an amazing job. The boy was probably not yet sixteen, but he was charming, open and more comfortable in his own skin than I could ever imagine being.

'We'd love that, thank you.' Something in me unclenched as though I'd been holding onto a problem that had disappeared of its own accord. Alicia caught my eye, anxious for approval. I nodded towards the pantry. 'Perhaps Connor could help you bring out the ice buckets for the beer.'

They scampered off. He looked so sturdy beside Alicia's thin silhouette. He bent his head to whisper something to her. I hoped it wasn't 'Got any condoms?' Somehow I was going to have to trust her again. I twirled round and scooped up a plate of mini beef wellingtons before more doubts had a chance to flood in.

Just as I reached Octavia, Nicole came bounding over to me, her skinny frame carrying off a white linen trouser suit on an overcast day with aplomb. I reminded her that she'd met Octavia at the wine bar.

'Octavia, hello again. How are you? Nursery still going great guns? Just met your husband. He's a clever man, isn't he? Honestly, computer programming. It's all I can do to cope with texting.'

I willed Octavia to be a little bit friendly. She'd sat through the sham speeches about the longevity of love at my parents' fortieth wedding anniversary, done the waltz with my grandmother at her eighty-ninth birthday, and cleared up sick when some vile child vomited at Alicia's sixth birthday party. But now, when all she had to do was eat, drink and be a bit flaming merry, she couldn't seem to raise her game. So she'd had a row with Jonathan. I'd have soon run out of invitations if I'd sulked every time Scott and I had arrived snarling at a host's front door.

Nicole persevered until Octavia started to unfurl, asking her for tips about dealing with her three-year-old's bad sleeping patterns, praising her knowledge. While they talked, I surveyed my little empire. Alicia was back with her best friends, and if she had to have a boyfriend, one who looked

205

like he would be kind to her. Laughter was bouncing from group to group against a background of chinking glasses, animated chatter and the soundtrack of *Dirty Dancing*. Finally, I could relish my new house where I felt so sure of having made the right decision. Nicole drew me back into the conversation by raising her glass.

'Here's to two clever businesswomen. One already successful and one bound to be.'

But that little moment I'd been relaxing into, a quiet satisfaction that even without Scott – or Jake – life still held the promise of good times to come, was sucked away in an instant.

Octavia jerked her head up. 'Businesswoman?'

Nicole gushed in. 'Roberta's going to be the new Kevin McCloud. Patsy over there was just telling me that you'd drawn up a fantastic design for her sitting room.'

Octavia looked puzzled. I wished Nicole hadn't chosen that exact second to appoint herself my business PR. 'I've decided to go ahead with that interior design business I was talking about. It's what I love and I think it will be good for me to go back to work.'

'I knew you were toying with the idea but I thought you'd dismissed it because so much has changed since you did your degree?'

Octavia was slightly open-mouthed, as though I'd said I was going to build a nuclear reactor from scratch.

Nicole burst in. 'I don't think it matters as long as you've got a good eye. You've only got to look at how Roberta's done her sitting room with that lovely rose paper on the chimney breast. I'd never have put it together with those curtains but it looks amazing. Can't wait till she starts on my bedroom.'

Octavia folded her arms. 'So when did you decide this? Didn't realise it was up and running.'

Nicole was looking puzzled. I shot her a desperate glance. 'I haven't exactly set up a proper business yet. Just got a few friends who've asked me to take a look at some of their rooms at the moment.'

'It's a big commitment, running a business. You can't just dip in and out of it. Something like that is going to be feast or famine, I imagine. I wonder if you'd be better off working for someone else while you get some experience?'

It was incredible how the people closest to me had the least confidence in my abilities, though of course, I hadn't ever had to prove myself. While Octavia had been juggling three kids and striving to make a success of her holistic nursery, I'd had a relatively easy ride with one child and organising the décor for Scott's properties. In our friendship, she probably thought she was the one with the monopoly on hard graft. But not any more.

I looked Octavia straight in the eye. 'I've checked it all out with the bank and the new business adviser. They think it's got potential. I don't want to work for someone else and be told what to do. I've had nearly twenty years of that with Scott. I'm going to make my own mistakes. I'm determined to create a situation so that even if Scott stops my money, I can support myself. And Alicia.'

'Good idea. Good for you.'

She sounded hurt. She backed off, though. It wasn't the right moment to explain that I hadn't wanted a plethora of opinions and well-meaning advice. I just wanted to take a chance, challenge myself without everyone chipping in with 'But have you thought about?' I had enough of my own doubts without withstanding everyone else's.

I picked up a couple of empty glasses. I should have told her. More and more I was finding it easier to confide in people who didn't know me so well, who didn't have a concrete view on who I was and what I was capable of.

I steered Nicole towards Brenda and went off in search of music. I put Van Morrison's *Brown-eyed Girl* on the iPod and soon a merry band of us were la-la-la-ing in a way that wouldn't have ingratiated us with the neighbours. As I swung round, I saw Octavia talking to Jonathan, jaw clenched, shaking her head while he was shrugging. Shortly afterwards, she came over and hugged me briefly. 'We're going to have to get back for the children. Thanks for a lovely time. The house looks fantastic. Great choice.'

Jonathan gave me a quick peck on the cheek. I watched them walk down the drive, both hunched up as though they were bracing themselves against a biting wind.

I'd never realised before that couples could look lonely.

Octavia

Jonathan and I were quiet in the cab on the way home. Hurt that Roberta was moving into a new life, one that had dropped me off her speed dial, had eclipsed my anger at Jonathan jaunting off to Sardinia again so soon. Roberta had even set up a business without telling me. I was obviously the friend for bad times. Nicole, Brenda and all those other blonde-haired looky-likeys were the good-time girls.

I put my hand on Jonathan's knee. He didn't move or acknowledge me. 'Sorry about today. I miss you. That's all.'

He inclined his head on one side slightly, in a 'bit late now' gesture. I felt a little prickle in my eyes as I realised that no one seemed to need me. Not Roberta. Not Jonathan. Not even the kids. The beginning of the cricket season meant Charlie would spend every minute of his free time whacking balls into the nets down at the club. Polly thought no one was more boring than her family and ridiculed my Enid Blyton notions of us all going for a walk together with the wildflower book in hand. Immi still liked to join in a bit of apple crumble-making but preferred to play zoos on her own in her room.

The house echoed with missing voices. Mum was bringing

the kids back after tea. We could have stayed at Roberta's longer but the more I saw her with her new friends, her new house, even a new business, the more stuck in a rut I felt. Maybe it was the after-effect of the food-poisoning that was making me feel so low. Surely I hadn't become such a dried-up excuse for a friend that I begrudged Roberta's life taking a turn for the better? I waited for Jonathan to scuttle off into the lounge and start tapping on his computer. I didn't think my ego could stand being sidelined for YouTube videos of computer troubleshooting.

'Do you want a cup of tea?' I asked.

'Not really, thanks.'

'Have you got work to do?'

Jonathan shrugged. 'Not really.'

I was sure I'd married someone with a wider vocabulary than 'Not really'.

'Fancy a shag?' I said it as a joke to see if he could answer anything other than 'Not really'.

He furrowed his brows, then took my hand and led me upstairs. I wasn't sure what he was intending. I wouldn't have put it past him to choose that moment to show me the mould on the bathroom wall 'because no one ever opened a window'. But he pulled me into our bedroom. I struggled to get out of scratchy-picky mode and into love's-old-dream gear, but since I was always going on about how predictable he was, I needed to embrace a bit of spontaneity myself. I chucked off my clothes while he folded his jeans, smoothed out his socks and added his boxers to the pile. I yanked the duvet up to my neck. Jonathan wasn't having any of it and ripped the covers back. 'Let me see you.'

I couldn't see how a close-up of my cellulite could possibly enhance his enjoyment but he launched himself with gusto. 'Where's your baby oil?'

It was so unlike Jonathan to think beyond the missionary

these days that I hesitated for a moment, in case there was some other meaning I hadn't grasped.

I ran to the bathroom and dug about in the cabinet, eventually coming up with a greasy bottle that had probably been there since Immi was a baby. I handed it to Jonathan, feeling self-conscious, as though we were pretending to be young and adventurous.

When we were first together, we were the Body Shop's best customer for lotions and potions. Seemed incredible to me now that I used to rush home from lectures to get my fancy pants on, ready to pounce the minute he walked in the door. During the last couple of terms at university, he'd moved into my tiny flat with rice-paper walls. Our antics often used to end up with the neighbours thumping their disapproval. Unsexy thoughts crowded in about how desire got lost in winding babies, clearing up dog shit and explaining fractions. I tried to focus on the slippery sensation of the oil as Jonathan massaged my back, but he'd obviously forgotten how ticklish I was and switched to doing feathery movements.

'Stop squirming.'

'I can't help it.'

Jonathan rolled me over and started massaging my breasts. I tried not to think of the last time we went to Pizza Express and I'd stood for ages with Immi watching the chefs kneading the dough. Jonathan leaned over and whispered in my ear, 'Are you ready?'

'Nearly.'

I scrabbled around in my mind for something to get me going so Jonathan wouldn't feel like he'd plunged his willy into a scouring pad. Maybe the food poisoning had sapped my energy more than I thought. I was trying to conjure up some images of us going at it in the shower when Jonathan stuck his tongue in my ear. My shoulders shot up around my ears and I shook him off. 'Don't do that. It's like having your ear gummed up with shampoo at the hairdresser's.'

His shoulders sagged. 'God above, Octavia. You know how to get a guy in the mood.'

'Sorry. You know I don't like you licking my ear.'

'Do you like anything I do?' He sounded irritated.

'Of course I do. Come here. We're just a bit rusty, that's all.' I did what I had promised myself I would never do. I dug deep into the recesses of my mind, came up with Xavi, my white limbs, thinner then, snaking round his brown legs, a slow-motion cine film across the back of my eyelids, his dark fingers probing and stroking and turning up the voltage inside me, caress by insistent caress. As Jonathan entered me, I reached out for the memory of us breaking into the Bains de Caldane at midnight and making love in the thermal pools, the warm water pressing between us, lapping, then splashing and slapping as our moans echoed off the surface.

Jonathan thrust inside me with the low groaning I recognised as my signal to get on with it. I pushed my head hard back into the pillow, gripping tightly with body and mind, the shimmering edge of betrayal unable to compete with the potency of Xavi's memory until I arched against Jonathan, then lay there quivering with aftershocks. I closed my eyes to let the moment continue for a little longer.

Jonathan collapsed back on to the pillow. 'We should get rid of the children more often.'

I reached out for his hand. 'Roberta said she'd have the kids, so I could come with you to Sardinia on Thursday.'

Jonathan stopped stroking my hand. 'Can Roberta cope with all of them together?'

'I'm sure she'd be fine.'

'Three kids are quite a handful when she's on her own. And she's got Alicia as well.'

'I know, Jonathan. I often deal with three kids on my own,

212

plus I work full-time as well.' I tried – and failed – not to sound grumpy.

Jonathan twitched away from me. 'It's not my fault the only job I could get takes me abroad all the time. Right now, my priority is to make sure Patri takes me on permanently when my trial period ends.'

I took a deep breath and tried out compromise, a technique I'd observed Roberta use to great effect, but that felt as alien as wearing a pair of deely boppers on my head.

'You're right. Getting signed on the dotted line has to be your main concern. It would be so nice for us to have a break together though, even if you are working.'

Jonathan shrugged next to me. 'We're transferring to a different server so it's going to be a very busy time.'

I bit back the 'Welcome to my world' and said, 'It's fine. I'll amuse myself. At least we'd have a bit of an evening together.' I snuggled into his shoulder. 'I'll call Patri's secretary and sort it out.'

'If you want.'

Result. Never before had I considered myself a woman who could get her own way with sex.

Roberta

I was clearing up the remaining party debris the next morning when my mobile went. I checked it wasn't Scott. We rarely had any contact these days that wasn't through our divorce solicitors. I didn't recognise the number. The eternally optimistic part of my brain hoped that it would be Jake.

That hope shrivelled as a rather haughty-sounding woman introduced herself as Mrs Goodman, friend of Mrs Walker. Once I'd snapped into gear and reminded myself that Nicole was Mrs Walker, I discovered that her publicity machine for my interior design business was a veritable runaway train. Mrs Goodman wanted a whole drawing room redesign since her husband, Sidney, had recently passed away. 'Sidney never would spend a penny on the house but I'm going to splash out on what I want now he's gone.'

Quite the merry widow. 'When would you like me to come and take a look?'

Mrs Goodman didn't miss a beat. 'Right now, dear. Time is of the essence. My sister-in-law is coming to stay from Canada in three weeks.'

I tried not to squeak in fright. Three weeks to revamp an entire room from start to finish. But I also knew that the only way to make a name for myself was by word of mouth. A large crow of doubt planted itself on my shoulder while I slipped into a suit, picked up my best handbag and gathered up a couple of the mood boards I'd used for my own home.

Mrs Goodman lived in a huge 1930s house where I knew avocado and brown bathrooms would reign supreme. I sat in the car mustering up the confidence to get out. What if I couldn't work out what to do? What if she bad-mouthed me to everyone? I gave myself a stern talking-to as I walked up the drive. She opened the door the second I rang the bell as though she'd been peering through the spyhole. She was tall and birdlike, very upright, almost as if she'd taken the postural advice to imagine a string stretching from your head to the ceiling a little too literally. I offered to take off my shoes.

'No need. I'm having all new carpets. And new curtains. The kitchen is next.'

Poor old Sidney must have been turning in his grave. She pattered through to the huge drawing room, a dark cavern hung with sludgy floral curtains and smoky-glass light fittings. A wealth of possibilities sprang to mind. 'What a fabulous space.'

'So you'll take it on?' Mrs Goodman was staring at me in a way that made me terrified to say no. 'Mrs Walker spoke very highly of you, said you were the best in the business because you do everything from the design to the painting. She told me about it while she was examining my—' She leaned forward, pointing to her pelvis. 'My down-there.'

I nodded hurriedly. I supposed all manner of subject topics provided suitable distractions. As I eyed the ceiling with its snug anaglypta covering, I regretted the 'complete service' tagline.

'I haven't seen my sister-in-law for twelve years. She was estranged from Sidney but we always got on well. She mustn't get the wrong impression and think Sidney was mean.'

I wanted to shout that I'd only done my own home and drawn up a few designs for friends' rooms. No one had ever paid me for my services and maybe what I liked as a thirty-nine-year-old, she would hate. Anxiety was clearing my mind of any suitable suggestions.

Suddenly she grabbed my arm, her bony fingers digging through my jacket. 'It feels rather odd doing this on my own.'

The old lady's intense face jolted me out of my fear. I pulled out my sketch pad. 'Let's sit down. Would you like me to give you some ideas and then you can have a little think?'

Over Assam tea and shortbread, we talked colour, textures and blending the traditional with the modern. Every now and again, Mrs Goodman shook her head vehemently and self-doubt consumed me. 'No. No. Perfectly dreadful.' Brushed aluminium lamps were obviously the work of Satan. But neon-striped curtains were angels' masterpieces apparently.

She clapped her hands. 'This is going to be wonderful. My sister-in-law will be so impressed. You will get it done in three weeks, won't you?'

Mrs Goodman had a knack of making rhetorical questions sound like an order. I'd have to work every second of every day. Maybe weekends as well. I was mentally plotting how I would cope. Much to Alicia's chagrin, she was due to stay at Scott's for a week because he was off to Australia again soon. I didn't want her to feel pushed out but it would be good for her to see me knuckle down and work for a living. Mrs Goodman's eyes raked up and down my face. She was relying on me to start her on the journey to freedom and independence.

I was too petrified to let her down.

Octavia

Ladies' Night came on the radio as I walked through to the kitchen to call Roberta. I stood drumming on the worktop for some time, thinking about our joint eighteenth birthday party six weeks before we left school for good. Roberta wore a pale pink knee-length dress. She hated it but her father insisted. That was pre-Scott, when she was still toeing the line. I was in a pair of yellow and black trousers with gold thigh-length boots, an exotic bumblebee. We were on countdown to spending the summer travelling. Every song was an anthem to our freedom which, when it came, didn't disappoint. We pointed to places we'd vaguely heard of on a map and hopped on a train. It was a joyous two months when responsibility meant using sun block.

Now I had a chance to recreate a tiny fragment of that freedom. If Jonathan was going to be working, I could tip up in places unknown again. Far more appealing than the windy weeks in Wales or the occasional crap package to sunny but indistinguishable Greek islands we'd had since the kids were born.

I felt guilty for being such a moody mare at Roberta's party. Especially when she'd offered to look after my kids.

While I waited for Roberta to answer, I danced about so wildly I could feel my buttocks flinging from side to side.

'Hi there. Just calling to let you know that wonders will never cease.'

'What?' Roberta sounded excited.

'Jonathan has agreed for me to go to Sardinia with him on Thursday for six days if you can cope with the kids. I never thought he'd say yes but I think even he realises we need a bit of time together. Can you manage?'

There was a long pause. 'Oh my God. Sugar. I'd forgotten all about that. When are you leaving? I'm working flat out for the next three weeks.'

Roberta gave me the whole sob story about 'Poor Mrs Goodman recently widowed' and how she'd signed up to do it all the day before.

'How long is he there for? Could you go next month? I'm so sorry. You sounded so doubtful about going, I didn't really think it would happen.'

'Doesn't matter.'

'I feel really bad. The problem is that Alicia's having a week with Scott and I'm going to be at Mrs Goodman's house all weekend. Maybe I could have them Thursday and Friday? Perhaps I could get a babysitter.' I could hear the anxiety in Roberta's voice.

'No. That's too complicated. I'm not that bothered about going. You've got to take the work when you can. Just bad timing, that's all.'

I slumped down into a chair. Sod's law that after years of fannying about with a few blinds, Roberta had a proper contract at the exact moment I needed her help. Lucky her having an ex-husband to dump Alicia on. Maybe Scott would start adding some value at last.

'Must go. I need to stop the secretary booking the tickets.'

'Another time, any other time at all, I'll do it with pleasure.'

The problem was, in my life, another time never came.

When I told Jonathan that Roberta couldn't help, he came out with his favourite phrase, the one I would put on his tombstone.

'Never mind.'

He could be next to the 'I did bloody mind' on my grave.

I told myself that there'd be a chance later on in the year. But as the week wore on, I found I could no longer empty the dishwasher without flinging the cutlery into the drawers with a great clatter. I hurled the children's laundry into their bedrooms. To the kids' delight, then consternation, I gave up on my usual five-a-day calculations and slapped pizza down every night. I made no attempt to stay within my weekly 14-unit limit. I'd find Stan stretched across the kitchen doorway, mournfully unwalked. Even at work, where I was paid to put on a jolly demeanour, I was spending less time on the lookout for butterflies and more time locked in my office. I'd even stopped trying to track down Xavi, disgusted by my pathetic attempts to inject some excitement into my life.

By the weekend, Jonathan was a living, breathing Alka-Seltzer, fizzing and twitching with irritation at the piles of newspapers, the mounds of shoes and trainers littering the hall, the fluff balls of dog hair cartwheeling around the kitchen. 'Have you done any housework this week?'

Usually I would get into a big slanging match about how it wasn't all up to me. Instead I simply said, 'No.'

Jonathan stood there, perplexed. The cogs of his brain were clanking round. 'Are you OK?'

'I'm fine.' I wondered whether Jonathan would be able to interpret that as 'I am totally taken for granted and no one would notice that I had keeled over in the garage while trying to find the screwdriver to fix the shower until a) there was no loo paper left or b) the terrible smell of my rotting body engulfed you all.'

219

In fact, it was a jolly good idea to keep no more than four loo rolls in the house at any one time to increase my chances of survival.

Jonathan absent-mindedly started sweeping crumbs from the work surfaces into his palm. I suppressed a smile when he encountered Immi's honey blobs from breakfast time. He walked over to the sink, soaping his fingers one by one. 'Is all this because you don't want me to go away again?'

'I don't have a problem with you going away again. I do have a problem with how you organise it without even checking to see whether it's OK with me. You assume that despite the fact that I work full-time and earn roughly the same as you, I should shoulder the entire burden of the house and three children while you dip in and out as you see fit.'

I waited for the whole change-the-record speech about not being able to pick and choose when he worked away but instead he said, 'I'm ringing your mother' and marched over to the phone.

'Denise? Jonathan. A rather wonderful opportunity has come up for Octavia to join me in Sardinia for a few days . . .'

Contrarily I wanted to stand in front of him and semaphore 'I don't want to go.'

I could imagine my mother scanning down her list of keep-fit classes, church fundraising meetings and funerals of anyone she was even on nodding terms with. I walked out of the room. I was not in the mood for overhearing a rundown of the final send-offs she'd have to miss, along the lines of 'You remember Mr Robertson? He lived next door to that lady who used to run the Sunday School, the one I wanted you to send Immi to? Throat cancer. Tragic. Such an awful way to die.'

Jonathan found me in the lounge a few minutes later. 'Your mum has come up trumps. You're coming with me the day after tomorrow. It's all arranged.'

Sometimes I thought that my capacity for joy had expired

at thirty-five, out of date like the half-used bottles of Calpol hanging around my medicine cabinet.

I should have been delighted, but Jonathan sounded as though I was an extra piece of baggage he'd have to lug to the airport. 'All arranged' was a relative term, which didn't take into account the logistics of the Shelton children or all the kit they'd need – dance shoes, wicketkeeper gloves, leotards – before they'd even packed a toothbrush.

I tweaked the tiny thread of excitement buried under the mountains to move before take-off. 'Thanks. I never thought she'd agree.'

Jonathan smiled. 'She always did have a soft spot for me. Rescued her precious daughter from a life of debauchery and aimless wandering.'

Frankly I couldn't wait to have another crack at aimless wandering. I didn't dare aspire to the dizzying heights of debauchery.

Roberta

When Scott was coming to pick up Alicia, I always called Octavia so that I wouldn't have to engage with him. I didn't even go to the door any more, just clamped my ear to the phone and waved to Alicia through the window. On the one occasion he'd tried to talk to me since he'd emailed Jake six weeks ago, I'd hissed 'You bastard' at him and disappeared back inside. If I'd experienced one moment of fleeting triumph, it was short-lived.

That one accusation, the only reference I'd ever made to it, unleashed a sustained campaign of emails and texts designed to destroy me. No perceived flaw was left unturned. His rants always started with some physical reference to how fat I was getting, my cellulite, even the ugly shape of my second toe. Inevitably his 'logic' then descended into an unfathomable stream of consciousness which, when condensed, more or less boiled down to the fact that every good thing that had happened to me in my life was down to my ability to perform in bed.

I hadn't quite reached the stage where I could delete his messages without reading them. I still spent hours constructing carefully worded rebuttals. If I ran my replies past Octavia, she'd always persuade me that the best revenge was to ignore Scott completely. 'Don't respond and he'll die off eventually.'

On this particular day, instead of waiting in the car, he came to the door and demanded to see me when Alicia answered. I wanted to refuse, to carry on moving around the swatches of cool blues and steely greys to find the perfect combination for Mrs Goodman's drawing room, lost in a world I could design rather than simply defend. I took a moment to ground my feet, to tell myself that Scott had no power over me any more. I would cling to the moral high ground, dignified and restrained whatever he levelled at me.

He stood on the doorstep, unshaven, dark circles under his eyes. I'd only seen him look like that once before, when he'd borrowed a huge sum of money to buy some land in New South Wales and it had turned out to be contaminated. I braced myself, but he seemed more lost than belligerent.

'It's Mum. She's had a stroke. I need to get out there fast. They don't know what the damage is yet.'

'When? Oh my God. Where is she?'

'She's in St Vincent's Hospital. They've got a good stroke unit but we won't know what's what for a few days.' His voice started to crack. 'I'm sorry. I can't have Alicia this week. I don't know how long I'm going to be away for. I'm catching a flight to Sydney this afternoon.'

Alicia sobbed beside me. She'd always loved Adele. Then Scott broke down. I put my hand on his arm. 'Come in for a minute.' I led him into the kitchen, competing thoughts reeling around. I didn't want him in my house. This was my safe place, away from Scott. Poor Adele. She always seemed so robust. Guilt crept in. What if we'd made her ill with the stress of our separation? I put the kettle on. I cuddled Alicia to me, smoothing her hair.

'Come on, we don't know how bad it is yet, darling. Let's not panic. People do make full recoveries from strokes.'

I handed Scott a cup of tea. His hand was shaking as he lifted it to his mouth. Part of me wanted to hold him until he calmed down. In the old days, I would have massaged his shoulders. That was unthinkable now.

Too much 'spoilt thicko, silver spoon, idle waste of space', still ringing in my ears.

The urge to make things right, at whatever cost to myself, was straining to surface. A harder, meaner part was battling through with 'Not my problem'. He'd succeeded in breaking something in me. The iron-strong bond, the loyalty that withstood other people's reproach, had splintered. The insults he'd thrown at me, the accusations of selfishness and sluttishness, had crowbarred open a gap that no promises, no apologies could ever solder closed.

So I hovered, uncertainly, not able to find any words to soothe this man whose skin, whose rhythm of breathing, whose cadence of voice were as familiar to me as my own. He took a gulp of tea. 'Will you come with me?'

'Where?'

'To Sydney. This afternoon.'

That had worked once. More than once. I'd dropped everything, let people down, even – to my shame – Octavia, on her thirtieth birthday, to jet off with Scott to Australia. This time, I didn't hesitate. 'No.'

I saw the jolt in his shoulders.

He turned to look at me, his blue eyes beseeching. 'Please. You were always so good with her. Mum is going to need our support. All three of us can go. If you pack your stuff quickly, you could make my flight, it leaves at 16.35. Or there's another one at 23.15.'

I put my hand on his shoulder. 'Scott, I'm genuinely sorry Adele is ill, but I can't come. People are depending on me. I've been commissioned to do an interior design job in a very short time. Alicia can't miss school for goodness knows how long.

This year's an important year for preparing for her GCSEs. And it's not right anyway. I don't want to give your mum false hopes if we all turn up together. Why don't you take Shana?'

Scott snorted. 'Shana? Shana doesn't do family crises well. She probably won't even be there when I get back. Anyway, Mum loves you. She doesn't even know Shana.'

So I was the one to roll out for the international dramas – though it was laughable that Scott thought I could play a part in anything involving hospitals without fainting. I'd always liked Adele. She was irritating but her heart was in the right place. I stumbled at the thought of not going to her when she was ill and alone. Still, I knew that whatever bribes or threats Scott wielded, I would never get on that plane. When I left him, all the other relationships that came as part of the package reverted back to his sole responsibility, family bonds fraying in a fraction of the time it took to build them up. Alicia's eyes were telling me that she didn't want to go either.

I picked up my cup and put it in the dishwasher. 'You need to go and get ready for your flight. We can't come. I want you to give your mum a huge hug from us and tell her to get better soon.'

Scott got to his feet. 'Robbie, don't do this to me. I need you with me. I can't deal with it on my own.'

I didn't want to stoop to pointing out that less than a week ago, he'd been emailing me to tell me he'd wasted the best years of his life on me. I was the woman who 'didn't know her arsehole from her earhole, a fat fucking fraud with no idea what work was and less creativity than a panda with a crayon in its paw'.

He came over to me and held my wrist, gently but firmly. I could feel the edge of the granite work surface digging into my back. I wanted to pull away so much, I couldn't concentrate on what he was saying.

225

'We should be together, Robbie. When I got the call last night, it made me realise that family is what matters. Mum. You. Alicia. The rest is superficial shit.'

I glanced over his shoulder at Alicia who was white-faced and watchful. The fact that he thought he could have this conversation in front of her meant he'd realised nothing. I shook him off and squeezed past him.

'It's too late, Scott. Way, way, too late.'

He opened his mouth to argue.

I put my hand up to stop him. 'No. No. Please leave now. Go and get your flight and look after your mum.'

He stared at me, as though he couldn't quite believe that I wasn't welcoming him back, wasn't rushing to appease him. I walked out into the hallway and opened the door. He pushed past me, shaking his head. I shut the door behind him and leaned against it. My knees were trembling but my heart was soaring.

I'd finally learnt to say 'no'.

Octavia

On the plane Jonathan buried himself in the *Financial Times*.
Still groggy from our 6am start, I drifted off into memories
of other journeys. Roberta and I stranded on a Swedish
station in the arse of the earth after misreading the timetable.
Gorgeous Italian *carabinieri* chucking us off a private beach,
then letting us sleep in the police station garden. Roberta
charming a chef in Antibes into lending us a saucepan so we
could cook pasta on the beach. And Xavi. Xavi everywhere.
Beach shacks. Nights under the stars. Mountain streams.
Even now, hurt scratched across the sunny pictures of him
in my mind. I tried to close down the memories by asking
Jonathan questions about Sardinia, but he seemed to find
mortgage rates far more interesting than anything I wanted
to talk about.

Every now and again, little sparks of angst about whether
I'd left clean cricket kit for Charlie and paid for Polly's tap
lessons dragged me back home. But as the plane glided
above the different shades of turquoise water surrounding
Sardinia, I wanted to fling off my seatbelt and dance. Even
Jonathan's cottering at the slow-moving passport control
couldn't piss on my party. The airport mayhem, the luggage

carousel with the suitcases piling up then plopping off the side, the children screaming, seemed vibrant rather than nerve-frazzling.

'I can't wait to see where we're staying.'

'Don't get too excited. It's a bog-standard Italian hotel.'

'Any hotel is good. Hotel means no kitchen. No kitchen means no cooking, no washing-up, no laundry.'

Jonathan burst out of the exit doors, looking about feverishly as though he was expecting an ambush. A handsome man in a jacket and dark trousers raised a tanned hand. Jonathan relaxed. 'Gianni. Good to see you.'

It was a short drive to the modern box of a hotel. I couldn't shake the feeling that it was sacrilege to stay somewhere that could have been anywhere in the world, nothing to mark it out as Sardinian, Italian or even Mediterranean with its angular brown furniture and beige curtains. The double bed was more like a single and a half. That could inspire intimacy or loathing, I wasn't sure which way it would go. Jonathan hung up all his shirts, folded everything into the drawers and lined up his toothbrush and razor in the bathroom.

I was battling to hang on to the rush of freedom that had welled up in me as soon as we'd landed. 'Do you want to go and find some lunch?'

'Not really. I feel a bit queasy from the plane. I'll just have a quick shower and get off to work.' He fiddled with the telly, moaning because he couldn't get Sky News.

'Are they expecting you?'

'Very much so. There's never any time to waste when I'm here.'

Jonathan Shelton, a legend in his Italian lunchtime.

'I might go for a little explore.' I wanted to clap my hands. Explore. I loved the way the word sounded.

'I'll check at reception whether Patri arranged to leave a car here,' Jonathan said.

'That would be brilliant. I won't go too far.' The idea of open roads leading who knew where sent a thrill through me.

'Up to you. I won't be home very early.'

'I know. Don't bloody worry, I won't be sitting here tapping on this nice brown furniture.'

Jonathan shrugged. Minutes later he was in the shower.

I couldn't help noticing how smart he looked as we walked into reception. Even the small flecks of grey in his ginger hair carried a certain gravitas of the international businessman. Sardinian style was rubbing off on him. He'd dug out a cream shirt he hardly ever wore, open-necked no less, the height of casual for Jonathan. The old guy on reception greeted him with a gnarly old handshake.

'I was just wondering if Sr Cubeddu had left a car here for my wife to drive?'

'Your wife?'

Jonathan pointed to me. The man nodded, looking a little confused. 'One moment.'

He shuffled round the corner. I whispered in Jonathan's ear, 'Perhaps women don't drive in Sardinia.'

'Judging by the way they all carry on, no one takes any tests.'

The old man came back clutching a key. 'Fiat. Italian. Very good.'

I smiled and took the key. 'Shall I walk with you to work?'

'It's too far. I'll get a cab.'

'Why don't I drive you? I'd feel better if you were in the car while I get used to driving on the wrong side again.'

Jonathan nodded. 'We'd better get a move on then.'

I wished Jonathan wanted to get a move on more often to spend some time with me.

Driving through the streets of Olbia brought an abrupt end to any navel-gazing. Avoiding the other drivers who swung across my little white Fiat 500 from both sides without

229

any indication and a lot of hooting focused my mind. Halfway through the journey, I began to enjoy myself, shouting '*Idiota*' and leaning on the horn as Jonathan gripped the seat and pressed his foot on a brake that wasn't there. After a little race through the traffic lights with a silver Punto, I deposited Jonathan in front of a building that looked more like a Venetian *palazzo* than an import-export nerve centre, taking great pleasure at double-parking. He leaned over and pecked my cheek.

'Thanks. I'll text you when I'm leaving work.'

'I won't be late. I might take a little trip up the coast.'

Jonathan strode towards the enormous arched door, while I screeched off, flooring the accelerator to beat a three-wheeled truck.

As soon as I left Olbia, the traffic thinned. I saw the sign east to the coast, the Golfo Aranci, and north to Santa Teresa di Gallura, the port at the northern tip of Sardinia. I'd be able to see Corsica from there. I indicated right to the sea, telling myself that my mission for the day was to find a little beach and plunge my sweaty feet into that turquoise water I'd seen from the plane. All the time my mind was urging me to head north. It was ages since I'd felt reckless. My foot was easing off the accelerator, my eyes searching for a suitable spot to do a U-turn. I pulled into the gateway of a field. I sat there for a second, then squiggled the car round, dust flying up behind me, and steered north, each blue Santa Teresa di Gallura sign calling me forward.

Excitement forced its way in like water through a gap in the rocks. I'd find a place on the cliffs, look over to Corsica and say goodbye to that part of my life. I'd buried it for so long, it would be ridiculous to develop some weird obsession with it now. Maybe I'd get closure, as Roberta would say. Usually followed by me taking the piss out of her in a cheesy American accent.

I counted down the kilometres. Forty-five, twenty-one, twelve. Then I was there, driving through the little streets, past the shops that made up Italian life. The deli with its piles of huge round cheeses. The baker's stuffed with saucer-shaped focaccia. The *tabacchi* with its bus tickets, stamps and fags.

I took a random road out of town, picking up a sign for Capo Testa. 'Capo' had to mean the end of something. How fitting. I drove towards the lighthouse. I got out and sucked in a great lungful of fresh air, struck by the smell of wild mint. Down below, the rocks were surrounded by water so clear you could never say to the kids 'Just do a wee in the sea' again. Immi would have loved finding the shapes of turtles and lions in the huge smooth lumps of grey granite. I almost didn't want to look across the waves. Xavi could be there. Just ten miles away. A little ferry boat made white tracks across the sea, Corsica-bound.

I found a flat rock to sit on. I texted Roberta to let her know I'd managed to make it here and that I wished she was with me to do a Thelma and Louise. She'd borne the brunt of my frustration with Jonathan's lack of enthusiasm for me joining him in Sardinia, which even I, queen of the non-apology, recognised as unfair.

The sun moved. A couple of hours passed and the ferry trundled back, a tiny dot that grew and grew until I could make out the people on deck. I gazed at the faces turned towards Sardinia and the ones still looking back to Corsica. Down there was a microcosm of feelings. Someone jiggling about impatiently, desperate for the ferry to dock to breathe in a lover. Someone ripped apart by a goodbye. Someone eager to explore Sardinia for the first time, someone jaded by the been-there, done-that. I lay on my back, a gentle sun on my face, fat clouds puffing past overhead.

Where was Xavi? Was he there, across the water?

I sat up and strained my eyes over the rocky outline of Corsica in the distance. After all these years, my yearning to see Xavi had clawed itself out of the deep place where I'd tried to put him to rest. The early evening breeze nipped at my bare arms. I stood up, brushing the dust from my jeans. Six o'clock. Still no word from Jonathan.

I lifted my hand in a silent goodbye.

Roberta

The day I started at Mrs Goodman's coincided with a letter from Scott's solicitor. I assumed it was a confirmation of the holiday schedule I'd agreed, allowing Alicia to go to Australia for one month in the summer while Scott supervised his mother's recovery. I scanned it on my way to the car. The words 'Reduction in monthly payments' leapt off the page. I put down my bag of fabrics and re-read the letter.

Now he was a 'full-time carer to his infirm and elderly mother', he'd scaled back on his business commitments and could only afford half of the sum originally agreed. A rush of panic shot through me. There was no way Scott was a full-time carer. It would be a miracle if he'd turned up with a bunch of garage flowers and a newspaper. No. He wanted to get his own back on me for not going with him. I knew he'd have all his little tricks ring-fenced. I could bankrupt myself trying to prove he was hiding money from me. The letter shook in my hands. I'd never be able to keep my house if I couldn't make up the shortfall. I couldn't uproot Alicia again. With Scott darting from continent to continent, I had to give her some stability.

Tears of self-pity gushed out of me as I drove to Mrs

Goodman's. I sat trying to stem the flow a little way from her house, dabbing powder on my flushed cheeks. I was twenty minutes late already.

I needed this job like never before.

Mrs Goodman was old-school, her bearing pernickety and pinched. I was still struggling to keep my breathing even as I sat down at the kitchen table with my samples, muttering apologies about being late.

She sat there tutting. 'I know you young ones don't have the same work ethic that we had. I dare say you find it terribly old-fashioned, but I find it simple courtesy not to keep people hanging around.'

I couldn't remember being told off for my manners in my whole life. I wanted to tell her that in the scheme of things, the demise of her net curtains and embossed wallpaper could wait. I swallowed hard, smoothed out some drawings and unfolded a swatch of fabrics, steely greys with some flashes of turquoise and green. I held them against my favourite colour of the moment, French Grey. 'I don't know whether you like this or not, but maybe we can consider it as a background for a bright contrasting colour?'

Mrs Goodman looked nonplussed. I ploughed on, trying not to sniff. 'It can look very sophisticated. We can bring in other hues with cushions and rugs.'

She was still looking at me as though I was putting forward a plan for a psychedelic seventies room. 'Of course, if I've misunderstood your brief, we can discuss other things.' I bent down to pull out another mood board. 'Cream is a slightly warmer option, but a touch less modern in my view.' My voice was coming out in desperate bursts. I couldn't separate my colour charts and they scattered all over the lino floor.

Mrs Goodman sat back in her chair. 'What on earth is going on?'

I started scrabbling at my charts. 'Have I got it all wrong? I was sure we discussed neutrals at our first meeting?'

'I don't mean the blessed paint colours. You're all over the place. Is it nerves? You've done this job before, I take it?'

'I'm sorry. I had some bad news this morning. I'm fine.' But as I vocalised the 'n' in 'fine' I dissolved, tears tumbling onto my carefully selected fabrics. The consummate professional, bawling her eyes out at her first proper commission. I'd been a monumental failure when I could least afford it. Scott was right. I was pathetic. Who *would* employ me?

Through my tears I was braced for a tirade. Mrs Goodman surprised me by putting her hand on my arm.

'Is it a man, dear?'

I nodded.

'Don't let the bastards get you down.'

I felt a visceral jolt at the word 'bastards'. Mrs Goodman looked like she didn't know anything stronger than 'blast'. 'I'm so sorry about all this. I can do this job, really I can . . .' Before I knew it, I was telling her the whole sorry story.

She nodded, interjecting with the odd 'cunning bugger' now and again.

When I finished, she said, 'Don't let yourself be bullied. My Sidney was a bully. Charming to all and sundry. Everyone thought he was such a lovely man except his sister, who knew better. I was too weak to leave him.'

'You sounded like you really miss him.'

'Of course I miss him. We were married for forty-eight years. But I tell you something . . .' She leaned forward. 'He was a nasty piece of knitting. It's just that in my day, it was shameful to get divorced. No one did that. You'd be ostracised. We all put on our best face and counted ourselves lucky if we had a husband to bring home decent housekeeping. But you, you're young. You've got another chance to get it right.'

I didn't think I would ever get it right, but the mere fact that someone on this earth thought I might stopped my hiccupping. I accepted the cup of Earl Grey she offered and felt the tension in me subside.

She stood up. 'Come with me.' I followed her through to the drawing room. 'See this suite? I wanted leather because we had a golden retriever at the time – Ruffles. She was a lovely dog.'

Mrs Goodman paused for a moment, fiddling with her sapphire earring. 'She moulted everywhere. I thought leather would be cleaner. But no, Sidney wanted this dark blue Dralon. Totally impractical, see every long white hair on it and my life, he didn't like it if everywhere wasn't shining like a new pin. I didn't often argue with him, especially not in public. But because the saleswoman in the shop was on my side, he was put out. We left without buying anything. The next day, when I was out shopping, he took the dog for a walk and she 'got lost'. I never saw Ruffles again but two weeks later, the Dralon suite turned up.'

I turned to Mrs Goodman. 'Then I think it's time to get rid of it now.'

She clapped her hands. 'I'll tell you what I always disliked greatly, those horrible decanters on the mantelpiece. I hated Sidney when he'd been drinking whisky.'

She pursed her lips as though she'd said too much.

Soon we were tucking the detested decanters into a cardboard box. I had a vicarious sense of rebellion. Mrs Goodman pointed at the little cocktail cabinet in the corner. 'That's going. Could I have a cream leather suite and pale wooden tables? Would that be over the top?'

'Not at all.' I had so many ideas about possibilities, I couldn't wait to get started. 'A big mirror over the fireplace. Is it a working fireplace? Could we take out the gas fire? Maybe some pale French furniture, a little ornate.'

Mrs Goodman stood with her hands on her hips. 'French. Sidney hated the French. *C'est parfait*!' She picked up a figurine of an Edwardian lady. 'Sidney used to buy me a figurine for every birthday and Christmas. I hated them all. Silly little ladies in fancy clothes, no doubt waiting hand and foot on a man.' She turned to me. 'Shall we?'

Before the day was over, we'd packed the tasselled cushions into bin bags, dumped the net curtains, rolled up the flowery rug and arranged for the council to collect the sofa and armchairs the following day. Mrs Goodman was fidgety with excitement, especially after pouring us both a sherry.

'I feel like I'm starting a new life. Fancy that. I'm seventy this year. Maybe I'll meet someone nice.' She flicked her head back in a flirtatious manner. 'Don't you give up, dear. You've got your whole life ahead of you. That husband of yours will rue the day he treated you like dirt.'

If I made a success of my business, I hoped he'd just become irrelevant.

Octavia

Jonathan was awake before me, humming in the shower by the time I opened my eyes. I'd been asleep before he came back the previous night. I pushed myself up onto my elbows when he appeared, towel round his waist.

'Hi there. How did you get on yesterday? Sorry I didn't make it for dinner, had a right palaver at work. I'm beginning to think they save up all the problems for my arrival.'

For a man who must have been going boss-eyed over his computers late into the night, he was remarkably jolly.

'It didn't matter. I had a nice drive up the coast. Dinner was a bit odd on my own.' I wanted to shake him, to tell him to get his nose out of work and give me a bit of attention. I couldn't find the words. I never had that problem normally. This meek wife as an appendage to the important husband/ businessman/the one everyone relied on almost frightened me. Who, what, when and where was my role. Everyone else just fell in.

Usually.

Jonathan seemed to speed up his shirt-buttoning process. 'I told you I wouldn't be around much.'

'I didn't realise not much would mean not at all.' I tried

for levity but my voice caught. 'Shall I sort out somewhere to eat tonight? Or do you want to meet for lunch? I drove past a fantastic bakery near your office. I could get a couple of focaccias.'

'Lunch?' Jonathan sounded as though I'd suggested bunking off for a lobster platter and a dozen oysters. I flumped back onto the pillow. 'Forget it. I'll catch up with you later.'

He stood fiddling with the buttons on his cuffs. 'I'm sorry. I knew that trying to mix my work with a holiday would be a mistake. You wanted to come so badly. I thought you liked exploring on your own.'

'I'd like to think we could grab a sandwich together.' As I said it, I knew it was futile.

He puckered his lips and leant over without quite managing to make contact with my cheek. 'I'll see what I can do. Have a great day.'

Impotence raged through me. One bloody shared plate of spaghetti plus the odd bottle of Prosecco. Was that so much to ask? No kids. A hotel room where we could shag away without Immi coming in. What more did the man want? One thing was certain, hanging around looking needy wouldn't bring him rushing. Well, I wasn't going to squander my opportunity to explore – I'd been dreaming about it for long enough. I'd take myself off for a night. It would still leave us three evenings together. I flicked through my guidebook, made a quick phone call to a hotel, then wrote Jonathan a note saying I wouldn't be back until tomorrow. Ha. See how that suited him. With a sense of regaining control, I headed down to the car.

I drove. This time with no hesitation. Just straight to Santa Teresa di Gallura, onto the eleven o'clock ferry for Corsica and off an hour later in Bonifacio.

Out of the port, I only had one destination in mind: Cocciu, Xavi's village. As I drove, flashes of home crowded in, worry about whether my mother would remember to rub E45 into the eczema patches on the backs of Polly's knees or tell Charlie to clean his braces properly. Then a hillside full of poppies, the way the sun caught the sea, the scent of wild thyme carried on the spring air would catapult me back to Corsica and I'd press a bit harder on the accelerator.

I was light-headed, as though I'd drunk lots of black coffee on an empty stomach. I was so rarely on my own that I kept glancing in the rear-view mirror to see if the kids were all right. A tiny wisp of freedom was spiralling up inside. The sort of freedom I'd felt nineteen years ago when I'd walked off the ferry from Marseilles with a suitcase strapped onto a pair of wheels with unreliable elastics and a determination to make the most of my teaching placement abroad before a career sucked me onto the work conveyor belt.

Lorries kept roaring up behind me, then overtaking on blind corners, practically squeezing my Fiat into the cliff as they coughed past. Occasionally I'd hear the throttle of a motorbike and some shiny beast would rev by, almost horizontal round the bends. I didn't see a single rider without a helmet. Clearly, the road safety rules had tightened since Xavi and I used to bomb down to the beach, helmets in the crooks of our elbows, invincible as only the young are.

I remembered the village as foreboding. Tall granite buildings, five or six storeys high, built straight into the rock. But as Cocciu came into view, with the May sun glowing behind the houses, it reminded me more of the Tuscan hill towns Jonathan and I had toured on our honeymoon.

My stomach was churning as I drove over the bridge on the outskirts of the village. Maybe his house wouldn't even be there. It was. That was his house, or rather, his parents' house, right there. They were probably all still living under one roof with his old trout of a mother ruling the roost. I almost didn't look, couldn't look.

Maybe I wouldn't recognise him.

What if he was standing there with a little daughter, his own Mediterranean version of Immi? Or maybe even a teen-ager, born soon after we split up, when I thought I would wake up with a shadow over me for the rest of my life. When I sat stubborn but broken-hearted, gazing at the map of the world, wondering where he was and who he was loving. Mourning the children we'd dreamed of taking island-hopping in Asia, all brown feet and tie-dye sarongs.

I breathed out. No one there. Not even the witch mother, if she was still alive. My heart slowed back to a normal beat. The chestnut tree we'd planted for his parents' wedding anniversary was full of blossom. No sign of kids' bikes or slides. For one mad moment, I considered knocking on the door. What would I say? 'Surprise!' My stomach dipped at the thought of some stick-thin wife opening the door, blank-faced and pouting. I dismissed the idea as unadulterated lunacy and sped on, straightening up behind the wheel as the house faded from view.

I drove up the hill, winding past the school where I'd taught English in my third year at university. The gates were still green. Before I'd met Xavi, they'd clanged behind me, leaving me to lonely weekends in the dark boarding house after all the pupils had disappeared back to their far-flung villages. I passed the tennis courts, scanning for those broad shoulders, a serve with a funny flick at the end. I had to remind myself not to search for a twenty-five-year-old, bouncing on the spot with pent-up energy. There was no one remotely near the age of, what, forty-two? Forty-three? Yes, forty-three on 8 May. Tomorrow, in fact. After all these years I remembered it as clearly as my own birthday.

I grinned as I remembered what I'd done for his birthday when he was twenty-three. Jonathan would be so shocked.

My hotel, San Larenzu, was just beyond. Still grey rock

but new, nearly pretty by the dour fortress standards of Corsican villages. Even now, everywhere looked ready to repel the marauding Genovese with boiling oil rather than to welcome tourists.

The girl behind the desk followed the same rule. Polite, efficient but wary, her heavy-set features remaining sullen. I questioned her about mealtimes, feeling something shift as the French I gabbled out effortlessly all those years ago rose to the occasion. I didn't sound like me. I sounded confident, blasé, as though my world was one of hotel liaisons, aperitifs in bars and skinny-dipping in a midnight sea. She pointed to a corridor and I headed off to my room, impatient to be walking those cobbled alleyways. I threw the suitcase on the bed and glanced out of the window. I didn't remember all those mountains.

Travel was wasted on the young. Xavi had blotted out the landscape of an entire island.

I changed into what Roberta called my 'hippie top', jewel blue and red. My reflection in the mirror grabbed back the little burst of confidence. Xavi wouldn't recognise me even if I did bump into him. My hair was much shorter now, and curlier. It went curly when I was pregnant with Charlie and never straightened out again. Eyes the same. Bit wrinkly at the edges. Of course, I didn't need glasses to read then. Cleavage. Ugh. Crinkled like a piece of corrugated cardboard. No, I didn't need a disguise. Age was my disguise. I put on my sun hat anyway.

Less *Room with a View* and more *Carry On Corsica*.

Back in the main square, I picked a seat in the café on the sunny side. Every head with curly black hair drew my attention. Maybe he was bald now. Motorbikes roared in and out of the piazza, my mind – against all logic – searching for a bright red Kawasaki. Memories were crowding in until they were criss-crossing over each other. Playing belote in

242

the bar opposite. Tucking our hands into each other's pockets to keep warm during the solemn Easter parade.

The past was multi-coloured, so vivid that it was as though I'd been living my life in beige ever since. I was too restless for café-sitting. I stood up, torn between dashing back to safety and finishing what I'd started. I'd told myself it was me I'd come to find.

But it was him.

I'd no proof he was even in Corsica, let alone Cocciu. If I did find him, what then? A dowdy middle-aged woman chasing an eighteen-year-old dream in which even the best outcome would be a nightmare. I defaulted to what I told the children when they were panicking. 'Let's deal with what is, not what if.'

I picked a direction at random. It was early in the year for tourists. People were staring. Every face was a face I thought I recognised, aged by two decades like a police photofit – kids I'd taught at the lycée, checkout girls, waitresses – now women in their thirties. There were many more shops now – even an internet café right next to the temperamental phone box where I'd stood shovelling in five-franc pieces to hear my Mum's voice straining out that Dad had had a funny turn.

I ran away from the memory, tearing off down some stone steps that were so deep and steep I threatened to crack my coccyx at any moment. At the bottom was a square with an art gallery in the corner. That was new. Among the bright canvases of sunflowers and poppies in the window was a huge picture of a little cove, typically Corsican with translucent water, pale sand and the ubiquitous grey rocks. It was the beach shack that drew my attention. Pietru's bar. Wine barrels for tables, scruffy thatched roof, old surfboards framing the door. I stared and stared. It was there that Xavi and I picked up a couple of beers and lay on the sand, still warm from the sun, watching the shooting stars flinging around the August sky. There that I gave him my heart and body so completely that I never quite got them back again.

I wanted that picture.

I started to push the door open, suddenly registering the name on the frosted glass as the bell jangled. Jean-Franc Santoni. Xavi's little brother. Just twelve years old last time I saw him. I darted round the corner out of sight, every nerve in my body pogoing away.

If I wanted to know where Xavi was, if I really, really wanted to know where he was, the answers were just next door.

Roberta

Alicia pitted herself against me when I stuck to my insistence that she was tested for STDs. But the spectre of chlamydia, gonorrhoea or worse transformed me into a parent who couldn't be won round. We fought, Alicia hurling insults about my failure to supervise her, to be someone to look up to. Each barb burrowed deep, threatening to unseat my determination. I dug my heels in; I'd messed up my own life, but I was going to sort out Alicia's. I chose a private clinic in London to minimise the chances of bumping into anyone we knew.

On Friday morning when Alicia and I left for the clinic, I could barely keep a piece of toast down. I'd texted Octavia, the only person I'd told that we were going. Even though she was on holiday, she'd texted back immediately.

Hope it all goes well. I know you were the Ice Maiden but don't forget that I'm an old hand at the morning-after pill, crabs and shagging men I wouldn't want to have a conversation with, so Alicia has got nothing to be ashamed of.

I longed to be young again. Even just to turn the clock back by a few months. Though I was glad I didn't have to share this particular episode with Jake.

When we got to the clinic I don't know who was more mortified – me or Alicia – as we stood before a very nice but very fat nurse. It never ceased to amaze me how many health-care practitioners were capable of single-handedly blocking corridors. Then again, she was no doubt struggling to keep her mouth closed at the thought that I was such an unfit mother that my daughter was having sex before she was allowed to drink in a pub.

I didn't want to be the parent who hadn't done enough.

I offered to go in with Alicia but the nurse practically shooed me out. I guess she figured that if Alicia was old enough to have sex, she was old enough to learn about the grown-up world of smears, scrapes and swabs. I resigned myself to wandering about the waiting room reading uplifting posters about herpes, chlamydia and HIV. Those three bald capitals, HIV, made something go weak at the back of my knee.

I would never forgive myself. Never.

Never mind that Mrs Goodman was so impressed with what I'd accomplished so far. Never mind that the hotel by the park had asked me to advise them on their new café area. The most important job I'd ever had was to steer my daughter to safe shores, and I'd failed. Turned the boat over and let her drown. If I deserved a second chance in life, now would be an excellent time to deliver.

The nurse beckoned me in with an 'All finished'.

'So what happens now?'

The nurse outlined how she would email the results, which sent a big rush of panic through me in case Scott could somehow hack into my computer. Any interaction I had with him still required me to gather my stomach before I clicked open his emails or answered his call. 'Could I phone for the results instead?'

The nurse delivered the face of someone who'd seen items

stuck in orifices they had no business to be in and still managed not to look shocked. I consoled myself that underage sex probably didn't even register on the scale. 'No problem. Results take a few days. Give me a ring after four o'clock on Monday.'

I handed her a pile of cash. If there was ever a reason for Scott to subpoena my bank accounts, he wasn't going to find a payment to a clinic that he could connect to vaginal swabs for his underage daughter.

No doubt about it. I'd failed Alicia. It wouldn't happen again.

Octavia

I dashed down the nearest alleyway, glad of the dark shadows. Out of the spring sunshine I shivered, tugging my thin cardigan around me. I'd only left Jonathan that morning and I was already getting myself into trouble. I ran my hand over the rough granite and looked at the two houses rising several storeys up only a few feet apart. You could jump across the alley from one window to another. Maybe Corsican mothers spent their lives saying, 'No jumping out of the window' instead of 'Stop at the zebra crossing'. Charlie, Polly and Immi seemed a long way away. I had to keep reminding myself that I had three children. Being in Cocciu somehow stripped away the years. I kept looking down expecting to see the white cropped trousers with a watermelon pattern I'd bought at the market for a handful of coins.

I missed those big five-franc pieces with '*Liberté, Égalité, Fraternité*' round the edge. Euros didn't carry the same sense of place, of history. Xavi had sawn one in half and given me the piece with *Liberté* on it – 'To remind you that you are free.' In the event, my dad dying had ended my freedom, plunging me into my first taste of responsibility. I threw my matching half of the coin into a skip the day after we buried him.

Xavi loved '*liberté*' more than he loved me.

When I needed him, he needed open roads and big skies, to convert our daydreams into real adventures. While he'd stuck to our plan of travelling to New Zealand, I'd stayed at home, stunned and bereft, trying to understand a world where my dad would never again look at Roberta and me in our ripped jeans and say, 'Lord help those lads'.

Xavi was probably dancing a haka while I lay on the floor curled up with the dog, struggling to get my head round a new reality where Dad's unconditional love – the sort that meant he smiled with his eyes even when he was giving me a right old rollicking – had gone forever. My own journey took place within the four walls of my room. Agonising, desperate and angry. Heartbreak just hitched a ride.

A young cat miaowing round my legs pulled me back from feelings that were still so jagged and raw they laughed in the face of the old cliché that 'Time is a great healer'. How much time? How much bloody time?

I shouldn't have come here.

After eighteen years of clamping down the lid of Pandora's box with a pile of concrete blocks, a couple of hours in Cocciu and I was dizzy with loss and betrayal. Roberta called it unresolved grief but I thought that was self-help bollocks. I should have had a good old ding-dong with Xavi when Dad died instead of cutting him out of my life and never speaking to him again.

I bent down to stroke the cat. I was just thinking what a pretty face it had when it lashed out and bit my hand. I shooed it away. Bloody Corsicans. Even the cats were two-faced. I walked back round the corner to the art gallery, telling myself that I was going to leave well alone. The other me, the me governing my feet and hand movements, put one flip-flop in front of the other and lifted my hand onto the art gallery door handle.

Jean-Franc. I knew him immediately. He was Xavi, though not as good-looking. Thinner, same features but arranged slightly closer together to less dramatic effect. Everything about Xavi was a statement. Big broad shoulders. Wide-spaced eyes with lashes you could sweep the floor with. A rumble of a laugh. And vision. There was nothing that he, we, couldn't do. He made island-hopping round Thailand sound like a train trip to Margate.

I waited for Jean-Franc to recognise me, but not a flicker, simply a polite 'Bonjour.' I did that awkward 'just looking' gesture and he shrugged, a half-smile so like Xavi that the hairs stood up on my arms. I wandered among the paintings. Every juniper tree clinging to a rocky outcrop, every black-capped fisherman holding sea urchins pulled me back, back to when I was happy, when the world seemed full of possibilities, when I hadn't taken a single decision to screw up the rest of my life. I wanted to sit on the leather stool in the corner, put my head between my knees and tantrum over my lost dreams, my lack of energy for the new and novel. I'd let stodge and mediocrity invade every corner of my life.

Jean-Franc stepped out from behind the counter. Part of me wanted to do some mad long-lost lover thing, demand to know where Xavi was, beg Jean-Franc to phone him, organise a meeting, whatever it took, to shake off this ivy-spread of unease. Maybe if I knew he was married with children, I could poke him back into the recesses of my mind, to be thought about at odd moments with affection rather than gnaw away at me centre-stage.

Even if I did see him, even if he was free, what then?

I'd never leave the children. I couldn't bear not to smooth Immi's hair before she went to bed, miss out on who did

250

what in Polly's day, not be around when Charlie came in, saying 'Now, don't start shouting, Mum, but . . .'

Out of the corner of my eye, I saw Jean-Franc approaching. I smiled at him and slipped out into a little courtyard where paintings were stacked against the wall and sculptures of boats, shells and mermaids were scattered among little metal tables.

'If you like to sit to look at the art, I can bring coffee.' His English was heavily accented, though the deep timbre was all Xavi's.

Before my logical mind could get a grip, I was nodding. I chose a chair in the sunshine. The burgeoning heat warmed my face. I lay back, flexing my neck from side to side, hearing the muscles cracking as I stretched. Even that old-lady sound reminded me of Xavi and how we sometimes pulled muscles trying out ridiculous sexual positions involving limbs where nature didn't intend them to be. I'd be lucky not to seize up tying my shoelaces now. I sat up straight when I heard Jean-Franc. He put down my coffee.

'So, you are on holiday? It's early, too cold now.'

'My husband is working in Sardinia, so I'm exploring.'

There. Jonathan was out there, alive and kicking, an articulated barrier to copping off with Jean-Franc's brother.

'Do you like Corsica?'

'I love Corsica.'

I must have sounded a bit more enthusiastic than the average punter because Jean-Franc's eyes shot open in surprise.

'Well, what I've seen so far, anyway. The scenery is absolutely wonderful.' I pointed to a painting of a beach. 'Is that near here?'

'Yes, Propriano. But I paint this from an old photograph, from when I was young. Now is lots of hotels and much more tourists. I prefer it when we have less people coming, but of course now is better for business.'

'I love your landscape paintings. The one of the beach bar in the window is fantastic.'

Jean-Franc smiled and a memory of Xavi flickered in and danced off again. I wanted to lie down somewhere with ice on my head. It was like watching split-screen TV. Images of Xavi removing the top of a beer with a rock, making coffee in the caravan, dragging the windsurf down to the water, competed with my middle-aged conversation with a guy who probably thought I looked like his mother.

Though actually I didn't look like his mother. His mother had skin like a saddlebag, hair so black it was almost blue, and a pair of bushy eyebrows able to convey enormous disapproval about her son's dalliance with a foreigner. The single greatest joy of splitting up with Xavi had to be missing out on eighteen years of her sticking her hands in her housecoat and sniffing every time we walked past giggling about our plans to run a youth hostel in New Zealand.

Jean-Franc walked to the other side of the courtyard and riffled through a pile of paintings. 'I like to paint people the best. Is easy to make life in the eyes and mouth.'

He showed me one of a girl leaning against a round Genovese tower, one of the many sixteenth-century garrisons dotted around the Corsican coast. She was intent on a dragonfly, her concentration and wonder jumping off the canvas.

'This is at Campomoro. My daughter.'

'Your daughter?' Jean-Franc was a kid. In my mind, he was still that little boy, sitting on our caravan steps, begging Xavi to take him out in the fishing boat. Now he'd had kids of his own. I felt one hundred and five. 'She's lovely. How old is she?'

'In this painting, about six. But thirteen now.'

'Thirteen!'

Jesus. Jean-Franc must have been having sex before he'd learnt to spell condom.

'I've got two daughters younger than that. You must have been a kid yourself.' In a distant corner of my mind, I patted myself on the back. Children acknowledged and talked about.

He frowned. 'I was seventeen.'

'Your mum must have gone mad. Did you marry your daughter's mother?' I forgot I was a polite Englishwoman Jean-Franc had never met before.

His head snapped round. Family business was nobody's business in Corsica. He ignored the question. The Santonis were all the same. They all had this fantastic scowl that rolled across their foreheads and scrunched up their eyebrows. I bet the dragon mother had done the scowl to end all scowls when Jean-Franc brought that happy bit of news home. At least the foreigner didn't get up the duff and steal her son away. Jean-Franc had been such a sweet twelve-year-old. To be fair, after the cinema once a week and a *café au lait*, there wasn't much left to do in Cocciu apart from shag like rabbits.

Jean-Franc snatched up his paintings. I should tell him who I was. He didn't deserve to be on the wrong end of my detective work, deceitful and cunning. As a child, Jean-Franc adored me, teasing me for my accent, my complete failure to pronounce the guttural French 'r'. In the end though, they were a bunch of tribal island warriors, the Santonis. Jean-Franc would chase anything that threatened the stability of his family down a dark alley and trap it there. They all would.

Especially anyone who encouraged Xavi away from Corsica.

I should just say, 'It's me. Tavy.' But I needed to know more, needed to stop him walking away. I leaned forward and pointed to a painting at his side. 'What about that one?' I saw him pause, no doubt hovering between the prospect of making a sale and ejecting the rude tourist. Reluctantly, he turned it round to show me.

'I painted this at Christmas.' His voice was guarded, unfriendly. Suddenly that face I'd known so well and loved so much

253

was right there in front of me. I made a squeak like I did when Polly hid by the bathroom door and jumped out on me. I coughed and took a swig of coffee. Jean-Franc frowned and stepped back, as though I might suddenly strip off all my clothes and start running amok. I cleared my throat.

I had to hand it to Jean-Franc, he had captured Xavi's eyes, watchful but always ready to light up. Xavi delighted in so many things. Heart-shaped stones we lined up along our caravan windowsill. Perfect water-skiing weather. Fish we caught, then grilled over a fire. Physically he didn't look that different. A few grey streaks in his curls. Sun-etched around the eyes. He'd lost that edgy leanness that made him look as though he was always about to dart off somewhere else. I swallowed. 'That's a great picture. Is he a friend of yours?'

A glimmer of a smile at the compliment. Jean-Franc shook his head. 'No, my brother.'

I waited. My brother what? My brother who lives in Ulan Bator? In Marseilles? In Sydney? My brother who was madly in love with an English girl and never recovered? Never let it be said that the Santoni family were a garrulous bunch. Blood, stone and all that. I was going to have to look nosey.

'Does he live in Cocciu?'

'No. London.'

'London? London in England?' My knee banged the table and made the coffee cup rattle. If he lived in south London, he could be less than an hour away from my home in Surrey.

'Corsicans do sometimes get on planes.'

He stared at me as though I was stupid. He didn't quite whip the painting away but he put it back against the tree in a way that meant our conversation was over. I wanted to ask more but Jean-Franc took my coffee cup and marched back to the till.

Xavi was in London.

No wonder I'd never found him. It never occurred to me that he could be in England. How long had he been there? I could have bumped into him on the Tube. Why England? Too much time had passed for Xavi being in England to have anything to do with me. Perhaps he was living in a converted warehouse in the East End stuffed with wooden carvings and Indonesian batik. With an exotic wife and free-spirited children.

Better not to know.

I pulled out a bunch of euros and picked up Xavi's portrait. I asked Jean-Franc to wrap it so I could pretend to Jonathan it was a present for Roberta. Even if I kept it in the attic, this Xavi at least was coming home with me.

Roberta

Alicia seemed to forget all about the big black cloud hanging over us the second she was out of the clinic. Her main comment about the whole experience was what a 'mahoosive' the nurse was. I, on the other hand, spent the day in a worried fog about whether Alicia would get the all-clear, obliterating my ability to concentrate on anything else. So in the evening, when Alicia burst through the door with Connor and asked me what I was wearing to the tennis club barbecue, I took a moment to grasp what she meant.

'Barbecue?'

'Mum, you know, you said you'd come and meet Connor's mum and dad tonight. What's the matter with you?'

Connor's presence probably saved Alicia. To her, there'd been a blip in her young life, something to get through and wipe from her memory. I was quite sure that when I died, 'daughter's early sexual experimentation' would be etched on my heart. I struggled to keep my voice steady.

'Sorry. I've had a lot on my mind. What time does it start?'

'Six o'clock. You're not going in that stripy shirt, are you?'

Connor smiled and said, 'Leave your mum alone. She looks

nice. I wish my mum was more like you, Mrs Green. My dad always says she gets dressed in the dark.'

'Thank you, Connor. I'm sure she has many other qualities to compensate. I shall do my best not to show you up, Alicia.'

I walked to the tennis club alongside Alicia and Connor with that familiar out-of-step feeling. Even my daughter was part of the Noah's Ark tribe, the people who didn't ever have to wonder where they would stand or who they would talk to at any social gathering because they'd brought their own partner. I felt as though all the people milling around the clubhouse were looking at me with pity because I had to tag along with my teenage daughter in order to have a ghost of a social life.

Connor spotted his parents and waved them over. I could see what his father meant. His mother was ruddy-faced, a stranger to foundation, wearing trousers that were too short and a high-necked jumper that did nothing for her sagging breasts.

She held out a hand that was rough to the touch. 'Lovely to meet you. I'm Catherine. Your daughter is absolutely delightful, a wonderful girl.'

I wanted to hug her for that, though she might have changed her mind if she knew where we'd been that morning. Catherine had a natural warmth, a friendliness, which made me feel mean for noticing her jumper. The relaxed way she joked with her husband, Stuart, a tall, lean man with a big shock of blonde hair like Connor's, made me wonder how I'd survived all those years with Scott, trying to anticipate which day he'd decide to take a flippant remark the wrong way.

Even when she said, 'Darling, manners, go and get Roberta a drink,' he apologised and asked me what I'd like. I could never ask Scott to do anything, however innocuous, and be sure he wouldn't launch into his 'What did your last slave die of?' routine.

We were just moving towards the tables and chairs when Connor grabbed the arm of another teenager in a baseball cap and did that funny-fist handshake that made me feel ancient.

'Angus, mate. You won the league. Well done.'

Catherine joined in. 'That's brilliant. Wimbledon next?'

I stood on the periphery, not wanting to cramp their style, while Connor introduced Alicia to his friend. Connor's fabulous manners didn't allow for that. 'This is Alicia's mother.'

I found myself shaking the hand of a young man with huge, blue eyes and a confident, open smile.

I tried to puzzle out why Angus looked familiar, then wished I hadn't. Bare breasts on Jake's sofa. I gasped and contributed a significant shot of heat to global warming. I willed him not to recognise me.

'Didn't you use to go out with my dad?'

I felt the heat creep up my neck, though Angus seemed amused. 'Yes, I did.' I tried not to look at Catherine or Stuart. 'How is he?'

'All right. Working hard. He said he might come along later.'

I wished that I'd worn something a bit more stylish than jeans and a shirt. I stopped myself from saying, 'What time?' and concentrated on stabilising my legs. I managed a neutral-sounding 'Good' before another boy clapped Angus on the back, a discussion about a tennis holiday in La Manga ensued and I lost my audience.

Alicia's whole body was a big question mark. I'd wanted to wait until I was sure of Jake to tell her about him and, of course, it had all imploded before I'd had a chance. Catherine rescued me by saying, 'Shall we go and find a table?' Every few paces she stopped to greet someone. She reminded me of Octavia, asking about holidays, children and even guinea pigs. I stood next to her trying to block out the excitement coursing through my body. I found company with a springer spaniel, which gave me an excuse to bend down and ignore other people without looking unfriendly.

When we were far enough away from Alicia and Connor, Catherine said, 'Horrendous coming to these dos on your own. You're very brave. I'd been divorced for several years before I met Stuart. I used to hide at home in my dressing gown. Stuart was my lodger while he worked as an engineer at Gatwick so I was lucky to meet him.'

Such a candid admission took me back. I was so sure everyone was looking down at me from their happy marriages – or worse, avoiding me in case I infected them with 'relationship disease'. I found it hard to accept that statistically one in three people would be like me. Scott had isolated me from my friends so well over the years that confiding in people didn't come easily. I wanted to blurt out what a monumental mess I'd made of everything but I confined myself to saying, 'I'm certainly finding it a challenge.'

That and not running around the crowd searching for Jake.

On the edge of my vision, I'd catch sight of a broad shoulder, short sandy hair, a bright blue polo shirt or any of the hundreds of details that made up Jake and swing round, heart beating. I kept pushing hope down, telling myself he wouldn't speak to me anyway, or that he might humiliate me.

I knew he wouldn't.

Finally we found a table and Stuart arrived with a bottle of Pinot Grigio. I chatted away, sipping my wine, trying not to make it obvious that I was scanning the crowds. As time and wine wore on, I became aware of a deflated feeling overtaking me. He wasn't going to come. I reminded myself that the presence or absence of men did not govern the life of the 'new' Roberta. Very quietly I said, 'No one can make you happy, only you can make you happy.'

I could hear Octavia cackling in my mind. 'New Age wankery! American shit! Give me money and a round-the-world plane ticket, then you'll see how happy I am.'

But I wasn't like Octavia.

Stuart and Catherine suggested getting some food. I clung on to my wine glass for something to do with my hands. As we walked towards the barbecue, I felt like the only singleton in the world. Women were picking bits of fluff from their men's jackets, men were pulling out chairs for their women, arms were casually flung around shoulders. My throat was tightening. Not the time or place to feel sorry for myself.

I'd just reached the steps by the barbecue area when the springer spaniel puppy came charging past me, knocking me off balance. I fell over with the effort of not squashing the dog and smashed my wine glass, gashing open my palm. My last thought before I came over queasy was how furious Alicia would be with me for making a spectacle of myself.

I'd had many years of practice at sitting down on the floor before I fainted. I put my head between my knees to stop the spinning before I blacked out. Blood was dripping from my hand and splattering on the steps. I fumbled for tissues in my handbag with my good hand. I heard the clicking of heels and the dull thump of trainers towards me, plus the buzz of panicking voices, the words blurring as I concentrated on stilling the whirling sensation wrenching at my head and stomach.

'Let me look at that.'

I had my face in the crook of my elbow, trying to stop the nausea. 'Sorry. I can't stand the sight of blood.'

I unfurled my palm. Strong, gentle hands straightened out each finger.

I could see a pair of Timberland boots when I looked down.

He shouted for someone to get the first aid kit. 'That's quite a deep cut. There's still a shard of glass in it.'

I knew that West Country accent. Before I could say anything, I threw up, all down my shirt.

Octavia

My first instinct had been to get the hell out of Corsica with all its scratchy old memories taking me to places I shouldn't go. Cocciu had suddenly felt suffocating with its imposing buildings, rising up and crowding round to keep outsiders at bay. Maybe I'd imagined that I was going to find Xavi staring out to sea over the Golfe du Valinco, willing me to pop up like a rotund mermaid. In fact, he was probably shopping for an organic brunch somewhere bohemian like Stoke Newington. I needed to stop my middle-aged moping and get back to my husband.

I called Jonathan on his mobile. It was madness to stay in a different hotel on a different island when we had so much to sort out. If I hurried, I could still make the last ferry back to Sardinia. Maybe we could find a little trattoria, share some pasta, talk. Talk about us, if we could find 'us'. A tall order when I was having difficulty locating myself.

I tried to work out when my marriage had gone from something stable that just 'was', to something off-kilter, as though I was struggling to stand on a lilo in the middle of a lake.

It was probably all in my head. Images of me roaring back

262

to Sardinia, my silly sortie to Corsica forgotten, no harm done, Jonathan walking out of the office and saying, 'Sorry, guys, I'm taking the missus out, see you tomorrow,' flashed through my mind.

The phone went to voicemail a few times. When I was about to give up, Jonathan came on the line, his voice all muffled as though he'd switched it on in his pocket and remembered he needed to talk into the mouthpiece a few seconds later. He sounded harassed when I told him I'd had a change of plan and was going to come back to Olbia.

'Your note said you weren't coming back tonight so I've arranged a load of meetings for this evening and tomorrow now. I can't cancel them; there's so much going on here, you know what the Italians are like, can't find their own pockets without directions. Doubt I'll be home much before midnight – so you might as well stay where you are. I'm sorry. Have you had a good day anyway? Where have you been?'

He wasn't really listening. It was tempting to tell him I was in Corsica and see if it rang any bells. There was a time when the mere mention of Corsica sent Jonathan into a jealous sulk. I could hear voices in the background, laughter. Italians clearly had a lot of fun at work. I muttered something about visiting a couple of nice beaches but the long pause before he said, 'Wonderful, good, as long as you're enjoying yourself,' gave him away. I said a quick goodbye but mentally he was already truffling about in computer heaven.

My carbonara/carafe fantasy shrivelled up like a plastic bag stuck on the hob. I marched straight to the hotel reception and booked for another night. I texted Jonathan to let him know he had all the time he wanted to work, that I'd be back two days before we went home.

So much for sorting out my marriage. Maybe I could put my past to rest instead. I decided to take the 'What doesn't kill me makes me stronger' approach and bring all the memories out into the open in the hope of finally laying Xavi's ghost. So, the following day, I tipped up at the beaches where we'd whiled away hours, talking nonsense and cloud-watching.

Cloud-watching. Who the hell had time to notice the clouds any more except in a 'Does that mean football practice is cancelled?' sort of way?

The car took me on autopilot to my favourite beach at Tizzano. More restaurants than I remembered, but so early in the season there were just a few German families on the terraces. I wandered away from them and lay down to stare at the sky. The sound of the waves, the sand under my back, the clouds drifting and merging overhead rolled back the years. Xavi was so real to me I could feel him. Little bits I'd forgotten kept coming back to me. The way he could swim for ages underwater. His face above mine, counting the freckles on my nose. How much he laughed when I swore in French.

How much I'd loved him.

I'd never held anything back, let it all gush out, never monitoring myself to reserve a vital five per cent to survive if it all turned to shit. I hadn't made that mistake with Jonathan. With him, I was eking out just enough love, allowing the minimum amount to squeeze through the sluice gates to stop our relationship grounding. Maybe if Charlie hadn't come along, we'd have called it a day after a few months, our attracting opposites starting to repel.

The beep of a text smashed through my memories. Polly. *Mum. Grandma is the official fun monitor. Can't wait till you come home on Tuesday! Miss you xx*

My finger hovered over the green button to call her, but I thought better of it. I might do something silly like cry. That would frighten her. I could count on one hand the times I'd cried since the children were born. There was no room for me amid all those tears over twisted tights, smudged homework and dead hamsters.

I texted back: *Sending you all a huge hug and big sloppy kisses. Can't wait to see you either. Be good for Grandma!*

I stuck in a smiley face. A second later: *Yuk to the kisses. Even Stan won't eat Grandma's cooking xx*

The invisible elastic that attached my babies to me like mittens stretched over the miles. I'd got so much wrong in my life, but I'd also got some things right. At long last, I understood why Xavi's mother had hated me so much. It wasn't hate. It was fear that she'd lose him. But he'd left anyway.

The next day I drove all the way to the Calanques de Piana, a funny fairy-tale landscape of red granite rock. I'd forgotten the narrow lanes and the sheer drop down to the sea. I was glad I didn't have Jonathan twitching in the car next to me.

Last time I'd been here was shortly before I'd got the call about Dad, when we still thought the world was ours, stretching ahead for a travelling eternity. We'd argued over which animal shapes we could see in the rock face, then hauled ourselves up the hiking trail in blistering heat with me moaning my arse off.

I'd planned to repeat the experience – without the moaning – and hike through the weirdly-shaped rocks with the funny chimney stacks to make the most of the view, but I simply couldn't summon up the energy. It was as though someone had let all the air out of me. I walked up to the Dog's Head where several tourists were leaning in for photos.

We'd done the same. In the photos that I'd had developed months after my dad's death, I looked like a girl on the cusp of adulthood, confidence and love radiating out of me, the naivety of youth. I could picture the exact spot where Xavi was standing. My eyes began to smart.

I hurried back to the road and sat on the wall, legs dangling over a huge drop into the valley. I didn't move. I watched the eagles soar, then dive. Listened to snatches of conversation floating past. Looked at the boats bobbing about far below until the sun started to go down, giving the rocks their stunning red colour. Sunset at its most romantic. My backside at its most numb. Never mind my heart.

Perhaps this experience wouldn't make me stronger. Perhaps I'd just keel over like a poisoned budgie.

I texted Jonathan.

Back tomorrow pm. Looking forward to dinner with you tomorrow night.

Time to call a halt to the pity party.

My stomach rumbled all the way back to Cocciu. I headed into the village square, pausing to dip my hands into the freezing fountain, remembering how often I met Xavi there. Summer hadn't kicked in yet. Cocciu was still waiting for the visitors to bring it alive. I could quite see why Jean-Franc had discovered sex so early.

I chose the café I'd always preferred: Chez Ghjuvan, a cosy cave-like bar hewn straight into the granite with tables made out of old wine barrels and candles stuck in wine bottles. It was there that Xavi and I had met. There that we had plotted our route from Auckland to Dunedin. As I got closer, I heard live music. I braced myself for the inevitable head-turning as 'the foreigner' walked in. Thankfully, all the attention was focused on a group playing mournful Corsican folk songs. Only a shaggy dog by the bar lifted its head in my direction. I sat down near the door.

The music was mesmerising, almost funereal in its intensity. The lead singer couldn't have been older than twenty-five, strumming his guitar and intoning about *Terra Nostra*, in a pure voice with a passion and sense of belonging that moved me. I tried to imagine Charlie tolerating, let alone embracing, songs dedicated to the mountains, sea and motherland, and failed. A whiskery grey-haired man who looked like he spent the daytime rounding up herds of Corsican pigs was on the panpipes. As he played the last eerie note, a rowdy table at the end burst into loud applause, bravos bouncing off the low ceiling.

I looked around. A few fairy lights, pink and fluffy, out of place among the ships' lanterns and old tin Pernod adverts, hung along the bar. A waiter came over, not quite rustling up a smile. He didn't bat an eyelid when I ordered a carafe of rosé, *grande*. He handed me a menu scribbled on a piece of brown paper in black felt tip. I'd only eaten a handful of peanuts since breakfast. I rarely ate meat but I had a sudden longing for *sanglier*, wild boar, served in thick gloopy gravy flavoured with wild thyme and rosemary.

As the evening wore on and the wine slipped down, I stopped feeling self-conscious, especially when I bribed the dog with a couple of roast potatoes to become my new best friend. The band continued with its haunting music full of desire and heartbreak. Just as I was wondering if they ever played anything verging on jolly, they broke into the Corsican equivalent of Happy Birthday. The table at the end went wild, clapping and shouting. A big pillar obscured my view. I could just make out a row of dark heads and the sort of skin that suggested the offspring of shepherds, fishermen and olive growers.

Then the lead singer said something about Corsicans being the warriors of the world and launched into *Sailing* by Rod Stewart. After all the lyrics about the women waiting and weeping for their bandit husbands, lonely trees on windswept crags and seas of tears, *Sailing* seemed positively upbeat.

The dog was snuffling at my plate, trying to get a long lick in. I pushed his nose away and headed upstairs to the loo, realising as I stood up that walking straight required concentration. As my foot touched the bottom step, the barman clicked his fingers at me.

I'm sure he meant 'Excuse me, madam'.

'*Toilettes, par là*,' he said, pointing to the back of the room. Two decades of progress – fairy lights and better bogs. I weaved my way through the chairs, squeezing past the football table where a bunch of teenage boys were bent over, four inches of underpants showing above their jeans. Charlie would fit in perfectly. I got held up behind a waiter, who was delivering plates of *figatellu*, pig's liver sausage, with the sort of insulting banter that comes from knowing the customers since they were babies.

I stepped back to let him through, steadying myself against the table behind me and catching the eye of a man opposite. Jean-Franc. He looked so much less morose after a few beers. There was a woman with long black hair next to him, lots of dark eyeliner and mascara. I wondered if she was his wife. She didn't look old enough to have a thirteen-year-old daughter.

I raised my hand in greeting, a fresh wave of guilt making me want to rush over and explain my behaviour. He nodded, then leaned forward and shouted down the table.

'*Ta compatriote. Elle est anglaise.*'

All the heads at the table swivelled in my direction. I did one of those 'nice to meet you, must be going' waves and tottered off to the loo.

A couple of minutes later, I tried to sidle back to my table without becoming the 'show and tell' of the evening' but Jean-Franc attracted my attention with '*Eh, l'Anglaise!*' on the way out. He pushed his chair back, pointing to me, explaining that I was the woman who bought his painting.

A man to my right handed me a beer. '*Bière* made of Corsican *châtaignes*.' Chestnut beer was a new one on me.

I raised the bottle to him and Jean-Franc, '*Santé*'. I hung back behind the pillar, swaying slightly, not quite sure whether I was being invited into the group or paraded as a gallery success story. I still wanted to make my peace with Jean-Franc, but an evening chugging back the rosé had affected the brain cells in charge of apologies. As I stood dithering, there was a touch on my arm from behind.

'Can I meet the woman who wants a picture of me in her house?'

I swung round.

Xavi.

I'd played this reunion a million times in my mind. The sultry way I'd walk towards him, pulling in my stomach. How I'd hold his eyes with mine. How the world would fade out, volume turned down. Instead I choked on my mouthful of beer until it came out of my nose. Through my watering eyes, I saw his dark brows furrow, a parade of disbelief, surprise and shock spreading across his features. He grabbed a serviette and led me away from the table while I spluttered to a halt.

He sat down next to me. I pressed the serviette into my face. Now he was there, I didn't want to watch his reaction to me.

'*C'est toi?* Is it really you?' He sounded as though he was holding back a giggle.

Not so fat then that he couldn't recognise me. 'You're supposed to be in London. You nearly killed me creeping up on me like that.'

Octavia Shelton. Romantic of the Year.

'It's my birthday. I always come home.' He pulled my hand away from my face. It didn't feel like a stranger touching me. Maybe hands were like memory foam mattresses, carrying the imprint of people they've loved forever.

I looked at him sideways. It pissed me off how well men age. His skin was a bit lighter than I remembered. The sun creases he used to get around his eyes in the summer were deeper. He'd never had that small chip in his front tooth capped. He still looked all olive oil and outdoor living, even if he was based in London. There was something more defined about him. The shirt and cufflinks. Sharp, urbane. I don't think I'd ever seen Xavi in anything other than a T-shirt.

I wanted to curl one of those funny ringlets that sat on his collar round my little finger.

He bent his head towards me. 'So, Tavy. My God. Tavy.' He kept rubbing his brow. 'What's the story, *ma petite* Octavia?'

He might live in England now but there was still so much French in his speech. He took my hands. My wedding ring sat there, dull gold suspended in slightly wrinkly flesh.

The story. I searched around for a sensible place to start but a rush of emotion, fierce and acute, had blocked my throat. 'I didn't expect to see you. I've had too much to drink.' Right on cue, I felt boiling hot. 'I need some fresh air. Don't spoil your birthday party with your friends. I shouldn't be here.'

'We've finished anyway. I'm staying with my brother and I still have two days before I go home. Wait for me outside.' He looked back over his shoulder. 'Please.'

I left some euros on the counter and blundered out into the dark square, tears cascading as though they'd been waiting to be released for nearly two decades.

Xavi came out, hands in the pockets of his leather coat, collar turned up against the cold. His shoulders were up and he had that look of excitement about him, the same as he did years ago when he had a plan, a little nugget of mischief he wanted to put into action. I was holding my breath, trying to get my blubbing under control. Instead of a seductive, witty one-liner, I managed a tipsy, 'Have I dragged you away?'

'It's fine. I am here for a week already. My friends are

270

pretty interested to know who you are, though. They think you are a secret birthday present, sent special-delivery from England.' He raised his eyebrows. 'Tavy?'

He still had that breathy French intonation when he said my name, which made me feel exotic and special.

He took my elbow and guided me towards the corner of the square. 'Why are you here? Eighteen years is a long time to come for me.' Xavi was joking but there was something sharp in his voice.

'I was in Sardinia.' My voice sounded shaky.

'Sardinia. Why Sardinia when you could be *en Corse*?'

'It wasn't really a holiday, more a business trip.' I tried to make a space in the conversation for Jonathan but the words kept closing over him. He would pop up soon enough.

Xavi rumbled out a laugh. 'What business? Cork? Wine? Sheep's cheese?'

'No, nothing like that.' Obviously the Santoni reticence was catching. I rummaged in my pocket for a tissue. Sniffing wasn't a good look.

Xavi stopped and turned me to face him. 'Tavy.' My stomach did a little flip. 'Do you trust me?'

'How do you mean, "trust you"? As a person, or to not slit my throat?'

I knew he couldn't be trusted not to disappear when the going got tough.

Xavi flicked his hands up, frustrated. 'I know what you are thinking about me. We will talk about this later. But no, will you let me take you somewhere?'

I nodded. Xavi was effectively a stranger. And yet I felt like I'd seen him last week.

'So, are you still the girl who likes adventure?'

I couldn't bear him to think of me as parochial, or his worst insult, *bourgeoise*. 'Of course.'

'Go on, then. Get on.'

I looked round. He indicated a motorbike parked by the wall. Not the puny Kawasaki we used to putter about on but a great big chrome beast that could snuff out life against a tree in ten seconds flat. He unlocked the helmet attached by a thick chain.

'You have this.' I hesitated, then took it from him. 'Tavy, Tavy, Tavy.' His tone was teasing. '*Allez*. Come on. I want to show you something.'

'I haven't been on a bike in years. I've had so much to drink. I'll fall off.'

'You remember I am a *pilote fantastique*. You just hold on. I will go slow.'

I crossed my arms. He swung his jacket towards me. 'Here. Have this. It can be very cold.' I slipped it on over my jumper, feeling his residual warmth. I sniffed the leather. The faint scent of aftershave. That was new. He pulled another jacket out of the bike panniers for himself and handed me some gloves. 'I remember your hands. Always freezing.'

A memory of me crawling into bed and putting my cold hands on his stomach to make him jump popped into my mind. I nodded, looking down to work out whether they were his gloves or the more petite pair of a woman, maybe a wife. They looked reassuringly large.

He got on the bike and patted the seat behind him. I'd put the helmet on but felt ridiculous, a middle-aged barrel in an alien's hat. My wine breath was suffocating me. I took it off again. 'I want to feel the wind in my hair.'

Xavi grinned and stuck the helmet in the crook of his elbow. 'At this time of night, we don't have much trouble with the police. Not where we are going.'

My inner thigh muscles complained as I lifted my leg over the bike. I had to look for the foot rests. Difficult to believe that I once saw myself as a biker bird, riding pillion to the most gorgeous bloke in town. It seemed a bit familiar to put my arms round him so I held his waist with my fingertips. He looked over his shoulder. 'Ready?'

The roar of the motorbike made me want to snatch the helmet back and jam it on my head. As soon as he let the throttle out I had no choice but to grab him round the waist. Every nerve in my body was clinging on, my knees gripping the bike, hands rigid. As we came to our first sharp corner, Xavi shouted back to me, 'Remember to lean.'

Remembering not to scream was more of challenge.

I kept wondering how the French police would explain to my children that I'd been found splattered over the mountainside.

Somewhere along the way, I felt the old stirrings of *insouciance*. I was no longer clawing onto Xavi as though the tiniest release of tension would have me skidding along the tarmac on my nose. I used whizzing round the corners as an excuse to press my face into his shoulder and breathe him in. My knees relaxed. My hair was flying all over the place, the cold air rushing through my lashes, making my eyes water.

As we turned off onto an unmade track that led through some olive groves, Xavi slowed the bike. '*Ça va?*'

I'd forgotten the way he asked simple questions made you feel as though he'd wrapped you in a cosy blanket. I breathed out. 'All good, thanks.'

'Do you know where we are?'

'No.' I considered it a success to have held onto my bowels.

He raised his hands in mock horror. 'You forgot all about Corsica when you left, eh?'

I shook my head. That funny lump was back in my throat. One minute I was smiling, a sort of dancing-through-the-daffodils smile when the world seems full of possibilities, the next moment great wells of sad emotion were corkscrewing up through my chest. Funky little ghosts of a younger me kept sticking their heads round the door, bringing in long-buried memories of what it felt like to be living, rather than existing.

Xavi opened the throttle again and we bounced down the rutted track, the beam of the headlight startling wild boars and sending them thundering off into the *maquis*. We arrived at a scrubby copse area encircled by trees.

I creaked myself off the bike and looked around. 'It's where we had our caravan!'

Xavi laughed. 'It turned to rust years ago. It was falling in pieces when we lived there. But I have something else to show you.'

Roberta

Humiliation squeezed every last bit of breath out of my body. The world had stopped spinning. Someone appeared with a bucket and swilled down the steps. Catherine sat on the non-sicky, non-bloody side of me and said, 'My mother was like you. Our Labrador once cut its nether regions on some barbed wire and she split her head open as she fell.'

I knew she was trying to make me feel better but I couldn't be sure that I'd finished vomiting for the day. Alicia stood near me, biting her bottom lip and leaning into Connor.

Jake had swabbed my hand and eased out the piece of glass. He didn't look at me. It was almost as though he didn't recognise me. He wrapped gauze around the wound. 'You should go to hospital and get that looked at.' Distantly, I was aware that he sounded concerned.

'I'm fine.' I got to my feet, then clutched at him for support as I saw the blood seeping through the gauze.

Jake seized my arm and held onto me. 'You must go. It needs dressing properly.'

Catherine backed him up. 'If there's still glass in there, it might get infected.'

'Mum. Don't be stupid. If it was me, you would make me go.' Alicia's face was pale and worried.

'I'll come with you in a taxi. Stuart can walk home with the kids,' Catherine said.

Jake sighed. 'I haven't been drinking. I'll drive you.'

Through the pain, a little burst of delight flared. 'I can't go like this, covered in sick. They'll think I was drunk.' The blood was spreading. The world wobbled again.

'I've got a T-shirt in the boot. It'll be a bit big, but it'll do the job. You missed your jeans.'

I was vaguely aware of Jake introducing himself to Catherine and of them making arrangements for Alicia. He pulled me to my feet and we walked to his car in silence.

'This is incredibly kind of you. I hope I don't make your car smell awful.'

'Can't be worse than Angus and his rancid trainers.'

Jake whipped a T-shirt out of the boot and helped me change, his touch firm and pragmatic. I couldn't blame him: the smell of vomit wasn't a great turn-on. I lay down on the back seat. Apart from 'All right?' he didn't say anything all the way to hospital. I pressed my cheek on the cool leather and waited for the motion to stop. I didn't dare pick at my feelings.

Jake led me to A&E. I wanted to ask him why he was bothering with me but I was frightened he would ask himself the same question and leave me on my own.

He stood back while I checked in. When the receptionist shrugged and told me it would be about an hour's wait, he stepped up to the glass. 'Hello there. I know you're very busy, but my friend has been bleeding for quite some time now and there might still be glass embedded in the wound.'

The woman behind the desk flicked her ponytail, smiled and said she'd see what she could do.

We sat down on orange plastic chairs that made me want

to squirt anti-bacterial gel on my hands. Jake leaned back, arms folded. I started to thank him but he shrugged. 'I didn't even realise it was you at first. I just heard the sound of smashing glass and someone groan.'

A woman in a woolly hat was knitting opposite. Metal clicked away. Next to her, a young mother kept saying, 'It's not bloody fair' into a mobile phone while her four kids bashed away on the xylophone, thumping drums and shaking tambourines. I never used to let Alicia play with anything at the doctor's. Jake contemplated his shoes. Hard to believe we'd stayed up until two in the morning whispering into the phone when we hadn't see each other. And even when we had.

'I met your son tonight.'

Jake nodded.

'He remembered our previous meeting.'

'I know. He came racing up to tell me that you were there. I never told him why we stopped seeing each other and I don't think he could understand it. But there was a lot about our relationship that puzzled me, too.'

I looked at the floor, then studied the geometric wallpaper, circa 1985.

'You didn't let me explain,' I said.

'Was there something to explain? It seemed quite clear-cut to me. You slept with me, then went back to your husband.' In that moment, the children's instrumental cacophony suddenly went silent and my sins boomed round the waiting room in Jake's deep voice.

I blushed. He flicked his hands out in a gesture of apology. I turned to face him, stared right into those gorgeous eyes. I dropped my voice to a whisper. 'Let's be clear, I didn't sleep with Scott. I don't want him and he doesn't even want me. He just wants to ruin any chance of me being happy with someone else.'

Jake shifted on his chair but he didn't look away.

I carried on. 'I was desperate to have a civil relationship with Scott so we could create some stability for Alicia. Over the years I've got used to going along with him, for the sake of an easy life, so when he made a move on me that night, I didn't know how to react without upsetting everything and going back to stage one. I came to my senses very quickly. I knew when I was kissing him that it was wrong, that whatever we had was over.'

Jake winced beside me. I ploughed on. 'I didn't mean to hurt you.'

'Maybe not. But you did.' He gazed out of the window.

My hand was pulsating with pain. I tried to clear my brain, to find the words that would help him see my world, when the old woman who was knitting opposite piped up.

'I don't know why you young couples make it so difficult for yourselves. If he loves you and you love him, you need to stop worrying about what's happened in the past. In my day we didn't ask too many questions and we were happy enough.' Clack, clack. She pushed her spectacles back up her nose and went back to knit one, purl one, without giving us another glance.

I mouthed, 'Was she talking to us?' Jake nodded. If I hadn't been whimpering in pain, I would have laughed.

The nurse called me through.

Jake didn't get up. 'Do you want me to come with you?'

I was horrified at the thought that he might not. 'Yes please.'

He followed me through. Straightaway he said, 'Roberta has a problem with blood. The sight makes her sick or faint.'

The nurse gave the sort of smile grown-ups reserve for children when they ask, 'Are ghosts real?'

'Sit down and look away. I'm taking the dressing off.'

278

Jake stood next to me, leaning into me slightly. The nurse's no-nonsense manner softened when she examined my hand.

'That's really nasty. It's quite deep, which means you're going to need stitches.' She asked me to bend my finger and thumb. 'I don't think the glass has cut any of the tendons, but let's send you for an X-ray to be on the safe side.'

The mere mention of tendons conjured up an image of something stringy and elastic. The room started to swim. When I came round, I was on a bed with my feet raised.

'Your husband wasn't joking when he said you didn't like blood, was he?'

I pretended I hadn't heard the husband bit.

The nurse put me in a wheelchair and asked Jake to take me down to X-ray.

'Thank you for coming with me. I don't do hospitals well.'

'It's OK.' His voice was tight, closed. One of the things that I'd loved about Jake was that he was so straightforward, so open with his feelings. Now I felt like I was watching TV with the sound turned off.

I slumped into the wheelchair, too miserable to worry about incontinent OAPs passing wind there before me. The silence turned uncomfortable. I didn't know how to rectify it. Everything I said seemed to intensify Jake's resentment. In comparison, having an X-ray was almost relaxing. Once they'd established that there was no serious damage, the doctor dispatched me for stitches.

This time Jake didn't mention my aversion to blood. I mumbled an embarrassed explanation. The young Irish nurse was very kind. She didn't look old enough to sew a name tape on, let alone skin.

She spoke to Jake. 'Just hold her good hand firmly for me and keep squeezing. Talk to her to take her mind off it.'

It was a tall order when he seemed to be finding it difficult to say anything to me at all. But when I saw her pick up a needle that looked like a fish hook, I grabbed his hand. Even through my fear, my stomach dipped at his touch. The nurse looked at him expectantly and he started talking to me in soothing tones, as though I was a dog hiding behind the sofa on bonfire night.

'So. How long have you been going to that tennis club?'

The nurse shot him an odd look. I guess it was a change from 'What shall we have for dinner tonight, darling?'

'It was my first time today. Alicia's boyfriend invited me. I usually go to Longridge Avenue.'

'Of course.'

I cursed myself. Longridge Avenue was exclusive, with a waiting list of several years.

I glanced over at the nurse as though she could somehow help me. Which was not terribly wise as she was injecting an anaesthetic into the wound. I yelped as it stung, forcing myself to keep my hand there.

'Keep chatting. Anything to distract her.' The nurse shielded my hand with her body.

'I was shocked to see you there today,' Jake said.

That won my attention away from the pain.

'Why?'

'I don't know. I wasn't prepared for it, I suppose.' Jake was so close, I could smell his aftershave. 'I was so happy when I met you, the happiest I'd been for ages. Doing what you did, well, I just felt like a complete loser.'

The corner of his mouth twisted up in resignation. I tightened my grip on his hand.

'I am so, so sorry. I wasn't thinking as clearly then as I do now.'

His voice had fallen to a whisper. He squatted down so that he was talking into my ear. 'Even though I hadn't been seeing you for very long, I was sure we'd end up together. I can't deal with someone else in the background, though.

What my wife did nearly broke me. I can't put myself through that again.'

I turned so I was speaking right into his face. 'There isn't anyone in the background. No one at all, of any description. But I've really missed you these last couple of months.'

My father would have thought I was very forward.

There was a definite relaxing of the tightness around his mouth. His eyes were searching my face. My heart, my whole being was straining to connect with him. I just needed a chance. 'What about you?'

Jake glanced away. I became aware of a man complaining about chest pains next door.

'I've met someone recently.'

I loosened my hand in his, hesitating while I got control of my voice. 'Good for you. Did you meet her on the internet?'

'No. She came to do some landscaping in my garden.'

Hope wheezed away. A great wave of tiredness rushed through me as the nurse snipped something and said, 'There, all done.'

'That was quick.'

'Not really. I just think you had other things to distract you.' She patted my arm and smiled.

Now I just needed my heart stitching up.

Octavia

Xavi parked the bike at the edge of the beach. A silence full of questions settled between us as we walked along the sand. After a few minutes, I crouched down and sifted the pale grains between my fingers. He knelt beside me.

'I don't understand why you're here now. *Curiosité*? *Nostalgie*? Are you still married?'

My wedding ring had done the talking for me.

'Are you?' I felt my stomach clench, ready to absorb the hurt.

'No. Never have been. No one would have me.'

I elbowed him. 'Don't give me that old shit. No one could tie you down long enough, more likely.'

'You didn't answer my question. Are you married?'

Xavi was barbecuing me with his eyes but I still hesitated. I knew once the words were out there, real life would crowd into this star-spangled corner of Corsica. Immi's little face filled my mind.

'I've got three children. And a husband.'

Xavi gave a little whistle. 'Three children. Wow.'

I waited for him to ask me ages, names, something, but he juggled a couple of stones, then got to his feet. He pulled me up.

'Come on.'

I followed him down the beach, the familiar smell of the gorse wheeling me back to simpler times. Washing in buckets of water. Collecting firewood. Days in sarongs and swimsuits. I shivered. The wind was whipping up little white frills at the edge of the sea.

Xavi pointed to a small boat, rising and dipping in a silver triangle of light, its tethered sails flapping against the mast. 'My almost yacht.'

'That's a step up from the old fishing boat that we had to bale out with a bucket.'

'I love it. Sometimes I live on it for a few days in the summer. Jean-Franc uses it when I'm in London.'

'London, Xavi. Why London? Is it permanent?' It was the first time I'd said his name, enjoying the shape of it on my lips.

He shrugged. 'Is anything permanent? I've been there for seven years. Set up the English branch of a New Zealand travel agency. Now I specialise in activity holidays worldwide. It was not necessary to travel here to find me. It was enough to take a train to West Hampstead.'

'I didn't come to find you, you great big-head. You never made any effort to get in touch with me. Disappeared like a puff of smoke.' I made a 'pouff' gesture with my hands.

He leaned into me and nudged me. 'You know that's not true.'

'No. I know that it is true. Dad died, you buggered off and left me to it.'

I lay flat on the sand and tried to pick out the shape of Cassiopeia among the stars. This wasn't a moment for confrontation. I wanted to enjoy the one evening I could spend with Xavi, not use the time to pickaxe at long-ago wounds. I watched sparse clouds, dark velvety chiffon, moving across the moon. Without the light pollution of the city, the sky was a different place.

Xavi leaned back on his elbow and stared down at me. His eyes were almost black in their intensity. 'She never told you, did she?'

'Who?'

'Your mother.' He got to his feet and kicked up an arc of sand. 'She didn't tell you. Bitch.'

That prickled me. I wasn't sure Xavi and I had the sort of closeness any more that allowed him to slag off my mother. 'Tell me what?'

'That I phoned. That I came back for you.'

I sat up. 'What?

'After your dad died. Yes, I went to New Zealand. But after two weeks, I kept trying to ring you. Your mother told me you were going back to university and I must left you alone.'

I dragged my memory back to the weeks after Dad's death. The months at home when I lay in my bedroom, listening to Dad's old Carpenters records, oblivious to everything and everyone until my mother coerced Roberta into coaxing me back to university for the start of my final year.

'How often did you phone?'

My mother was steely but she hated me to be unhappy. Though she would have hated me to drop out of university and hightail it to New Zealand more.

'Jesus, Tavy, a lot. It cost so much then to call, not like now with email and texts. I spent a fortune on two-minute earaches from your mother. She keep saying to me to forget you.'

'You've managed to do that quite well for eighteen years.' Though to be fair, that was more Mum's fault than his.

'So have you. Husband. Children. I don't see you crying for Xavi.'

'I didn't leave you. You left me.' I was like a child poking a slug with a stick to see if its guts spilled out.

Xavi hurled a pebble into the sea. 'Water under the bridges. You cold?'

I nodded, wanting to pick, pick, pick a bit further. Xavi hated small-mindedness. He was the master of the Gallic shrug. The damp from the cold sand was creeping right up into my soul.

'I know where we can get warm.' He nodded towards the boat. 'I have everything we need there. Just one problem.'

I gave him a sarcastic smile. 'What? We have to swim there?'

'*Beh, oui*. It's not very far.'

'No. No. I was joking when I said that. That's silly. That water is going to be freezing. People die in water like that.'

'When you were here, we used to swim in March. You survived it then.'

'I know, but I'm nearly forty now, not twenty.'

'That's it then? Life over? No more fun? No courage any more?'

Xavi was rattling me. In my life, my real life, I was the one who challenged people, told them where they were going wrong. I'd got used to the children, Jonathan, even Roberta, looking to me for guidance. Now Xavi was making out I was lacking gumption because I didn't want to die of hypothermia.

'I'm just trying to live long enough to see my kids grow up. Some of us have responsibilities.'

Xavi stood with his hands on his hips. 'And some of us have *joie de vivre*. Come on, take a new memory of being young now back home with you.'

Stripping down to my underwear in front of a guy I loved when I had a flat stomach *sans* stretch marks was not a deal-clincher. But I hadn't done anything crazy for so long. I thought about recounting the story to Roberta and a little giggle rippled at the back of my throat.

Now. It had to be now, before I remembered my sensible self.

'Let's go then.'

Xavi swung round to see if I was serious. I paused. 'You first.'

He threw off his jacket and started stripping off his clothes as though we windsurfed together every weekend. It was so long since I'd noticed a man, any man, but he still had those broad muscly shoulders and well-defined biceps. Doing a bloody desk job. Nature was so unfair. He was wearing boxers, not the baggy parachutey type Jonathan favoured, but the snug butt-huggers models wear. I turned away.

He drew a heart in the sand with his toe, then scuffed it out with his heel. 'I'm going to start swimming in ten seconds. I'm not looking at you.'

I paused when it came to taking my trousers off. Eventually, I folded them into the jacket.

Xavi started shouting. '*Allez, allez, allez!* I'm freezing.'

I stood there in my knickers and T-shirt. I couldn't take the T-shirt off. Lord, no. Xavi's patience had run out. 'That's enough. Let's go.' He bundled the clothes into a heap, then took hold of my hand.

'Ready? Don't stop running.'

He pulled me along straight into the sea. The sand was soft beneath my feet. I was knee-deep before the cold registered. 'Keep going. Keep going. When I say dive, you dive with me.'

The water was lapping around the bottom of my T-shirt and I was letting out little shrieks as the waves touched my stomach. Still Xavi pulled me on. 'Come on, thirty metres and we're there. Dive. Now.'

I plunged under the freezing water. The cold stabbed at my scalp and emptied my lungs. I went from drunk to sober in an instant. Xavi was treading water, looking as though he was on a Sunday outing at the local pool, as I half doggy-paddled, half breaststroked my way towards him, sucking in uneven gulps of air, my chest shaking. The moon disappeared behind a cloud and for a moment, I flailed about, panicking in the inky blackness of the sea. High-pitched whimpers were escaping from me. I tried not to think about squid sucking onto my legs.

'Tavy, I'm here, follow me.'

I kicked towards Xavi, forcing down my fear. His hand closed around my upper arm, yanking me the last few metres to the boat. He positioned my hand on the steel ladder. 'Hold on. Let me go up first.'

He hauled me into the boat. My chest was heaving but my whole body felt invigorated, any wine fuzziness long gone. He opened a hatch to a tiny living area and disappeared down the steps, re-emerging with a towel. 'Come inside and take off your T-shirt. I have blankets here.'

Joy at not being fish fodder made me laugh. I couldn't remember the last time anyone had ordered me to get my kit off. I draped the towel round me and climbed gingerly down the steps. Through the hatch I could see Xavi silhouetted on deck in the moonlight, tan lines framing his gorgeous arse, drying himself unabashed.

I, on the other hand, was like Great Aunt Gladys on Brighton beach under my towel tent, trying to peel off my soaking T-shirt and underwear without exposing more than an elbow. Thank God I'd painted my toenails. I wished I'd had my bikini line waxed.

Xavi jumped down, landing lightly on his feet, then dug about under one of the seat cushions. He produced an enormous fleecy blanket, which he wrapped round me.

He lit the gas. 'You still can't resist to a challenge, can you? Now you feel great. Good decision.'

I doubted that Jonathan would agree. A galley kitchen-diner was an intimate space for two naked people with a sexual history.

Xavi morphed into a Stepford Wives hostess role. Every time we were settling down, the boat rocking us, letting old memories of life in the caravan resurface, he jumped up to get coffee, then tangerine wine, Cap Corse liqueurs, pistachios. His towel kept threatening to slip and put his bare buttocks within grabbing distance. I batted those thoughts away. My life with Jonathan and the children was closed, a circle with no random openings for outsiders. I'd found Xavi, assuaged my curiosity. I had one of my own adventures to tell Roberta.

That had to be enough.

I pulled my blanket tight until I was swaddled like a Bedouin baby.

'You still cold?'

'I'm warming up, thanks. The liqueur helps.'

Xavi told me about Jean-Franc and his premature fatherhood, making me laugh when he imitated his mother threatening to go and shave the girl's head.

'She act as though Jean-Franc is a little boy, taken advantage of by some evil predator. Eventually, she was OK. She loved the granddaughter. Now, of course, my mother is dead, a few years ago now.'

'I'm sorry.' I was, but I also had a shameful surge of relief that there was no chance of bumping into her. Maybe now I would just see her for what she was. A mother who wanted to protect her son, rather than the evil black crow I remembered.

We dipped in and out of our families, Roberta, his friends and their lives, catching up on the present and delighting in recollections from the past. Every time we approached the meaty stuff, the me and him, the husband and children lurking in the corners of our conversation, one of us would skitter off, burying ourselves in anecdotes about the caravan practically floating away in a spring deluge or Xavi's patient removal of sea-urchin spines wedged in my foot. It amazed me how much we laughed, real amusement boiling out of us with its own energy.

I couldn't remember the last time Jonathan found me funny. Whenever I got the giggles, he just looked bemused.

Somewhere along the way, the space between us had diminished and Xavi brushed against me, the hairs on his arms sending little shockwaves up my skin.

I turned Xavi's wrist to look at his watch. 'My God. It's quarter past two.'

'Are you in a hurry?'

'No. I just never go to bed this late.'

Xavi turned to me. 'Are you tired? Do you want to swim back?'

I wished I hadn't mentioned it. I didn't want to go, didn't want to open my hand and let these precious moments fly away. The thought of getting back in that freezing water made me shudder.

'Do you?' I didn't want to be a sad cling-on either.

'*Non.*' He put his head on one side. '*Non.* Not at all.' His eyes skimmed over me taking in my hair, lingering on my mouth in a way that made me want to check for errant pistachios, and finally looking directly at me. We sat for a second, our eyes steady, reaching into each other.

I waited for him to leap up and start fannying about with bloody cashew nuts. Instead he took my hand, twirling my wedding ring. I let my fingers relax into his.

'So?'

'So what?'

'So. *Ton mariage.* Is it happy?' He'd been doing that all evening. Lapsing into French whenever the subject was difficult.

'It depends how you define happy.' Xavi wasn't someone you could fob off.

'Let me make it easy. Do you love your husband?'

'Yes.' There was only one answer to questions like that.

Xavi shifted beside me, opening up a chilly gap where the warmth of his thigh had been.

'So why aren't you in Sardinia with him?'

Even though I was trying, I couldn't meet his eye. 'He was busy with work so I thought I'd go exploring.'

'But you're not exploring. You come back somewhere you know.'

I took a sip of wine. 'Just fancied seeing what had changed.'

'And me, have I changed?'

'Not much at all. More mellow than I remembered. When you were younger, I always felt you might get into a fight at any time.' I paused. 'You're a bit greyer.'

'Still handsome though?' Xavi ran his hand through his hair in mock film-star mode.

'You always were so vain.'

Xavi lowered his voice. 'Have you changed, Tavy?'

I flicked him playfully. 'You can judge for yourself. I'm not going to tell you.'

Where would I start? Couldn't go on a trampoline without wetting myself. Old-woman chilblains in the winter. Often looked in the hall mirror and wondered who the granny was standing there.

'I think you are more sad than I remember.' He leaned his chin on his hand.

I reminded myself that he didn't mean 'sad' in the way Charlie meant sad – embarrassingly fuddy-duddy. The words still hit a sore spot. 'What do you mean, sad? I'm not singing and dancing all the time. Who is?'

'I see serious in you, you didn't have it before.'

Christ. I'd laughed more that evening than in the preceding

six months. Maybe I could get a job as a professional mourner. I shrugged. 'That's family life. There's always something to worry about. You can't be as light-hearted as you are at twenty. Marriage changes you. Children change you.'

Xavi stretched. His blanket fell away, revealing that chest where I'd put my head for so many nights. My eyes were itchy with tiredness but I knew the next day would carry me away again.

Forever.

He cleared his throat. 'I came back after a year. To ask you to marry me.'

'Marry you? My God.'

Flippancy was on the tip of my tongue but something raw flashed across his face.

'Did Mum know?' My mind was scrambling. What could have, might have been.

'No. She told me you were going to marry Jonathan. That you were having a baby.' The words sounded harsh on his lips. 'I was shocked you loved someone else enough to have a baby so quickly. I had nothing to offer you – just a surfboard and a camper van. No life for a baby. Sometimes life is a Russian roulette. I thought I wanted to adventure. But I wanted you and it was too late.' Xavi looked sideways at me. The swish of waves against the boat filled the silence.

My eyes tingled with unexpected tears. 'I wish I'd known.'

'Would you have come with me?'

'I don't know. The baby wasn't planned. I got pregnant just before we finished university. I ended up with a very different life from the one I'd imagined. But Jonathan was – is – very reliable. I knew he wouldn't leave me. I couldn't have got through my final year of university without him. You know, after Dad died and you leaving me. I was a bit of a wreck.'

291

I expected Xavi to sneer at Jonathan's conservative attributes but his face clouded over. 'I can be reliable. I know I did a bad thing. The responsibility, *ça m'a fait peur*, you know, scared me. In the end, it was me that lost.'

While I was still forming my platitude about us never knowing whether we would have been happy or not, Xavi kissed me with a passion so ferocious that everything went red behind my eyelids.

A biscuit crumb of brain was arguing against it. I was reaching out, trying to clutch onto my marriage vows, conscience, decency, anything. But my body had no reverse gear. It was as though I'd lied to myself. My body knew what I'd come here for but my mind was still pretending to be a respectable wife. And underneath it all, the shamefully superficial consideration that Xavi might take fright once he got a close-up of my scrambled egg stomach.

But I didn't want him to stop. His hands were everywhere, pushing away towels and blankets and caressing me in a way that annihilated my ability to think.

Xavi paused for a moment, searching my eyes until I wanted to close them against him in case my entire soul was spilling out. He wasn't questioning or asking permission. He didn't need to. My body was giving him all the answers he needed. He plunged into me, familiar yet different, aggression and possession hovering on the edge of his lovemaking.

An unwelcome thought about whether Xavi would feel like he'd fallen in a quarry in my post-children fanny threw me off rhythm. I opened my mouth to speak, to make a joke. Xavi shook his head and put a finger to my lips, slowing his pace and silencing me with a kiss so gentle I felt as though I was falling. Falling somewhere I'd never want to leave. Then, as if a new train of thought consumed him, he held me by the shoulders, pumping into me with such intensity that my body sucked him in, drawing him up into my core until my poor knackered pelvic floor rose to the challenge and we strained against each other in a release that carried eighteen years of love and loss.

Xavi lay on me, his body trembling, pushing my hair back from my face, searching out my lips. He kissed me in a way that made me think back to lying on the beach so long ago, watching the sunset, unaware that the egg-timer had been flicked over. I studied his face. Xavi had that Santoni grit, that hard edge I wasn't sure I'd ever worn down. Now, right in front of me, was a tenderness, a vulnerability I didn't recall. He eased himself off me, pulling up a blanket and tucking it round me.

'He's lucky. Your husband.'

Xavi had always had a knack of sounding angry when he was sad.

He flipped onto his back, chewing at his lip.

I lay cramped up beside him, trying to formulate an answer to that.

To any of it.

Xavi Santoni had blown open the closed circle of my family and now I needed to find a way back. I'd made a mistake thinking that I wasn't romantic. I wasn't romantic with Jonathan. I could have lain there stroking Xavi's face and telling him all the things I'd missed, all the dreams I'd had, the sheer yearning inside me until the sun came up.

Jonathan had no clue about what I wanted out of life, except perhaps a new dishwasher and a man round to clean the gutters.

I could have spent the rest of the day running my hands over Xavi's olive skin, reacquainting myself with every mole, every little scar old and new. I could barely be bothered to have sex with Jonathan if he took too long taking off his socks. We'd stopped watering our marriage and it had shrivelled up like a forgotten basil plant on the kitchen windowsill.

Instead of getting out the Baby Bio, I'd lit a bonfire somewhere else.

Roberta

As I lay in bed trying to ignore the throbbing in my hand, I don't know what made me more nauseous – looking at the bandage or the thought of Jake making love to someone else. I kept picking up my mobile, willing his name to appear. I was so sure he would call to see how I was. At midnight, I couldn't stand it any more. I texted him: *Thank you so much for looking after me. It was lovely to catch up with you. R.*

But nothing. I tossed and turned, convincing myself that he wouldn't want to disturb me in case I was asleep.

In the morning, I deluded myself I was looking to see if the newspaper was on the doorstep, but really, I half-expected to find a bouquet of flowers or a note tucked into the letterbox. I dialled 1471 to check that I hadn't missed the phone while I was in the shower. As the morning wore on, the time I should have spent sourcing Mrs Goodman's globe chandeliers dwindled as I checked my inbox every two minutes on the grounds that he might find it easier to email than to talk to me on the phone.

By mid-afternoon, I was raking through plausible but increasingly far-fetched reasons why I hadn't heard anything. Maybe he'd left first thing for a conference? An emergency at the printing plant? I did understand that he was seeing someone else, but I knew I hadn't imagined that chemistry between us. Perhaps I'd been too aloof. Octavia was always telling me that men would never guess that I liked them because I was such an old 'Frosty Knickers'. Either that or 'He's just not that into you.' 'He's in love with someone else.' 'He's not worth worrying about.' And her favourite: 'Move on.'

But how?

Octavia

I woke up with a crick in my neck. Bright light was shining through the porthole right into my hungover eyes. Xavi was still clutching me to him, dark shadows under his eyes, his lips twitching lightly in his sleep. I rummaged around in my heart for guilt. It was there all right, simmering under the surface.

Right next to the rush of love that had only ever been dormant, not extinguished.

I lay wide-eyed staring at the ceiling, trying to take in the new me. Without waking, Xavi pulled me closer.

Shame that I wasn't the mother my children thought I was – practical, caring, reliable – crashed down on me. When I picked at that sensation a bit more, a desire to cuddle them, to explain that this was not about them, but about the me I was before them, pulled me taut. Far beyond that was an ache, a heaviness that would be my penance, the herculean effort of locking away this strength of feeling, this craving for Xavi in the pokiest corner of my heart.

Xavi stirred. His eyes flew open and his hand shot out. '*Putain*. Tavy. I thought you were a dream.' He sat up. 'I am too old for sleeping squashed in a little bed. Next time a big matrimonial bed.'

Something fish-hooked deep inside. 'No next time.'

Xavi rubbed his eyes. 'No. Wait. Wait. I can't think with no coffee.'

I stared at his back while he lit the gas, simultaneously recording the moment and locking it away. I wrapped myself in a towel and threw the hatch open, blinking in the sunshine. We were so close to the shore, the distance seemed laughable now. Xavi handed up a coffee to me, then joined me on deck. 'Tavy?'

'There's no next time, Xavi.'

'So. You leave me again.' He pulled at a rope hanging from the railing and tied knot after knot in it.

'No one is leaving anyone. We're not together in the first place. I've got kids, Xavi. I can't go home and tell them I'm off with a guy I knew twenty years ago.'

'I show you something.'

Xavi disappeared down the steps. He came back with a little square box made out of olive wood. 'You know what's in here?'

'Dead mouse. Marble. Shell. Sea urchin. Haven't a clue.' The fact that I'd be leaving him again, so soon, cancelled any desire for stupid games.

He lifted off the top. I hung back, expecting him to make something jump out at me. No insect. No dead animal. Just half a five-franc piece with '-*lité, fraternité*'.

'Have you still got yours?'

I shook my head, explaining how I'd thrown it in a skip in an effort to forget him.

'I never forgot you, Tavy. I never will. I have tried. I don't know what is so special about you.'

'Thanks.' I'd always found it hard to take Xavi seriously, even when he was being earnest.

'No, that's all wrong, I do know what is special. You're kind, but tough. You make me laugh. You don't follow everyone else. Your mind is ready for any possibility. If you didn't have a family now and I said, "Right, we go in Africa and set up a school," you'd come. I know you would.'

I loved Xavi for his belief. The truth was, my open mind had eroded over the years until it was a narrow passageway through which I forced the occasional independent thought. I felt like an anarchist when I took the kids out of school on a sunny day and buggered off to West Wittering to splash about in the waves. But I wasn't about to shatter the illusions of the last man standing who thought I was Wonder Woman.

'I see you have a family. I understand family, but I don't want to let you go. What if we wait? For the children to be grown? How long? Nine years? I will be wrinkled. We can be old together.' Xavi was trying to smile but melancholy hung between us.

'No more waiting, Xavi. I can't spend the next decade wishing my children's lives away so I can be with you. It's not fair on Jonathan, either. He's a good man. We need to let each other go. Maybe in another life we'll get it right.'

My voice was catching, high-pitched, a flood of emotion rising and falling in my throat. I tried to imagine going home, packing my stuff, leaving the children with Jonathan, becoming a weekends-and-holidays-only mum. I couldn't.

Xavi was drawing patterns in the sand on deck. 'You looked for me. Now you have found me, you want to walk away. I spend eighteen years staying away from you so I don't hurt you. You wouldn't be here now if you were happy.'

Was he right? Was I unhappy? Certainly what I felt for Jonathan appeared pedestrian and sickly compared with how I felt right now sitting next to Xavi. But maybe that was the thrill of a different body after so many years of the same one, rather than a deep, enduring love begging to be heard. Perhaps after a week with Xavi, I'd be nagging him to 'get his nose out of the bloody iPad and feed the dog'.

'I shouldn't have come.'

'I never find love after you. Maybe I get close once or twice. In the end, they are not you. I never meet no one with that *spontanéité*. No one who sees the world as *une grande possibilité*.'

'I don't believe that for a minute. I'm middle-aged, a fat bat with all kinds of baggage. You're gorgeous, you're successful, you're free. What woman wouldn't want you?'

Jealousy scrabbled inside me like a cat up a curtain at the thought of Xavi finding someone else.

'You.'

'Xavi, it's not that I don't want you. I can't have you.'

Round and round the arguments went until Xavi followed my car down to Bonifacio on the motorbike and stood cuddling me, telling me all the reasons I needed to see him again until a bad-tempered steward threatened to close the gates to the ferry if I didn't get on that second. I breathed Xavi in, stared hard into his face to create a memory to last me forever and walked away, still feeling the sensation of his hand in mine.

I couldn't look back.

Roberta

By the evening, despair pervaded every room in the house. I didn't want to be in the kitchen because it reminded me of fantasising about sunny Sunday lunches with Jake. I couldn't bear to be upstairs because I remembered him talking about 'christening' my bedroom as though it were yesterday. I kept making cups of coffee, then forgetting to drink them. I Googled holidays for Alicia and me but nothing appealed. I was constantly picking up my phone to text Jake, then putting it down again.

Life had taught me that one-sided love was never enough.

But when the doorbell rang about seven o'clock, my heart lifted for the first time that day.

It had to be him.

I smoothed my hair back and straightened my T-shirt. I readied my face for one of complete surprise. When I opened the door, my fake astonishment turned to genuine disappointment. Not Jake. A slender, blonde woman of about thirty.

'Hello there. Sorry to disturb you. I'm looking for Roberta.'

Her tone was steady, reserved even, but there was something gritted and taut about her, as though she was sieving her words through a fine mesh.

I felt my whole demeanour shift into a ready position. 'I'm Roberta Green. And you are?' I just managed to get a friendly upswing onto the question.

Today, I simply didn't have the patience to endure a Jehovah's Witness speech before disappearing inside to direct a *Watchtower* magazine straight into the recycling bin. A 'No thank you' was forming before I even knew what this woman had come to say. The only thing that stopped me from twitching the door into a closing position was the outside possibility she was looking for interior design services.

'I'm Lorraine.' She raised her eyebrows, waiting for a reaction. Her eyes, the palest blue I'd ever seen on anyone outside a husky, looked huge in her angular face. I shifted my assessment of her from 'slender' to 'skinny'.

I knew who she was, even though Jake hadn't told me her name. Of course I knew. The landscape gardener. But rotten luck for her: my injured hand, Jake despair and general malaise didn't lend itself to welcoming meet and greets with the woman who was sleeping with *my* boyfriend. I'd still think of him as that, even if he married her.

I wasn't in the mood to be generous-spirited. I doubted she was here to discuss the best plants for my rockery. 'Do excuse me, but should I know you?' I could feel the poshness that I'd toned down over the years creep back into my voice, the plummy tones leaping onto my middle-class words and cranking them up a level. Octavia always said I did outraged dowager very well.

She shifted, managing to combine a certain shyness with emotions that looked like they might form a marching band at any moment.

'I'm here about Jake.' She had such a soft voice; her speech almost melted away with minimal disturbance to the airwaves. Totally at odds with the nerve required to present herself at the house of an ex-girlfriend.

'What about him?' Common courtesy dictated that I invited her in. But I didn't feel courteous, so we stood, watchful, adjusting our positions slightly. I kept my face neutral, but my body was opting for a slight slouch on the doorjamb and a bit of hip jut.

'I think you know I'm seeing him.'

'I do.' I wondered if she could feel the antagonism fizzing in the space between us.

She tucked her hair behind her ear. 'I'm aware that things didn't end well between you but I just wanted to make sure there was no chance of you getting back together.'

I hated the idea that Jake had told her what had happened. It was hard to see how any recounting of the story – 'got out of my bed, then directly into her ex-husband's' – wouldn't put me on the back foot somewhat.

'Shouldn't you be asking him that?'

'He won't discuss you. He just keeps saying what happened between you two isn't relevant. But I can't help thinking he wouldn't have spent the whole evening at A&E with you yesterday if it was all so cut and dried.'

Her marshmallowy voice was beginning to sound more nut brittle.

'That was because everyone else had been drinking. I needed stitches and he was the only one sober enough to drive me.' I waved my hand in front of her. 'He was just being kind.' As I said it, I had to squash down the tiny hope that wasn't the whole truth.

'Is that all it was?'

I'd taught myself to be so slow to anger over the years, I rarely confronted anyone directly. So it was particularly unfortunate for Lorraine that the stars had aligned in the wrong way for me to retreat into a hole today. No one was going to turn up on my doorstep, give me the third degree and get away with it.

I did an elaborate shrug. 'You're asking the wrong person. He told me he was going out with you and seemed content enough. How would I know what plans he has for you both?'

A flash of hurt flitted across her face. Bitchy old me had hit home with 'content'. She'd hoped to hear he loved her and our little dalliance was dead in the water. She glanced away, her mouth twisting with emotion, stuck between wanting to question me further and a desire not to give me another chance to tell her something she didn't want to hear.

I stayed silent, more like my father than I'd ever admitted. He always won arguments by pausing until the other person raced to fill the silence. I dithered. I could wreck their relationship forever. Sow just enough doubt that she'd never trust him again. If she did stay with him, I could force her to live under the shadow of insecurity for the rest of her life. But he wasn't coming back to me. Whether he loved her or not was irrelevant. I was history anyway.

She looked up. If I stopped thinking of her as the enemy, I could see similarities between us. Proud, insecure and desperate to hang onto the nicest man she'd ever met. The difference was she was young enough to build a baggage-free life with him, have his children, make him happy.

I sighed, feeling the last bit of resistance in me give. 'Go home to him. I promise you, he doesn't want anything to do with me.'

Her face relaxed. 'Are you sure?'

'One hundred per cent.'

For the first time she smiled, and I could see why Jake was attracted to her shy charm. I wondered if that breathy voice irritated him. Maybe she thought it somehow enhanced her standing as someone who communed with nature, finding light, brightness and nodding daisies everywhere she poked her trowel.

She shuffled on the spot, casting about for the right thing

to say. 'Loser' was probably the most accurate. Now I'd surrendered instead of blasting the competition out of the sky with a double-barrelled shotgun, I wanted to dive inside and shut out the image of her skipping back to him, fears allayed, future glittering.

But she wasn't going to let me off that easily. 'Thank you. You've been very understanding. I'm sorry to have turned up on your doorstep like this, but I was driving myself mad worrying that he'd go back to you. I wouldn't blame you for wanting him, he's such a lovely man.'

She held out her hand to me.

I hesitated, then shook it. I nodded. 'I know.'

I really did know.

Octavia

Jonathan was late to meet me at the Da Alberto restaurant on the marina. I couldn't relax. I swigged back the red wine. My head needed San Pellegrino, but my heart needed the oblivion of alcohol. Two glasses later, I finally saw Jonathan winding his way through the crowd, looking quite the native in a linen jacket I didn't remember seeing before.

Guilt hung from me. I wasn't who he thought I was. I wasn't who anyone thought I was. Every time I thought about Xavi, I felt as though I was toppling off a cliff. It made me want to clutch the chair.

Jonathan saw me and nodded. I took a deep breath and smiled. He hurried over, red-faced and harassed, and swung himself into the seat opposite me.

'Hi. You made it then. Sorry I'm late. Find your way here all right?'

No kiss. Jonathan wasn't one for over-the-top greetings in public places. Or anywhere.

He picked up the menu. 'I'm starving. Came here the other night after work. Food's good. Pricey though, but I thought we'd have a little blow-out. Job's going really well. Spoke to

Patri and I'm going to have to come out at least twice a month from now on, maybe more.'

Jonathan seemed more animated than I'd seen him in ages. He twittered on about the team he worked with, describing them one by one until Fabritziu merged into Pasquale and Dominigu.

'Not bad for a bunch of Ities, some smart brains among them. I was surprised that there are even a few women in senior positions. Thought it would be quite a chauvinistic company with Patri at the helm,' he said.

I wanted to be interested, but my mind kept leapfrogging over who was leading the installation team, back to Xavi and the look in his eyes when we said goodbye. I was glad when the waiter interrupted Jonathan to take our orders. My appetite had disappeared. I stuck with a plate of antipasti. For a meat-and-two-veg man who usually piped up with 'Aren't there any potatoes?', Jonathan amazed me by choosing stuffed anchovies and a bowl of clams.

'Like the jacket.' I stopped myself spoiling the moment by mentioning that he'd had time to shop but not to spend a second with me.

'Yeah. It's so hot. Had to get something a bit lighter.' He shrugged. 'Food's surprised me. Some of the people I work with insisted on me trying all their different specialities. Found that I quite liked it, especially their seafood. We never eat a lot of seafood, do we?'

I resisted pointing out that every time I suggested mussels, Jonathan screwed his face up and made a comment about them being the sewers of the sea and looking like vaginas.

I waited for Jonathan to ask me what I'd been up to. If I said anything about Corsica, I'd give myself away. I'd Googled the distance between Santa Teresa di Gallura in the north and Cagliari in the south, and decided my best plan of attack was to invent a time-consuming scenic trip around the Sardinian coast. From the slow progress I'd made when I'd been on the winding back roads, I could easily get away with a couple of overnight stays en route.

Jonathan was listing the colleagues he liked best, pausing now and again to scoop up a clam with flatbread. I should have been thrilled that he was becoming more cosmopolitan but it was like watching the scene from above. My body was present but my mind was jet-lagged.

Eventually Jonathan ran out of work steam. 'So. Did you have a nice time? What did you see?'

Xavi pulling me into the boat. Xavi looking into my eyes, really seeing me. Xavi cuddled up close, singing me the songs we used to listen to on Radio Cuore. I dragged myself away from those thoughts.

I took a slug of wine and found my bright jolly voice, the one I used for the children at nursery when I wanted them to wash their hands before lunch.

'I took a really slow drive around the coast. I almost covered the whole island.'

Reading about it in the guidebook, anyway.

'I saw a fantastic campsite near Palau with ready-pitched tents. You can camp right on the tip of the peninsula among the gorse bushes, gorgeous beaches on both sides. The kids would love it, we should think about bringing them in the summer. I bet Charlie would be brilliant at windsurfing.'

Jonathan wrinkled his nose slightly. 'Camping? Do you think they'd enjoy that? I don't imagine that Sardinian shower facilities are up to much. Though I suppose it would be cheap.'

'It's not great luxury but the kids would have a lot of freedom. It might be a bit of fun for a week. Immi and Polly never get a second without us helicoptering over them. They could learn some Italian.' I tried not to think about the adventures we could have had with Xavi, squatting around camp fires, eating coconut in Ko Samui.

Jonathan shrugged. 'No one really speaks Italian, do they? Spanish would be more useful.'

'It's a lovely language, though. Presumably you'd find your job easier if you spoke it?' I tried to keep the sarcasm out of my voice.

'Not really. If the people I need to deal with don't speak very good English, they just get one of the secretaries in to translate.' Jonathan dabbed at his chin with his serviette.

'Wouldn't it give you a sense of satisfaction to be able to communicate in their language?' I said.

'English is the language of business. Anyone who wants to compete internationally has to learn it. That's the way it is.'

I had to let the subject drop. I could find a million and one reasons to pick at Jonathan tonight. Learning Italian, Spanish or bloody Swahili was the least of it.

We turned back to safer ground, discussing the children and whether we'd have to pay for a private school for Immi if she turned out to be dyslexic. I felt myself relax as Jonathan came up with sensible solutions, guided by facts rather than unfounded emotions. I reminded myself how I'd clung to him in my last year at university, frail from Dad's death, barely able to keep up with my work. He'd been there, making decisions for me, waiting for the time when I could stitch myself back together. Sticking by me when I decided to keep my baby. I couldn't let my mind wander down the avenue of thinking what might have happened if I'd known Xavi had wanted me.

Enough to marry me.

I reached over the table to hold his hand. He gave it a perfunctory squeeze then shrugged me off in favour of his fork. When we'd finished, I suggested a stroll round the port to buy an ice cream and choose our fantasy yacht.

Jonathan patted his stomach. 'It's so busy down there and I'm stuffed anyway. Done nothing but eat these last few days.'

And there was me thinking he'd been working his arse off. But given I wasn't exactly camped on moral high ground myself, I tried to salvage the evening. 'Come on. You can have a coffee. Let's make the most of our last couple of evenings together. You know what it'll be like when we get back on Tuesday, rushing about with the kids. I won't speak to you properly for a week.'

Jonathan nodded and we walked along the marina. I slipped my arm through his. We walked awkwardly, out of time, until he disentangled himself and shoved his hands in his pockets.

I tried to enjoy the surroundings, the glamour and bustle of it all. All the women in their designer dresses, the little girls with their frilly skirts and white ankle socks like something off a soap powder advert. Even the old ladies had fashionable glasses and elfin haircuts.

'I want to try one of those *sa carapigna* ice creams. I read about them in the guidebook, they're handmade from lemon and sugar. Shall we sit down on one of the terraces?'

'I'm pretty knackered. It's been a long week. Buy one to eat while we walk back to the hotel. I've got to get up early for work tomorrow.'

I gave up my feeble notion of sitting on a café terrace, people-watching, enjoying the moment. Jonathan had to have a focus. He would go to a restaurant because it was eight o'clock and he needed to eat. He wasn't going for an insight into the regional cuisine, the local customs or to reconnect with his wife. He was there purely to stop his stomach rumbling. Once that had been achieved, he couldn't see the point. The doors to freedom that had flung wide open while I was with Xavi were closing in on me again.

I'd have to accept that, if I wanted a stable life for the

kids, 'What do you want to do that for?' was going to be part of my future.

I queued for the ice cream I no longer wanted, watching a young couple at a table snogging each other as though they were alone on a hillside. I glanced round for Jonathan. He was standing, arms folded. He could have been waiting for the two-thirty to Leeds in the middle of King's Cross station. No pleasure in his surroundings or interest in what was going on around him.

I ordered my ice cream, feeling old and invisible as the barman continued his banter with the long-haired girl working next to him, showing off with a cheerleader twirl of the ice cream scoop. Some men had Porsches, some had ice cream scoops.

Some had a zest for travel and a little boat on a Corsican sea.

I licked the lemon sorbet, relishing the sourness on my tongue, and turned back to find Jonathan. He had shifted from his waiting-for-a-delayed-train stance and was chatting, quite enthusiastically, to a couple of women.

I wandered out and stood at his side, waiting to be introduced. Eventually, Jonathan indicated a petite woman with cropped black hair framing her face. 'This is Elisabetta. She works for Patri. This is her friend, Alessandra.'

They shook my hand and smiled. Then they both did that thing I'd noticed a lot in Italy. Their eyes gobbled up what I was wearing, almost as though they were pricing up my outfit. Florence & Fred probably didn't compete very well with Max Mara. I promised myself that I would buy a trendy pair of sandals when I got home to replace my Tesco flip-flops.

'I'm Jonathan's wife, Octavia,' I said, filling in the gaps in case they thought I was some random tourist who'd happened to come and stand next to them. A hideous discussion then followed about what I'd seen in Sardinia. Apart from one sticky moment when Elisabetta asked me whether I'd visited some ultra-famous tombs I'd never heard of, I managed to sound quite convincing for someone who'd barely spent twenty-four hours on the island. I prayed Jonathan wouldn't invite them to have a drink with us. Thankfully, he soon hurried me off to the hotel with both women saying how pleased they were to meet me.

No doubt I'd keep them in 'English women have no idea of fashion' conversation for some time to come.

Tonight it was me who leapt into bed and pulled the sheets up. I gave Jonathan the big bottom and curled into a ball. This would be the last time I would let myself think about Xavi. A great wash of fright swept through me. Fear that I'd never be able to go back to my old world. Fear that I'd never see Xavi again. Fear that I'd wreak havoc in Jonathan's life, in the children's lives, and all fingers would be pointed at me.

When I got off the plane in a couple of days' time, I'd dig a deep dark place in my brain and bury Xavi forever.

Roberta

When I met up with Octavia shortly after she got back from Sardinia, it seemed as though she'd been away for ages. Over coffee, I filled her in on my relief that Alicia's tests had ruled out any horrendous diseases. When I'd phoned for the results earlier in the week and heard the nurse tapping into her computer, I'd felt sick.

'She did say that the tests weren't foolproof because the incubation period varies so much.'

Octavia shrugged. 'You've done what you can. Stop worrying now.'

She sounded lethargic, not at all like someone who'd just been on holiday. Maybe she thought I'd made a big fuss about nothing. Then, in a big rush, she said, 'I've got something to tell you.' She sounded so serious, I braced myself for bad news. When she announced her dalliance with Xavi, I was both relieved and horrified.

'You went with the express purpose of finding him?'

Her answer that it was circumstance – that Jonathan hadn't had any time for her, that she simply wanted to revisit a few places, see what had changed – didn't fool me.

I couldn't compute what she'd told me. For all Jonathan's

endless twitching about with cloths and mops, his parsimonious attitude to money, his oft-repeated mantra of 'Don't get involved' when Octavia wanted to 'fix' people, I thought she loved him. While Scott and I had always teetered on a fragile footing, Octavia and Jonathan were the couple that no one ever discussed. I'd always been in awe of the fact that as soon as she got pregnant, Octavia had diverted her travelling energy into creating a rock-solid family life without a single moment of self-pity.

After Octavia had rushed out her confession, she sat there, eyebrows raised, waiting for me to laugh as I used to when she would bound into afternoon lessons, cheeks flushed from kissing someone else's boyfriend on the hills behind school. What seemed funny at sixteen was life-ruining at thirty-nine.

'Don't you feel bad about breaking your marriage vows?'

'I feel terrified about getting found out, though I can't bring myself to regret it.'

Octavia seemed both shamefaced and defiant. My stomach was knotted. I'd taken it for granted that she'd stay with Jonathan forever.

'If you're not going to go off with Xavi, why would you risk everything like that? You're not intending to leave Jonathan, I assume?'

'No, I'm not. How can I?' Her voice trailed away. 'You think I'm awful don't you?'

'I don't think you're awful.' I took a breath. 'I'm just rather shocked. When we talked about Xavi a few months ago, you gave me the impression you never thought about him. Being bored isn't a reason to go off and have an affair. I'd have loved to have had the chance to get bored with my marriage. You've always had stability. Your kids have stability. You can't underestimate how important that is.'

Octavia's eyes flew open. 'This isn't about you. I don't

want to feel like I'm some big ferry lumping through life with a sophisticated anti-roll system. I know you've had a huge trauma but you've no idea what it feels like to be so insignificant all the time. I'm not looking for the big romance but I'd like to think that I can expect more from a relationship than a subscription to *Practical Pre-school* magazine at Christmas.'

I realised I'd touched a nerve but before I could backtrack, Octavia raged on. 'You're used to getting male attention. I'm not. No one looks at me. No one has looked at me for years. You know what? For once, I felt special, as though there was something about me that no one else had. That I wasn't just someone who mops up the fucking Oatibix and knows where the Sellotape is.'

I knew this was a good time to stop the conversation before I said something I couldn't rewind. 'At least you've got someone backing you up, not working against you all the time.'

'I haven't. He's not here half the time. I've got the worst of both worlds. I'm stuck with a husband who isn't here and when he is, doesn't give a shit what I'm doing, thinking, saying.'

Octavia was marching about the kitchen, waving her hands around. 'It's all right for you. You have every other weekend and two nights in the week to do what you want. You've only got one child, so when she's not there, you're done. I've got three kids wanting a little slice of me. When do I have time to do what I want? I barely recognise myself. I used to sing, dance, go to festivals, have people over for dinner. Christ, I even used to laugh sometimes.'

The heat of injustice was spreading through me. 'It's all right for you' must be one of the brightest red flags known to humans. I hung onto my temper.

'As you are well aware, I would have liked another baby.'

That wound was still raw after all these years, ready to seep open at the slightest rub.

Octavia nodded in apology.

I heard the anger in my voice, even though I was trying to stay calm. 'I do get some free time but I also have to work incredibly hard to make up for all the chaos Scott and I have caused. I feel ashamed every single day that we failed Alicia. I don't think marriage is something you can jettison on a whim. Who's to say the problems won't be exactly the same with Xavi in a few years' time?'

Octavia sat down again. She put her head on her arms, mumbling from the depths of her jumper. 'Don't worry, I'm not going anywhere. I just wanted to feel young again. Like me. The me I was before I became this dowdy old bore that no one recognises.' She paused. 'I know that sounds selfish.'

Octavia was the first to admit she had plenty of character flaws, but she wasn't selfish. She possessed a generous spirit and warmth that I could only dream of. I couldn't let her throw everything away.

'It's no picnic on the other side. The grass is not greener. It's a universe populated with weirdos, eccentrics and Elvis lookalikes,' I said. 'Even when you do meet someone decent, you've got so many issues, you're predisposed to messing up. You have to consider the children. You can't just think about yourself.'

Octavia's head shot up. 'That's the problem, I never get to think about myself. There's always some other sod whose needs are far more important than mine. I never stop considering my kids.'

I dug deep for a conciliatory tone. 'You're a great mum, I know you are. All I meant was that having an affair won't make you feel better in the long run. It will just complicate things. You're privileged to have such a strong family unit. It's not worth destroying for a fling.'

'Xavi wasn't "a fling". It wasn't as though I went on a website and started hooking up with any old bloke with his own teeth. I went back to someone I love. Loved.' Octavia ran her fingers through her hair. 'Unfinished business.'

'And is it finished now?'

'It has to be.'

Octavia

In the fortnight since my return from Corsica, the falling feeling didn't go away. Roberta's disapproval had made an already big bad deed seem much more enormous. I plodded through the days, still functioning, managing to remember who'd got a new dog at nursery, which mum had just had a baby, who'd started a different job. I could still do what was expected of me, though I had to try harder to make it seem natural. My addiction to Googling Xavi was not so much cured as killed. I couldn't know any more about him, have any contact with him, if I was to be the mother I'd set out to be.

Too late to be the wife I'd set out to be, but I could still be the mother.

Polly was the first to notice the change. 'It's much nicer now you don't come bellowing into the bedroom shouting at me to get up.' That morning I'd sat down gently on the end of her bed and stroked her foot to wake her up, marvelling at how those tiny baby toes had grown into near-teenage feet.

Charlie had grunted, 'You're not half as stressy any more. You been through the menopause?' after I shrugged when he knocked a pint glass of Coke over the lounge carpet.

Now and again, my longing for Xavi consumed me. To make up for it, I forced myself to focus on Jonathan's qualities, praising him for his hard work with Immi and her reading, admiring the shed he'd built rather than moaning about how long he'd spent arsing about with it.

My self-punishment was to become the woman he wanted. Late in life I had discovered my mother's favourite saying was true. The devil does indeed make work for idle hands. As soon as the children were settled at night, I raced round the house like some kind of supermaid, squirting all manner of unecological things on the bathroom taps to remove the limescale, replacing dead light bulbs and hoovering under the bed. My new regime of housework left me exhausted. When Jonathan wasn't there, I didn't even bother getting undressed properly, rope-tricking my bra off under my T-shirt and collapsing into bed in my knickers. Sleep couldn't come quickly enough to blot out Xavi.

As the days passed I trained my thoughts away from him. Occasionally Jonathan even noticed my efforts to be a good wife. He was delighted with my faux-antiquing of our old pine chest of drawers. He'd been deflecting my request for new bedroom furniture for a while and spent a whole weekend telling me how much money I'd saved us. I didn't spoil it by telling him that all the sanding down knackered me out so much that I'd gone to bed for a whole afternoon. He always thought that my ability to nap in the day at the mere sight of a duvet proved that I was innately lazy.

One Saturday morning when Jonathan had taken Charlie off to cricket, I struggled out of bed at 9.30 to answer the door to the postman. I felt hungover even though I'd only managed a couple of glasses of wine before drifting off to sleep in the armchair. I stood groggily at the door, vaguely embarrassed by my Dalmatian dressing gown, while he asked me to sign for a Jiffy bag. More crap from one of Jonathan's computer magazines. Then I realised it was for me. I pulled it open, expecting some more free tights that my mother periodically sent off for, in the hope that I would turn into the dainty daughter she'd always wanted.

Half of a two-euro coin.

I knew without reading the note who it was from. I crept past the lounge, where Polly was busy belting out Passenger's *Let Her Go* on the karaoke machine. Very fitting. I sat down at the kitchen table feeling more energetic than I had since I'd come home from Sardinia. He hadn't forgotten me.

The note was very Xavi, that distinctive curly Mediterranean writing.

Tavy, here is a modern version of our coin. I keep the other half. You have my heart. It is up to you what you do with it. I will always love you.

Plus his phone number.

Dimly I registered the relief that Jonathan wasn't here to see me open the package. I should have been cross with Xavi. We weren't a family who guarded phones, computers or post. But I was so happy to hear from him. Now he knew my married name and town: Google had obviously worked its magic. I smelt the note, breathing in a bit of his world, trying to ignore the fact that I now had his number. I made a cup of tea to distract myself but the first gulp made me feel sick. I was desperate to hear his voice, to soothe the ache that had plagued me since I'd come home. In the end, I gave in, found my mobile and ran out into the back garden. I yanked some sheets and towels off the washing line. The children wouldn't disturb me if it looked like they might get roped into a chore. Then I punched in the number at the top of the letter and watched the screen flick onto 'calling'.

I stabbed the red button.

My kids were in there without a care in the world. It wasn't their fault I'd decided to sleep with an old boyfriend while their dad was buried in work. I wasn't going to be the one to blow their lives apart. I shoved my phone in my pocket and brought in the washing. Instead of stuffing it into the airing cupboard willy-nilly, I folded each pillowcase into careful quarters and smoothed the duvet covers into hotel-like neatness. I'd make it up to Jonathan, starting with an embargo on secret phone calls to Xavi.

I had two hours before he got back from cricket duty. Just time to clean all the toothpastey spit off the mirrors. It was one of the thousands of things that made Jonathan start shouting about 'changes needing to be made in this house'.

I found something therapeutic in polishing everything. My mother would have said it was rubbing away my sin. I lined up Charlie's various deodorants on the windowsill. Thrill, Lure, Inspiration – ridiculous names for something that made him smell like loo freshener. I piled Polly's bath cubes into a neat corner. I picked up the empty pill packet that I'd finished a few days ago and added it to my rubbish pile.

No. More than a few days ago. A week ago.

I sat down on the loo seat and thought back. I always finished on a Saturday. I should be starting a new pack that night. No period. My heart was speeding up. I hadn't missed any pills. I couldn't be pregnant. Christ, it was like being eighteen again, trying to think back to when you had sex and doing complicated calculations about when you might have ovulated. No, it had to be a hormonal thing. Or the stress of meeting Xavi again, then having to hide it.

I abandoned my bathroom cleaning. I'd just double-check what might cause it on Google. Panic was subsiding. I'd been on the pill for years. Since I'd got pregnant with Charlie, we hadn't taken any chances. Why would it let me down now? I was sure it was my guilty conscience playing havoc with my body. I ran downstairs and Googled 'on the pill, no period' and found the usual gormless answers of 'u shd see your doc' and 'u might be pg'. I ran my eye down the others. 'My doctor said it's normal to miss a period sometimes.' 'If you get too thin, your periods can stop' – I could rule that one out. 'I got food poisoning with throwing up and the trots for two days. Doc said I should've used condoms for a week afterwards.'

I let out a little shriek that made Stan leap to his feet. Out-of-date scallops just before I went to Corsica. Oh God. Oh God. I couldn't have a baby. Not now.

Especially when I didn't know who the father was.

Roberta

I hated being at odds with Octavia. Our communication had been brief and terse since she'd told me about Xavi three weeks ago. She was much better at delivering home truths than hearing them. However, once I'd finished Mrs Goodman's sitting room to her satisfaction – 'A Gallic triumph, dear, a triumph!' – I tried to make peace. I convinced her that she needed a day out to revamp her wardrobe as she'd been moaning about feeling frumpy for ages. It might help her feel good again, and maybe even Jonathan would sit up and notice her.

'Shopping? Do we have to?'

I persuaded her that she could sit down on every available bench and I would gather up things, bring them to her, deal with the hangers, plus feed her sandwiches at regular intervals. As we drove to Bluewater, I waited for Octavia to launch into our usual pattern of a Shelton family round-up followed by a discussion about my work, relationships and Alicia. This morning was different. Octavia sat in the front seat like a worn-out old Labrador that couldn't be bothered to get out of its basket.

'Are you OK?'

'Yes. I'm fine. Just a bit tired.'

This taciturn Octavia was unnerving me. Here was a woman who had sweeping opinions on everything. I preferred it when she teased me for still moping about Jake. We drew up outside John Lewis.

'I don't know that I'm in the mood for this,' she said, as we made our way up the escalator into the women's department.

I ignored the comment and parked her by the changing rooms, bribing her with a promise of sushi, and ran around snatching up V-necked T-shirts, three-quarter-length tops and sandals.

I poked the clothes through the curtain and just as quickly they came out again. 'It's not me.' 'I'd feel ridiculous in that.' 'Too top-heavy.'

When she pushed out a glorious pink wrap-over dress, I pulled back the curtain. 'Trust me. You will look amazing in this. Just try it on again.'

Octavia folded her arms. 'No. I don't feel like it. Sorry. Nothing looks right today. I just look fat and past-it.'

Octavia's petulance was beginning to rankle but I concentrated on my desire to make amends for my reaction to her fling with Xavi. The last six months had obviously turned me into an evangelical defender of other people's marriages despite walking out on my own. I didn't want to become someone who waved sticks about at Speaker's Corner, droning on about 'Thou shalt not commit adultery'.

I attempted to make shopping attractive. 'I'll tell you what. Why don't we get you some new lingerie? If you've got the right bra on, it makes everything look better.'

'No. No. I'm not messing about with bras and pants.'

'A good bra hauls everything upwards and streamlines your silhouette.'

324

Octavia started pulling on her jeans. 'Roberta, I'm sorry, I can't do this.'

'Let's just find one thing you feel great in.' I'd never earmarked Octavia as a sulker before. Opinionated. Acerbic. Stubborn. But not a sulker.

Without responding, she clapped her hand over her mouth and ran towards the exit. I snatched up my handbag in time to see her splatter sick across the one bit of tiled floor that didn't have a rail of clothes on it. Even Octavia's vomiting was practical.

I gave myself a stern talking-to. This was not a throwing-up competition. I lifted my hair off my neck, pointed out the mess to the nearest assistant, then marched Octavia away.

As soon as we got outside, I guided her to the public lavatories, taking care not to breathe too deeply.

'You won't mind if I don't come in with you?' My stomach was starting to whir.

When she came out, I looked at her. 'You poor thing. Must be a bug going round. You should have said you weren't feeling well.'

She looked at the floor. 'I'm pregnant.'

I felt a rush of surprise, followed by the painful little jab of envy I always did whenever anyone said they were pregnant. I studied her face. 'Are you pleased?'

The vehemence of her 'no' shocked me. Unlike me, who greeted every blue line with a rush of fear as the start of a journey I was unlikely to finish, Octavia positively bloomed, as though she'd found her perfect niche in the world.

'So what happened?'

She was too glum to make any stupid jokes about seeds and eggs. 'Remember I ate some scallops that gave me sickness and diarrhoea? Mucked up the pill. Should've used extra contraception for seven days afterwards.' She tried to smile. 'Would have to be that week I picked to get lucky twice.'

325

'Does Jonathan know yet?'

'No. He mustn't ever know. I've booked an abortion for the first day of his next trip to Sardinia, in two weeks' time. I should be OK by the time he gets back.'

The loo door banged as an elderly woman struggled out with her bags and a couple of grandchildren. I was aware of people moving in the shopping centre, colours and shadows passing around us. I closed my eyes. The grief of my two miscarriages was always there, ready to surface.

I'd tried so hard for another baby, my two little boys who never got a chance to live.

I concentrated on keeping the horror out of my voice. 'You've already booked a termination? Are you sure? You could cope with one more, couldn't you? The children are old enough to help you out a little. I can see it's not ideal now they're all at school, but you'd manage.'

Octavia looked at me as though I was the slowest person on the planet. 'I don't know whose it is.'

A big gust of rancid lavatories wafted over us. 'Let's find somewhere to sit.' I dragged her through the shopping centre, practically elbowing a mum with a toddler out of the way to commandeer a table in Pret. 'Have you thought this through properly? You only slept with Xavi once, didn't you?'

Octavia looked down at the ginger beer I'd bought for her. 'I only slept with Jonathan once in that time frame as well. It's a straight fifty-fifty chance.'

'He has a right to know you might be carrying his baby.'

'Who? Jonathan? Or Xavi?'

'Jonathan.' I thought for a moment. 'And Xavi, I suppose. Oh God, Octavia. Maybe Jonathan would understand if you told him.' My voice trailed off. Straw-clutching sprang to mind. 'A termination. That's so final. Getting rid of your children's sibling.'

Octavia winced. 'Cheers for pointing that out. I know. I

can't think what else to do. I've gone round and round in my head. I can't have the baby. Not if I'm staying with Jonathan. There's no way I could let him bring up Xavi's child. Sooner or later I'd have to tell him and that would be far worse.'

'How long have you known?' I picked at the rocket in my sandwich.

'A week, but I only did the test today. Kept hoping it was stress that was stopping my periods but no, Octavia Shelton, babymaker extraordinaire, strikes again. I've already had the consultation with the clinic. Just the business end to sort out now.'

Octavia's cold matter-of-factness wrenched at my heart. I tried not to think about the unfairness of it all, the praying for a missed period, the endless rushing to the loo to check, the deflecting of the question, 'So when are you going to have a little brother or sister for Alicia?'

'Have you contacted Xavi?' Only superhuman effort kept my voice neutral.

'No.' Her voice dropped to a whisper. 'You were right. I was being selfish. Anyway, I'm not going to put a gun to his head like that. He loves me, yes, but who knows whether he'd want the baby even if it was his.'

On any other occasion I would have pulled Octavia's leg about admitting that someone else was right. I tried to think logically.

'You can't have a termination yet. Promise me you'll take time to reflect on it.'

'I already have. Everything else, all the other options, are worse. This way the only person who gets hurt is me.'

There were times when I envied Octavia's decisiveness, her unwavering view of the world while I dithered and vacillated, always wondering, 'What if?' even after I'd made a decision. But everything in me was fighting her now. I searched for a way to change things, to find a way through. I cleared my throat. 'Don't you want another baby? You always seemed so fulfilled when they were tiny.'

'I love babies. I hadn't planned to have another one, but I'm sure I'd cope. But I can't cope living a lie, knowing it's Xavi's baby and letting Jonathan think it's his.'

'It might not be Xavi's. It might be Jonathan's.'

'What if it isn't? What if a dark-haired olive-skinned baby pops out? What if I don't know whose it is straightaway?'

'Can you get through the rest of your marriage never breathing a word?' My voice was catching. Terminations were for fifteen-year-olds caught out before their lives began, not capable mothers of Octavia's age. 'How long will Jonathan be in Sardinia for? Are you going to be well enough to hide it from him when he gets back?'

'He's been a bit vague on how long he's going to be away for, but probably ten days or so. I think because it's early, I'll be OK. It's just a suction job at this stage.'

Octavia had a knack for gathering herself up. She'd pulled me together so many times, I owed it to her to return the favour. But I couldn't get past that little baby who was never going to see life. 'Sorry. I just think it's so sad to get rid of a baby, any baby.' I started to cry. 'Promise me you'll think about telling Jonathan. You don't have to mention Xavi.'

'I can't run the risk. I can live with it. I'll survive.' Her chin was set. Octavia never ceased to surprise me. Under her easy-going exterior was a steely core of iron.

'I can't sit here fretting about things I can't change. I've got to make plans.' She piled our discarded sandwich wrappers onto the tray. 'I'm going to need some cover at the nursery. I'll tell my mother I'm going on a course and get her over to look after the kids. Must find out how soon I'll be able to drive afterwards.'

I was shaking my head. This was the woman who had

sung to her babies every day of their lives in and out of the womb. The one who still snuggled up with all of them on the sofa like a big German shepherd with her puppies. The mother who had the patience to make food into faces, to play endless games of Uno, to join in dance routines, to allow her children to grow without the rigid rules and regulations that seemed fundamental to my own parenting style.

I couldn't see how she was going to walk away from a termination and still be the same person. Every time I tried to speak, sorrow, agonising and fresh, carried my words away.

Octavia leaned back in her chair, flicking at crumbs on the table. 'I know you don't approve but I can't see any other option.'

I had to get my words out. 'It's not about approving or disapproving. I don't want you to make a mistake you'll regret for the rest of your life.'

Octavia picked her bag up. 'It's too late for that.'

Octavia

'I need to talk to you.'

The phrase was so unlikely for Jonathan that I automatically said, 'Pardon?'

I forced myself to look him in the eye. He was leaving for Sardinia the next day.

I was leaving for the abortion clinic as soon as he'd gone.

I'd laced up my emotions like a bodice, not allowing myself to think about what I was doing. I couldn't remember what a neutral, non-guilty face looked like.

'What about?' I turned away to put the kettle on, anything to escape his gaze.

Jonathan inspected his fingernails. 'I've got something important to tell you.'

I prepared myself for him being made redundant again, no summer holiday this year, his usual diatribe about finding one of Stan's hairs in his food.

'I'm staying out in Sardinia for six weeks this time.'

'Six weeks?' The longest he'd ever gone for before was ten days. Typical Jonathan, leaving it till the day before to tell me. I suppose he figured I'd only have a day to huff and puff. My first thought was that I'd have much longer to recover. My second was that he'd miss sports day.

Before I could say anything else, he rushed out, 'I'm considering a permanent move out there.'

I must have put on the sort of face that waiters in France use whenever I try to speak French to them.

'What?' This was the husband who got an upset stomach when we went to the Isle of Wight. Now he was planning to move all five of us to another country without consulting me. 'What about the kids? Are there any international schools there? What about my nursery business?'

Jonathan tucked a chair under the table and squared up a couple of magazines.

A tiny part of my mind was already rising to the challenge, conjuring up images of a sun-kissed Immi playing in a piazza with other children while Charlie buzzed about on a Vespa, sunglasses balanced on his head.

Jonathan eventually tore himself away from polishing smudges off the table with his sleeve. 'I'm sorry.'

'I hope you haven't already agreed to do it. It's not really a decision you can take unilaterally. There are five of us in the family. And Stan.'

Jonathan lifted his head.

'I've met someone else.'

I stared. Round-eyed, gob-open, legs-threatening-not-to-hold-me-up staring.

'Who?' My voice was harsh. My hand went instinctively to my stomach. That solved whether Jonathan would want the baby – if it was his – or not.

'Someone I work with.'

'Very original. Don't tell me, one of those knitting-needle women we bumped into when I was in Sardinia?'

Jonathan nodded.

'Christ, they must have been having a right laugh. The

wife that doesn't know the husband is fucking the woman standing right in front of her. Classy. Which one? The one with the big hooky hooter or the one with no tits?'

'Don't do this, Octavia. You're better than that. Her name is Elisabetta. You must know that things haven't been good for a while.'

'Maybe I thought that was what marriage looked like after a decade or so. I didn't plan to throw in the towel, though.'

Even I could hear my voice lacking the outrage of the innocent. While I imagined I'd been doing Jonathan a favour by forgetting about Xavi, Jonathan was forging a life with someone who wanted to be with him out of love rather than duty. It made me wonder when we'd stopped noticing each other, a bit like a cabinet you plonk down in the corner of the lounge on the day you move in and don't touch again for ten years.

I wasn't out of anger yet. Yes, I'd slept with someone else, no credit to me, but I hadn't just decided I was off, never mind the carnage left behind.

'What about the children?' I couldn't even bring up a picture of what Immi would look like when she heard.

'I didn't plan this.'

Fear of their pain made me ferocious. 'Plee-ase. Save me the "I didn't plan this, it was love at first bloody sight" bollocks. I don't care if you had your little diary out, plotting your work stints in Sardinia round her periods. I don't care if you saved up your Air Miles for a little in-between-time rendezvous in Rome. What I care about is how you're going to explain to your children that you've decided to leave them, with no discussion, no debate.' I still couldn't quite get the antagonism into my voice that I would have expected to manage.

That Jonathan would have expected me to manage.

Jonathan became very interested in his fingernails. 'I will explain to them. Of course I will. I'm not just going to disappear. I'm hoping that when things are settled they'll come and visit me in Sardinia. I know they're at the age when they're more interested in their friends than us, but I've really missed them these last few months. I still love them, you know that.'

The subtext – I don't love you – was loud and clear.

I was beginning to understand why Roberta had found it hard to leave Scott, despite it appearing a no-brainer to me. Staring down the barrel of total uncertainty was terrifying. It hurt me to think that Jonathan was saving his thoughtfulness for another woman. Maybe another family.

'Has she got children?'

'No. She's too old now. Forty-six.'

I felt a flare of reluctant admiration. Those bloody Italians knew how to look after themselves.

'So that's it. You're definitely going? Not interested in hearing a plea from me, for the family? Just happy to put yourself first and bugger the consequences?'

'It's too late for that, Octavia. I'm forty next year. I can't envisage another thirty years like this, or even another ten.' Jonathan had been saying he was nearly forty since the day after he turned thirty-one.

I butted in. 'So this is a mid-life crisis?'

He picked at a loose thread on his jumper. 'No, I think we are fundamentally wrong for each other. You're so restless all the time. You want to try new things, expand the business, visit weird and wonderful places. I just don't. I like my own bed and my own routine.'

Frustration was building in me. 'Sorry. I didn't realise wanting to grow the business made me bad wife material.'

'You know what I mean. You're never satisfied, and I can't give you what you want. I feel as though you're always looking at me and wishing I was different. The truth is that if you hadn't got pregnant with Charlie, we'd have probably gone our separate ways years ago.'

333

'But you can't regret having the kids, surely?' I was feeling an urgent need to stay away from baseball bats.

'Not at all. Not for a minute. Which is precisely why I think we need to split up.'

I laughed out loud at that, hollow and sharp. 'Saint Jonathan, leaving his wife to live in another country for the sake of his children.'

'I don't want my kids growing up thinking that love is about whose turn it is to do the school drop-off and sort out the science homework. I want them to know it's about finding the right partner who makes you feel that you could be a better person than you ever imagined.'

All that lyrical Italian was rubbing off on Jonathan. I wished I could have sneered at him. But I knew what he meant. Xavi made me feel the most interesting, the most capable and the most cared-for person alive. I couldn't believe I hadn't spotted the fact that Jonathan had someone else. I prided myself on being eagle-eyed. I was the one who noticed how a husband looked at his wife, how she touched him, how they spoke about each other. But I still hadn't realised that him not wanting me in Sardinia had nothing to do with work pressure and everything to do with penis pressure.

Adventure wasn't quite so enticing when I had to protect three children. I was pretty sure the kids wouldn't follow Jonathan's logic. I took a deep breath. 'Promise me you'll come back after this stint and we can work out a civilised way to tell the children that we're separating and you're moving to Sardinia permanently.'

'Of course. It's for the best. While we're still young enough to build another life.'

Jonathan, least likely adventurer in the world, seizing the opportunity of happiness with both hands. Octavia, most likely adventurer in the world, shit-scared.

Briefly I considered playing the 'I'm carrying your child'

card. But Jonathan was right. What I'd mistaken for comfortable married love after sixteen years was not love at all. Just boredom and habit. I'd got my wish for adventure but somehow I'd envisaged it with walking boots and rucksacks rather than a series of ready meals for one.

Freedom didn't look quite so bloody thrilling after all.

Roberta

I saw Jonathan leave in a cab at 7.30am. I watched the next-door neighbour walk off to school with her own brood, plus Polly and Immi. Charlie finally shuffled out of the house about 8.30 with Octavia shouting instructions from the front door. I'd parked up the road, watching her house in my rear-view mirror.

I knew Octavia wouldn't have let me come if I'd phoned ahead. She viewed asking for help as a weakness. I'd wrestled with myself. Every time there'd been a shadow of trauma in my life, Octavia had been there. Scott. Jake. Alicia. She might not have agreed with me. On some occasions, I'm sure she thought I was the most ineffectual person in the world. Unlike my tennis friends, she never told me what I wanted to hear. But when push came to shove, Octavia was the person who was there, door open, corkscrew in hand, whatever was going on in her life.

Now it was my turn to step up.

I had to stop thinking about my own losses. Terminations were abhorrent to me. When I thought about what she was about to do, I felt impotent, verging on angry. Although Octavia would carry on as usual, sorting out swimming

336

costumes, cricket gear and packed lunches, refusing to buckle under the enormity of what lay ahead, inside she'd be petrified.

She had to be.

I walked up to the house and knocked on the door. Octavia appeared in clothes that looked like they'd hung around on the end of the bed for a fraction too long. 'Roberta!'

Her hair was matted down one side. I hoped it wasn't sick. She looked blotchy. Definitely not bonny.

'I'm coming with you,' I said.

Octavia let out a long, controlled breath. 'Thank you.'

Then she clung to me and sobbed.

Octavia

Roberta drove. I sat in the passenger seat wondering when I became this great big drip of a woman who snivelled through her problems. Since Roberta had turned up I hadn't managed to speak more than a couple of words. It was as though I was crying my insides out. I hadn't blubbed like this since Dad died.

When my kids were small and cried when they were tired of walking, I used to tell them to save their energy for doing what needed to be done. I wanted to follow my own advice, but I couldn't. Every time I thought I'd run out of grief, a picture of Immi with chocolate round her mouth aged two would flash through my mind. Charlie, in goal, eyebrows knitted together, aged six. Polly putting glass baubles on the Christmas tree, tongue out in concentration, flyaway hair sticking out like a dandelion clock. Then I'd think about this little mite with its downy blonde hair or dark thatch and my stomach would lurch.

'You don't have to do this,' Roberta said.

I didn't answer, just turned my face to the window. I didn't recognise myself. If anyone cried in meetings at work because they felt underappreciated, tired out or stressed, only

338

employment law stopped me going bonkers. Of the millions of things that had me gritting my teeth, people who couldn't cope were probably top of the list. Or parents who put their happiness above their children's. Or mothers who thought extra-marital sex was the answer. Which, as life had shown me, it definitely wasn't.

Now I was going to do the thing that no mother should do.

I reminded myself that my baby was only about as big as a blueberry, a cluster of nothing. It couldn't smile, wave or kick a foot. I'd tested my resolve searching the internet to see how developed it would be. Apparently he or she would have hands that could bend at the wrist, eyelid folds and, the bit that made me shut down the computer immediately, the beginnings of a nose. Charlie had had the most wonderful button nose as a baby, squidgy and wrinkled. I'd have posted pictures of it on Facebook if it had been around then. If I was that sort of mother.

I hadn't yet told Roberta that Jonathan was leaving me. I'd been drama-free for sixteen years and had managed to pack an extra-marital affair, pregnancy and marriage break-down into a couple of months. I needed all my strength to get through the abortion. There was no room for a debate about an expired marriage. I leaned back on the headrest and battled to stop my tears.

Roberta parked at the top of the steep drive. 'Serving your health needs for the future' seemed a strange slogan for somewhere that dealt mainly in abortions and HIV testing.

'I'll come in with you.' Roberta yanked the keys out of the ignition.

'You really don't have to. You know what you're like with hospitals. You'll be fainting at reception.'

'I won't. I promise.' Roberta unclipped her seatbelt. 'Let's get it over with.'

Roberta went through the front door first. The receptionist was trained to act as though I was popping to the dentist for a quick whizz with the tooth polisher.

'Ms Shelton? You're in to see Doctor Washington at 10.10. Take a seat in the waiting room on the left.'

Maybe dealing with people who were getting rid of their babies all day long made it more acceptable. Or maybe she spent every dinner party slagging off women like me who messed up their contraception, then couldn't cope with the outcome.

We sat down. I eyed the other women there. Not a single teenage girl. In fact, no one under thirty. All women who looked old enough to know better. One was in a smart trouser suit with boots with red soles, that shoe designer that Roberta liked. I imagined her baby to be the product of a rich married man who reached for his wallet as soon as the line turned blue.

Then there was a thin woman, serious straight haircut with severe fringe, pointy nose. I couldn't imagine her forgetting the condoms in the throes of passion.

I was wandering off onto the story of the woman in the tweedy clothes – mother of four already? Gardener to some country squire? – when a nurse called my name.

'Shall I come?' Roberta started to get up.

I shook my head. The chances of Roberta staying vertical while they sucked the life out of me were zero, but I loved her for offering.

She squeezed my hand and whispered up to me. 'Are you sure you're doing the right thing?'

I whispered back. 'Jonathan's leaving me for someone else. I can't have a baby now. He wouldn't want it even if it was his.'

'Jonathan's leaving you?' Roberta's voice came out so loud, I think we managed to distract the whole waiting room from their woes for a moment.

The nurse's smile was stuck in a transition between 'I am a kind and non-judgmental person' and 'Chop, chop, there's a queue after you.'

As I walked away, I glanced back. Roberta had her head in her hands. I averted my eyes from the other women sitting there. I followed the nurse down the corridor, her plastic shoes squeaking on the lino. As we got to the door, she patted my arm. 'Don't worry. You'll be fine.'

Platitudes were obviously part of the job.

Dr Washington, a slim black man, introduced himself and invited me to get undressed behind a curtain. The nurse handed me a gown. The doctor confirmed that I had chosen no anaesthetic. I'd had a variety of drugs, epidurals and gas and air when my children were born but I felt that I shouldn't let myself off with this one, as though the pain would somehow atone for the act. I unzipped my boots.

Would I be mourning my baby's should-have-been birthday forever more?

I undid the button and fly of my jeans. I'd read somewhere on a 'what to expect when you have an abortion' site that it was a good idea to wear loose trousers, nothing too clingy. I'd chosen an old pair of superfat jeans that I'd lived in during the months after Immi was born when my extra weight hung around like a rejected boyfriend. I figured that there'd be room for the great raft of sanitary pads I'd waddle out with.

The nurse's voice came through the curtain. 'Everything all right in there?'

Presumably I was taking up valuable operating time. 'Just coming.' As I folded up my jeans, a tiny pink sock fell out of the pocket. I picked it up, marvelling at how minute it was. Hard to believe that Immi's feet now required such an array of trainers, tap shoes and flip-flops.

I'd never hold this baby.

Never watch it pull off the socks I'd struggled to get on. Never straighten a hat. Or see little legs kicking up, chubby and squeezable on a changing mat. Never feel the inexplicable happiness that comes with a baby eating butternut squash puree without protest.

I put my jeans back on.

My marriage was finished anyway. My old life was over. But I could still let a new one begin.

Roberta

I brought Octavia back to my house that evening. The next night the children arrived from her mother's. Stan slept in the utility room. I hadn't seen Octavia vulnerable and unsure in decades. Now when I went out of the room, it was as though she wanted to follow me. She'd told the children she wasn't feeling well and needed me to look after her.

I dropped the kids at school on my way to work at my new job – a glorious glass orangery for which I was to source the water features and plants. After an initial pout about the influx of the Shelton children, Alicia had embraced their love for karaoke and every spare moment was taken up with dance routines, singing competitions and homemade videos.

Her boyfriend, Connor, was becoming more and more of a fixture. Since I'd met his mother, I'd relaxed to a point where I'd ceased worrying. Almost. Connor and Charlie hit it off together – watching them playing rugby in the back garden filled me with a bittersweet gratitude that I hadn't had a boy. I wanted to rush out and stop them tackling each other, fearful of necks, collarbones and future ugly ears.

When it came to children, Octavia was usually at the centre of things. Now she was absent. She listened to Polly reading from *Alone on a Wide Wide Sea*. She helped Immi with her project on the Victorians. She even explained some Spanish grammar to Alicia that I had failed to get through to her. But the enthusiasm, her sheer verve and joy, had faded like a pair of curtains hung too long in a sunny window.

I'd never been the sort to caper round the garden, dance to the radio or flip pancakes in a flamboyant manner. I tended to be the person chasing around after the children with the Mr Muscle, mopping the loo floor and organising discarded trainers. However, in an effort to give Octavia a bit of breathing space, I became like one of those over-enthusiastic dog trainers you see on television who makes a squeaky ball in a sock seem like the most fun ever. Fairy cakes? Let's do it! Cow-racing on the Wii? Moooooo! Game of tennis down the club? Trainers, please!

The children were a tad bemused but I received little rewards along the way. Polly slipped her hand into mine. Charlie looked at me one day like he'd never seen me before and said, 'I never got why Mum found you funny but I think I do now.'

Nothing seemed to help Octavia, though. I tried kindness: 'Do you want me to take you home to fetch some more belongings? I don't want you to feel like a temporary vagrant.'

'No. We'll manage. Thanks.' Then she shuffled off upstairs, as though I'd made her feel in the way.

I tried appealing to her competitive spirit: 'Did you know that a new nursery is opening on the other side of town?'

'Yeah, I'd heard.' She flicked open *Hello!*, a magazine she'd always disdained, explaining, 'Makes me feel better reading about other people's car-crash lives.'

I preferred it when she lambasted the competition, raging about 'crappy management' and 'stifling traditionalism'.

I tried reminding her she'd have to face the music at some stage: 'What are you going to tell Jonathan when he comes back?' To that, she just shrugged.

I was starting to panic. Unlike her other pregnancies when she was snuffling in the fridge at quarter-hourly intervals, she'd lost her appetite. I cooked her favourite dishes – shepherd's pie, haddock chowder, toad-in-the-hole. She pushed them all around her plate. I bought blueberries, pomegranate juice, mango smoothies to get vitamins into her. She was always grateful, but none of it made it into her mouth.

Stan slept directly underneath my bedroom, letting out little barks and sighs in his sleep, which were enough to rouse me out of mine. I'd lay there, watching the room grow lighter, fretting about what would happen to Octavia. When I gave up on sleep, I'd often find her folded up in the armchair in the kitchen, cradling ginger tea. She'd been trying to lose weight for a decade and now she needed the sustenance, it was dropping off her.

I couldn't see how the baby could be thriving. It was almost as though having changed her mind about a termination, she was starving the baby to death instead. I didn't know how to fix her.

Or perhaps I did.

Octavia

During the week I'd stayed with Roberta, she'd transformed herself into Mary Poppins. I half-expected to see her hovering a few inches above the floor under an umbrella. On the second Saturday, so I could 'work out a strategy for dealing with Jonathan', she twirled all the kids off to Westfield shopping centre for retail therapy. Normally, I would have banged on about 'It's not what you've got, it's who you are' but I was fast discovering that principles were a luxury I couldn't afford.

Roberta had made me shower and get dressed because she said it would focus my mind. She was right – dressing gowns did not sharp decisions make – but I was still doodling squares of diminishing sizes on a blank pad, blundering down every dead-end option of unstitching my life from Jonathan's.

When the doorbell went, I assumed it would be a delivery of more beeswax candles, coffee capsules or the super-wicking tracksuit bottoms that Roberta couldn't live without.

It was Xavi.

I had too many emotions for a single response. I didn't know whether to swear with surprise, scream with joy or cry.

He stepped inside, put his arms around me and kicked the door shut with his foot. Crying got the upper hand. We stood in Roberta's hallway while enormous out-of-control tears poured from me. For the first time since I found out I was pregnant, the world steadied a little. When I lifted my head, the shoulder of his shirt had turned dark.

'*Bien. Tu as fini?* That's it with the tears, my little cabbage?' I smiled at that. Xavi had always translated the French for 'darling', *chouchou*, into English.

'How did you find me?

'A little bird.' He lifted my chin and planted a solid kiss on my lips.

'Roberta? I can't believe she did that. She was so disapproving.'

'That you meet me? Or you sleep with me?'

'Both.' Plus getting up the duff. I'd let him broach that little detail.

'I tell you what she told me later.'

'You'd better tell me now. Come through into the kitchen.' Thank God I was at Roberta's where all the skirting boards were licked clean, hand towels changed, empty loo rolls put in the bin on a regular basis. No mad dash to grab the knickers drying on the radiator or brandish the loo brush on skid marks.

I busied myself making coffee for him, realising that the deep despair weighing me down had lifted slightly.

He came up behind me and put his arms round my waist, which was just beginning to thicken. He still didn't comment.

'*Alors.* Roberta tells me that Jonathan leaves you? He has someone else, *non?*'

I nodded. His words scraped at something sore. My love for Jonathan was nothing like my love for Xavi. Nothing burned, nothing ached, nothing longed but still, there was a cosiness, an underlying shoulder-to-shoulder solidarity that comes from bringing up children together. Maybe I didn't love Jonathan, but it didn't stop me feeling that a whole chapter of my life was about to be ripped away like a super-sticky plaster, leaving everything oozing underneath.

Xavi put his head on one side. His long lashes swept up. Even when Xavi was vulnerable, he still had a lick of defiance about him. 'So. Are you sad?'

'I am sad. I don't know why. Failure, I suppose. I don't know what it will do to the children.'

I walked over to Roberta's cream settee. I always felt the need to check I didn't have any chocolate stuck to the back of my trousers before I sat down. Xavi followed. I put my legs across his knees. He massaged my feet.

I took his hand. 'Everything has changed, Xavi.'

'Can it be good change? Can I hope that I might grow old with you?'

He looked so earnest that a trickle of life, of joy, stirred in me. He leaned over and kissed me. My body was surrendering, on the verge of brushing away the fact that the whole package was three kids and a baby with an indeterminate father. I lay back, feeling him shift position to lie next to me. My fatigue was melting away, taking with it my resolve. His hands were working upwards, skimming my stomach. I glanced at him but he made no move to linger there. I struggled into a sitting position and pushed him away. He drew back. 'So, you have a response for me?'

'There's a lot you don't know about me now.'

As a cue for getting the baby business out of the way, I couldn't have been more obvious if I had employed a band of morris dancers to jingle their bells and shout, 'Wha-hah!'

'I want to discover the things I don't know about you, your family. For me, there should never have been a gap of eighteen years. So we continue now, before it is too late.'

The first wisps of panic were stretching out to pull me in.

'So what else did Roberta tell you?' I wish she had warned me what she was going to do. I would have flossed my teeth for a start. And prepared my 'You might be a father, but you might not' speech.

Xavi smiled. 'What do you think she told me? Apart from the fact that I'd better not fuck it up this time?'

Despite myself, I grinned at Roberta's unfamiliar use of the F-word. She was becoming more ferocious as time went by. Xavi wasn't going to make this easy for me. He still answered everything with a question of his own. The delight I'd felt at seeing him was descending into alarm.

'So why did you come?'

He threaded his fingers through mine. 'You know why. What I said when I sent the coin. I love you. I can wait.'

'Wait for what?'

'For you to be free. Free to love me.' He made it sound so simple.

'Free from the kids?'

Xavi shrugged. He hesitated. 'No. Not free. I don't think a mother is ever free. I am worried to sound arrogant but I would like to be part of their lives. I'm thinking it is always difficult for children to accept someone else, so maybe it will be easier for us when they are more independent.'

Shit. He didn't know. I thought he'd just been having me on, reeling me in and teasing me. He didn't have any idea he'd be waiting for the next eighteen-plus years. I had to tell him. I could feel dread gathering, panic that he would walk away, just as he had all those years ago. The expression on his face when I told him I couldn't go to New Zealand, my own moment of realisation that he was going anyway, without me, would be etched on my mind forever.

Right on cue, my bladder turned into a thimble. 'Back in a mo.' I didn't want him to hear me clattering into the little loo next to the kitchen so I went upstairs. I ran my wrists under the cold tap. I studied my lips in the mirror. A little pinker than usual. I'd never understood yearning before. Yearning was for people who weren't busy enough. Far too Cathy and Heathcliff.

God knows, I understood it now.

Xavi might be able to stomach the kids I had, even love, or at least like them, eventually. But a baby was a commitment, one where real fathers often faltered. Xavi was used to sailing in Corsica, kite-surfing in Brazil, trekking in the Atlas Mountains. He had no idea what it was like to walk the landing with a grizzling baby all night, eat to the background of screaming, be so tired that words swim around your brain without the energy to arrange themselves into a thought.

And that was without staring at every crease, every fingernail, every toe, and wondering whether half of that baby was yours – or just some other man's burden.

I started back downstairs. Defeat was filling the place where hope had been. The pull of adventure, the unknown, the world to explore had tempted Xavi away when he only had me to contend with, without my current tangled web of ties. Back then, he couldn't even wait a couple of months for me to deal with Dad's death. There was no reason to suppose he'd join me on this uncertain and lifelong journey. No point prolonging it. I marched into the sitting room, ready for history to repeat itself.

Xavi grasped my hands and pulled me to him. I made my back as concave as possible, delaying the inevitable. I had to say it now. Right now. No build-up.

'I'm pregnant.'

His dark eyes flashed wide. 'Pregnant?' He slumped back against the sofa. I tried to read his face but he'd gone all Corsican on me. The stone-wall barriers were blotting out any emotion. If he felt any joy, he was doing a damned fine job of hiding it.

He stood up. 'Wow.' He ran his fingers through his hair. 'Is it mine?'

'I don't know.' I was going to have to get used to that over the coming months. Octavia Shelton, owner of an establishment dedicated to the welfare of other people's babies, had no idea who the father was.

Or rather, could offer a choice of two.

Xavi walked over to the French windows. 'It could be mine?' Those shoulders were up around his ears.

'It's an equal chance. I'm sorry. I haven't slept with Jonathan since I slept with you.' I felt more ashamed admitting that I'd slept with my husband than I had telling Roberta that I'd been to bed with Xavi.

'*Bien.*'

'Well what?

'I don't know what to say. I don't know why, but I never thought of this. Though at my age, I should know how babies are made.'

Hormones weren't on my side. I rolled my eyes. 'So you don't mind the kids but you don't want the baby? Because it might be Jonathan's, or because it's a baby?' My body was tensing, warding off the inevitable.

Xavi sighed and pressed the heels of his hands into his eyes. 'I didn't expect this.'

'Neither did I.' I filled him in on the scallops but I think he thought I was some stupid woman who hadn't got to grips with contraception – again. 'You haven't answered my question.'

I realised I was hanging out for the fairy tale, the 'Never mind, darling. I love you so much we can survive anything. I will love the baby whether I'm the father or not. It's still part of you.'

I waited. Xavi kept shaking his head and raising his eyebrows. I couldn't compete with his macho pride. His silence said it all. The possibility of another man's baby was stronger than his desire to be with me. I walked over to him.

'Go. Go now. My baby needs unconditional love.' I left off the 'So do I.'

'Tavy. Don't be silly. I'm not going anywhere. I love you. If the baby is mine, you know I am going to be the happiest man in the world. I need a moment to think if I can accept a baby that isn't mine. I must be honest with myself and you. I don't want to make a big promise I can't keep.'

I cut him off. 'Don't make any promises at all. I will survive perfectly well. I did last time.'

'*Putain*, Tavy. Today it is a big news you tell me. I am trying to understand it all.'

'What is there to understand? I'm pregnant, might or might not be yours, on my own with three kids. You're either in because you love me, or out because you don't love me enough.'

I should have known better than to set an ultimatum trap.

Xavi folded his arms. 'I hurt you a long time ago. I don't want to do the same again. This is not a thing we can say, "OK, no problem". This is something we have to think about as adults and make plans.'

I knew a let-down gently when I heard one. 'Don't worry. I couldn't rely on you then and I'm obviously not going to be able to now. Some things never change.'

Xavi stepped towards me but I backed away. 'Tavy. Stop. You are not fair. You can trust me, but we have to think about other people also. Maybe Jonathan will decide he wants to come back. Maybe the children refuse to accept me. And in the middle of all this, maybe I am a father. Or maybe I am not. I don't want to make mistakes this time.'

I knew where this was heading. Again.

'No, Xavi. No. If you really wanted me, you wouldn't need to think about it.'

I walked to the front door with Xavi arguing and trying to take me in his arms. I all but pushed him out into the street.

'I don't need anyone. Not Jonathan. Not you.'

Roberta

I left an inert lump on the sofa and came back to find a whirlwind. Everything was super-bright and breezy. Octavia had mopped the floor, stripped the beds and put it all in the washing machine. The windows were open. I half-expected to find Stan sitting in a big bubble bath in the garden. She ushered the girls in, exclaiming over Immi's sweep of all things purple and sparkly from Claire's Accessories, Polly's new bikini and Alicia's cache of halter necks that only a fourteen-year-old could work. She busied about making tea, telling me to put my feet up, but somehow avoided my eye until I almost imploded with curiosity.

The second the girls disappeared for a trying-on session, I said, 'Any visitors this morning?'

I caught the brief wobble in her lip.

'I think you know.' She smiled. 'Thank you for trying to help.'

'And?'

'He didn't want to know about the baby.'

'No! When I tracked him down to his travel agency, he said he would do anything to be with you. I told him not to even think about darkening my door if he wasn't serious.

I grilled him for ages before I gave him my address. He was falling over himself to tell me how much he loved you.'

'You didn't mention the baby to him?'

'I wanted to. It didn't feel like it was my secret to tell. What did he say? Tell me everything. From start to finish.'

I listened. I didn't interrupt, though I desperately wanted to. She'd had a chance to get together with the love of her life, but because the conversational choreography hadn't quite matched her expectations, she'd blown him out.

Octavia petered to a halt. She looked rather sheepish, as though hearing it out loud made her realise how ridiculous she was.

'Cut the chap some slack. He didn't say he didn't want to know. He said he wanted to think things through before making promises he couldn't keep. Not everyone is as black and white as you. The rest of us have shades of grey. We're not like you, not little armies marching as the crow flies towards our goals. Some of us waver and wobble and need half a day to consider how we feel, sometimes half a lifetime.'

Octavia put her hands on her hips. 'He's either in or he's out. I've spent my entire adult life with a bloke who was indifferent to what I wanted or what I felt. No more compromise.'

I nearly choked on my tea at that pronouncement. Octavia had some tremendous qualities, but compromise didn't figure. 'So that's it? You've found him after all this time, you love him, you might be carrying his baby, and because he wants a couple of days to think it all over before promising he'll stand by you, no matter what, you've ousted him.'

'Perhaps he wouldn't have promised me anything. I can't rely on him anyway. Can't rely on anyone except myself.'

I felt a stab of injustice at that. 'I hope that doesn't include me.'

'No, I meant men. You've been wonderful. Which is why I'm going to leave you to it now. I've cleared out our stuff.

355

I hope you're not going to be finding all our old rubbish under the settees for the next six months. I'm going to take my brood and get out of your hair.'

'You don't have to leave. You were going to stay here until Jonathan gets back.' This was not what I had intended.

'I need to move on with my life. It's better for the kids if they're in a proper routine at home. I can't keep expecting you to pick up the pieces.'

Just when I thought Xavi had tapped into her vulnerable side, Octavia's harshness was back and with it, her scathing judgment of everyone else, including herself. I tried again. 'I'm your friend. We all need a little help sometimes.'

'You've got your own shit going on. You can't carry me. I know you're still mooning over Jake the Peg. You don't fool me with your trips to the Co-op down his road. You've never shopped anywhere except Waitrose. Nice olives though.'

Nothing escaped her. 'Guilty. Sad middle-aged twit that I am. I know it's ludicrous. I keep hoping he'll get rid of the gardener and realise he can't live without me.'

'I'm envious that you still believe in all that lovey-dovey bull.'

'I'm furious that I still hanker after the Disneyland dream.' I started folding up the carrier bags from our shopping trip.

'That's how you grew up. Scott jetting backwards and forwards, flying in on Christmas Eve, turning up at New Year's Eve parties when you weren't expecting him. I've never had that. Jonathan's idea of a romantic killer gesture was coming to pick me up outside Aldi when it was raining.' Octavia bent down to retrieve Stan's chew toy from under the sofa. Just looking at the mangled old thing made me want to wash my hands.

'Are you sure you can't patch things up with Jonathan?'

'If I was going to throw myself at the feet of any man, it would be Xavi. I don't even miss Jonathan except in a

Pavlovian, it's-what-I'm-used-to sort of way. At least he's still phoning the kids, even if he doesn't appear to give a shit whether I've got my head in the oven or not.'

She folded up Stan's horrible hairy bed. The Dyson was beckoning to me.

'Jonathan wasn't one for big emotional confrontations though, was he? And you're pretty terrifying when you get into one.'

'Sod being terrifying. This is our marriage, our family. I could never simply disappear, not knowing if the children were howling into their pillows every night.'

For the first time ever, I didn't envy the fact that she had a baby on the way.

Octavia

Three weeks after I returned from Roberta's, my household was in meltdown. Immi was crying at bedtime because she was missing Jonathan, which didn't bode well for when it became permanent. Polly, usually the sweetest-natured of my brood, told me to fuck off when I asked her to empty the dishwasher. Even my carefree Charlie was shutting himself away in his bedroom rather than watching the telly with me. It was as though the children could smell uncertainty, despite the adults trying to pretend everything was OK. I'd ignored the battery of texts that Xavi had sent since I'd been home, though there'd been times when I'd nearly weakened. With so much change rushing towards us, I couldn't afford to gamble on a man who might be gone again before the baby was even born.

Today, he'd rung again. Before I gave in and answered, I decided to text him and close down any hope. If we spoke, it would be harder to keep what was right for the children at the forefront of my self-centred brain.

I cannot risk my children's happiness any more than I have done already. I hope you understand and respect my wishes to be left alone.

I keyed in *I will always love you*, then deleted it and pressed send. I allowed myself a short but vocal sobbing session on the kitchen table, while Stan nuzzled my hand and whined. Then I washed my face and unwrapped a family-sized bar of Galaxy. The tiniest sliver of an upside: there was no one to care whether my arse took up one seat or two.

Much dabbing of chocolatey crumbs later, I was resting with my feet up. I'd moved on from the chocolate and was now wading my way through a box of liquorice allsorts, washed down with liquorice tea. It was weird how liquorice usually made me retch, but I craved the taste when I was pregnant. I'd put my iPod on, quickly switching from Paolo Nutini's *Last Request* to the upbeat sounds of The Beach Boys. I was just willing myself into a state of mind where I could envisage any kind of hope for the future when Jonathan marched into the kitchen. I jumped. He started.

'Octavia! I thought you'd be at work.'

I snatched my earphones out. 'Bloody hell! You scared me to death. I was knackered so I left work a bit early. I thought you weren't coming back for another two weeks?' Everything in me rushed to adjust to the idea that he might be back for good.

Nothing danced. Nothing sighed with relief.

'I wanted to see the children. And we really need to start sorting things out.'

He suddenly sniffed the air. 'What are you drinking?' He glanced at my box of sweets. 'Is that liquorice?' His gaze suddenly shot down to my stomach, which didn't yet have a noticeable bulge. Heat was spreading up my face.

'You're not pregnant, are you?' He laughed as though the suggestion was ridiculous.

'Yes.'

Jonathan looked as though he was trapped in the corner of a cave with a huge bear racing at him with gaping jaws.

He slumped onto a chair. I waited for him to speak. He looked crushed, his freedom to start a new life gushing away like water over a weir. Eventually, he stammered out, 'How pregnant? Aren't you on the pill? What the hell happened there?'

'About twelve weeks. Do you remember I got food poisoning from scallops? That's what happened, stopped the pill working properly.'

His face tightened. 'Our timing wasn't very good.' He put his face in his hands, then started massaging his temples as though my 'happy news' had made his brain ache.

I stood up. One word from me and the whole baby fiasco would take on another dimension entirely. 'Is this a fleeting visit?'

Jonathan looked away. 'I wanted to explain things to the children.'

'So you're not coming back?'

I wasn't even hoping for a yes but felt I had to ask out of some perverted politeness.

Jonathan flicked his hands in a gesture of 'What's the point?'

'Do the children know about the baby?'

My turn to look at the furthest corner of the room. 'Not yet.'

Jonathan picked at some dried-on Weetabix on the table. Presumably he was used to sitting at gleaming Sardinian oak now rather than knackeredy old pine.

I stood up, feeling my breasts ache as they adjusted to gravity. 'Do you want a coffee?'

I'd rehearsed a million times in my head how I was going to tell Jonathan, get him back for leaving me, hurt him as he had hurt me. Now, when I had my chance, my overriding emotion was regret. I wanted to protect him. After all these years, it didn't seem necessary to score a victory. I watched the kettle boil. When it clicked off, I'd blurt it out.

My voice came out in a thin quiver. 'The baby might not be yours.'

'What?'

That got his head out of his hands.

I passed him his coffee. 'I'm sorry. The baby might not be yours.'

I poured out the whole story, glossing over the odd detail here and there, such as my endless cyber-stalking. I paused occasionally to swallow and blow my nose. I couldn't watch the emotions on Jonathan's face. I didn't want to see the hurt – or the relief – that he might not have to take responsibility for the baby. He listened without interrupting, looking bewildered as though he was trying to choose between two TV programmes on at the same time. I wanted to shake him and ask if he could hear what I was saying.

The only time he showed any reaction – one of total agreement – was when I said I didn't think we had brought out the best in each other. His enthusiasm for our failings stung me.

'It wasn't all bad though, was it?' I didn't want to believe that our whole marriage had been a miserable slog.

'I don't think I thought so at the time.'

Big fat bulbous praise indeed. 'So what do you want to do?'

'I don't want any involvement with the baby.'

I gulped. The one thing I thought I knew about Jonathan was that he did his duty.

'Not even if it's yours?' I couldn't compute his reaction. When I'd got pregnant with Charlie, he'd practically force-fed me spinach and trollied me down the aisle.

'No.' Jonathan looked at the floor. 'Are you sure you want to have the baby when we're splitting up? It's not really an ideal time to bring a child into the world, is it? And it's still early enough to think about other options.'

'Abortion, do you mean?'

Jonathan nodded.

'No way. No. I am not doing that.' I had no problem grabbing back the moral high ground now Jonathan was acting like a lily-livered lump. I decided to gloss over my near-miss at the clinic.

'Promise me you'll think about it. I know it's not something we thought we'd ever have to do, but having a baby now would be mad.'

'It's not something *I'll* ever do. I am not getting rid of my child just because it doesn't slot neatly into your world view.'

'Octavia, listen to me. I'll be living in Sardinia and you'll be over here. You're not going to send a three-month-old to me for a fortnight's holiday, are you? How could I possibly be a father – of any sort – to a newborn? It's going to be hard enough staying close to the children I've got.'

Jonathan looked desperate, as though he was about to cry. 'You made the bloody choice to move to Sardinia with "Betta". Don't start whining to me about the difficulty of keeping in touch with the kids. You. Chose. That.'

Everything about him sagged. 'Be honest, Octavia. Did you really want to trudge on for another forty years like this? If you do go ahead with this child, you can count me out completely. I'm not giving up my chance of happiness because you've been stupid enough to mess up your contraception.'

I waited.

'For a second time.'

For a fleeting moment, I considered cracking a chair over his head. When my voice came out, it reminded me of the noise Stan makes when another dog tries to mount him.

'I can hardly be blamed for a split condom. Though since you mention it, it was me who gambled on not needing the morning-after pill. And do you know what? I'm bloody glad

362

I did because I haven't regretted having Charlie for one single second. But since you're so keen to apportion blame, let me just point out that I didn't even want to get married. You were the one banging on about responsibility and whittling about getting a ring on my finger. Looks like you've changed your tune on that front over the last sixteen years.'

I wanted to howl at the surge of protectiveness I felt towards this little butter bean, clinging onto life in my stomach, tiny nails forming, mini-fists opening and closing. In that moment, I understood women who chopped off their husbands' penises. I could have fried Jonathan's willy with onions and garlic and served it up to Stan, hooting with hilarity as I did so.

Jonathan scratched his chin, looking as though the accusations I was hurling his way were deeply unjust. 'It's not about shirking responsibility. I'd stand no chance of forging a relationship with this baby – who, let's not forget, might or might not be mine. Even when I was living at home, you've always encouraged the kids to poke fun at me, the square, the geek, the plod in the corner. They probably don't miss me half as much as I miss them. Last time I tried to Skype Polly she said she was too busy.'

I wondered if there was any truth in his words. I felt a glint of recognition water down my rage. I was so secure in the kids' love that I'd never thought about how it would feel to doubt it. 'Children are like that, they're selfish, it's how they survive. It doesn't mean they don't love you. Judging by their behaviour, they're definitely missing you.'

His face relaxed slightly. 'Elisabetta and I would like them to come and spend some time with us, so they can get to know her. You've always wanted them to experience other cultures. Elisabetta's really keen to teach them Italian. They're still young enough to become bilingual.'

I stared at Jonathan. All the times I'd tried to persuade

him to take a sabbatical, move abroad, think outside the narrow little life we'd been leading, he'd been like a racehorse refusing the bloody water jump. Now, he was Mr Fricking Cosmopolitan, suddenly appreciating the brilliance of my argument but slipping in a new mother figure to reap the rewards.

I put my hand on my tummy and promised the baby I'd make up for choosing such a poor father – whether he turned out to be a Mediterranean fly-by-night or a pale-skinned duty-dodger.

Roberta

Surrey World had done a spread on my work that morning, under the title 'One to Watch'. I sat reading about 'the amazing eye for detail of Roberta Green, upcoming home interior designer' and my 'thriving business', 'edgy but accessible style' and 'the name on the lips of the Surrey set' over breakfast. There were photos of Mrs Goodman's sitting room, Nicole's bedroom and the orangery, tailor-made for sipping wine. I didn't even look at the pictures of myself and cringe.

I'd done something no one had thought was possible. The vain housewife, the woman whose greatest skill was picking out a vintage chandelier or making a room seem larger, had stood on her own two feet – and made a success of it. Alicia was so proud, she'd taken one of the magazines to school to show her friends. 'Mum! You are so cool!'

Before I'd finished my muesli, my mobile rang. A local businessman wanted me, little old me with my sketch pad and pencil and ideas in my head, to come and look at a 1970s hotel he'd just taken over with a view to working out a shabby-chic revamp. I did a first-over-the-finishing-line punch in the air. Roberta Green, woman in control of her own destiny.

I owed it to Jake.

I'd never have had the courage to offer a single opinion on other people's houses if he hadn't encouraged me. Euphoria at my moment of fame, of proving that I wasn't just someone who could match a handbag to an outfit, made me reckless. Jake deserved to be thanked. I picked up the magazine and snatched some champagne from the rack. I wouldn't knock on the door, I'd just leave them on the doorstep with a quick note. I didn't want to bump into Lorraine digging up the dandelions.

As I drew up at his house, my nerve faltered. The curtains were still shut. I hoped they weren't having lazy early-morning sex. I was surprised how much the thought hurt. I crept up the drive, peering round the hedge for any sign of Lorraine whispering breathily to her hollyhocks. I popped my little message inside the magazine and was positioning the bottle on top when Angus came out.

'Hiya. You OK there?' He swung his school-bag onto his shoulder. 'Is that for Dad?'

'Yes, I needed to thank him for something.'

'Shall I get him for you?'

'No, I don't want to disturb him. Just let him know I left this.' I scrabbled up my offerings and thrust them into his arms. I started down the drive, poised businesswoman morphing into tongue-tied twerp. Angus was yelling up the stairs in the unselfconscious way of teenage boys.

'Dad, Dad, the woman who cut her hand open is here.'

I wanted to run but I wanted to hang back: my feet couldn't decide whether to speed up or dawdle. I made it to the car, glancing back to see if Lorraine was racing out, brandishing her shears. Instead Jake was in the doorway, hair sticking up, bare-chested in pyjama bottoms. Longing shot through me. He stood with the champagne in one hand, reading the note in the other. I unlocked the car, feeling as though I would disintegrate with shame at my soppy words. As I flung my bag in, I caught a glimpse of Jake hurrying down the drive, barefoot.

He was beckoning to me.

I stood by the car door, ready to disappear.

He shouted over. 'Thanks for the champagne. I can't take the credit for your amazing success. But hey, I'll enjoy the kudos where I find it. Have you got time to come in for a coffee while I read what they say about you?' He came closer, grimacing as the gravel dug into his feet.

'No, you can't read it while I'm sitting there. That would be far too mortifying. Anyway, half of it is poetic licence on the journalist's behalf. She makes me sound like Wonder Woman.'

'You look like you've done pretty well to me. Come in for a minute.'

He'd put on a bit of weight since I'd last seen him. I hoped it was high-fat ready meals for one, rather than multiple romantic dinners.

'Is your "friend" here? I don't want to intrude.' I missed the neutral enquiry tone.

'No, just Angus, who's going to school any minute, and me, who wants to hear your news.'

I ignored the stab of disappointment that Jake didn't say Lorraine was ancient history. 'Go on then, five minutes. I've got to meet someone who wants me to revamp his hotel soon.' I wondered if he could spot the half-truth, that 'soon' was in a week's time.

'Hark at you. Roberta Green, adviser to the great and good.' Jake came round to my side of the car.

'I didn't mean it like that. The business is very much in its early stages, I'm still finding my way but I've had a few lucky breaks.'

He ushered me up the path where Angus was crouching

down, shuffling through great bundles of dog-eared papers in his school bag. He smiled the cheeky grin of someone who loves a bit of a wind-up. 'I was talking to Connor's mum about you. We think you're perfect for my dad.'

I felt like the dense girl in class who doesn't know whether something is a joke or not. I didn't answer in case he fell about laughing, so I went for some kind of 'haha' grunt instead.

Jake pretended to push him over. 'Hurry up. You can't be late on the last day of term.'

Angus tried to rugby-tackle Jake, Jake flipped him over onto his backside, with more pushing and shoving in a way only boys could do. I'd have been worried about scuffed shoes, dirty trousers, neighbours' disapproval.

While Jake popped upstairs to get changed, I had a quick flick through the post on the side. Bills and bank statements. No letters addressed to Lorraine. Not living here yet, then.

By the time Jake came back with damp hair curling round his collar, I was sitting at his table, all butter-wouldn't-melt. I needed that coffee Jake was whipping up.

Now I was here, I didn't know why I'd come. The silence was threatening to become embarrassing when Jake said, 'I met your husband the other day.'

'Where?' My stomach contracted.

'We were one of three businesses he contacted about printing the brochures for a new development in Australia. We'd been recommended by one of the estate agents in town.'

I waited. He grinned. 'Forthright sort of man.'

'Bully, you mean?'

'I'd say ruthless. And charming, actually. All that matters is what he wants but somehow he delivers it to you in a way that makes you feel he's doing you a favour.'

'I haven't seen him for ages. He spends so much time in

Australia these days. We mainly communicate about Alicia by text now.'

Jake started slicing bread for toast. 'I'm not excusing you, though I can see how he could trap you into a corner. He was pretty sharp at getting concessions out of me. I've dealt with a lot of slippery fish, but he's very clever at dancing a couple of steps ahead, then claiming as his right something you vaguely discussed half an hour earlier.'

'Did you know he was my husband – my soon-to-be ex-husband – before you went?'

'I Google everyone I deal with.'

'You didn't discuss me with him, did you?' I couldn't stand the idea of Scott judging the one who came after him.

'Of course not. He obviously didn't connect my name with what happened before. I didn't even tell him I knew you. Wouldn't have got our working relationship off to a good start. He did indicate he was looking for someone to work on several different property portfolios, so potentially there's a lot of business there.'

He passed me a coffee and sat down opposite. I watched the precise way he spread butter – nothing 'lite' or margariney – into the four corners of his toast. The new boho floppy fringe suited him. I hoped that pumping me for information wasn't the only reason he was prepared to let me into his house.

'Did you win the contract?'

'Yes, I did.'

That made me shudder. It was like finding out your best friend was going on holiday with someone you hated and thought they did too.

I had no right to feel betrayed. But I did.

'Be careful.'

I slugged my coffee down, scalding my tongue. 'Anyway, I wanted to drop in the magazine and thank you for your encouragement. You pushed me in the right direction.' I reached for my handbag. Jake put out a hand to stop me.

'I didn't say I accepted the contract.'

'Didn't you?'

'No. I had no intention of accepting any work from him.'

'So why did you go in the first place?'

'To begin with, I didn't realise it was your ex. Then when I Googled him, I came across a picture of you at some charity dinner with him. You looked absolutely gorgeous.' He stopped abruptly as though he hadn't meant to articulate that thought. He sighed. 'Do you want the honest truth?'

I refrained from my usual pedantic observation that truth was intrinsically honest. 'Yes, truth generally works for me.' I realised too late that I'd probably laid myself open to a charge of hypocrisy.

'I wanted to see who it was who had such a hold over you.'

I felt a little rush of joy, followed by frustration.

'Why? I thought you were in love with the gardener.' Only superhuman effort kept the spite out of my voice, though I managed to omit 'landscape'.

'Lorraine? No. Definitively no. That's all I'm saying. You can ask Angus. He's quite a fan of yours, if you hadn't noticed.'

'You know she came to see me?'

'I do, yes.'

'And?' I forced myself not to look away.

'And I'm sorry. If it's any consolation, I finished with her straightaway.'

Everything went quiet. The expression on Jake's face was gentle. I had a chance to make the dice fall in my favour if only I could find the correct answers.

'Just so you know, Scott doesn't have a hold on me now.'

'You sure about that?' The harshness was back in his voice. He bent his fingers back until the joints cracked.

'Absolutely one hundred per cent sure. I've been sworn at once too often.'

Jake looked disgusted. 'He wasn't very pleased with me either. Couldn't believe that someone had said no to him. Kept offering me more and more money and then turned nasty.'

Hearing about it made me feel sick. 'Scott hates it when he doesn't get his own way.' I wanted to leap to my feet and hug him for standing up to Scott.

Or any reason at all.

'I'll probably end up buried in an old quarry in a ton of concrete.' Jake gave me a wide-open smile that contrasted so strongly with Scott's ironic grin.

He came round to my side of the table. I felt hot and shaky. He stood in front of me and put his hands on my shoulders. I didn't dare look up in case what I was hoping for wasn't there.

'Do you know who has a hold on me? Who I've tried to forget and can't? Who has wrecked me forever for other women?'

I sat still. If I didn't speak, hopefully I couldn't mess up.

'Look at me.' With enormous effort I met his eyes, which were intense and serious. 'I hated you for a while. But my gut instinct kept telling me that you were essentially an honourable person. Trying to marry up what you did with what I knew, or at least, was pretty sure you felt, it didn't make any sense.'

'I'm sorry. You couldn't have hated me more than I hated myself.'

I dropped my head forward, breathing him in. He didn't move. I froze, wondering if I'd misread the signals. Then I felt a kiss on the top of my head. Firm hands pulled me to my feet.

Jake drew away from me slightly. 'No more Scott?'

'No more anyone. Just you.' The kiss when it came was full of promises, of desire, tender yet covetous, protective yet fierce.

For once, I overlooked getting into an unmade bed.

Octavia

Jonathan wasted no time launching himself into the domestic chores I'd gaily let slip during his absence. For a brief moment, when I found him ironing sheets in the kitchen, I was almost grateful for his help. Then I found him tucking hospital corners round the knackered old settee cushions and realised he was too bloody tight to spend money on a hotel.

'What are you doing?'

'In the circumstances, I don't think it would be appropriate to share the marital bed.'

'Oh please. Don't start talking some corporatey-lawyer bollocks to me. It's not flaming "appropriate" for you to be here at all.'

'I'm not the only one who has transgressed. Potentially with less far-reaching consequences.'

'Jonathan. Please do not get all holier-than-thou with me. Why don't you just find a B&B?'

He carried on smoothing the sheets. 'Why don't you? I need to conserve money if we're to divide our assets shortly.'

'Because I am the one looking after the children. What is it with all this pseudo-lawyer speak?' The penny suddenly dropped. 'My God. You've already seen a solicitor, haven't you?'

Jonathan nodded. 'I don't see the point of prolonging this situation.'

I'd now become a 'situation'.

There was a danger of me fetching Charlie's cricket bat and rampaging through the house with a swipe at Jonathan's head for my grand finale, so I put my hands up. 'Fine. Glad to see money considerations take priority over everything. Does the glorious Elisabetta mind you being under the same roof as your wife?'

'She knows it's been over for a long time.'

That dart still pricked deep. Had he been tapping his fingers for years, sizing up a replacement while I was ploughing on through family life, aware that I wasn't delirious with joy and laughter but thinking I was happy enough?

'Let's hope the baby's not yours then, otherwise that's going to be a little tricky to explain,' I said.

Charlie coming home sweaty and starving after a cricket match saved Jonathan from a further tongue-lashing. I couldn't bear Jonathan's ineptitude. Charlie was doing a bit of teenage swagger and what I called 'bled, innit?' handshakes, but I could see he was thrilled to see Jonathan. After an awkward hug, Jonathan showed his delight at seeing Charlie by carrying out a detailed investigation into where he'd left his stinky trainers and shin pads.

'So how long you home for then, Dad? Mum, can we move out to Sardinia? The women are wicked out there. It's sunny. I could learn to windsurf.' He grinned round at Jonathan. 'And I suppose we'd get to see you more often.'

I had a sudden urge to sob. I'd planned to take Charlie quietly to one side and tell him the truth when Jonathan wasn't there so he could cry, rage, kick out, without Jonathan banging on about boys of his age being too old to 'boo' as he put it. I didn't know how to soften the blow.

In the end, I panicked and said, 'I'd definitely be open to moving abroad.' When Charlie started leaping about, working out who he was going to invite in the summer and whether we could come back sometimes for Christmas so we didn't forget what winter looked like, I wanted to point to my stomach and to Jonathan's bed on the settee and shout, 'It's *not* that easy' until my throat vibrated.

'Sit down. Dad and I have got something to tell you which might be a bit of a shock.'

Jonathan was lurking round the kitchen units, looking like he wanted to crawl under the skirting board.

I scrunched up my eyes, grabbed Charlie's hand – which startled him – and said, 'Dad and I aren't going to live together any more.'

Charlie took on an expression of disbelief as though we came as one congealed lump, incapable of taking on separate identities. 'Why?'

'It's a bit complicated but Dad has fallen in love with someone else, who lives in Sardinia, so he's going to move out there on a permanent basis and—'

'Your mother is pregnant, but doesn't know who the father is.'

'I was just about to tell Charlie that it wasn't all one-sided, if you give me a chance.'

'I didn't think you even had sex any more. Oh my God.' Charlie twirled his fringe round his finger, like he did when he was a toddler. 'Are you actually going to have the baby?'

Despite Jonathan's best efforts, it appeared that Charlie had overlooked the crucial element of multiple candidates for fatherhood. He did, however, seem clued-up on abortion. I nodded. 'I am, darling. I'm not going to do the "It will be wonderful for you to have a little brother or sister" because

I get that you might not feel like that right now. But I hope you will come to accept it.'

Charlie looked bemused and a bit disgusted. 'For God's sake. Can we still move to Sardinia? Then at least my friends won't see you waddling about. Who's Dad copped off with, anyway?' He sounded incredulous that anyone would fancy his father.

I looked round at Jonathan. He was scratching at some imaginary stain on his jeans. I raised my eyebrows. That was one question I wasn't going to answer.

Jonathan launched into a lengthy explanation about relationships, how people's needs alter over time, how the pressures of work sometimes change one's perspective on life, how it was important not to live a half-life. Charlie glazed over. Frustration hissed through me. Just when I thought I was going to have to fill in the blanks, Jonathan finally harrumphed out the name 'Elisabetta'. He then had the audacity to say, 'She won't replace your mum, but I hope over time you will see her as a sort of wise aunt.'

That I managed not to snort like a charging rhino must have guaranteed me a place in heaven. The strain of not launching into Jonathan with the gusto of a menopausal Jack Russell was giving me indigestion. I got up and took a surreptitious swig of Gaviscon.

Charlie sat nonplussed for a moment. 'Fucking hell.'

Neither of us reacted to the bad language. Charlie got up and made himself a huge doorstep of a ham sandwich. Jonathan was itching to tell him to wipe the butter off the counter top but even he managed to hold back on the J-cloth until Charlie mumbled that he was going to play the XBox, and wandered out.

'He seems keen on coming to Sardinia,' said Jonathan. 'Perhaps he could come and stay for the summer.'

I resisted the impulse to shout, 'Shut up!' The thought of

handing over my gorgeous son to stay in some other woman's house, where she could buy his affection with ice cream and pizza, made me shudder. 'We do have three children. Are you going to have them all and take the summer off to supervise them, then? Or is "Betta" going to be a stay-at-home stepmum and trot off to the beach with them every day?'

Even to my own ears I sounded bitter. My heart hurt at the thought of Immi skipping along holding the other woman's hand. As I knew she would. The best thing for all the kids would be that they adored Betta. I wasn't sure whether I was grown-up enough to encourage that.

I lowered my voice. 'We're going to have to handle the girls a bit better than we managed Charlie. Perhaps you'd like to tell them your version first, then you won't feel the need to jump into mine. We've both made mistakes here. I'm not trying to pin the blame on you. Let's make this as painless as possible.'

Jonathan nodded, but there was nothing about him that looked proactive. I went to find Charlie.

He didn't look up from his XBox killing frenzy. I sat on the arm of the chair in a two-fingered salute to Jonathan. I put my hand on his shoulder. 'Are you OK?'

Grunt.

I grunted back. 'That means I love you and I'm sorry that I've messed up.' I grunted again. 'That means please can you not say anything to your sisters until Dad and I have had a chance to speak to them?'

Charlie pressed pause. 'Mum, stop grunting. It's freaky and weird.' He looked up at me. 'I'm all right. Loads of people in my class have got divorced parents. I still don't see why we can't go and live over there as well. When Dad lost his job, you were always on about moving abroad. Now I want to go, you don't. Is it because you've got a boyfriend here?'

I turned his face towards me. 'I haven't got a boyfriend at all. I'm afraid I made a huge mistake and thought I was still in love with someone I used to know. Instead of trying to work things through with Dad – I know I'm always telling you not to give up – I didn't follow my own advice about that or, er, safe sex.' Charlie's mouth contorted with revulsion. 'Sorry I know you don't want to hear this, but I feel the need to explain.'

Charlie put his hand up. 'Mum, it's all good. I don't think I need to hear any more. So you haven't got any reason to stay here.'

'Except the business.'

'Couldn't you get someone to run that and then you could take the money but not do the work? You wouldn't be so worn out all the time.'

'I couldn't do nothing,' I said.

'You could learn Italian. You're always telling me to seize the moment, that it's so important not to get to eighty-five and say "coulda/woulda/shoulda". And you're going to have another baby so you won't be able to work for a bit anyway.'

He went quiet. 'If it's a boy, do you think you'll love him more than me?' He tried to make it sound like a joke but something caught in his laugh.

'How could I ever love anyone more than you? Ever, ever, ever?' I hugged his shoulders and, for once, he relaxed into me.

'Will you think about moving to Sardinia?' he said through a face full of my hair. 'A proper think, not just a fobbing-off.'

I squeezed Charlie's hand. I loved his adventurous spirit. Thank God he'd inherited at least one good trait from me. 'We'll see. I'm not sure Dad would be very keen to have me on his doorstep.'

'We don't have to live next door. That way we could be a sort of family. Still see him at least.'

When the kids were born, I hadn't envisaged being a 'sort of family.'

It never occurred to me that one day we'd sit them down and say one of us was leaving voluntarily. I was twenty-one when my dad died and on occasions, I still missed him so much I wanted to rush out into the garden and scream at the unfairness of it all. It seemed heartless to deprive the kids of a father when he was still alive, for them to suffer that agony of longing, that need to connect. Presumably a bit of Jonathan, tidying and fussing, would be better than nothing.

As soon as I allowed myself to speculate on how wonderful it would be to start again somewhere new, an array of images paraded through my mind in sunny technicolour: a terraced house, stone steps leading up to an oak door, paths weaving down to the beach. Bare feet. Balconies. Growing up in a community rather than a faceless Surrey suburb. Weekends at the beach collecting sea urchins. Autumn walks collecting wood for the open fire. In fact, everything I'd always dreamed of for my kids.

A tiny apple pip of excitement forced out a shoot.

Roberta

'That is absolutely insane. You are not going to move to the tiny island where your husband lives with his mistress. I am simply not going to permit you to do that.'

Pregnancy had fried Octavia's brain. She had come over all fired-up about sea views, pizza places and roof terraces with geraniums, just like she used to be when she was planning a trip round Asia on two pounds a day.

'You've got no sense of adventure,' Octavia said. 'Charlie's really keen. We're going to let out our house here. Jonathan is moving in with "Betta" and we'll look for somewhere to rent. The schools are keeping their places open for a year. I'm thinking of it as a sabbatical.'

'What about when the baby comes? You won't know anyone to help you.'

I'd seen Octavia like this before. Once she had an idea in her head, no argument would sway her. I could point the pitfalls out until I was purple.

She shrugged. 'Italians love children. I'll find some teenager with ten siblings to help me. Can't be worse than being in Britain where the kids are expected to sit with a poker up their arses whenever they're in public. I might even be able to go into a café and breastfeed without everyone falling on the floor in shock.'

Octavia sounded belligerent. I knew I should keep quiet and wish her well, but I felt obliged to cover the things she was overlooking.

'I bet Polly doesn't want to go. She'd miss all her friends.'

Octavia didn't exactly concede but admitted that Polly had holed up in her room when they had revealed the Shelton shenanigans in all their glory. She gave me a half-smile. 'I did promise her a Vespa when she's old enough, which softened her up a bit.'

'What about Immi?'

'She's closest to Jonathan, so she'd do anything as long as she can still see him. Immi will be the one who needs him most when the baby comes. She's used to being the youngest. Her main concern was Stan but I think we can take him with us if we can find somewhere that accepts dogs.'

'What sort of place are you going to rent?'

Octavia suddenly found a corner of the table rather interesting. 'Not sure yet. Have to see what's available.'

An image of the Shelton gang getting off a ferry with an assortment of battered possessions and Stan pulling on a rope came to mind. I couldn't imagine how Octavia would ever clean up her house enough for anyone to part with money to live there. She'd need to paint over those turquoise walls in the sitting room. And the lime-green kitchen was an acquired taste.

Octavia was so animated, it felt wicked to pour cold water on her plans, but the woman was deranged. The mere thought of clearing out all the knick-knacks from her travels, the children's artwork from the year dot, the jeans Octavia deluded herself she would slim into, was giving me a migraine.

'Are the children OK about the baby?'

'Charlie's a bit jealous I think. He keeps being really rude to me. He might not mind so much if it's a girl. I thought Immi would be the one to go through the roof, but she's excited about it. Keeps pressing her ear on my stomach to see if she can hear him breathing.'

'Him?'

'I've convinced myself it's a boy.'

'Do you have an inkling about whose it is?'

'I daren't think about it. Poor little bugger will grow up without a father anyway, so I suppose it doesn't make much difference. Getting away from here will be a good thing, though. It would be so hard for the kids with everyone gossiping at school – can you imagine what nursery will be like: all the mothers wishing me well, then bursting out to whisper in the car park?'

'What about me? Won't you miss me?' I was only half-joking. The thought of not having Octavia in the same town was alien to me. We'd ping-ponged around the world but come back to live within fifteen minutes of each other. I knew I was being selfish but Octavia was like family, just nicer.

'You can visit whenever you like. Email me every day. I shall expect all the gossip. You're all loved-up anyway. And you'll be too busy to miss me now you're the top designer in the county.'

I could hear the doubt in her words. For the first time ever, my life was stable, underpinned by a lucrative job. I had Jake, and my dad's relief that I had finally found a 'decent chap' meant that parental olive branches were in the process of being extended and accepted.

Octavia, on the other hand, was experiencing the rockiest ride of her life. Moving to Sardinia seemed as foolhardy as standing on the deck of the Titanic instead of dashing for the lifeboats.

'Is Jonathan pleased?'

'On one level, he wouldn't care if he never saw me again,

but he was really receptive to the idea of the kids being close by. I can't see him flying backwards and forwards every month to spend time with them if we stay in England, once he gets properly settled into his new life. As for this little one . . . who knows?' She stroked her stomach.

'Have you told Xavi your plans?'

'No. I haven't spoken to him at all. I told him to stay away and he has. Ultimately, he could never tolerate someone else's baby.' At that, she pressed her fingers into her eyes. 'Don't ask me about him.'

I softened my voice. 'You are going to tell him?'

Octavia frowned. 'No. He had his chance to come on board and he couldn't commit. Anyway, now we're off to Sardinia, it's irrelevant. There's no room for me to be wobbling about all over the place. I've got to stay strong for the kids. I can't be fretting about whether Xavi's suddenly going to feel trapped and head for the hills.'

I'd always gone along with Octavia's mad plans before, even when I'd thought she was plain wrong. But this time, someone really needed to be the voice of reason.

Octavia

Summer and the start of the school holidays barely registered as I unpicked our sixteen years of marriage. Jonathan stayed for a week, sorted out his workshop and grumbled off into the attic, where he heaved down Christmas trees, boxes of school reports and business presentations from half a lifetime ago.

'That's it, then. I think you can manage the rest,' he said, as he packed the last must-have screwdriver into his bulging suitcase. Frankly it was a damned good job he hadn't left his hammer lying about, as I might have been tempted to rearrange his teeth.

I couldn't get over the fact that marriage took two people who loved each other – because I had loved Jonathan – and turned them into worse versions of themselves until they were practically mouthing 'arsehole' behind each other's backs at every opportunity.

On the morning he left, I hid in the kitchen while he said goodbye to the children, afraid of their pain. Charlie stomped upstairs. Immi's distress was so loud and catastrophic, I felt helpless in the face of it. Polly was reined in. Even her moving about the house became considered and purposeful, as though she was concentrating on walking.

When it came to my turn, he stood on the doorstep surrounded by bags and said, 'I'll be in touch then,' as though he'd just been to give me a quote for lagging the airing cupboard. I had to train my brain not to give him a perfunctory hug. It was like learning to do everything in reverse.

Over the next few weekends, Roberta toiled away with me, God bless her, clearing out cupboards and wrapping up my crockery. She'd stopped calling me crazy, but I could tell from her attempts to point out the drawbacks of my plan that I was definitely in her category of irresponsible mothers.

The more I saw of Jake, the less I worried about leaving Roberta. He helped out heaving furniture into various vans, carting mouldy plastic chairs to the tip, all with humour and kindness. When I caught sight of him in the garden, smoothing back Roberta's hair and kissing her gently as though she was a jewel he was lucky to find, I had to look away.

Jonathan sent me a barrage of emails, all on the same theme:

I do not consider us to be sufficiently well off to give away things we could sell. I am quite sure there could be a market for my computer books, remaining tools and sports equipment.

Sadly for him, I didn't consider myself sufficiently arsed about making £2.50 to sell the flippers he'd been hanging on to since university. I'd need more than an old snorkel to get me out of the shit. Instead I gaily Freecycled most of our tat. I eBayed my paltry collection of jewellery, including my engagement and wedding rings. I put the half of the two-euro coin Xavi had sent me in a matchbox. I couldn't bring myself to send it the same way as its predecessor.

By the middle of August, we were camping in the lounge and I was preparing to let the children fly out to stay with Jonathan for the next fortnight so that I could tie up all the loose ends in peace.

Every time I thought about the children leaving, I wanted to cling to them and bottle their smells, their laughs, even their moods. I'd promised them a holiday by the sea as soon as I got there. I'd booked a huge family tent on a campsite, not far from Jonathan.

When I told Roberta, she looked like I'd stirred her peppermint tea with one of Stan's bones. 'A tent? For goodness' sake, Octavia! Don't tell me you'll be using communal washrooms?'

'It's got all the mod cons, like a fridge and lights and stuff. It's only temporary, while the kids and I look for somewhere to live. I want us all to decide together.'

'What will you do if you don't find something quickly?'

'Nothing. I'll stay there until we do, I suppose. We used up most of our savings when Jonathan was out of work. I'll have some income from the nursery, of course, but I've had to pay through the nose to get a decent manager in. I'll be better off when the rent for the house kicks in.'

I wish I'd had a camera for Roberta's face.

'You can't stay in a tent. You're pregnant. Please don't do this. You need to be resting. How are you going to eat properly on a campsite?'

'Roberta. Some people live in tents all their lives and survive perfectly well. I don't need five-star luxury.'

'You could stay here in a four-bedroomed house and Jonathan couldn't do a thing about it. What about the washing?' Roberta didn't understand roughing it, only room service and chocolates on her hotel pillow.

I tried to pacify her. 'I promise I'll come back to England if I can't sort myself out before the weather turns cold.'

'Octavia! You cannot stay in a tent until October. What are you trying to prove?' Roberta's voice was rising in horror.

'I'm not trying to prove anything. It's an adventure. We'll be about twenty metres from the sea. Just think, no dancing lessons, no bloody cricket practice, no parents' evenings with middle-class mothers worrying about the pasta play of their two-year-olds, none of that Year Six stress for Polly – will she, won't she get into the grammar, and are we all going to hell in a handcart if she doesn't? I can't bloody wait.'

Roberta unfurled another length of bubble wrap. 'I was beginning to think that Sardinia might be the right decision for you. But you're not thinking things through. Camping's not practical in the long term. Where are you going to keep your passports? What if you go into early labour?'

On and on she went until Jake picked her up and they drifted off for dinner at the French bistro in town. I wished it would only take a bottle of Sancerre and a few *cuisses de grenouille* to make me happy.

Roberta

Jake took us to the airport for our flights to Sardinia. God knows how Octavia was feeling, because I wanted to cling to Jake myself. I'd waited while Octavia walked around her house the night before, checking everything was ready for the tenants to move in the following week. She wouldn't admit it, but she was saying goodbye to her old life. Her courage humbled me. She walked down her little path, glanced back over her shoulder and said, 'I never liked that house. Just bricks and mortar anyway. Adventure here I come.'

I'd forced her to let me go with her. Alicia had gone to France with the school and I persuaded Octavia that I required a dose of sunshine before my big hotel project started in the autumn.

At first, she resisted. 'You don't want to come and live in a tent. Don't be soft. You'll hate it.' She was hell-bent on proving that she was stronger, steelier, more capable than any mere mortal moving to a new country with three children and one on the way.

I stood firm against the battery of Octavia's objections. 'You're always pointing out that I would benefit from broadening my horizons. So here I am, ready to stretch them far and wide. If it's truly intolerable, I'll go and stay in a hotel.'

Saying goodbye to Jake almost had me clutching onto his jacket in an unseemly manner. We kept it brief but he whispered, 'Take care, I will miss you so much' in my ear, which filled me with a warmth I could lock away, then revisit when required.

Once we got on the plane, Octavia withdrew, burying herself in a book, her habitual survival tactic when she was overwhelmed. I was glad of the silence. I forced myself to relax into my seat, focusing on images of Jake, some so strong I could feel the draw back to England right down deep in my stomach. I noticed Octavia was wearing her half of the two-euro coin on a chain around her neck. I didn't pass any observation.

She squeezed my arm as we started to descend into Sardinia. 'Thanks for coming with me. I'm glad you're here. I hope the campsite is bearable. No butler, I'm afraid. But the awning's all yours.'

I looked away as the plane juddered to a halt. I didn't want her to read anything on my face.

Octavia jumped up immediately, dragging her bags out of the locker. I peered out of the window, narrowing my eyes to see if I could make out any details on the ground. I sent up a silent prayer.

There was no turning back now.

Octavia

I paused on the steps of the aircraft and stroked my bump. 'Welcome to your new life, baby.' Just a cab journey between me and the children. I couldn't believe how long a fortnight had seemed. Roberta had been a godsend – persuading Jake to have Stan until I got settled, sorting out the flights and the taxis – while I tied up all the last-minute issues back at the house. I wanted to be excited, but by the time the luggage was creaking round the conveyor belt, I felt as though I might burst into tears. Bloody hormones.

'Is the taxi driver going to have a sign with our name on it?'

'I think so.' Roberta was squinting through the glass into the arrivals hall.

'What company are we looking for?' My ankles were swelling up and the idea of slipping into an air-conditioned car with the minimum of fuss was very appealing. Originally I had tried to convince Roberta that we'd manage on public transport. She'd looked at me and said, 'I don't do buses. Ever.'

'I can't just recall the company, I'll know it when I see it. I've got the details in my bag.'

We grabbed my huge holdall and dragged it along beside Roberta's sleek aluminium case. Roberta had refused to let me travel in a tracksuit. 'Start as you mean to go on. You can't look a wreck. The children haven't seen you for two weeks. You don't want them thinking you fall apart when they're not there to look after you.'

Frankly, Charlie wouldn't notice if I turned up with a baboon on my head, but I put on Roberta's good-luck gift – a beautiful indigo blue top and black linen trousers from some ridiculously posh maternity shop I'd never heard of. I'd got through my three other pregnancies in leggings but I didn't want to seem ungrateful.

We jostled our way out into the arrivals hall. Roberta hung back a bit, fiddling about in her bag. The crowds were making me claustrophobic so I pushed on ahead, a protective arm defending my baby, looking for a space to breathe. I made it past all the relatives blocking the exit with their hugs for returning grandchildren and looked back for Roberta.

A hand grabbed my arm. 'So you think you can bugger off to Sardinia, not a word?'

My hand flew to my mouth. I stared at Xavi, the epitome of a fierce Corsican, throwing his hands up in a 'What the hell?' gesture.

'What are you doing here? How did you know?' It was too much for me to take in. A rush of relief made me light-headed. He was here. He'd ignored my request to be left alone. Ignored my bloody-mindedness.

Maybe he really did love me.

'I'm here because you won't speak to me and there is something we need to sort out.' But there were no open arms, no declaration of love.

He marched me away from the crowds, his shoulders rigid. He parked me in a seat and started the pacing I used to see years ago when something stood in the way of his plans to travel. 'What is this nonsense, Tavy? I hear nothing, just two lines of "Leave me alone" and then I find you are going to live in a tent with a baby. Disappearing without saying nothing to the father? I am not having my son or daughter born on a campsite in Sardinia like some immigrant with no home.'

I was my own worst enemy. I had been wrong to hope. This was about pride, not about love. 'I've got three – soon four – children to look after and not much money to do it with. It's summer. We can survive. You've lived in tents yourself in the past.'

Spoken out loud, it did seem a bit of a flimsy parenting strategy.

'Anyway, the baby "you don't want born on a campsite" might not be yours.'

'I know that,' Xavi said quietly, instantly making me feel petty.

Roberta caught up with us, looking sheepish. Xavi hadn't been bugging my house or hacking into my emails then. They greeted each other with a complicity that infuriated me. I glared round at Roberta.

'I had to tell him. I couldn't not.' She grimaced.

'I was supposed to be coming to Sardinia for a fresh start.'

I didn't know what to feel. I had no doubt that she had my best interests at heart, but Roberta was not a friend who should go behind my back. Going behind my back was for lesser friends, acquaintances, people I didn't trust with my life.

I looked at Xavi who stood with his arms folded, one eyebrow raised. My mental map of his body language had faded over the years. But there was no disguising that he had the monumental hump with me. I forced down the desire to tease him out of his temper, to fold myself into him. To make up for all those lost moments.

He didn't deserve a second chance.

Roberta turned to me. 'I've got a driver. I'm going to stay

at a hotel tonight. You go with Xavi. You have some things to talk about.'

I stood up. 'No. I can't. The children are expecting me today. I'm not letting them down.'

Roberta started staring over my shoulder. 'I've already arranged everything for tomorrow. I spoke to Jonathan and explained there was a hold-up with sorting out the house and we'd be coming a day later instead.'

All my maternal adrenaline was rushing. I'd been thinking of Immi's blonde hair, her little fingers in mine, Charlie lumbering towards me, too cool to kiss me until no one was looking, Polly jabbering away, filling in the detail of their time in Sardinia. My distress was instant. 'I can't not go. They'll be wondering why I haven't phoned them myself. Jonathan will be telling them all sorts, turning them against me as an unreliable mother. Did he even believe you?'

Sands were shifting beneath me. People were making decisions without me and for me.

Roberta nodded. 'I think he was happy that you were sorting the house out so he didn't have to. He said the kids were spending their lives at the beach, that they barely know what day it is, anyway.'

I had to trust that Roberta wasn't trying to hurt me, though my reaction was visceral. Not pining away for their mother at all. Their emails and texts had been full of swimming and ice cream and 'awesome pizza'.

'Why didn't you tell me? Then I could have prepared myself.'

Xavi butted in. 'If Roberta had said anything, you would say no. I try for all those weeks to speak to you and you tell me you can't be with me because of the children. You decide what the truth is and you never let anyone say their words.'

The fury in Xavi's voice shocked me.

My hair was sticking to my neck. 'I didn't want to talk to you because I couldn't risk falling apart when you suddenly disappeared again.'

'You have no idea what you are talking about. I wanted to support you.'

'Like you did last time, I suppose?'

A string of French swear words followed so fast that I didn't quite catch them all.

Roberta clicked up the handle on her suitcase. She didn't even bother to address me. 'Xavi. You didn't come all this way to row. You need to talk to Octavia, so why don't you do just that? You could always drop her off at the campsite tonight.'

I never thought of Roberta as someone who could deal with dominant men, but Xavi stopped his pacing. He stuck his hands in his pockets. 'In the long plan, it is much better for the children that we reach a conclusion. I am not kidnapping you. I drive you to the children any time you want.'

The emotion of leaving England had sucked the fight out of me. 'I'll phone Charlie from the car.'

Roberta hugged me and disappeared. She managed to combine apology and defiance. I would rake through the embers of my emotions later. Since my mother shooed off Xavi so I could marry Jonathan, I don't think anyone had ever again risked deciding what was best for me. I watched her go, the confident stride of a woman used to instructing drivers, secure in the knowledge that if she didn't like her destination, there was always enough money to decamp elsewhere.

Xavi helped me to my feet. His voice was still taut but a fraction friendlier. 'You look well. The baby is suiting you. Come. I take you to the car.' He heaved up my holdall, shaking his head. The searing blast of the sun outside made me blink. He clicked open the door to a convertible BMW. 'No motorbike today.'

'Where are we going?' I still couldn't tell if he was planning to take me to some dodgy solicitor to sign papers waiving any claims on his future income, or whether I was simply in for a cards-on-the-table conversation. Xavi was a man with opinions. We were well-matched. He ignored the question, taking care to pull the seatbelt gently round my bump.

Xavi wove slowly out of the airport. I kept glancing at him. He was a good-looking old sod. The demand of an explanation hovered in the air. He took the road north, past Palau, where I knew the children were. I phoned Charlie, fighting to keep my voice steady.

'*Ciao, sono Carlo.*'

'Very impressive. Go-go-go with the Italian, Charlie. It's Mum. Are you OK? I'm so sorry about today. There was a last-minute hiccup.' I couldn't bring myself to tell a direct lie. Longing to ruffle his untidy hair dragged at my heart.

'Chill out. We've been out on the banana today. We're at the beach. Immi and Polly have made some friends, so they're fine.'

'Banana?'

'You know, one of those inflatables that drags you through the water.'

'Oh God. Did you wear life jackets?' I was aware of Xavi listening. It made me self-conscious, as though he was judging my ability to be a good parent to his potential child.

'Yeah. It was awesome. We're seeing you tomorrow, aren't we?' He sounded moderately enthusiastic.

'Yes, can't wait. Tell Dad I'll phone him later. Give my love to Immi and Polly.' My voice started to crack. 'The reception's not very good. I'd better go. See you tomorrow.' I added, 'Love you,' but Charlie had obviously returned to gawking at bikini-clad babes.

Xavi looked over at me. 'OK?'

I nodded. Confusion was whirling around me. I didn't

know where I was going, I didn't know what Xavi wanted, my kids had adjusted to life without me. I recognised a deep ache of longing for what had never been, for the simple life I might have had with Xavi if everything had worked out first time. If, if, if.

And in among all that, I was hungry, the ravenous sort of hunger that you feel when a baby has sucked all the goodness up, leaving you with the equivalent of a packet of Haribos and a tube of Smarties to sustain you.

'Xavi, could you tell me where this mystery tour is going to end?'

'Relax.' Said the man who was gripping the steering wheel like a lifebelt.

'Thing is, I need to eat, otherwise I feel sick. It's the baby.'

Without missing a beat, he reached behind the back seat and pulled out a bag full of rustic rolls – wild-boar ham, goat's cheese with fig jam – which made my nasty little work lunches from the corner shop look as though they were in need of mouth-to-mouth resuscitation.

'Can I eat in the car?'

Xavi looked at me as though I'd gone doolally. 'Am I the sort of man who makes a fuss about a little crumbs? If you are hungry, you must eat. I even find the goat's cheese pasteurised for you.'

I thought about Jonathan going bananas when he found chocolate wrappers in the glovebox of his car and wondered again how two such different men had dominated my life. I was just hoovering up the last salty bits of goat's cheese when we came into Santa Teresa di Gallura. It seemed decades since I had stood on the cape and gazed across the water, my marriage still intact, my baby not yet conceived.

Life as I knew it.

'Xavi? Are we going to Corsica?'

'Yes. It seems right that we go back to the beginning for this.'

I stopped trying to second-guess what the hell was happening. 'I must be back tomorrow.'

'Don't worry. I'll take you first thing.'

I looked at Xavi properly for the first time once we were on the ferry. I couldn't remember seeing him so serious before, drawn away from me. The idea that he had flown out to do the big romantic gesture was looking pretty unlikely. I'd been right not to expect anything from him.

'Are you OK?' I asked.

'Nervous.' He'd softened a bit. That gorgeous mouth wasn't quite so tight.

'Speak to me. What's this all about?'

'I have been trying to speak to you for months. Now I am going to show you something.'

I felt like I was viewing the world through swimming goggles. I couldn't figure out why Xavi would make the effort to meet me at the airport, simmer away, barely speak. Why not just stay at home in a cold, damp room and sit on drawing pins for fun? I was too weary for games. I turned in my seat and kept my eyes on the horizon. I'd get through this. I should have stuck to my guns and refused to let Roberta derail me. I could be with my kids by now.

Xavi relaxed once he was on home turf. The wheel glided through his hands as he threaded his way up the coast. A few miles from Propriano, Xavi started to fidget. Radio on, radio off. Seat more vertical. Window down, then up. We took a sharp turn down an unmade road. I felt the craters in my bladder. We ground to a halt just in time for my pelvic floor, thirty yards from the sea in a clearing ringed by oak and olive trees. A grey stone house with a wooden verandah stood to the right.

Xavi climbed out of the car, stretching his back like a cat. 'Come.'

He helped me out. My skin tingled where his fingers were. He took my hand, his grip firm as though I might run away.

He stopped in front of the house, pulling the chain he always wore round his neck out of his shirt. He unclipped a key. 'This is your new home. It is not luxury but I hope you like it.'

I stared at him. I wished afterwards I'd been more eloquent and gracious than 'What?'

'This is one of my houses. Normally I rent it out. Now I give it to you and your family for as long as you want.'

My eyes filled at the unexpected offer. 'It's absolutely gorgeous, but why would you do that? I'm not your responsibility.'

Xavi flung his hands up in a gesture I remembered well. 'You might have my baby there. That makes you my responsibility. Let someone help you, Tavy. Jesus. You are so *têtue*, so stubborn.'

I couldn't let go of my resistance even though I wanted to. Xavi pressed the key into my palm.

'It's yours. Take it.'

Hot tears were starting to run down my face.

'I can't. Because then I'll be tangled up with you forever. I'll start to hope.'

'Hope what?'

'You know what.'

'I don't know anything at all when it comes to you.' He took a step forward and pulled me into him by the shoulders. He whispered in my ear.

'What did you say?' I needed to be sure.

'You heard.'

Xavi let go of me, picked up a rock and hurled it at a tree. 'Tavy. Enough. I love you. I love you so much it makes my heart hurt. I want to be with you, all the time. I spend these months thinking you don't love me any more so maybe better for me to stay away. I imagine you want to go back with the husband and forget me. I wait, still hoping you will ring when your mind understands what you have to do for the baby.

'But no. I made a mistake, *une erreur si grande* eighteen years ago and you never forgive me. I spend all my life looking for another girl who make me annoyed like you. But do I find her? No. Instead, I am waiting for another chance for all these years. This is my another chance. I give you the house so you will be "tangled up" with me forever. I want you. The baby will come and we will love it. I hope the baby is mine but if it isn't, I will love anyway.'

I stood, pleating the bottom of my tunic. I was waiting for the 'but' or the joke.

Men didn't make speeches like that to women like me.

They mumbled things like 'All right?' and patted my hand. They didn't stand in front of me, imploring me to listen or swivel me towards them and take the fear out of my heart. They didn't present solutions to my problems, they didn't promise to be there no matter what, and they definitely didn't find me sexy.

All the emotions I had sandbagged away came pouring out. I dropped my head onto his chest. 'Thank you. Thank you so much.'

I'd never known Xavi speak like that before. When we were young, we took love for granted with the occasional playful '*Je t'aime*' as we flipped another top off a bottle of beer.

We didn't know how big love had to be to survive back then.

There in the scorching midday sun, Xavi kissed me until the rushing in my ears mixed with the sea flopping onto the rocks. When we paused for breath, he took my hand as though we'd been walking across the sand forever, with a mere eighteen year blip in between.

'Come and see in the house.' He pulled me up the steps and pushed open the door to reveal a bright living room, all white wood with a view over the sea. We stepped out onto the little balcony. I leaned on the railing, imagining a little table and chairs where I could sit with Xavi under the stars and dare to dream about the future.

'This is paradise. Absolute paradise. The kids will love it here. I'm going to have to find a windsurf.' My heart was leaping with relief at being able to provide a decent home for them. Still an adventure, but a Boden sort of adventure, with hot water, pillows and toilet paper. Extreme survival could come later.

'It's the favourite of my houses. Private. Safe for the children. Maybe too lonely?' The hard flint had gone out of his eyes, but something uncertain was still there.

'Depends on you.' A brief glimpse of the flirty me from long ago.

Xavi smiled, his whole face relaxing. 'I'm planning to set up a travel agency in Propriano, about ten minutes' drive. I still keep the one in London. That is my income. The one in Propriano, more of a hobby.'

He led me upstairs, showing me a couple of little bedrooms with whitewashed walls, decorated with shells, fishing nets and driftwood. Then he opened the door to the master bedroom, a dazzlingly light room with a view over the cove. He pushed me gently onto the bed and put his face against my stomach. 'I have thought a lot about this day.'

'I'm frightened. What if the baby isn't yours and you can't love it?'

Xavi lifted his head. 'I will love it. It will not always be easy but even people you love drive you mad.' He raised his eyebrows and pulled himself up to kiss me. 'Can we?' His hands started to move down. 'If I am gentle? Is it safe?'

I nodded and gave myself up to him, feeling his love fill

me up. He looked down at me. 'I wait all these years to have you in my home, in my life. I promise you that I am never going anywhere, never. I travel the whole world and now I see you were always the destination.'

I felt as though I'd been standing with pistols drawn for months and I could finally accept that no baddies were going to burst through the saloon-bar doors. All the jagged, raggedy feelings melted away into something warm and soothing. I even managed to whisper 'I love you,' without feeling a complete dork.

Sometimes friends could see the things that blind us.

Epilogue – Three Years Later

Roberta

I gripped Gabriel's hand tightly, watching his sandy hair fly up with every jump of the waves. It was so long since Alicia was small, I'd forgotten how fascinating tiny children found the beach, exclaiming over shells, digging for stony treasure, mesmerised by footprints filling with water. Immi came along to scoop him up. 'Come and see the sea urchins.' He trundled after her, chubby little legs stumbling on the sand. He was so pale compared to the others.

Charlie, in particular, had become very Mediterranean. He had the shades, the tan, the teenage swagger. Even Angus had turned a deep golden brown. The two of them zipped off every morning on Charlie's Vespa – ostensibly to play tennis – but it turned out there was more hanging out with the long-haired girls in short skirts than serving aces. Alicia sat under a big umbrella, huge sunhat on her head, Kindle in one hand, mobile phone in the other, still elated with her brilliant AS results.

Jake had adapted very well to the holiday pace of a Corsican cove. 'What's not to like? I know you really miss Octavia, the kids are having a ball and I'm spending time in a place I've never been to with a native guide.'

I walked over to him in his favourite hideaway – one of

the hammocks that Xavi had strung up so that the kids could sleep outside under the night sky. 'Move over. I'm coming to join you.'

'Never a moment's peace, is there?' he mock-moaned as my clambering into the hammock threatened to deposit both of us onto the sand. 'Can't a guy have two seconds to himself without you crowding into my den?' He stretched round to kiss me. He glanced round. 'Do you think it would be possible to make love in a hammock without falling out?'

I laughed. 'In your dreams. We'd never get to first base without Gabriel deciding to join us. Let's try and have a few days away on our own before Christmas.'

Jake stroked my hair. 'You wouldn't be without him though, would you?'

'God, no. Wouldn't have minded a bit more time together without a baby but I can say that now I have Gabriel. I waited so long for this one. I suppose it was the ultimate test for us too.'

'Roberta! Please stop looking for proof that I love you. How much more do you need?'

'I know. I do know.'

Jake snuggled up to me. 'Shall we make another one?'

'At the risk of sounding ungrateful, I'm going to turn you down.'

'Ungrateful about what?' Octavia asked, walking out with a tray of chestnut beers that Jake and I had developed an addiction to.

'He wants another baby. I'm feeling blessed but replete on that front.'

Octavia laughed. 'Me too, I think. Too damn old now.'

Xavi walked up from the beach with Polly. Luc was on her shoulders, his tanned toddler legs contrasting with the white soles of his feet. Octavia put the tray down. 'Did you catch any fish?'

Xavi swung a bucket towards her. 'A couple of *raies*, you know, skate, and three monkfishes. Not bad. Polly here is getting very good with the fishing rod. So, enough for the barbecue tonight.'

Octavia lifted down Luc and kissed his head. 'And how about Lukey? What did you catch?'

Luc stretched his arms as wide as they would go. 'I catched a *requin* this big.'

'A shark? Oh my life. Were you scared?'

'No. It was a friendly *requin*.'

Xavi nodded in agreement. 'The *requin* knew you were so big and brave he didn't dare challenge you.' He swung Luc into the air, squealing.

I was staring again. Every time I looked at Luc I changed my mind. He looked a lot like Charlie when he was small. The same gestures. His eyes were dark, little gypsy sparkles of mischief. His hair was mid-brown, close to Polly's colour. He had an intensity just like Xavi, a way of sizing you up. I could see Octavia's grit in him, her manner of getting stuck in. So far I hadn't noticed any of Jonathan's finicky ways. Who knew if fussiness came from nature or nurture?

When I dared – after a few glasses of wine – to ask Octavia what she thought, she shrugged. 'As far as I'm concerned, we're concerned, Luc is Xavi's son. Jonathan has been true to his word. He hasn't shown a flicker of interest, let alone tried to claim paternity rights. Xavi's already taught him how to fish, play boules, speak French, have an open mind, seize the moment, embrace adventure . . . I don't need to know.'

Octavia and I took our beers to the swinging hammock on the veranda. She clinked her bottle against mine. 'Here's to life after divorce, to friendship, to surviving, to finding – and rediscovering – good men in the end.'

I raised my bottle to her. 'Here's to adventure – preferably one without tents.' I looked over at Jake. He looked over at Gabriel. Gabriel ran to Alicia.

The universe did seem to be unfolding as it should.

If only it were the kids who
had the tantrums . . .

A hilarious, straight-talking read for
anyone who's ever despaired at the politics
of the school run.

Follow Avon on
Twitter@AvonBooksUK
and
Facebook@AvonBooksUK
For news, giveaways and
exclusive author extras

A V O N